Praise for Leanna Renee Hieber's
Strangely Beautiful books

"Tender, poignant, exquisitely written."
—*New York Times* bestselling author C. L. Wilson

"A strangely beautiful tale indeed! An ethereal, lyrical story that combines myth, spiritualism, and the gothic in lush prose and sweeping passion."
—Kathryn Smith, *USA Today* bestselling author

"A delightfully lush and richly imagined tale. Transcendent."
—*Fresh Fiction*

"I cannot recommend this book, this series, or this author enough."
—*True-Blood.Net*

"Strikingly rich, dark, and beautiful imagery."
—Alethea Kontis in *Orson Scott Card's InterGalactic Medicine Show*

"A secretive, gothic, paranormal world . . . a character who will resonate with anyone who has found the beauty in being different."
—*Booklist*

TOR BOOKS BY
LEANNA RENEE HIEBER

The Eterna Files
Strangely Beautiful
Eterna and Omega
Perilous Prophecy
The Eterna Solution
Miss Violet and the Great War

MISS VIOLET
AND THE
GREAT WAR

LEANNA RENEE HIEBER

TOR

A Tom Doherty Associates Book
New York

MISS VIOLET AND THE GREAT WAR

Copyright © 2019 by Leanna Renee Hieber

All rights reserved.

A Tor Book
Published by Tom Doherty Associates
175 Fifth Avenue
New York, NY 10010

www.tor-forge.com

Tor® is a registered trademark of Macmillan Publishing Group, LLC.

Library of Congress Cataloging-in-Publication Data

Names: Hieber, Leanna Renee, author.
Title: Miss Violet and the Great War / Leanna Renee Hieber.
Description: First edition. | New York : Tor, 2019. | "A Tom Doherty
    Associates Book."
Identifiers: LCCN 2018046255| ISBN 9780765377463 (trade paperback) |
    ISBN 9781466855892 (ebook)
Subjects: | GSAFD: Occult fiction.
Classification: LCC PS3608.I326 M57 2019 | DDC 813/.6—dc23
LC record available at https://lccn.loc.gov/2018046255

Our books may be purchased in bulk for promotional, educational, or business use.
Please contact your local bookseller or the Macmillan Corporate and Premium
Sales Department at 1-800-221-7945, extension 5442, or by email at
MacmillanSpecialMarkets@macmillan.com.

First Edition: February 2019

Printed in the United States of America

0 9 8 7 6 5 4 3 2 1

MISS VIOLET AND THE GREAT WAR

PROLOGUE

IN THE CHILL WINTER OF 1889, A SMALL CERAMIC URN FLOATED in the English Channel. If one were to put an ear to it, the contents could be heard hissing quietly.

A boatman, bound for a respite in Verdun, caught the object in a net, feeling oddly obsessed by the smooth, tightly sealed jar, only to deposit it into a French river just a few days later. He blamed the urn for the onslaught of nightmares, visions of a gray netherworld where towers of skulls marched off into eternity. He hadn't opened it and tried to forget the sounds. "Back into the water then, with you," he murmured, depositing it overboard, and continued on, his small craft winding along the Meuse River, which ran its lovely, lazy course through Verdun before it fed its gentle current into several European provinces.

He could have sworn the contents hissed at him in response.

It was an irony that the river to which the urn had been returned so closely resembled the name of the sworn enemy of what was inside.

Curse them all, the ashes of a Gorgon hissed. *The fool Muses always loved mortals more than their own divinity . . .*

So die, then, with the whole world . . .

The creature that had once loved the Whisper-world labyrinth, a creature with hopes and dreams of its own, was gone. Only hatred and wrath stirred the trapped ashes; all that remained of her once beautifully monstrous body was misery, pain, and a need for violence. A potent, deadly compound.

The Muses who had fought this beast for the ages had left their mortal hosts and cozied up inside strong bricks to enjoy a well-deserved rest.

For such a thing as this to be alive and awake when heroes were asleep . . .

Woe to hapless mankind.

A farmer who had brought fruit from his village to sell in town sat on the riverbank, pausing in his labors to soak his tired feet in the water and appreciate the life and greenery of Verdun, as verdant a place as its name might suggest.

A small, gray-white urn bobbed gently along the Meuse. It brushed against the rolled cuff of his trousers.

"Ah, what are you there?" he asked.

He bent to lift the vessel. Shaking it, he heard only grit and tiny sifting bits, something light.

The lid, poorly sealed, slid free as he examined the canister.

"Ah, no!" the farmer cried. "If you're someone's poor remains, I can't have you blown about on the wind, but I don't know that the priest would be willing to take you, he's mistrustful of strangers. Come, come, we'll give you a proper place in my garden. You'll love the flowers. So many flowers. I live in a village named for flowers! Come to Fleury!" He rose, put on his socks and shoes, and hastened back to a small cottage teeming with blooms.

The Gorgon had always hated flowers.

They had grown in her enemy's step, and though they rotted immediately in Whisper-world air, they were brief, horrible spots of beauty.

Soon enough, the farmer's flowers died.

The grapes on his vines soured.

The vines died.

The farmer died.

The withering of his once verdant farm chilled the air as misery seeped into the soil and water.

Misery spread through the land, running through deep veins, and rubbing the scabs off old wounds at the lines drawn between two sometime enemies. Their recent war wounds bled again and the Gorgon drank deep of their mounting fears.

The tang of tensions; she tasted the bitterness in the soil, souring the world, borders chafed, and unrest bubbling up as a new century loomed. The old-world order was unsustainable and a hissing pile of ashen power thrilled to these burgeoning new urges born of colonial brutality and ravenous greed.

Yes . . . the brittle scraps of a vengeful monster whispered on the wind. Her death rattle carried to growing armies and armadas on land and shore. She'd never thought much of mankind and their wars, bloody spots on her ancient timeline, but if mankind would erupt across its whole map, she might finally get what she wanted.

Yes . . .

She would make mankind dig for mercy.

She would ruin everything her enemies loved.

She would, in due time, bury the whole world in ash . . .

CHAPTER
ONE

London, England, 1897

VIOLET HAD TO BE DREAMING. AS FAR AS SHE KNEW, ONE COULD not walk through a hail of bullets without being harmed. Though she often had odd experiences, she was fairly sure a body couldn't *deflect* a sword or fist or bullet. Yet hers did, as she walked numbly through an utter hellscape.

She was surrounded by gunshots, flashes of light, flying dirt, and unnatural shrieking sounds descending from the sky. Men in uniforms fell all around her, tumbling into the mud in a place she did not recognize. She walked in a body that was not her own—it was a tall, adult body, when she knew herself to be only eight years old.

She looked out upon a barren, alien landscape; all mud and gray light, posts, and wire with jagged edges . . . and bodies . . .

A dark, plain skirt flared out as her boots descended an uneven set of wood-plank stairs, into what looked like a maze whose walls were, in some places, made of boards, and in others, made of bags stacked like bricks. The bottom seemed to be eight or ten feet below the surface of the earth.

The men around her were all young, all wearing uniforms and helmets; they appeared gaunt, grim, and even at death's door. Most of them held rifles. A horizon of mud shifted into new craters and peaks as heavy projectiles landed and changed the face of the soil.

Descending the last wooden stair, Violet tucked herself into a corner. Paltry boards laid down to serve as the maze floor hardly kept puddles and mud at bay and she felt her boots sink into the muck.

Even at eight, she had read of wars in some of her many books and knew she was in the middle of one. But what war was this, so waged in the ground? Nothing about her looked familiar in any way.

Along with the clatter and the screams, there came a faint strain of music, lovely and soothing, a sound that could heal all . . .

Was it a waltz? She so loved waltzes.

Violet Rychman awoke. Bright moonlight filtering in through lace curtains illuminated her bedroom and bathed her face, making the strands of hair over her eyes the slight magical purple that had led to her name.

From far off in the opposite wing of her family's estate came the faint sound of a harpsichord. Mum was playing again, likely at her father's request, something she was hard pressed to ever turn down. Violet jumped out of bed, yearning to be closer to her parents' love and the sounds of sweet music to purge the terrible sounds of explosions and gunfire.

She knew she wasn't supposed to be awake, but the dream rattled her, and her mother was soothing; a marble angel come to life. Violet chose to think of her entirely colorless mother as angelic rather than ghostly, though she saw how people stared at her in a mixture of apprehension, fear, and fascination. Her mother, Persephone's, smooth cheek was as white as snow or bleached paper, her hair the very same, her eyes like pearls with slivers of ice-blue.

It was hard to see strange things and not be affected, Violet understood. But strange could be beautiful. Her father, Alexi, certainly thought so, and took every opportunity to praise their family as different, unique; special.

As she crept down the long hall that separated her room from her parents' set of rooms, her toes curling on the floral carpet runner, she saw her father standing by the instrument, his coat, vest, and cravat all undone. Locks of black hair tucked behind his ear made his expression visible. As usual, his hard, angular features were made soft when he looked at his wife.

The bounce of the waltz was inescapable. She'd seen her parents dancing at a party the month prior and squirmed out of the too-close grasp of Auntie Rebecca—who was decidedly not as much fun as Uncle Elijah and Auntie Josephine—to demand to be taught the steps. Now, in and out of shafts of moonlight shining through the beveled glass windows of the hallway, Violet practiced her new dance to the music she so craved. Whenever she was unnerved, music was the answer, any kind, any instrument. The phonograph downstairs could never be cranked too often. She was already adept at melodies on the keyboard herself, encouraged by her parents.

Enraptured by the music, her waltzing grew more and more grand, dramatic enough to attract attention . . .

"Violet! What are you doing awake?" Violet heard her mother call. She had a preternatural ability to sense where Violet was, which made making any mischief terribly difficult.

She stopped abruptly; momentum kept her swaying a bit on her feet before she stepped into the moonlight to make a calm reply. "Why, I was waltzing! What *else* is a girl to do when she hears a waltz?"

Her father peered out into the hallway, a long lock of black hair falling into his face, his sharp features scowling. But if Violet wasn't mistaken, he seemed to be trying to hold back a laugh. Violet loved that look. But it was hard to tell. While she had no doubt he loved her, he did not suffer her to be undisciplined. She froze at his tone:

"Violet Jane Rychman, what on earth are you doing waltzing after midnight?" He strode briskly toward her. Violet bit her lip and looked up at him a bit fearfully. "Without inviting your father?" he added, whisking her up into his arms.

Grinning, a giggle turned into a roaring laugh as he began to grandly waltz her about the foyer, holding her, one arm out, the other grasping her against him as she threw her arm around his neck and smelled the familiar mixture of clove tea, leather-bound books, and his evening bit of sherry.

"Carry on, Percy, my dove," he cried, "carry on! We must have music!"

Violet heard her mother's soft laugh as she sat back down at the keyboard, playing and watching them over her shoulder. She beamed whenever they twirled by, and blew them a kiss.

The waltz ended, and her mother moved to join them. Violet was returned to her room, ever filled, at her own request, with potted flowers. Both she and her mother had a particular way with plant life.

Alexi tucked Violet under her white lace covers, and her parents sat on either side of the bed. As had become their custom, they clasped hands together over her. Violet placed her hands atop theirs. She should tell them.

"The truth is, I couldn't sleep for a nightmare," she stated.

"Would you like to tell us about it?" her mother asked.

"It was a war. In the ground. It was very strange."

Violet watched intently as her mother turned to her father, perhaps trying to hide the sudden and sharp unease on her face. Seeming unruffled, her father placed his free hand fully atop all their entwined fingers. "Don't worry about any nightmares. Your mother and I are always here to protect you."

"Oh, yes, your father has protected me against the worst of nightmares indeed."

"Because you're a nightmare, Father? And you can fight those best?" Violet asked. Alexi furrowed his brow, prompting Violet to explain; "Will Page told me all the children at the Academy think you breathe fire and steal the souls of naughty children! I haven't dissuaded them, should I?" Here, Violet grinned, taking great pride in the idea of a mythical beast of a parent. Her mother stifled a laugh.

"If their being scared of me makes them behave, then," her father began carefully, "I suppose their overactive imagination has its uses . . ." He leaned closer to Violet. "If *I* am a famed and frightening nightmare, then I can frighten away your dreams." He snarled, a low growl, and Violet squealed in delight. This made him smile, a dancing light in his dark eyes. His tone grew soft and earnest as he added, "The darkness won't find you. Not while I'm here." He turned to his wife. "We're here. You've warriors on your side, my dear, don't ever forget it. None of us battle alone."

Violet found this greatly comforting and was glad they had not dismissed her dream as nonsense, as she'd feared. "Promise?"

"We promise," they chorused.

"Are there people who go through walls?" Violet asked. "Pale ones, much like Mum, but . . . transparent?" She looked first into her mother's ice-white eyes, then her father's burning dark ones.

A shudder seemed to collectively course through her parents.

Her mother swallowed once, placing her white hands upon the folds of her skirts and squeezing. Her father's angular features remained impassive.

"Yes," her father replied. "Ghosts. You've read about ghosts in books."

Violet made a face. "They're not like in books."

"Where have you seen them, Violet?" her mother asked carefully.

"Around and about. Home, the times I've been to Athens, in

your office. The city streets. Sometimes the Heath. I used to think they were just sunbeams, or tricks of light, but they've begun to look like people now. Can you see them?"

There was a long pause. The Rychmans glanced at one another, then back at Violet, as if they were measuring something.

"Yes," her parents chorused.

"Don't worry," her mother assured, "they won't hurt you."

"I know they won't. Are you upset?" Violet said, seeing the unease in their faces.

"No, of course not." Persephone clutched her daughter's hands. "We . . . simply hoped you wouldn't be troubled by them is all. You're not frightened, are you?"

Violet shook her head.

"Not everyone can see ghosts, Violet, and not everyone wants to talk about them. They can be a contentious subject," Professor Rychman explained. "So, we'll not discuss ghosts with anyone else, all right? It's a unique gift the rest of the world has difficulty understanding or appreciating."

"Like how everyone looks at Mum?" Violet asked.

Persephone sighed. "Precisely so, my dear."

Violet nodded. Seemed simple enough. It was all a part of their being a special, unusual family.

Violet closed her eyes, murmuring. "I'll dream of angels, then. I think Auntie Jane's not a ghost but an angel, looking after me between here and heaven . . ."

HAVING LEFT THEIR DAUGHTER TO REST, PERCY PACED IN THE room where she had been playing and Alexi closed the door.

"What of the dream?" Alexi asked. "And the ghosts?"

"I'm not surprised about Jane. I've seen her look in on Violet, I just wasn't sure if Violet looked back." She sighed. "As for the dream, I've no idea what to make of it," she replied, crossing toward the harpsichord, her dainty step making an old floorboard creak. When she moved back, something fell to the floor from behind the music stand.

Percy bent to find a sealed envelope. "That's odd."

"What is it?" Alexi asked, coming closer, moonlight filtering through the window and over his shoulder, casting the paper in half shadow.

"A letter. Addressed to 'the Rychmans.' How in the world would that get tucked all the way back there . . . ?" Percy lifted the missive and opened it, pulling Alexi next to her as she sat on the piano bench to read.

The first of the pages was a note from Alexi's father, a departure note, leaving him the house at too young an age.

"I dimly recall that note," Alexi said, examining it. "Mother and Father left this place because they were scared of me, the year I became the Leader of the Guard, the year my life became ghost-riddled." He scowled, his eyes flashing. "But this, I've never seen . . ." Behind it was another letter, written in a beautiful, looping script.

Over his shoulder, Percy read aloud:

> *To the strangely beautiful woman I hope to become:*
> *The hand that writes this is a hand that would take yours*
> *and hold it if I could. As I am, I will pass on to become you,*
> *you whom I see in my visions as a ghostly pale girl who stares*
> *at her prophesied husband with all the love he well deserves . . .*

She gasped. "It's from *me*?"

"The goddess," Alexi whispered, visibly taken again by old, blurred wounds. His shaking hand gestured for her to continue, and Percy took the letter and did. Her voice was true and clear.

"Some have called me goddess, some have called me our Lady, and some have called me angel. A force of nature, I answer to all. But of all my mortal names, I remain fondest of Persephone, which I hope you've accepted in my honor.

"What is built between you and Alexi is strong. I have seen it, seen this very moment in a vision—the Liminal and fate willing—and so I leave this note for you. You are meant to hear it from me, a herald from your past affirming your present. I made a promise to Alexi, a promise he likely only remembers as an echo in his heart, but a promise that he will be loved, supported, adored. I believe that he is.

"He comes from a lineage of Guard Leaders, via the grandfather he never knew. He was intended for this destiny, though he had to walk it blindly. I see now that this must always be the way, for only through honest human choices can any power or destiny be effective. Only through mutually earned love is the old vendetta truly healed. Without that, the vendetta lives on.

"I die. My form fails me; the last drops of my life force are bled into the Whisper-world to set the Guard free. But you, dear girl, will set me free. You must live on, live well and love. No matter the storms, no matter the nightmares. You are my eyes, my heart, and the whole of my light. You are the future I would wish for myself.

"Goodbye, my beloveds. I give my light unto you and pray for Peace.

"One final thing: Ahmed, the Heart of the Guard before yours, warned of a war in the ground. "Do not close every door," he said. The dead must pass. I trust that you will know what that means when the time comes. Love unto you."

Finished, there was a long silence before Percy registered that she was aglow. Light shone at her bosom, a reactive luminosity in times of danger or extreme emotion, the power borrowed from a goddess but sustained by her passionate, mortal heart.

She gripped her husband's arm, thinking again of the goddess that was both her and not her. No matter how things had come to pass, this whole family was her greatest gift.

"I was left so in the dark," he murmured. "We *both* were left in the dark." Alexi took the letter from Percy's trembling hand and put it down. "If we'd just been told, all the trauma of our coming together could have been avoided. All the danger—"

Percy, aware that she was particularly luminous in the moonlight, placed a radiant hand upon her husband's cheek, cupping it gently. "You heard the goddess's words, and I have maintained—and will always maintain—that falling in love with you of my own accord was far better than being told to do so. How else can one gain sure footing but to stumble first along the way?"

He stared down at her; the weight of adoration in his eyes could have anchored a steamer. "Again, you prove wise beyond your years. My *goddess*." He bent to kiss her and she accepted eagerly.

"I have to wonder; will it ever end?" she murmured once she'd drawn away to tuck her head into his shoulder.

"We can't know," Alexi replied. "But I have you. Together we have a treasure." He reached out and combed his fingers through a lock of her pearlescent hair, pressing his lips to her temple and speaking softly against her ear. "And for you, for this family, I will suffer anything."

He smiled suddenly, pushing her away far enough to gaze at her, so she could see the conviction in his eyes. "I believe I've strength enough for one last fight, should Phoenix again come to call and the Grand Work press us back into service. We have our promises and I intend to keep them."

Percy loosed a weary chuckle. "I've been quite enjoying retirement. But perhaps our daughter will outshine us all."

Alexi nodded. "For she embodies our love. Darkness can never again ascend the same throne. Light crowned us the victors, and while we yet live, we shall walk in its promise. No matter what dreams—or nightmares—may come."

HOURS LATER, BEHIND THE THICK CURTAINS OF THEIR BED, ALEXI Rychman held his wife close. They'd been unable to sleep, discussing their daughter's dream, the echo in the letter.

"I say we tell her the whole of it. The goddess, Phoenix, the Muses, the Gorgon, Prophecy, everything. We should tell her that for over twenty years, ending just before she was born, we were the Guard; spectral arbiters guarding the barrier between this world and the Whisper-world," Alexi declared after a long silence. "If she is having nightmares and seeing ghosts, we ought to be honest about the fact we used to police them. If some sort of power lingers in her, she should be aware of where it came from."

Percy took a deep breath. "A normal life, Alexi. I want her to have a normal life." Her calm tone was belied by the way her hands shook. Her mind flooded with memories, and the murmurs of being called a freak while growing up were hot upon her ears.

"Can't we just . . . wait to see if she asks? Wait to see if something actually needs our attention? I don't want to give her the pressure of an unsure fate; you and I both know that's maddening."

"More maddening than saying nothing?"

"What could we tell her?" Percy asked anxiously. "We are as the Muses left us; without collective powers. We perceive only a vague few omens in dreams and the whispering of spirits. What could we tell her that would be of use?"

"The story of our pasts."

"When she's older," Percy insisted. "The stuff of the Grand Work ages a soul. Let the girl be a girl. At least for a while."

Alexi folded his arms. "Should we stop inviting over the 'extended family,' then?"

"No, of course not! The Guard is family indeed, her aunts and uncles . . ."

"The Grand Work of the Guard still defines us," Alexi stated. "It always has, as it did those who came before us, defining us still even in death. We should not pretend it is not of the very fabric of our existence, of why you and I are together at all . . ."

"I know, my love. I just . . ." Percy looked away. Her voice became very small and sad. "I wouldn't wish my own childhood upon her. I want a joy for her that I never knew until I came to Athens."

"Trust who we are, Percy." He cupped her cheek, lifted her face to look at him, and spoke definitively. "I will do as you request but I will not lie to her. If she asks a question, we must answer it."

"Entirely agreed."

"Let's keep her close at Athens," Alexi suggested. "She's bright enough to continue tutoring there, with more than just we two teaching her; that way she'll always be accessible to us."

Persephone lit at the thought. "I'd love to, but she's so young . . ."

"*Nearly* nine. Going on nineteen," Alexi muttered. Persephone chuckled.

"She hardly wants to go anywhere without Will Page. Her dearest friend. I imagine she'll ask if he can come. He's a sharp lad; shall we ask Marianna and Edward if they'd permit our godson to have a head start on his education?"

Alexi shrugged. "And *that* child, too, goodness. Eight going on *eighty*. He's got a stare that could unnerve a warrior. What did I do to deserve old-soul children around me, children who are far too intelligent for their own good?"

"To keep you young." Persephone smiled, offering a kiss.

Still, she trembled. Perhaps it was the goddess within her, rest-less beneath her skin, ready to protect her own at any cost, even that of her life.

CHAPTER
TWO

WILL PAGE WAS IN THE LIBRARY, WINDING A COPPER WIRE around a small spool, a book about alternating and direct current open in his lap, when his best friend burst in without being announced.

"Willificent the Terrificent! You're coming to Athens with me!" Violet Rychman stormed into the modest, well-kept Page household south of Hampstead Heath, crossing the parlor in a few swift bounds.

"It's my first day there and it *promises* to be an adventure," she said, pausing at the library's threshold. "You must come with me."

Violet must have learned such entrances from her father, Will thought. Professor Rychman always made Will feel he should dodge out of the way, lest he be knocked to the ground by a billowing fold of black fabric.

Looking up from his book with a small smile, Will took in the black-haired, luminous-skinned girl standing with arms folded across her waist. Her pose and imperious air made her a near-perfect imitation of her father.

Will was obsessed with watching people; he learned so much doing so, and he loved watching Violet most. Especially when evening moonlight tinted her hair the color of her name.

"Alexi and I struggled to name her," Persephone Rychman had explained when Will had once asked about it. "She was just so important to us, how could we pick *one* word to encapsulate our entire world? When she was born, and we brought her into the moonlight, clouds parted and a shaft of light fell directly upon her head. There was a violet halo about my angel's head."

"God must've anointed her an angel right there," Will had replied. "I mean, *you're* one, Mrs. Rychman. That's what Mum says; that you're like snow all over because you're an angel. That makes Violet half angel," Will had stated. He remembered that Persephone had grinned broadly and pressed him into a warm embrace that made his tumultuous mind clear into something serene; proof she was an angel, how else could she make him feel so at peace?

Violet often had that effect, too. But not always. Sometimes she roused something else in him—something far darker.

"Will, are you listening to me or have you gone away again?" She tromped up to him, peering into his eyes.

He returned to the present. Violet stood before him in a lavender pinafore that brought out the amethyst tint to her eyes—there were many shades of violet to Violet.

"I'm sorry, Violencia the Magnificenzia," he said, returning her grand nickname with a bow of his head, "I suppose I was lost again. What do you demand of me?" he asked with a partial smile. He learned that expression, he'd been told, from his father, Edward, a gamesome man who was delightfully bewildered by the women in his life.

"I *said*, I'm going to Athens to sit in on classes. If it suits, I'll start attending. You must come. You're smart enough," she said, gesturing to his wire and electrical book.

Will thought a moment. "Aren't we too young?"

"They take the best ones early."

Usually the first years at Athens Academy were bright ten- or eleven-year-olds at the very least. They had to be exemplary to be admitted so early.

Will had strict rules for himself. The whispering darkness would come for him, if he was bad. He had to be a very good boy indeed.

He had always known that he lived on a precarious ledge. A whispering darkness would come for him and everyone he loved if he wasn't careful. But he shook that off and focused again on the purple streaks in Violet's eyes, shrugging as he answered, "I suppose you're right, we're smart enough."

"I'm usually right, Will, you should know that by now," Violet stated.

"Come now, Violet. Don't be boastful, it's unbecoming." An angel appeared at the library threshold.

Thanks to her spider-silk white hair and glittering ice-blue eyes, there was a constant glow of loving warmth about Mrs. Rychman. Violet's eerily colorless skin was an inherited effect of her mother's extreme albinism. While Will noticed most people reacted to her with a start, he didn't understand how anyone couldn't find her beautiful. He considered Persephone and Violet Rychman, unique as they were, the two most beautiful things God ever fashioned.

"Violet simply *wouldn't* come to Athens today without you, Will," Persephone stated. "So I asked your family. If you like the Academy, you may begin, too."

Before Will could reply, a raven-haired man all in black, a greatcoat on his arm and top hat in hand, towered at the door behind his younger wife.

"What do you say, young Master Page? Do you accept the challenge?" Professor Rychman asked in his low, thundering voice, stepping into the room and taking air out of it as he did. Will felt as though the little library wasn't meant for this many overwhelming presences.

Even though the professor terrified him, Will preferred not to make it evident. He raised his chin, squared his chest, and looked up into those fearsome dark eyes.

"I accept, sir."

Professor Rychman deigned a curt nod.

At the Rychmans' fine carriage, Will's mother, Marianna, lavished no end of affections in German upon him, making him blush. Mrs. Rychman and his mother, her blond curls bouncing, shared a fond embrace. They were best friends and had been, his mother proudly declared, from the moment they met, the day they both arrived as students at Athens Academy.

"So young. I arrived at Athens at fifteen . . ." His mother clucked her tongue, looking at both children. "Too young . . ." A melancholy expression passed over her fair face, her green eyes clouding.

"Our children are special," Professor Rychman declared as he helped his wife and daughter into the cab, swirling his black great-coat behind him and placing a black-booted leg on the stair. "And there is no more special place in all the world than Athens Academy."

Will did not take any hand; he nimbly hopped up the stair and into the closest seat, realizing with some trepidation that it would place him beside Professor Rychman. Violet quickly bounced across to sit next to him and all was well.

Most of Will's formative memories generally involved the Rychmans. Violet was his earliest and best friend. Will found it impossible to express in words the magnitude of what she meant. He felt as though she were an extension of his own life; that his world only ended at the tip of her fingers.

However, Will's *earliest* memory was of darkness . . . a large, roiling darkness that had many hissing heads. It slunk about his room in vague, slithering shapes. It murmured near his ear. Grains of ash occasionally tumbled across his bedclothes.

From then on, he owned sadness and pain, stony grains lodged in an otherwise healthy heart, along with his brighter joys. He thought of those memories as tiny portraits hung in a dusty, cob-webbed room. Perhaps Athens could help supplant those shad-owed corners with new ones.

The Bloomsbury district of London was upon them, full of grand shops and museum plazas. One narrow corner was turned and there was the impressive fortress that was Athens Academy, all Richardson Romanesque red sandstone. The buildings sur-rounding the complex turned their backs upon it, bordering the school with alleys, making it a rather well-kept secret indeed.

It was the first time and certainly not the last that Will won-dered what sorts of secrets sat silent between him and this family. He knew his. What were theirs?

"While your father and I check in with Auntie Rebecca—ah, that will be Headmistress Carroll to you now—wait in my office," Persephone instructed.

Already tearing up the steps, Violet called assent. Will was quick behind her. The few times they had visited Athens, it always seemed magical.

"Isn't your mother's office on the second floor?" Will asked as they swept past the landing in the opposite direction.

"Yes, but I had visions of something, upstairs *this* way. Let's go and see!" They ran up and their smooth shoes slid them out onto the marble tiles of the third-floor foyer, all stately and open, colonnaded, and bordered by huge windows with gauzy curtains making the room glow gray in the London daylight.

"Yes!" she said in a conspiratorial whisper. "This is what I know. This is what I've been seeing, *feeling*, since I can remember!"

Violet giggled and began bobbing, no, *waltzing* around the open foyer, her small booted footfalls echoing on the marble in a bouncing three count. He'd heard his mother say that waltzing led to indecent behavior. She'd said it with a giggle, however, and with her arms around his father.

Looking down, Will studied the seal of Athens beneath his feet. A circle of reflective mosaic tile surrounded a bronze plate stamped with a great eagle, talons outstretched and seemingly ready to snag him by the leg. A small pain throbbed in his head. His vision spun a bit. The motto of the Academy swam before his vision:

So Promethean Fire Banished Darkness: So Knowledge Bears the Power and the Light.

A strange noise filled his ears. Music and voices. Beautiful music and singing.

"William Page," said a deep, resonant voice. "You may never hear our voices again, so listen close. It is our fault that there is a shadow that haunts you. It is from an old, old wound. We'll do our best to help you fight it. But when in doubt, look to the light."

Violet moved to stand with him on the seal, looking first at the powerful bird, then at the boy.

In that moment, young Violet shone. She was engulfed in fiery light, blue and blinding at first, then a bright eruption of every color of the rainbow, as if a prism were made a bonfire.

Will gasped, sure their lives would never be the same.

Violet had never felt such happiness.

She stared down at the seal, the wide-winged eagle flying bold and triumphant over the motto of Athens Academy, there on the third floor where hardly anyone traveled. She felt that if she stared hard enough she could see whatever was itching at the side of her mind, wanting to show her great wonders. Looking up, she noticed Will was staring at her as if she were a different creature entirely than his best friend. As if she had become *more* just by standing in this place.

Athens had now become a magical castle all her own. Not just because her family worked here. Her place was here, in four adjoining halls and grand courtyard, and she felt certain that the building itself had claimed her. As she stood on the seal, so did it seal its place in her heart. She could almost hear it saying her name.

She dropped to her knees, the cool brass and stone biting through the thin layer of her bloomers. A warm current of air eddied around her small body, carrying a gorgeous musical note into her ears.

"I'm here," she said to the eagle.

A hazy, pearlescent glow rose from the seal like a bas-relief, threaded with a snaking line of cerulean-blue fire. The flames illuminated part of the mosaic more brightly than the rest; Violet softly said the words that were most vibrantly lit.

"The Power and the Light . . ." As she murmured, the blue flame wrapped around her suddenly, sending her to her feet, fire arcing up from her back, snaking around her arms, and she gasped.

"We are entwined, my child," the fire whispered. "If you need me, we will all awake."

Violet looked at Will, who was staring at her in amazement, biting his lip, seemingly in conflict between worry and exultation.

"Do you . . ."

"See the light?" he finished. "Yes. It's blinding. And I hear something, too." This was perhaps the most excited she'd ever heard him, the most relieved. "Something far nicer than the voice I've tried to fight as long as I can remember. This feels like the opposite of that dreadful hissing."

"Is it an angel we're hearing now, I wonder?" Violet whispered, looking around to be sure they were alone. This was the sort of thing her mother would tell her not to say in front of strangers.

"What else?" Will replied. His brow furrowed as if any other possibility was unconscionable. The light dimmed, the thrilling, rushing sensation faded, and a new sound was heard: footfalls on the stairs.

The children turned to see Violet's parents ascending. Violet stood straighter, though she could still feel the tingling echo of what had enlivened her skin, spirit, mind, and heart. If the elder Rychmans saw anything different about the space, they kept it well concealed.

"Exploring, are we?" her father asked in a tone that reverberated through the hall. "When you were told to report directly to your mother's office?"

Violet nodded. "I'm sorry, Father, but I couldn't help myself. This place is so beautiful!" she exclaimed. "*This* space in particular!"

"Yes . . . it . . . holds many memories," her father said, and here, he turned to her mother. The love he shone upon her was such a stark contrast of warmth against an unfailingly icy, stoic exterior. Violet considered how in love they were to be vaguely nauseating, but she had grown somewhat inured to it.

"Your mother and I shared our first dance right here," he explained, "right where you stand."

"Did the space sing for you, too?" Violet began with an exclamation that faded to a whisper at the end, as her mother reached out a cautionary hand.

A student scurried past, glancing nervously at her imperious father.

"This place has . . . curious acoustics," Alexi explained.

Her mother offered a hand, first to Violet, then to Will. "Come, let us show you to your classrooms."

The children followed, looking at one another as if they wanted to say so much more. It wasn't just acoustics. It was *magic*, angelic magic, something beyond description that seemed as though it had been waiting there, just for them to find.

Violet was beaming. For the first time, she had something to combat her inner war, the visions and nightmares that terrified her. Sounds she heard echoing in her ear in terrible tattoos. And from what she knew of Will's own struggles, so did he have a new salve. She was sure she was too young to worry about death, dying, and war. About fighting and protecting. And yet, if they were cursed, here was help.

She prayed she wasn't imagining it all, and most importantly, she begged that angelic music to remain in her ears. To drown out the explosions and screams, before the din finally drove her mad.

Her mother looked down at her curiously and for a moment Violet wondered if the woman could read her mind.

CHAPTER
THREE

THE WHISPER-WORLD WAS A BREATHTAKING PLACE. THAT'S what the four Keepers had come to realize after thousands of years in the sifting place of the dead. Its grayscale nature was of so many delicate hues; as a snow-bound culture having innumerable words for snow, so did the Keepers comprehend the vastness of charcoal and shadow.

The world was born of an old violence; when ancient divinities struck out in murder and woe, and mankind's restless miseries became more complex as society evolved. The melancholy of the species was enough to populate a realm and the Whisper-world became a plane separate from mortal experience but a place all would ultimately waft through after death.

The Whisper-world was populated by the listless dead, the ones whose souls carried a certain weight, sorrow, or pressing attachment. The viler sort slunk off to deeper depths and the buoyant floated on to heavens knew where. The Keepers liked to think of their world as representing all the rich shades of aching possibility; a precarious promise of a better life floating like a brittle leaf along the onyx river that flowed through its heart. Never mind the bones in the waters.

Relegating themselves to the shadows entirely, the Keepers did not involve themselves any further in the ancient vendetta they avoided. This could be characterized as cowardice, however they preferred to think of their actions as maintaining a cautious arc of history. When the whole place threatened to crumble after Darkness fell in the Guard's war, they silently kept up the great stone eaves.

But the old foundations of this special place were weakening. The Keepers noticed widening cracks at the bases of their great columns where before there had only been smooth hewn stone moist with tears. Whatever rumbled in the parallel mortal world could shake the base of both realms.

The great clock over the Liminal proscenium was ticking loudly. A telling sign. A rectangular viewing space set aside from the great Whisper-world dais, the Liminal was built for divinities to project prophecies and wreak fates. Its clock showed all possibilities of time and destiny. Its otherworldly, crystalline light went so far as to snake out toward the Keepers' shadows, as if reaching out a hand, bidding they come and see. The Liminal was wholly on the side of mortals and so for the Keepers to have received this gesture was sounding an alarm indeed. They followed the trail of light to the distinct Liminal edge and watched.

Its great clock ticked forward and showed the Keepers many scenes of the coming century; if mankind so chose to take a poisoned bait left buried in the earth, a harrowing toxin that magnified all their worst sins.

"Oblivious fools," the leader of the Keepers, the tallest shrouded form, said in its dusty death rattle.

"What to do?" queried a soft sigh from the smallest form behind the leader.

"What else is there but to rouse those who forsook us?" growled the tallest shroud in response. "How could they have let such a stage be set?"

* * *

FIVE MUSES, GREAT BEINGS OF BEAUTY AND MAGIC THAT HAD served mortals since ancient times of gods and monsters, were awoken from their much-needed rest in the bricks of Athens Academy after the Guard waged war there. They had found peace in the Guard's Sacred Space, a lovely, circular stone chapel full of celestial music and starlight that existed in the sliver between mortal and spirit worlds. There they had slipped away from consciousness and the tick of mortal time for a period of recovery.

However, their rest proved impermanent. Their glowing, iridescent forms were drawn from slumber into sharp alertness at a wretched tearing sound. A rectangular portal now stood open before them, obliterating anything else from view save the wet, gray, labyrinthine corridors of the Whisper-world of the dead, endless halls of silver mist that trailed off behind four dusty, hooded, shrouded figures who stood in the foreground.

The closest of the four figures spoke, a rattling, wheezing sound of something brittle unused to speech.

"What are you going to do about your mess, Muses? You waged a war and you didn't clean up all your casualties. Some of it got away, already causing trouble; poisoning your beloved earth."

Of the five Muses, Intuition was the leader and it spoke. Its luminous, violet-tinged form was incorporeal but its voice was resonant and clear. The rest of the Muses that had embodied and powered the Guard wafted close to Intuition, their wispy mass so colorful and warm compared to the cool gray winding-sheet figures before them.

"That's *your* mess, Whisper-world, not ours," Intuition countered. Its violet form flickered like a candle. "And who are you to accuse us so?"

"After your murder of Darkness," the foremost shroud replied in a wheeze, "in the absence of a leader, we four old souls took it upon ourselves to settle what you threw into chaos. Darkness had his faults to be sure, but he kept our world protected. *Your* mistake threatens to destabilize not only your precious mortal world, but ours as well. The Whisper-world is not an endless void. As the mortal world grows in population, our capacity has limits. Whatever is left of the Gorgon doesn't now care *what* it undoes."

"We destroyed her completely," Intuition scoffed.

"*Not* entirely. Part of her remains escaped into mortal soil. Her base materials have transformed into something far more terrible than the Whisper-world alone would ever have fashioned. It is unrecognizable to us now. Her forces pull at the edge of the Whisper-world like a thread, unravelling the foundations she once helped build. Our ancient fortifications are cracking from strain that will only worsen with the weight of a new century and the disasters that will befall it if visions go unaltered."

"Then take care of your own, once and for all," Intuition instructed. "*Your* mistake. That creature was born of your world."

"She once loved this world; now there is only hate and the virulence leans too easily into mortal tendencies."

Intuition floated forward toward the edge of the threshold the shadows had opened. "We'll stand in the way of whatever violence we have to, as we always have."

The foremost shroud snorted. "You proud fools. Your limitations will be proven to you in time."

Intuition peered closer at the forms who seemed made of nothing more than grave-clothes and dust. "Who *are* you, though? Do we know you?"

One of the forms laughed bitterly and the Liminal window between worlds snapped shut with a concussive thunderclap that threw the Muses back onto the stones so violently that Intuition felt the depths of their own weakness.

They hadn't recovered enough. The truth was, these divinities couldn't rally even if they wanted to. Their essence settled back into the bricks again in hopes of better healing and renewal, with no idea of the grinding fault lines across mortal Empires.

The last thing that could be heard was a faraway hiss; an old familiar death rattle to give them nightmares as they slept.

CHAPTER
FOUR

ELIJAH WITHERSBY NAPPED IN THE SPACIOUS SITTING ROOM OF the fine Kensington mansion he shared with his wife, Josephine. The gray English light filtering in the bay window fell across his eyes at an angle, lighting his closed lids with a grim glow. His dreaming mind saw the familiar ghost, in that same gray light. His tragic mistake.

He never slept well near the anniversary of Aaron Willis's death.

It was trivial, what had prompted him to abandon the Grand Work in 1877. A fight with Josie, when they were still young lovers, and a fight with his family about property—a marquess's second son had little responsibility, but little to say about what was left him or given him to do. Whatever led him to slough off his Guard duties as the Memory paled in comparison to the wrath he endured in the aftermath. The full Guard needn't be present at every ghostly admonishment or poltergeist corral, but with a violent possession, the full and fated six were required.

Elijah had wrongly assumed he could take a holiday, deal with his family drama, and return to the group when he was in a better place.

Elijah's duty, as chosen vessel of the Muse of Memory, was to alter the minds of passersby during a spectral incident. He was called to make families remember nothing of terrors endured. It was his job to ensure the Guard and their gifts went unnoticed and unsung throughout haunted London.

But the rest of the Guard, who had rallied to the side of a possessed child during an exorcism, faltered and failed when Elijah didn't show. Their chain of celestial song and holy fire was broken and the preternatural force that overtook the young Aaron Willis pressed the very life out of him.

Alexi had tracked Elijah down to a flat he and Josephine used as a private rendezvous. The Leader had kicked down the door, then lunged at Elijah in a swirl of black fabric and fury, knocking the other man across the room.

Hand to a bloody split lip, Elijah scrambled back. Alexi plucked a newspaper clipping from his breast pocket and threw it at the young nobleman. The headline shouted:

CHARING CROSS OCCULT MYSTERY LEAVES BOY DEAD, FIVE SUSPECTS ON THE LOOSE

Elijah read the gruesome report about a boy who had been found self-mutilating when five people broke into the house of a shop-keeper and his wife, seemingly trying to "help" while a priest officiated. A housekeeper in the building saw the intrusion and alerted a local officer. The strange group had escaped in a mysterious pyrotechnic display of blue fire.

"You're going to clean up the mess you made," Alexi seethed. "You're going to go to every person involved and wipe their memories clean of us and of what went wrong in that flat."

"Alexi, you can't force me—" Elijah winced, shrinking back from Alexi's lifted hand and gasping in a sudden sharp agony. Since Elijah had ignored the Pull that psychically called them all together in times of crisis, he'd been having chest pains as if knives were at his heart. Clearly, physically and psychically, he and the Grand Work were tied and nothing could sunder it while he was alive. He supposed he could kill himself . . .

Rather than land another angry blow, Alexi sighed, ran a hand through his mess of black hair, and took a different tack.

"I doubt we'll ever have children of our own, Withersby," Alexi declared. "So, you might do, as the rest of us have done, to begin thinking of the children of London as our own. The lives we save by banishing evil spirits is our one and *only* calling. *Nothing* else matters. Not your comfort, not your status, not your class, not your heart!" Alexi ground his teeth.

"I pray this boy haunts you," Alexi growled. "To remind you of your selfishness. Your faults. To remind you to keep the Grand Work ever foremost."

It was as if Alexi had cursed him right then and there.

Young Willis did haunt him. In a modest schoolboy's suit, floating in grayscale at Elijah's bedside, staring down at him accusingly as he slept. The shirt that should have been pale was stained dark. Bloodied, Elijah assumed, from a puncture wound where the boy had stabbed himself, spurred on by the offending spirit. Their healer, Jane, had been unable to mend him well enough before they were intercepted. Thankfully, Alexi's holy fire distracted the authorities long enough to allow the Guard safe retreat. If Elijah had been there as Memory, all would have been kept in line, their duties uninterrupted.

"Traitor," came a whisper at his ear. His mind manifested infinite cruelties of haunting damnation. Elijah started in his chair, bolting awake, then recoiling in fright as the ghost bobbed before his face.

Tears rimmed the lord's tired eyes. "I'm sorry. How many times must I tell you?" he pleaded.

The ghost shrugged, as if he wasn't sure when he'd be satisfied. Not that he could have heard the child if he had said anything. The Guard could see spirits and once had power over them, but as far as they were concerned, the ghosts were silent. Only their prophesied Persephone could hear what the spirits had to say.

Sighing, Withersby put his head in his hands. Usually he wasn't one for prayer, but now he prayed for a sign or message, a task to make this nightmare finally pass. When he lifted his head again, the boy was gone.

The balance between the mortal and spirit worlds was delicate, mercurial; fragile. Now that the Guard were no longer responsible for maintaining that balance, Elijah thought he alone remained sensitive to this razor-thin edge, that he himself was balanced precariously on the rim of a precipice. He wasn't sure how long he could keep upright before tumbling into the abyss.

"Ah, good, it's time you got up, I don't want you sleeping the day away," his wife said, entering the room in a fine, plum-colored day gown. She was carrying a tray bearing a tea service, which she sat upon the lacquered table between two chairs.

Of the six disciplines that the Muses bestowed upon their chosen coterie, Josephine Belledoux had been the Artist. The countless canvases hung on every wall of their home were all from her talented hand. During their time in the Guard, she had primarily painted spiritual subjects; now, her images were almost entirely of flowers.

Dark-haired—save for two white streaks, one at each temple—and proudly French, Josephine was stunningly beautiful, with dusky skin thanks to distant colonial island relatives. They'd been in love from the first, a passionate, often tumultuous partnership, but devoted nonetheless. Despite Elijah's snide arrogance and elite airs, he'd always secretly wondered what in the world he'd done to deserve her. His vague disbelief at his lot and his dangerous listlessness formed a subtle undercurrent to some of their arguments.

Pouring tea, Josephine examined him with an artist's scrutiny. A rose-blossom, probably from a still life she'd been painting, sat tucked behind her ear. Its gentle scent wafted down to his nose.

"You've got that look about you," she said, running an olive-skinned hand over his blue-veined one before handing him the teacup and saucer. "Willis again?"

Elijah nodded.

"We've got to do something about that. We can't have you haunted forever."

"I keep asking the boy what he wants. Eventually he has to tell me in a way I can intuit."

"Let's take this to the group," she urged.

"I've already been trouble enough where this is concerned!" Elijah said sharply. "I'll not waste anyone's time on it but my own. This is my penance. The least I owe."

Josephine didn't push the subject further but Elijah could feel a gulf widening between them, a dread gnawing at his nerves. He felt sure he would, in time, get an answer from the child about what would set him to rest . . . and equally certain that it would be too much to bear, or that he'd fail yet again.

CHAPTER
FIVE

AFTER VIOLET'S FIRST VISIT TO ATHENS, PERCY WAS IN THE parlor, absently tending to some needlework, when a familiar presence wafted into the room. A ghostly hover at the corner of her eye. Percy smiled warmly and turned to her departed friend.

Jane.

The former Healer of the Guard, who had sacrificed herself so that Percy and the newly conceived Violet might live, floated at eye level. A polarizing rush of emotions filled Percy: the lifting joy of reunion and the plummeting wrench of guilt at being a reason for her death. But Jane would have no sadness.

"Your daughter," the healer, who hovered at the French window, nearly blending in with the white curtains, replied warmly, "is talented. In many ways that will yet prove themselves." She drifted closer, an earnest expression on her grayscale face. "You have to let her fully become the girl she's meant to be. Just like you, only with a streak of her father that will give the world a reckoning." Jane's Irish lilt made her words bounce in a way Percy loved to hear.

"You weren't protected when you came into your own," the spirit continued. "You underwent trials by fire. I know Violet's dreams worry you, but she's better advantaged than you were at her age."

"I would wish my sad orphan's life on no one—"

"You mustn't worry. She's got the best of you and Alexi. She's not unprotected. Besides, the Muses are watching. She's *not* alone and the old powers haven't forgotten you."

"Thank you, this is just what I needed to hear," Percy replied.

"They may all be back before we know it," Jane murmured and before Percy could ask anything further, the spirit, seemingly taken by the sight of a butterfly landing on a rose, wafted through the lace and the windowpanes to become a part of a beautiful picture. Percy lost sight of her transparent form in the glow of a blue-gray sunset.

Small footsteps were suddenly closer. A small form at the threshold.

"Mummy, who were you talking to?" Violet asked.

"No one, darling." Percy smiled. "Just myself."

Violet shook her head. "The madwoman doesn't suit you—"

Percy chortled. "Doesn't it? Well, I've been called far worse."

Violet sighed. "You don't need to protect me from everything. Was it Auntie Jane?"

Percy stared at her child and saw that the true, piercing effect of her own ice-blue eyes could unsettle her child when sharply focused. "That is what a mother does, protect. And, yes, it was Auntie Jane, who says you're very talented."

After that brief moment, Violet evenly met her mother's gaze. Percy saw the old soul within her daughter whose mind, language, and spirit were all beyond her years.

"In my dreams," Violet began, not countering her mother, but matching her, "it's *me* doing the protecting. And that's the only thing that makes any of the dreams bearable."

Percy reached out her arms and Violet fell into them. "Being protectors is a family tradition, for all your aunts and uncles, too. You're not alone. How well could you hear Auntie Jane?" Percy asked, genuinely curious as to what her daughter may have over-heard.

"Bits and pieces. I have to concentrate."

Percy nodded. "Will you tell me if your sensitivities change and if anything needs attending to? I wish I could wipe the grim things you see from your mind."

"Only time can do that, I think," Violet said. Something in her child's expression made Percy wonder if she would, in fact, be told when her daughter's gifts and visions changed. She feared a gulf would develop between them, an expanse that was not merely the yawn of years between adult and child, but a difference of experience, a working not of time but of destiny. But for now, she had a lovely child who was unique and precious and she had to cherish every moment afforded her.

She rose, keeping Violet by the hand and gesturing forward. "Shall we to the symphony tonight?" she asked.

"Oh, yes please!" Violet jumped, dragging her mother out of the parlor and toward the stairs, eager to put on finery.

"To music?" Violet lifted her arm as if leading a charge.

"To music!"

A sweet battle cry for culture.

"You know, Mum, what I think will save the world, if the world is ever in trouble?"

"What's that, love?"

"Art. Music. Books!" Violet exclaimed. "Those are the ways to make sense of terrible things."

"That is precisely so, how terribly wise," Percy said in agreement.

"We'll understand the future even if we can't in the moment," Violet continued, as if willing a future into existence. "*I'll* understand my dreams someday. In poems. I can wait for those . . . Poems make some sense of the senseless . . . Art can lead us." Violet looked away and hummed a melody Percy recognized as the freshly beloved carol "Silent Night." Why that, of all things?

CHAPTER
SIX

THE GUARD GATHERED AT THE WITHERSBY ESTATE FOR DIN-
ner, and the distinct personalities sat at the long mahogany table
trading tales and fond barbs, the bright new electric lights lending a hearty glow to all the white lace and gilt trimmings.

It was a motley crew that had been gathered together in their
youth from various backgrounds and class strata. Despite their dif-
ferences, they remained family even if their duties patrolling the
spectral realm had faded.

Violet, the only child of their number, was adored by all, and
as she was well behaved, was allowed to sit at the table and dine
with the adults. Percy couldn't bear for her little visionary to
have seen the profound depths of what she saw and yet still be set
aside for the simple fact of her age. The love on every face whenever
Violet joined their full company was unmistakable.

As far as Violet knew, her unusual family had worked in secret
for the Crown and there was nothing further to be said about it.
That's what Percy felt comfortable sharing, for now.

"I hear you visited Athens, Violet," said Headmistress Rebecca Thompson-Carroll, a tall, thin, intimidating woman with
graying brown hair and piercing, unrelenting gray-blue eyes. "Will
you be joining us for classes, then?"

"Yes, Headmistress," Violet said eagerly, nodding at both the
headmistress and her husband at her side. The radiantly pleasant

Vicar Carroll eased the severe edge of his wife. His glittering bright eyes, white bushy hair, and full moustache always curved upward by a smile gave him the air of a jolly old elf.

"And Will, he'll join us there, too," Violet added. She turned to an empty chair across the table from her before looking up at Percy. "Mum, why isn't Will here tonight? I thought the Pages were coming."

"He isn't feeling well," Percy replied.

"Headaches again," Violet murmured. "You should help him with them, if you can." Violet offered her mother a winning smile. "I think you can fix anything."

"She certainly fixed your father," Lord Withersby said from the head of the table.

The constant battle of barbs between Withersby and the professor was the stuff of legend. Elijah was Alexi's foil; the nobleman's constant teasing and bright, foppish airs were the antithesis of Alexi's black attire and stern demeanor. It had always amused Percy greatly, and Violet, too, who took to the game.

"All while you remain a helpless case, then, Uncle?" Violet replied to Elijah. At this, the group crowed laughter, none so much as Lady Withersby, who passed the child an extra helping of pudding in victory.

"By God, Heiress Incorrigible, forsake thy acerbic ways, there is yet time for you!" Elijah pleaded dramatically, tossing back a lock of his flaxen blond hair he'd let grow longer than was fashionable.

"Time enough for me to keep sharpening my young wit on your aging one!" Violet replied and grinned when her father beamed.

Percy laughed along with the group but her sensitive heart, always attuned to the complexities of her chosen family, turned to where she felt a weight settle in. Particular cares aged with them each in their own way, old wounds with internal scars.

Percy noticed Josephine's eyes were on her. Dressed in the latest French fashion and an elaborate coiffure, Josie, their consummate artist, was as immaculate as ever, but there was a visible strain around her eyes and mouth, and her olive skin seemed more ashen than vibrant.

Looking across the table at Elijah, Percy found a similar weariness. The couple were generally the picture of joviality and warmth, and they were putting on a good show of it, but Percy knew something ate at them.

After dinner, while Michael eagerly entertained his wife and Violet at the piano in the parlor, and Alexi and Elijah took to cigars and sherry in the den, Josephine took Percy aside to the back veranda of the house, lit brightly by the moon across the heath. Josie spoke quietly in French, a far more comfortable tongue for her when worried or impassioned; due to her supernatural augmentations, Percy was able to understand all languages.

"If you have a moment, my dear, and it seems natural . . . Elijah is . . . having a hard time. He'd not want me to bring it up but something is eating him alive."

"Oh, I'm very sorry to hear that he's troubled," Percy murmured in the same language. "How can I help?"

Josie sighed, then replied in a torrent. "Years ago, long before you were with us, he abandoned the Guard in a fit of pique. I know he didn't mean for any ill to come of it but . . ." The Frenchwoman wrung her hands. "A child died during an exorcism while Elijah was away. You know we needed *all* our talents, especially when dealing with a possession."

Percy nodded as Josephine continued. "Elijah didn't really understand the weight of the Grand Work until then. He's been haunted ever since. By the dead boy himself. He tries to hide it from me, but you know how we women know . . ."

Reaching out, Percy touched Josephine's elbow in commiseration.

"We can always tell the subtle shifts," Percy agreed.

"I hope something can be done about it. If you see and speak with the boy, if Elijah dares open up to you . . ."

"I'll do whatever I can," Percy assured her friend, "to ease his suffering, and the spirit's, too. It remains one of my primary missions upon this earth to grant peace to spirits where I can. I'm glad to help." The women embraced.

When they returned to their sitting room, Michael was playing the piano and singing a colorful song that a vicar shouldn't necessarily know. He was changing the most suggestive words to silly ones, which made Violet, who was bouncing in a little jig by the side of the piano, laugh, to the vicar's evident delight. Rebecca stood towering over them, turning music pages and scoffing whenever her husband made a terrible pun.

Elijah had challenged Alexi to a game of chess and was obviously already regretting it.

Though Percy didn't see her, she could feel Jane nearby, and out of the corner of her eye Percy glimpsed the Gaelic ghosts as she and her beloved Aodhan danced in the Withersby rose garden, hovering feet above the slate stones.

Counting their few ghostly additions, they were the happiest of chosen families. Here they were, relishing simple pleasures and preoccupations; a normal life Percy had prayed so fervently for. A sudden violent pang pierced her and she sent a wrenching prayer unto God that nothing could tear them apart, that their paradise wasn't temporary after all.

At the same moment, Violet turned toward her and the look on her daughter's face made Percy nearly gasp with a secondary sort of pain, the kind a mother feels sharply when she sees that her little girl is now a lady. There was something in the child's eyes, a weight, a knowledge, a foreshadowing. Percy could feel the elder quality of her daughter's soul begin to truly take shape and form.

From Violet's early days, Percy had tried to cultivate a particular bond, a psychic closeness that would allow her to be in tune with her daughter. Percy valued a person's privacy too much to want to hear her daughter's thoughts or see through her eyes, but this gave her a way to know that Violet was not hurt or in need. She had honed a sense of her whereabouts sight unseen, an inner compass magnetized toward Violet with a secondary gauge upon her spirit.

While she didn't know if Violet had crafted a similar sense in reverse, it was quite clear that her daughter had picked up on that momentary pain. The girl shook her dark head and smiled faintly, an expression that was as weary as it was amused: *Don't worry about me, Mum. I'll be all right. My journey is my own. You cannot take it for me. But I promise I'll fight for us all.*

The girl was happy and strong, Percy saw, and she had to content herself with that. Just then, Violet winced.

"What is it, my dear?" Percy asked, placing a hand on her daughter's shoulder.

"That wretched pain here," she murmured, touching the back of her skull. "Not my head, Will's."

If Violet didn't have one of her senses tuned to her mother, then she certainly had one attuned to Will. He, Percy thought with some trepidation, was a part of the unknown. He always had been. None of the Guard knew it, really, not in the way that Percy did, but the poor child was born of the Abyss.

CHAPTER
SEVEN

THE SOUND OF SOMETHING TUMBLING AND FALLING WOKE LORD Withersby from a restless nap. He squinted at the inlaid table to the side of his Queen Anne chair and saw that the laudanum bottle he'd placed beside his teacup had fallen over. Its contents had dripped onto the floor.

"Damn," he muttered, picking up the small, empty bottle. He'd put a few drops into his tea, hoping to foster a decent nap, as his nights had been so sleepless of late. He knew he had to be careful, as within any opiate's clutches lay a yawning abyss.

Wishing to avoid a maid's silent judgment or concern, he decided to clean up the mess himself. He used a tea towel to wipe up the liquid, which gave off a heady mixture of sweet and bitter scents. The metal flower that served as a stopper had wound up caught in the fringed edge of a Persian rug; he picked it up and placed it back in the bottle's mouth, then wiped his fingers on the towel.

He wondered what could have tipped the bottle and sent the stopper flying. Given the position of the armchair he'd collapsed upon, he didn't think his own hand had been the cause. A chill blew through the room as the spirit of the boy who haunted him wafted up from behind the chair.

Badly startled, Withersby almost cursed the child but restrained himself, thinking better of it. Biting his tongue, he managed to suppress a growl.

The child began an elaborate sequence of gestures. Pointing first to the bottle, he mimed picking it up and putting it inside the pocket of his grubby jacket. Then he bobbed on the air, moving toward the door. Elijah sighed.

"What now?" He rose to his feet, buttoning his azure waistcoat and smoothing his mussed hair. The spirit sped toward him, creating a breeze of chilled air, and then back away, urging the aristocrat to follow. The ghost paused to point again to the laudanum bottle. Elijah began to assume that the boy had somehow managed to knock the vial over.

"You'd like me to bring this with?" he asked. The child nodded. "Whatever for?"

The boy folded his arms and frowned. Obviously, the explanation, if there was one, was not something that could be communicated in mime.

Shaking his head, Withersby placed the empty laudanum bottle into the breast pocket of his blue and white frock coat. "As you wish, then . . ." He glared at the spectral child. "Anything else?"

The spirit considered this a moment before deigning to smile and shaking his incorporeal head, shagged hair floating this and that way in weightless freedom.

Grumbling, pocketing a house key, and making sure a few notes were folded into his breast pocket, Elijah wound his way through the house, out the entrance foyer, and put his hand over his forehead as he strode down the lane, his eyes slowly adjusting to another glowingly gray day.

It wasn't easy to keep up with the translucent shade ahead of him. The spirit flickered in and out of view, making Elijah often stop or change direction abruptly. At one point he very nearly ran into a nanny with a pram; at another he was himself nearly run over by a passing carriage. Cursing under his breath all the while, Withersby tried not to call out to the maddening child, lest he garner too much attention and be labeled a madman.

Soon enough it became clear that the boy was leading him from Kensington to Bloomsbury. Any number of places important to the Guard could be found there, yet none, as far as Elijah could tell, directly related to this child. What was he up to?

At long last, following the wispy trail of the child's worn scarf that trailed limply behind his floating body, Withersby turned a sharply angled corner and stopped at the sight of an imposing, Romanesque, red sandstone fortress, hidden behind alleys and behind the backs of buildings.

"Athens?" he murmured. "Why?"

The ghost shook his head and pointed to an upper floor, as if there were something there that he needed to see.

Elijah lifted his hand. "Lead on, then," he said wearily.

Glad to find that the front doors were unlocked during school hours, he slipped inside, trying to appear to any passing students as though he belonged there, and hoping desperately to avoid any of his colleagues. It was hard not to notice that the bright colors and finer fabrics of his clothes did not harmonize with the school's prim and proper aesthetics.

The spirit had floated up a side staircase to what Elijah knew to be an open, upper foyer. He'd been here a few times and had often felt that there was something about that wing of the school that was particularly, thrillingly, eerie. The energy that coursed up and down the back of his neck wasn't the caress of a ghost but something altogether else. Athens had always been a living part-ner in the Grand Work.

If the spirit had continued along the first floor, it might have led him to their old chapel, which had once opened into their Sacred Space, from whence great mysteries flowed. But the Muses had left them years ago . . .

First darting up toward the stately ceiling and then down toward the floor, the spirit at last whirled to face Elijah, his ratty scarf floating out slowly, as if immersed in water. He pointed at the floor, at the seal of Athens, a great eagle bearing a torch and declaring power and light.

The spirit in question was emphatic, pointing at Elijah as if demanding he pay attention.

"What are you saying?" Elijah hissed. The boy then pointed to the seal, floating down to it, placing a transparent palm upon the eagle, gesturing for him to join in.

Elijah set his hand on the intricate texture of the eagle's brass feathers. The metal seemed not to be solid, to feel more like . . . sand. When he drew his hand away and turned his palm up, he saw grit, ash, and a bright smear of crimson blood on his skin. Elijah swallowed hard.

The boy smiled, as if to reassure him this was all entirely natural, then gestured toward the pocket where Withersby had stowed the laudanum bottle. Withdrawing the little container from his embroidered frock coat, the nobleman carefully scraped the residue into the bottle. The boy gestured that he take a further sample of this gruesome mixture. He did and when there was nothing further seeping up, he was sure to wipe any evidence of the marring, jarring substance from his palm with an embroidered handkerchief, tucking the soiled linen back in the breast pocket he'd plucked it from. Rising, he looked down again at the seal, which had regained its solidity and unwavering form.

"What is this for?" he asked the spirit. The boy tapped his temple. "I should know, or I will know?" The boy swept his hand forward. "I *will*, then . . ." He sighed. "I wish I could hear you to help this whole matter along."

Percy. Perhaps he could bring Percy here; it was a school day, so she would be present on the grounds. Surely she wouldn't mind a little translation from across the veil . . . Even as he formed the thought, the ghost faded from sight.

"Damn it all . . ."

Closing his eyes, Elijah took a deep long breath and ordered his heart to slow its alarming gallop in his ears. He looked down at his palm, using a fresh kerchief to wipe the last trace of blood from the deepest central crease. What was going on? It felt like magic—but that was no longer part of their lives. Why was it coming back? What did the great forces know about the future that they, foolish mortals, didn't?

THANKS TO JOSEPHINE'S QUIET COMMENTS AT THEIR RECENT dinner, Percy was not surprised when Lord Withersby showed up at her offices. Knocking quietly upon the frame of her open door, he entered her office with a bit of a sheepish smile when she waved him in, closing the door behind him.

The nobleman looked tired. His flaxen hair had gone limp; his bright eyes were dimmer and lacked their usual mischievous glimmer.

"Why, Lord Withersby, to what do I owe this pleasure?"

"Percy my dear, hello. I . . . hope you may have a moment to spare me?"

"This is a perfect time. Alexi is immersed in the longest of his lecture sessions and Violet is entirely preoccupied with library studies until dusk."

"Good then. I . . ." The lord pressed his hands together. "I don't even know how to begin. You have been, in your time with us, the sort of presence one confesses to, unburdens oneself to."

"And I am glad to be so," Percy stated, rising and going to the samovar by the bay window to prepare tea. She soon handed him a cup, noting the slight rattle on the saucer before he set it down at the edge of the wooden desk.

"Before you came into our lives and saved us all, in the earliest days of the Grand Work, I was led astray by my own selfish idiocy."

"You've seen, firsthand," he continued, "what happens if a Guard splinters. You saw the disaster of Prophecy leading up to you. In our less talented youth, I failed London. And a child—" Elijah winced. He spat the next. "—*died*. Because I neglected my duties. And because of that I have no peace." He reached forward and drained the cooling tea as if it were a draught of alcohol.

"Forgiveness is the hardest of all God's directives," she said gently. "But that does not mean it is not a heavenly request; to forgive. That includes yourself."

"I don't know what he wants."

"Who?" Percy pressed softly.

"The spirit. Aaron Willis. I can't ignore him anymore . . . Sometimes, I'm compelled to visit the place where he died. Recently, he's been more agitated. I thought it was merely the anniversary of his death, but I think now it's something more. Today he bid me take a bottle and go to the seal."

Elijah withdrew a small glass bottle full of dark material from his breast pocket. "He had me place . . . residue from the seal of Athens, the one on the upper floor, above the ballroom—"

"The seal, where we placed the key to unlock the Whisper-world war. It is the resting place of holy relics, of the Muses."

"Yes, right. That." Elijah made a face of discomfort. "Well, there was an . . . unseemly residue, perhaps from the war, perhaps fresh, I don't know, but he insisted on collecting a sample. I need to know why."

"We should all know. If you'll show me the way, I'll speak with him and we'll see what is to be done."

"You would do that?" Elijah asked hopefully.

"Of course," Percy said with a smile. "Isn't that what you came here to ask?"

Elijah shrugged. "I didn't dare presume." His eyes flashed. "Don't tell your husband. He'll be angry with me all over again."

Percy shook her head. "I will not lie to Alexi, but I have been known to be careful about what I include, and I believe I can keep you out of it."

"You are a gentlewoman through and through, the old bat doesn't deserve you."

"Oh, of course he does," Percy chuckled. She glided toward a line of hooks near the door, one of which held a long scarf and a small beaded bag.

With a careful sort of ceremony, she placed the scarf over her head and draped it to hide her hair and neck. Opening the beaded bag, she withdrew delicate blue gloves and a pair of dark blue glasses. These she kept in hand, turning to Elijah with a slight smile as she leveled her shoulders and took a deep breath.

"Now that I've my armor for the outside world, let's go while we've got time and light on our side."

At the end of the hall, Percy opened a door in the wall, revealing a steep, wood-paneled stair that took sharp corners around into shadow. "A staff staircase," she explained. "Alexi doesn't use it as he prefers to visibly stalk his kingdom, but these passages make me feel like I'm a part of a haunted castle full of old secrets. I love them." She grinned and led the way down the angled stairs, picking up her layered skirts of eyelet lace and soft muslin. At the bottom, the door opened into an alcove to the side of the main foyer.

"The secrets and wonders of this building never cease!" Elijah said quietly.

"I know," Percy said with pleasure. "I adore it. Though we have to keep so many things locked, lest we lose students to adventuring." She made sure that the door latched tightly behind them.

As Elijah opened one of Athens's massive front doors, pressing a bit of his slight weight onto the heavy wood and iron portal, Percy donned her shaded glasses and lace gloves. Together they descended the main stairs toward the quiet alleys that carefully guarded the school. When they stepped onto the slate stone sidewalk, the nobleman held out his arm for Percy.

Only when she took Elijah's arm did Percy realize his offering wasn't for the show of being a gentleman, but to help stop him from trembling. A brace against his torment. This moved Percy as much as it concerned her. He had never seemed capable of being so shaken. She was glad Josephine had prepared her for this moment, and that he hadn't further delayed seeking help. There was no sense in any of their family suffering alone.

They walked for some time, into a part of the city where the buildings drew closer and alleys grew dark and full of the struggle for survival. They traded simple, pleasant conversation until a comfortable silence won out. Percy was well aware that she attracted attention, her shrouds making people curious, but hoped that she and Elijah merely looked theatrical and odd rather than a threat or target. While her own dress was of the moment, Elijah's rather loud and colorful clothing was just out of modern fashion and might be thought to mimic the style of some old French prince.

At one point a man in a worn bowler and a long, tattered black coat approached them; Percy did not like his expression. In the instant, a soft glow radiated out from her and the man glided past them, stepping just out of their way so as to not collide with Percy's shoulder.

Exhaling as the man moved on as if she and Lord Withersby were invisible, she found Elijah staring at her, partly in wonder, a bit in envy.

"You . . . you lit up."

"You remember, it's been a while since you've seen it but when I feel at all threatened, it happens. The light is sort of instinctive, not something I'm always conscious of. It can protect and sometimes it just . . ."

"Wipes the mind . . . I see. It has similarities to my old power," Elijah said dejectedly. "I miss it, you know. The rest of them won't tell you they miss it—"

"But they do," she and the nobleman chorused.

"I know. It made everyone feel important," Percy continued, "I understand. But none of that is gone entirely. You were more than your powers and you are all still important. We are all still aware of the spirit world and its goings on, and you are attuned to this issue, here," she said, and at the sound of a murmur she turned to the building across the street, a Tudor-style structure painted black and looking rather gloomy. They crossed to the door.

"This is it, how did you know?"

"Because that little boy there said, 'Here, miss,'" Percy said, turning to the floating, grayscale specter who wafted out from behind the grimy window and cast them in a cold, sudden gust. The round-faced, mussy-haired child, eyes dark gray and wide, wore a worn schoolboy jacket. A thin scarf trailed in the air from around his neck as though he floated in moving water; the weightlessness of death.

"Ah yes," Withersby murmured. "So we meet again."

"Can you tell me why you haunt Lord Withersby, young master Willis?" Percy asked. "Unlike Elijah, I can hear you speak. I understand you were the casualty of a possession . . ." Percy said with a mother's gentleness. "What may bring you and Elijah an eternal peace and set you to rest?"

"Many things are necessary before a rest," the boy replied with the breathless urgency Percy had come to expect from spirits. They never knew how long they could connect with a mortal before they faded or the mortal stopped listening, so they generally spoke in haste.

"The spirit world is worried," Aaron stated. "The mortal world shifts and tilts. Things will change in ways we can't expect. I'm tied now to your fate." The boy shifted his translucent focus from Elijah to Percy and back again. "You'll be called upon again. All of you. Great, terrible maws will open, ready to receive your bodies. Be ready when the time comes and create protections in the meantime."

Percy relayed the words to Elijah as if she were a translator, the last sentence making her shudder.

"What protections?" Percy asked. "Is this what the bottle was about?"

"Yes! It's all for a final door," Aaron said emphatically. "Between there and here. Find a safe place in England to build a doorway. And there . . . you'll know.

"But you must know this, and so must he. Don't close every door. That's what the blood and ashes are for. To keep a door open when all else fails."

Percy repeated Aaron's words to Elijah as best she could while listening, her voice a soft echo of the child's plaintive but insistent tone.

"Elijah," Aaron said, his translucent gaze fixed on the nobleman. "Be ready when you're called. You will be called and you must go."

It was Withersby's turn to shudder. With a little jump, the spirit turned, as if hearing something behind him. Percy saw a strange flash of light, felt an odd rumbling in the air, a tremor like an earthquake or thunder. The child faded toward the shadows between the buildings, becoming one with their gray darkness.

"Don't close every door . . ." Percy repeated. Her blood chilled. "Elijah . . . I know that phrase. It's a warning that was left in our house. From *me*, rather . . . what I was before . . ."

"The goddess?" Elijah asked in breathy reverence. Percy nodded.

His eyes wide and glazed, he patted his breast pocket. "I'll take great care, then, with this . . . And I'll go where I'm bid when I'm called?"

"Indeed. I'm sorry he wasn't more specific, but ghosts often aren't."

Elijah looked at Percy with a bit of awe. "I sometimes forget . . ." His bright eyes watered. "Just how lucky we are to have you. All that was in place trying to lead you to us . . . You were *divine* and you never hold it over us. Perhaps you should sometimes . . ."

"Oh, hush," Percy said with a laugh. She squeezed the nobleman's hand, noting through her gloves how cold his thin fingers were.

He recovered himself but stared at the empty air where the spirit had been.

"The times I miss the Grand Work, I feel entirely worthless," he confessed quietly. "I never knew how to be a member of the landed society other than to be insufferable, arrogant, flamboyant."

"You mean there's another way?" Percy asked with a grin. Elijah chuckled.

"There is more, yet, for my life. I believe Aaron is a part of that. Josie, too, as every part of my existence entwines with her. I will obey. I confess there's something wondrous about having one's own prophecy."

"I wish I could tie up every one of my own prophecy's loose ends," Percy stated. "Though *my* part of the Grand Work was too extreme to have been sustained. For that, I am glad of retirement from its rigors."

"I struggle with meaning, really, more than anything," Elijah said, staring up at thick clouds above made heavier for soot and industry, the signs of churning toil. "Our Guard family has always teased me for being a listless noble with no head or heart for work, but . . ."

"I know that's hardly the whole of you," Percy assured. "You all are far more than you seem, and more than the sum of parts."

"And you are the infinite," Elijah breathed. He shook his head. "Now you know my burden."

"But now," Percy said in a rallying tone, turning back in the direction of Athens, bidding Elijah follow. "A burden has become a mission."

THE PALMS OF FATE WERE RUBBING TOGETHER, CREATING FRICtion and heat, as Violet sat in the library with her favorite mentor, Mina Wilberforce. Violet had been attending Athens now for a few months. Will kept up as best he could, when his headaches didn't keep him home. Out of everyone Violet had met, she cared for the librarian most.

A dark-skinned woman whose black locks were wound up in a white wrap upon her head, the head librarian and classical literature tutor kept the same smart and simple style as the headmistress and many other teachers. Her only flourishes were the lace cuffs on her linen sleeves, the intricate threads splaying across the well-worn wood of their study table. Violet found herself staring at the patterns in the lace when the librarian, who had been guiding their discussion, paused.

"And into what underworld corner has our hero journeyed now?" the woman asked, allowing a flash of a smile before her full lips closed into a sterner press, cocking an eyebrow at her pupil.

Violet leaned in. "Do you ever get the feeling, Miss Wilberforce, that this building . . . that Athens, is alive?"

When the librarian's warm, dark eyes widened, she knew she had unwittingly struck a nerve.

"You think so, too, then," Violet said. "Please don't . . ." Violet searched for the most impressive word. ". . . *prevaricate* like my parents. Please tell me if something is odd, special, supernatural and don't avoid it, uncomfortably, like some sort of sin."

Mina took a deep breath.

"There was a time, the year before you were born, that the building . . . changed . . ." She looked around at the dark, gaslit room, its towering bookshelves and arched windows. "I can hardly describe it other than it seemed as if this building were larger. There were extra doors, windows, panels, and tiles, as if it were growing; becoming an infinite place.

"I brought my concerns to your parents. I knew they, of all people, would not criticize me nor deem me mad. And while they thanked me for my insights, they did not explain exactly what the phenomena were, why the building was . . . expanding, as if arming itself for battle. The staff were all sent away for an early holiday, and when we returned, all was normal."

"Arming itself as if for battle . . ." Violet echoed. "That makes me think of my dreams and visions. It's a war, in a foreign place and time. I have had these glimpses as long as I remember. My family talks around them. None of us can make sense of it. Not yet."

Miss Wilberforce studied Violet intently. "Oh, the divine path is a long one, all right. Just think of my people, of any people longing for freedom. But that path bends toward peace and justice, I pray.

"I do not pretend to know the meaning of your visions," she continued, "but there is plenty to invest in, here. Plenty to ward and protect, right here." She ran her hands over the hefty mahogany table, a complement of smooth brown hues. "Athens *is* always an infinite place. That much I know. And that isn't paranormal, or otherworldly, it's the mundane magic of this place, allowing it to be a place of equality. The world outside is hardly gracious to women, to those of other skin tones, faiths, life choices, pressures to be a certain way or adhere to certain societal demands of mind, spirit, body, and family. You are of this place and this history. You will not, you must not, ever do it a discredit by living anything but its truth of peace and equanimity. You may see war in your mind, dear one, but you are a child of peace. *That* fact may be at odds with England."

Violet furrowed her brow and at this, Wilberforce continued.

"I am descended of slaves; the name I chose was one of a reformer and liberator. I'm not blind to what the Empire does around this globe. It has taken, and taken, hungrily, ruptured and redrawn the sides of countless countries, piercing their very heart with the English flag.

"But *here,* I am whole and I've every belief in the England I see within these walls, educating with generosity, ingenuity, kindness, and peace. If you see a war, see to it that you defend these walls above all others."

The great clock behind Wilberforce's dais, her librarian's castle throne behind a carved wooden gate and counter, chimed deep reverberate tones.

"We didn't even *talk* about Ulysses," Miss Wilberforce said in a tone that admonished them both.

"I'm sure he'll be fine, regardless if we analyze him or not."

Her mentor chortled. "Indeed. Give my love to your parents."

Exiting the library, Violet turned the corner into the wide corridor between Promethe and Athene halls and stopped at the sight of her mother ascending the stairs ahead of her. It was a ghostly vision: a woman dressed in white lace nearly indistinguishable from her pearlescent, intricately arranged hair, the light from leaded-glass sconces giving all an ethereal glow.

At the top of the stair, her mother turned and looked down, perhaps sensing something, and smiled.

"Hello, love, you caught me just back from an errand," she called, her soft voice easily reaching Violet thanks to the building's uncanny acoustics. "How is *The Odyssey*?"

"As advertised," Violet replied, ascending to join her mother. "Though Miss Wilberforce and I wandered off topic. But she sends love and regards to you and Father."

Percy smiled. "She was so good to me from the moment of my arrival here. When I needed to feel like I belonged, she championed me like no other, besides your father. She's brought so many here who need this haven; we are such sisters in vision and heart."

Violet nodded, seeing the similarities of passion and kindness, and ability to see the world beyond five senses. Faith wasn't a sixth sense, but it seemed to bolster the gifts that could be described biblically as charismata. Her fond supposition that her mother was part angel was renewed.

"Any news of Will?" Violet asked as they walked toward her mother's office. From there they would gather their things while Alexi called for their carriage.

"Marianna hasn't been by, even though I sent her a note. We'll have to pay a call and insist we see him."

"I wish I could help him," Violet said, entering the office and darting to the bay window, flouncing down upon the cushions. "But he's so stubborn. And proud."

Her mother pursed her lips, moving to her desk to collect papers. "And you would know nothing about that now, would you?"

"Blame Father," Violet said, holding up her hands as if she were guiltless.

"Oh, I do."

There was a sharp knock on the office door.

"Speaking of," Percy said with a chuckle. "Come in, love, I'm just gathering my things."

Alexi entered in his school robes, like a raven with great black professorial wings. He swooped toward Percy's white form, their fabrics and hair a merging of contrasts as he pressed his lips to her brow.

Now that Violet was a student at his school, he no longer kissed her on the cheek. Instead, he stalked over and awkwardly patted her on the head, which Violet found irritating. She scrunched up her face.

"Hello, Father. Yes, before you ask, I did well on my geometry exam this morning."

"Good. Good. I see you haven't inherited your mother's dislike of the subject."

"I liked geometry just fine," Percy protested. "It's the equations I could do without."

"What of Will?" Alexi asked. "I didn't see him in my afternoon class. If he thinks he can miss school as a friend of the family he has another—"

"He's out ill again," Violet interrupted. "We must press Marianna to let us see him. I'm worried."

"I'll ask around for a specialist. Headaches mostly, is it?"

Violet nodded. "And other things he won't tell me about."

"Well, perhaps he will tell a doctor, if we force one upon him."

"Maybe Auntie Jane could pay a visit?" Violet asked hopefully. Her parents turned to her with reprimanding looks. "When he's sleeping! He wouldn't even know she was there, goodness!"

"Just because this family has an . . . unfortunate habit of attracting ghosts, it doesn't mean we set them on others," Alexi stated. "Even if they are family."

"Why have access to and interaction with the world of the dead if not to make the living one all the better?" Violet insisted. "I'm not afraid! Stop acting like I'm fragile, or that Will is, or any of us are. You're not the only people in the history of the world to see ghosts, you know."

"All right, you needn't be impertinent about it," Alexi muttered wearily, storming toward the door, gesturing for his family to follow.

THAT NIGHT, AFTER A QUIET DINNER, VIOLET ASKED TO BE excused on the pretense of homework. The truth was she wanted to see if she could summon Auntie Jane to discuss Will. Perhaps, she thought, if she cut herself, the blood alone might summon the healer. But that was a bit too dramatic, even for her taste. That was something the voice that plagued Will would have suggested.

Sitting in the moonlight of her bay window, she thought about times when Jane had appeared, and the solution hit her. Music.

Turning to face the windowpane, she closed her eyes and quietly sang an old song drawn from her earliest memories, in a language she did not understand. After a few bars, a ghostly, grayscale, and transparent figure appeared at the threshold between her bedroom and the adjoining reading room. The woman, in a plain dress, with long waves of hair worn in a mussed braid over her shoulder, wafted toward her, singing along.

Then Violet remembered. This was Jane's lullaby; she'd sung her to sleep with it since she was a baby, making sure she was watched over from both sides of the veil. Tears sprang to her eyes in the instant.

"Hello, Auntie!" Violet whispered excitedly, jumping up from the sill and closing the distance between herself and the spirit, feeling Jane's aura of cold sap the warmth from her body and turn her breath visible. "I'm whispering to you because Mum and Dad are worrying about spirits again. I don't know if I'll hear you this time, but it's always good to see you."

"And you, love," Jane replied in the faintest of whispers carried on a faraway breeze. "Were you singin' or were you callin' for me?"

"Calling. Thank you for coming. I'm worried about Will. He's ill. Headaches, but I think that's only part of it. He's haunted. Something cruel takes a hard toll on him.

"I can't say I understand it fully. Could you look in on him? You can discern things; I'm sure, between your gifts and your position in life . . . Well . . . I mean—"

"Yes, child, I shall."

The sound of footsteps on the stair made Violet scurry to her bed, get under the covers, and feign sleep, but not before blowing a kiss to her spectral aunt. Jane waved and wafted out the window and into the beam of moonlight as if it had snatched her up.

"Were you talking to someone, my dear?" her mother asked quietly.

Violet opened her eyes. There was no sense in lying.

"I was singing a lullaby when Jane appeared. As we'd discussed, I asked her to check on Will."

"Oh. Good then. Good night, love."

"Good night, Mum."

Her mother closed the door. It was dizzying. Violet couldn't keep up when it was permissible to talk about spirits and when it was forbidden, when her parents were scared for her or when they were proud. Perhaps that was the life of living between worlds; one had to be prepared for the moods of either to govern at will.

CHAPTER
EIGHT

THE NEXT DAY, THE RYCHMANS CALLED UPON THE PAGES AND A delightful late lunch was had. The gentlemen went to Edward's study for a cigar and the ladies followed the children outside, who, when granted permission to leave the dinner table, were off like shots to dart about the property creating tall tales and bold myths.

Percy loitered for a moment inside the house, trying to get a read on what might be troubling Will to give him fitful sleep or pains to the head. Nothing was immediately apparent, at least not from a spirit world source.

She joined Marianna on the veranda where her friend was keeping a motherly but respectfully distant eye on the children. Violet and Will ran through the garden, weaving through hedgerows Edward had planted at intervals with the hope they would one day grow into an actual hedge maze.

Percy touched Marianna on the arm and the women exchanged complicated looks of gratefulness and weariness.

"Would you be so kind as to give your old, dear friend a few turns around the garden?" she asked gently.

Marianna nodded and took her best friend by the hand, leading her down slate steps to the garden where neatly ordered rows of red primroses with bushy green leaves met squares of marigold and lavender, a quilt of plantings.

"I envy your meticulous way with your garden," Percy stated. "Mine grows a bit wild; I can't get a handle on it."

"That is because your light makes things grow," Marianna replied. "Catalysts, even forces for good, often make things around them spin a bit out of control." There was no edge to her friend's tone, but Percy couldn't help but feel the weight of the words.

"I say constant prayers asking you and God to forgive me for putting you in danger back in those days," Percy said. "Inadvertently, of course, but still . . ."

"If not me, the Gorgon would have chosen someone. And, thankfully, I've many champions. I would not, were I given the chance, give up our friendship, or everything that has occurred since those early days."

"You are one of my greatest treasures, my friend," Percy stated.

The women sat on an iron bench beside a small, classically tiered fountain that had been a gift from Percy and Alexi when the Pages had taken possession of the home. Marianna had surrounded the basin with blue German cornflowers, a token of her heritage.

Taking a deep breath, Percy said, "Violet tells me Will suffers from headaches. Has he spoken to you about that?"

Marianna stared at the fountain. "Yes," she replied quietly. "I worry about him."

"How so?"

"There is a . . . look in his eye, a quality in his movement. There is sadness in him. Something older than himself. Darker than himself." Marianna looked at Percy urgently. "He is a safe, loving boy. He is not a danger."

"I know, my dear," Percy reassured her. "I want him to live his best, most comfortable life. I'm no stranger to difficulties," she added, lowering the dark shades of her glasses and exposing her eerie orbs to further her point. "Once they're done running about, may I ask him a few questions? A cursory examination?"

Biting her lip, Marianna nodded. "That would be good, I think." She shifted on the bench.

"That dark time. When I was . . . not myself," Marianna continued heavily. "That's when . . . I came to Edward. That's when we first . . . you know . . ." Marianna blushed. "It was silly, it was too young of us, and it was not what we planned, but Edward loved me. I loved him, even if I was not myself . . . I do not regret giving myself to him, but for the timing. It may have . . . affected Will. I mean . . . do you think so, Percy?"

Percy was struck by the weight of how long Marianna had been holding this fear, this burden. Her first instinct was to assure her friend that her harrowing possession could not have affected an unborn child, but really, how did she know? Percy didn't like to deal in false promises or blanket comforts.

"I cannot say," she replied quietly. "I wouldn't think so, but then again, my life often presents me with unexpected situations and I have frequently had to make sense out of extremity. What I do know is that you have not *damaged* him. I can see Will's heart as if it were the written word on a page. He has too good a soul for anything to be born of evil within him."

Relief passed over Marianna's fair face.

Percy took a deep breath and continued. "Perhaps Will's head pains and fitful sleep are due to nightmares or visions. He is sensitive. He feels more than he will ever say. I can see that plain as day. Violet, too; I've watched her piece his nature together. I'm sure she understands something of her own nature by his mirror."

"They are mirrors, aren't they?" Marianna exclaimed with a smile. "Intersecting pieces. Complementary parts."

"Will isn't the only child conceived in hell. We were both in the Whisper-world, you and me," Percy murmured. "I'm so glad you don't remember any of it. If it weren't for me, you'd never have been in danger and we wouldn't be concerned for Will."

Marianna shook her head. "I've told you, stop that. Regret is ungrateful. If not for you, would I have any of this? Would Edward and I have our beloved boy? Our hand was forced. But I love the hand I was dealt."

"That is gracious of you, and it is true that you have two wonderful men in your life. Edward has always been a treasure, and your son, well . . . I think Violet says it all."

The children were playing near the fountain. Violet threw her arms around Will in an embrace of pure happiness. Will rested his head onto her shoulder as if it were the most sumptuous of pillows. It seemed they granted one another joy and peace in alternate turns. Percy couldn't say she'd ever seen anything like it between two young people. Or two adults, for that matter.

"This life of yours," Marianna continued, "the way you must live with uncertainties and a reality that strains all credulity, tests all sanity . . . I cannot imagine how you have been able to come to peace with it."

"I haven't entirely," Percy answered. "That's part of what has kept me alive. Sharp. Learning."

Marianna nodded. "Will is so quiet. I fear he will suffer his peculiarities all alone in his mind, trapped in silence . . ."

"Ah, no," Percy assured her softly, taking her friend's hand again, trying not to feel responsible for the way it shook in her colorless palm. "In my darkest hour, when the whole Whisper-world was coming down to bear upon me, I was alone. Save for you. *You* were all I had in that painful darkness and you were enough to keep me here. Will has all of us. A whole battalion, to keep him safe."

There were sudden tears in Marianna's eyes. "Yes, he does.

Thank you. Do ask him about his pains. See if he'll tell you something he's reluctant to tell me."

"I will."

Edward and Alexi appeared at the open rear doors, snifters in hand, looking elegant and content by the light of the setting sun, staring at their wives like they were still getting used to the idea of being married. Their expressions reflected their delight at the prospect. Marianna rose and went to her husband, nearly floating to him like a ghost. Edward was her tether. He had helped her back from the precarious netherworld, nursing her and professing his undying love. Percy realized yet again that many of the couples that had formed in the midst of the Grand Work were complementary yet distinct. Mirrors and puzzle pieces.

Percy wanted to watch Will and Violet for a while, placing herself at an angle behind a tall rosebush where the children, who had run back into the larger garden, would not immediately know they were being observed. They had delineated the corners of the hedge maze by setting rocks into certain positions and were making their way through it as if they couldn't see one another.

With their eyes closed as much as possible, the children navigated the nonexistent twists and turns, their invisible labyrinth leading them to the inevitable center; a large willow tree that Violet exclaimed was the Minotaur. She snatched up two willow fronds and began goring Will with their bending tips; Will retaliated with his own fistful, the Minotaur battle devolving into an inelegant, slapping swordfight of fronds.

When Violet noticed her mother, she came trotting over to sit beside her, one hand immediately going to an open flower on the rosebush and caressing it. Will followed, both children breathing heavily, and Will took the liberty of sitting down on the other side of Percy. He didn't say much, but when he did, it was generally worth the wait, and this moment was no exception.

"I beg you, Mrs. Rychman," he began between deep breaths, "do not enroll your daughter in a fencing class. I fear for any living thing. Positively barbaric. Nothing gentlemanly about her sport."

Percy and Violet both laughed.

"I'll take your observation under advisement," Percy said, amused, before shifting tone and topic. "Now Will, my dear, may I ask you something?"

"Yes, Mrs. Rychman."

"You know you can call me Percy, dear."

"All right, Mrs. . . . Percy."

"You're such a gentleman," Percy declared. Will's mouth thinned in an expression that was far beyond his years.

"I have to be." He spoke as if there were no other option, lest some other nature take over.

"Violet has told me you suffer from headaches."

Will flashed Violet a look as if she'd betrayed a confidence. Violet folded her arms. "Mum is made of *magic*," Violet declared. "She can help. Let her."

"I don't know about magic," Percy countered with a chuckle, "but I would love to help, if you'll permit me." While her tone made it clear that Will should submit to her inspection, she'd learned that old souls, no matter their body's age, had to feel that they had a say in the matter.

"If you like," he replied with a shrug.

Percy placed a hand on Will's forehead. Immediately and instinctively, a luminosity began emanating from the center of her palm. Will gasped while Percy tried to remain calm. Hers was not a healing light necessarily, not like Jane's.

Percy's light activated around a threat.

A tremor passed through the muscles behind Will's eyes and across his forehead. He looked at her, in a mixture of pain, sadness, and fear. Suddenly something flashed across his eyes, which seemed to go onyx for a blinking moment before returning to their usual hazel. It was Percy's turn to gasp.

A breeze rustled suddenly and in the flurrying rattle of leaves, a whisper sounded on the air.

"Hello again, my *sweet* old friend . . ." came the gravelly, sibilant murmur.

Percy rocked back.

"What's wrong?" Violet asked.

"Just . . . something . . . familiar," Percy said, fumbling for an explanation.

"An old haunt . . ." came the voice. "I haunt him. I lay claim to him . . ."

"You do not," Percy nearly growled in reply. She turned to her daughter. "This is a . . . troublesome spirit who has come to taunt me," she said more calmly. "One who knows me from long ago."

"It's a voice I . . . hear more often than I'd like," Will stated with evident fear and discomfort.

"Unhand this boy," Percy declared. "You are vanquished."

"Never entirely, my dear . . ." the murmur retaliated. The breeze picked up. A cloud of dust rose, suddenly animate. "Ashes to ashes, for eternity . . ." The murmuring, swirling voice of steam and air went quiet for a moment. When it sounded again, it was directly against Percy's ear, wet and cold.

"I'll bring him to me, in time . . . *jusssssst* you wait . . ."

Then it was gone.

"I . . . I have never understood what it wants." Will stated, pained.

"How long have you heard it?" Percy asked, trying to make sure her own fear didn't register in her voice.

"Since I can remember," Will replied.

"But *I've* never heard it until now, just taken Will's word for it," Violet said. "It must be getting worse. What *is* it?"

Percy fumbled for some way to describe the ghost of an ancient, Whisper-world Gorgon, the eternal nemesis of the goddess who preceded her. "Some spirits cling to others, to old wounds, more tightly than they should. This is one such."

She turned to Will. "Whenever you feel that presence, hear that whisper, fight it. Think of my light. Think of the brightest things, what you care about most; that which makes you happiest."

Will's gaze went to Violet. She stared back at him unflinchingly, then held out her hand. He took it. There was no blush nor awkwardness, they were direct youths who made no secret of their bond.

Wondering if they could grow older and still maintain such a connection, or if their hearts, much less the world, would force distance between them, Percy loosed a silent vow; she would do all she could to keep this forever-haunted family as together and safe as she could.

The guilt she had felt about Marianna was now crippling, thanks to this added layer of responsibility. Her eldest enemy, the ashes of the ancient Gorgon, had somehow, through Marianna's possession, bound her son in a lineage of spite. Were Will's young soul not so stalwart, the poor child might have already buckled under the strain. It took every ounce of Percy's restraint not to strengthen her protective light and hug any lingering darkness out of him, clutch him so tight there was no room for doubt or fear. But she had to maintain her composure, lest the children take panic as a cue.

"Can you do that, Will?" Percy asked enthusiastically. "Every time you feel a pain? Every time you're kept up at night? Can you hold to our light?"

Will nodded.

"I'll bring a few things for your room," she continued, "things that helped us when we were particularly haunted."

With old Guard magic, she'd bless his room. Josephine's paintings of angels, which had graced every structure they'd entered, still retained powers of peace and benediction, so she'd hang one on each wall. Perhaps Jane could provide a ghostly healing hand and watch over him. Before it unraveled anyone any further, she had to clean up some of the mess Prophecy had made.

THAT NIGHT PERCY DREAMED FOR THE FIRST TIME IN SOME time. Having grown up with visions, seeing things that were beyond the pale, it took more than just a fleeting image or passing fancy, a trick of the light or the eye to affect her. But in the dream world, she was a bit more susceptible.

She was wandering through what appeared to be a stone maze. Long corridors, wet slate, dim light. The only light in the space came from her. Her senses must have pinpointed a threat.

The great deal of whispering that surrounded her meant she could only be in the Whisper-world, a place full of soft, sad laments, murmurs of things left undone, gasps of unfinished business, and hisses of broken dreams. Her former home, when she had had another form. In her current life, when she'd visited this place, Darkness had told her she was with child. Before that, Percy had not known.

This world had almost taken everything from her present life, and everything in the life before. It was a terrible place.

Yet it was not the Whisper-world's fault it was a place she detested. It was not hell, exactly, more purgatory, a wailing wall of endless shadow.

Distantly, a beautiful sound cut through the oppressive pall: the laughter of children echoed off the slate. Familiar laughs that she'd heard all afternoon. Violet and Will. In the maze of the Whisper-world.

Percy picked up her pace, turned more corners, her light

brightening. She tried not to notice the flowers that grew and died at her feet, a heartbreaking cycle, a remnant of her previous self.

She tried not to notice the hissing of that familiar foe, but it seemed to rattle around every corner, louder at the dead ends.

Spirits floated to and fro about her. Percy tried not to acknowledge them, tried not to be seen by them, but this was futile. Those who did notice knelt.

"My Lady . . ." they would say, and bow or try to reach out, shrieking, trying to cling to her, beg for intercession and light.

She ignored them and broke into a run. Trying to hush them so she could hear the children. But the giggles had been replaced by a growl. The old rattle of bones that was Darkness's rallying cry.

They had vanquished him, but perhaps some part of the idea of Darkness would always remain. How could he not? He was born of the most abject pieces of human misery, a god made from compounded human sorrow. Would he not inevitably build again, a sum of terrible parts?

Her light grew brighter and the path became clearer. Finally, she saw an opening in the maze: its center, a long platform, and a dais with rushing water on either side.

A familiar place. Darkness's old throne. And the children.

"Darlings, come away from there," she said frantically, trying to be heard above the dread river's gurgling rush without awakening any undesirables.

"Hello, Mummy," Violet said, turning to greet her mother in a crisp white pinafore, Will beside the girl, wearing a child's sailor suit. They smiled. And then they were skeletons.

Percy cried out, throwing a hand to her mouth, her light growing brighter in reactive horror.

"We are children of two worlds," Will's skull said. "Our mothers made us so . . ."

Flesh. Bone. Flesh. Bone. Tick. Tock. Child. Skeleton. Alive. Dead. Flesh. Bone.

Percy felt a wail rise within her. Her light was attracting countless dead. A drifting, shuffling horde . . . The children just kept smiling. Staring. Flesh. Bone.

The wail drove her to sitting straight up in bed, throwing her arms to each side. She struck Alexi squarely in the chest, startling him awake beside her.

"Nightmare," she gasped. "Sorry." He reached out to enfold her in strong arms.

"Care to tell me about it?" he asked.

She shook her head against his shoulder and let his embrace be soothing comfort.

OVER THE COURSE OF THE NEXT SEVERAL YEARS, WILL'S PAIN eased, or so Violet told Percy. Violet's own nightmarish visions of battle also seemed to subside. Or so Violet told her.

Percy enjoyed herself, her life, her family.

But every now and then, due to some trick of light or distance, she thought she saw bone when she saw the children's lovely faces.

The empirical evidence of her life proved nothing was ever finished, nor wholly settled, nor vanquished forever. She tried to make peace with unease. Periods of calm were only ever prefaces before storms.

CHAPTER
NINE

Spring 1904

VIOLET'S VISIONS HAD NOT GONE AWAY. BUT THEY WERE HER burden and she bore it as best she could. Just like Will. In this, stubborn practicality served them well.

Every year the glimpses and sounds increased incrementally. By the time she was fifteen, she wasn't sure her senses would be able to handle the onslaught if it continued to expand into her adulthood.

She still saw ghosts. They remained a nagging itch at the corner of her mind, a little flutter at the corner of her eye. Her parents still talked around the topic more than they addressed it, and to be honest, Violet wasn't sure what questions she should be asking them.

To be at the edge of gifted was maddening.

Sitting in an intermediate art class, Violet paged through a large sketchbook she had been utilizing as a journal for years. One entry caught her eye:

> *The turn of the twentieth century.*
> New Year's Day.
>
> I awoke to a bright sun and the taste of blood in my mouth. It wasn't my blood. It was something on the air. In my heart.
>
> "Now . . ." I said softly at the breakfast table where my

family sat quietly pecking away at their breakfast like agitated birds. "Now it begins to change. Everything we knew, everything we are . . . it begins to change."

Mum looked at me, curiously, and then moved her tongue as if she too tasted the metallic, sour notes. Making a face, she lifted her colorless hand to a small gilt flute glass, lifting it to sip a bit of a red, syrupy cordial that made her white lips look just as bloody as the taste on the air. A garish sight that made me nearly recoil.

What I didn't say, because I hope it is not true: *Now the world begins to live into what I've seen. Now for the dreadful, trenching pit, now for the sound and fury.*

God, please show me how to avoid it all. The twentieth century has to have some beauty in it somewhere. It has to. I'll make it.

Following this, three words were repeated boldly across several pages.

Art. Education. Empathy.

These were the three tenets she'd built her heart and her Athens studies around, the qualities she thought were most vital to a civilization. A counterpoint to her barbaric, muddy, exploding visions.

Like a slap to the face came her most intense vision to date.

A train station, hazy and full of men in uniform. Soldiers. Not English. An announcement boomed out over the crowd; a sure voice that got the men moving onto plain train cars with open doors. French. The announcement was in French. The truth of the dream came in a secondary beat after the sights, smells, and distinct, eerie lighting. Sound came in at a distant fourth.

In as much as Violet could gather, having been woefully remiss in her French studies—she would apologize to Auntie Josephine for this lapse—the men were, via the announcement, being sent off on trains.

Violet tried to turn toward the center of the train station, hoping to pick up some clue as to where in France she might be. She found herself floating through the station until she hung suspended below metal latticework, large clocks, and a set of signs.

GARE DU NORD. Paris. Parisian trains full of eastbound soldiers, it seemed, from the announcements she dimly understood.

Suddenly she flew.

Out through the steam and smoke, up toward the arching rafters.

Paris, gaslit, electric lit, dark in parts, a patchwork of light and dark, fell away below her. She followed the trains until she was completely lost, both land and sky growing dark around her.

A single gunshot rent peace asunder.

The sound made a ripple in the air, echoing far longer than a single shot should, as if it were the roar of an insatiable dragon. Then everything below began to groan and scream.

From the shadowed ground speckled with firelight, there were explosions, eyes of blood-orange fire opening all across the lands. The earth itself seemed to yawn open and everything shook, shook to the bone, rattling teeth and human morale.

Fissures opened in the land below, drawn along what seemed to be the borders of countries. Everywhere, people were yelling.

The whole area below her flooded with dark water. Violet felt herself descending. A distinctive scent of copper accosted her nose; her voluminous nightgown billowed around her as she sank toward the glistening surface. As the muslin hit the water, the fabric blossomed with crimson.

Blood. The earth was awash in blood and she would drown in it . . . More cloth turned white to red, the blood quickly seeping up through the thin, porous layers. Her toe dipped into the thick warm fluid and she tried to scream but the sound was strangled in a wrenching gasp. Now her whole foot was in the blood and the lower half of her gown was drenched. Violet tried to claw upward at the air, but this only propelled her further down.

From below the surface a hand grabbed her ankle and yanked her down into the mire.

With a violent exhalation, Violet came to herself again, glad she hadn't screamed and rent the quiet of the art room, which was silent save for the scratching of charcoal and pastels on paper. No one seemed to notice her start; fellow students had long ago written her off as odd and didn't pay any mind to her.

The professor wasn't concerned, either, an airy old woman who was always staring out the window and murmuring profundities instead of critiquing their work. Violet sometimes wondered what the teacher was seeing and wished the aging woman would sketch out her fanciful imaginings for them.

Focusing on quiet, measured breathing to regain herself, to shift from the panicked animal of her nightmares to a cooler and more rational human, she reviewed the images at the beginning of the vision. Her journal handily open, she took note of everything she heard and saw, better at hearing the French and transcribing it than actually understanding it. She profoundly wished she had inherited her mother's preternatural skill of understanding every language—a most useful power. Still, she would be able to translate her words later.

She would have to go to France, and for more than a mere visit, as this vision seemed to suggest. An encampment. An interminable digging in. Whatever her visions wanted to show her, warn her of, demand of her, it seemed to require a significant phase of her life. If she went *now*, could she avoid it? Could she stop the needless suffering? She had to try. Anything.

When the dream opened wide its dreadful maw of scope and

height, the journey was antithetical to her hopes, the exact opposite of these safe bricks where a distinct power coursed through its walls just for *her*. This place had spoken to her in powerful recognition. Out in the world there were no such protections, just open air and a thick fog and the world breaking open piece by piece. The surrealism of the imagery was no comfort. The book of revelations was terribly surreal, in parts. Armageddon did not look familiar; the alien qualities led to greater terror.

From Paris, blood and bodies would flow into unknown boundaries and tributaries. The question was when would she need to be there to become a part of this terrible unfolding? And who on Earth should she tell about it? Her poor mum. A vision like this might break her in two.

As she was taking down notes, still more rapid-fire images came to her, as if answering her question.

Next, she envisioned a building, floor, and door. A paper with a seal the details of which she couldn't quite make out. The image of someone who would be greatly important; someone she had to go talk to.

The visions left her with clues she could attend to immediately. The fever of needing answers overtook her. She was not without recourse or resources. There was no choice but to follow the trails.

She would not leave her family entirely in the dark. It would be easy enough to leave a note for her mother in her office and slip out while the day was yet long.

PERCY WAS EVENTUALLY ALERTED TO HER DAUGHTER'S ABSENCE by the very pragmatic note the young lady left on her desk. The corner had been slipped under a book of French folklore to be translated into Russian and the day's mail had been set over the top of that, so Percy didn't see the note until she cleared her desk after two tutorials, one teaching a Chinese girl English and another teaching a Bengali boy both English and French. As she read the note, she knew immediately she had to take it to Rebecca.

The formidable woman opened the door herself, taking one look at Percy and gesturing her wordlessly inside. Thankfully, the headmistress wasn't one to make any uncomfortable jokes about her looking like she'd seen a ghost.

"I just found this," Percy said, handing her friend the sheet of paper. "I brought it to you directly because I recall you have a government contact. I'd like you to find them now."

Rebecca remained expressionless, placing wire-rimmed glasses on to read:

Dearest Mother,

Because you are a superb woman of strength and intellect, and because I love you dearly, it is my duty to inform you that I have undertaken a mission to find out more about my preternatural gifts. I am well aware that you prefer to shield me from the supernatural, but it unfortunately is an inextricable part of my life, as it has been of yours.

I long for the day when you'll actually unburden your heart and tell me the whole, complete truth about your history. But because neither you nor Father feel comfortable doing so, and because our respective callings are different, I must discern mine. You know visions don't just go away.

I'm going to a place where secrets are kept in the nation's trust. I have seen a seal and a location. If they are to assign me somewhere, I will go immediately. If I can somehow delay, or even stop, the visions I see, then I must try. To ask you not to worry would be foolish, but I'll be all right.

We are lucky in that we have a distinct tie, Mum. You have

a light. I see that light. I have it, too, and I feel yours even when
you're not near. That binds us no matter where we are. I strive
to live in that light. Love, your daughter.

While Rebecca read, Percy let a few tears flow, dabbing at them
with a lace-trimmed handkerchief pulled from her pearl-buttoned
cuff. "What if she's right, and some secret department sends
her away without even a goodbye?" Percy murmured, her voice
breaking.

"She's quite the writer and I don't doubt her convictions, or her
gifts, or that she'd go somewhere if she thought she could help
stave off a terror," Rebecca said. "I take it you've not yet shown
this to Alexi?"

"No . . . I wanted to try to find her before . . . You know how
he'll—"

"Overreact? Oh, I'm sure of it," the headmistress said sharply.
Here Rebecca studied Percy for a long moment. "I know you're
worried, my dear. But I admire your fortitude. I always have.
You've been the strongest of us from the very start, despite your
youth. Now, my dear niece is as clever as both her parents, but as
stubborn, too. There was no stopping this, and if Alexi blames
himself, or you, I will set him *very* straight."

"You read my heart so well," Percy murmured.

"I haven't always been so keen. I owe you a few back pay-
ments," she said with the weight of an old sorrow. "This is a test,"
Rebecca continued, "of your powers as she tests hers. It's daring
and impetuous, but then again, have not all of us done something
similar?"

"Not me, not as a child . . ."

"I think staring down the entire Whisper-world by yourself
counts," Rebecca countered.

"Violet believes we are all retired from the Queen's service. I've never known what to tell her. This is my fault for trying to shield her—"

"*Stop*," the headmistress scolded. "Let me see if I can call up my rusty old Intuition. Even with the Muses having abandoned us, there are traces of what they built in us that still stand strong."

Rebecca closed her eyes and placed her hands on the solid hardwood of her desk, the scattered papers strewn about its surface cleared gently aside so she could place bare palms against the wooden surface. After a long moment, she patted her hand on the wood and opened her eyes.

"Whitehall," she declared, rising to her feet. "You're right about my government contact. I'll go now."

The great clock down the Athene Hall corridor chimed a quarter of, and as if on cue, loud and firm footsteps came closer to the office. Predictably, the door burst open without knocking or announcement and the imperious Professor Rychman stood at the threshold with a quizzical look.

"The headmistress and I are discussing an important matter," Percy stated.

Alexi eyed them, as if he were suspicious of women talking. Rebecca shooed him off. "She'll be with you in a moment. Some concerns are best left to ladies." No one moved. "Alone. If you please."

"I'll meet you in your office," Percy said. "In a moment."

Alexi retreated with a wary look and let the door close reluctantly behind him.

CHAPTER
TEN

WHEN ROSE EVERHART SPIRE HEARD THE KNOCK AT THE DOOR of her office in the heart of Whitehall, she felt the same sinking feeling in her gut that had woken her early that morning. She'd known from the moment she'd slipped out of bed at dawn, kissing her husband's forehead softly, that today would be a strange, fateful day.

"Yes?" she called. Maria Velazquez, her dark-haired protégée in all manner of brilliant bookkeeping, opened the door with a somewhat baffled look on her face.

"There's a woman outside, ma'am, who insists on seeing you. She said she knows you from the . . ." and here she whispered, "*Omega* days, but I've no record of a Rebecca Thompson-Carroll."

Rose's blood chilled. How could a stranger know her from Omega? She'd gladly left the cavernous Millbank offices behind, trading paranormal attacks for civilian paperwork and a cozier, wood-paneled office in the heart of Whitehall. Omega was retained only in one capacity; refreshing the city's protective Wards against dark forces.

Some years were easier than others. 1888 had been the worst since Moriel's death; what with the Ripper and a host of reported hauntings. The turn of the twentieth century, while anticipated with trepidation, had gone relatively without incident, Her Majesty's death notwithstanding. Rose shuddered to think that might soon change.

Miss Velazquez stared at her expectantly. Rose frowned. "Show her in, please."

The woman who entered was a stately, striking woman in her fifties, dressed primly head to toe in navy wool without an ounce of frippery—a woman of functional fashion after Rose's heart. She was immediately familiar.

Rose nodded to Maria and her aide excused herself and closed the door.

"You won't necessarily remember me and I don't expect you to," Thompson-Carroll stated.

"I do remember you," Rose murmured. "You're one of the ghost patrol my dear Lord Black would go on about so often, *years* ago." At this, the woman smiled; a ray of sun peeking out from behind a cold curtain.

"There was a day," Rose continued, "on Westminster Bridge. You saw me staring your direction . . ."

"I pressed my finger to my lips to hush you," the headmistress finished. "I did not have your memory wiped. I knew you could keep a secret and were more like us than not. Intuition told me I'd need your friendship someday. I am so pleased you remember, and that Intuition has proven true."

"Your company doesn't make you easy to forget," Rose said carefully, "but we are not yet friends."

At this, the woman chuckled. "No, I don't suppose we are. I have need of your assistance. There's a missing girl."

"Oh, dear. You've come to a civilian office when you should instead go to the police, I can recommend someone in the Metropolitan—"

"While I'm sure your husband is very capable in his position at

Scotland Yard, this is a matter that requires the utmost discretion and the hands of sure women."

Rose sat back in her chair, her eyes widening. She did not hide her discomfort at the realization that her details were well known to this woman. "My husband is the surest hand and the picture of discretion."

The visitor shook her head. "This dances close to what gets a young woman committed if we're not careful. In our old days, our coterie would have handled this all with our powers, but our gifts have flown on to different skies. My niece is likely making someone's job very difficult as we speak. She thinks the secrets to her strange gifts and visions can be found in a government office and she's trying to find it. She has also made it known she will avail herself to any government institution that might have use for her warnings."

"Do you have any sense of what government office she may target?" Rose asked.

"Anything . . . *paranormal*. If Omega were still active, she would target you. Whatever happened to it?"

Rose tensed up. "The Queen . . . her attitude toward the department changed. She closed us down. I was shut right out.

"It seemed that the Queen turned to a fascination with the manipulation of time. Harold and I had no taste for it and he longed to get back to the police force. But that's beside the point. How long has she been gone?"

"The disappearance was announced by a note to her mother this morning."

"Well then, let's see if Lord Black can shed some light before she gets herself into trouble. Anything *interesting*, he will know of it. He was rather obsessed with finding your coterie, never quite did manage it, so it will *thrill* him to meet you."

The headmistress offered a distinctly strained smile. "Indeed?

Well, if I can oblige him after all these years, perhaps the day can turn out to be mutually beneficial."

REBECCA WAS LED OUT ONTO THE BUSY STREET, WITH THE distinctive gothic spires of Parliament in the distance, the tip of the clock tower's hands just barely visible above the rooftops. A sharp wind blew loose a few graying hairs.

Putting a hand to her forehead to shield her eyes as they adjusted to the brighter than average day, Rebecca, as was her habit, tested the air, checking for a spiritual disturbance. It was so natural that even fourteen years after having lost the powers of the Guard she still physically reacted as if she had the Muse of Intuition at hand. Every time it was like turning to a friend you were certain was walking with you, mid-conversation, only to realize that friend had passed away and you spoke only to memory. Every time there was a pang.

Looking to the sky she yearned to see her old familiar, Frederic, a grand and wise raven who had been a scout and companion, hovering above. But he'd flown off the day the Muses released them all. Long past his prime, she hoped he'd simply flown straight to heaven.

If she'd had the same care for the Muse and her powers as she had in their absence, in her early years, at Violet's age, life wouldn't have been so difficult. Why could human beings never quite wrap their hearts around happiness, appreciation of their circumstances, while they were living them? Why did it take loss to be found?

Dappled sunlight cut sharp golden angles in the courtyards between the various Whitehall ministries, alternating light and shadow as the clouds played games with the sun. London seemed pleasantly at peace on a fine autumn day.

A group of women turned the corner toward them, most clad

all in white from hat to heel. They held banners and signs and wore sashes, all supporting votes for women.

"Ah," Rebecca said. "The important cause of the day."

A line of wary police officers followed as the chanting crowd approached Parliament.

"Someday," Rose said softly.

"Someday," Rebecca echoed.

A striking, fierce woman at the forefront of the procession turned to them as if she were responding to their hope like a call. Rebecca recognized her as the infamous Mrs. Pankhurst and she clapped loudly. Taking Rebecca's cue, Rose joined in.

"For us working women," Rebecca stated, "is there anything more insulting than being told you could be trusted with a school or a department, but not a vote?"

"It boggles the mind," Rose replied. "But what I've learned, working in government, is that those who hold onto power zealously do so as if clutching on to a life raft, believing sharing voices undermines their authority. Those who govern for the power of it cannot fathom parsing another viewpoint to half the population. For we will hold them accountable for their promises, and they do not want to be mothered by our votes."

The suffragists strode onward toward Parliament and disappeared from view but were hardly out of earshot or out of mind.

"I should mention, Mrs. Spire, that the girl in question has been going on about a war," Rebecca added to her earlier description. "She's been dreaming of war. Considering tensions in Europe, I can see where she might extrapolate prophetic fear, though I hope it doesn't come to that."

Rose frowned. "There are rumblings, to be sure. Just . . . far away for the moment."

"I worry she may turn up at some secretive place, asking the wrong kinds of questions. Someone might think she was some sort of spy, and with her willingness to help, take her directly into custody when she came merely to share a possible precognition. I don't know if you believe in such a thing," Rebecca said quietly.

"I've been forced to accept . . . expanded senses," Rose replied carefully.

"That's an innocuous way to put it," Rebecca said.

"We needn't be veiled. I *saw* you with ghosts, all those years ago. You chose not to wipe my memory. That was a moment of trust that made me feel part of something beautiful and important. I am sure the girl you seek feels this same way."

"Your empathy does you credit."

"My work with the Omega division took place during a period of constant, paranormal madness that now feels like a fever dream. But at the time . . ."

"It was all too real. Quite a decade, the eighties. Goodness. We were circling around one another, each group with specific tasks and destinies but whose paths gently entwined."

"Do you think this girl will start a new, otherworldly cycle?"

"If my old gifts were with me in full I might know. Mine was a preternatural intuition."

"Intuition is native, it never leaves you. I'm not sure we need 'paranormal' permissions to do our jobs as we've always done. I ask again, what do you think?"

Rebecca considered this; the woman was daring her to trust in herself again. She closed her eyes and felt within for a deeply uncomfortable truth. "Yes," she stated finally. "She's going to kick something off."

Continuing with a cautionary tone, Rebecca looked at Mrs. Spire directly. "She won't start a war, but if there is one, she'll have something to do with it. Someone needs to be ready. Her parents, God bless them . . ." A complex knot of emotions welled up in her throat. "They cannot be without resources."

"We must start with Lord Black. He is somehow always at the heart of things."

"I'm very glad to know you, Mrs. Spire."

"Rose, please."

"Rebecca, please."

The new associates set off for Lord Black's office.

PERCY CLIMBED THE STEPS TO ALEXI'S SECOND-FLOOR OFFICE, an act she had performed a thousand times by now. A delighted shudder went through her body and she was transported to the first awkward, aching moments of their acquaintance, when she was a timid student attending a private tutorial in his luxurious academic quarters.

Every time she ascended in those early days she had steeled herself, in awe of, intimidated by, and in love with him from the very first. Her attraction to him had been the first awakening of her own power. He was the bow to her arrow, drawing her slowly and agonizingly against his strings until she loosed a goddess's force.

Knocking on his door, when she could have simply walked in, provided the same old thrill, as did pressing her ear to the door and letting her fingers alight like a skittish bird upon the door-knob. His firm "come in" sounded clearly from within.

In the early days her entrance had been hesitant and his greeting detached, cool; entirely inscrutable. All the while they'd been burning for one another in agonizing secret, until fate made them collide in an explosion of passion and tumult. Those old patterns remained engrained, etched in her every move as she repeated the magnetized walk to the chair across from his desk. His unbridled smile upon sight of her, the unfolding of time's thorny rose, made every look between them full of a library's worth of poetic sentiment.

She took her seat, no longer wearing the shielding accoutrements she used to hide behind, and he took the seat opposite, his hand reaching across the desk to hers; his warmth upon her cool alabaster skin. He'd aged with the distinction she'd expected; a couple of elegant shocks of white had grown in, exacerbated by a stubborn daughter, and in part the fault of a life with ghosts.

A soft smile played at the corner of his mouth, a slight curve that made her want to kiss him, to lose herself wholly in him and forget that anything else mattered, that anyone else mattered. Of course a child was first in one's heart, but they were not the only thing in it. Alexi held the original claim.

"What is it, love?" he asked quietly.

"Violet is gone," Percy replied finally.

Alexi's dark eyes narrowed. He leaned forward. "What?"

"She is gone from the Academy; she left a note with me this morning. Rebecca has gone to try to collect her at Whitehall." Percy tried to keep the worry from her tone but her shaking voice betrayed her. "Visions are leading her. She is following."

He stood quickly, nearly toppling his chair, his robes whipping out behind him as he began to pace the room.

"You were the one who encouraged me to tell her everything about us and our past from the start, Alexi," Percy said. "I should have listened to you. This is my fault."

"No, it isn't."

"I can feel her. She's not in danger yet. But she said in her note that she will avail herself if anyone thinks she can stop what she sees, that she would be willing to be sent somewhere in the instant if she could be of use. This could be terribly misconstrued. If Rebecca can intercept her contact and stop this, perhaps I needn't have come to you at all with this news."

"Would you not have told me?" he asked incredulously, swooping to her side.

"I was considering it. In fact, Rebecca instructed me not to."

"Why wouldn't you?" he bellowed, whirling on her and pounding his fist upon his desk.

Percy just stared at him.

He glowered, and then a terribly complex set of emotions washed over his face.

There were moments she recognized a certain monstrosity within him. It had happened in their early days, when his concern for her safety had him grabbing her just a bit too hard, his tone barking too sharply. She didn't stand for it, and pushed back when necessary, though she didn't think punishing him for being passionate, for loving her more than he could physically or emotionally contain, was fair. He was contrite then, as now; she didn't need to drive the point home any harder.

"I'm sorry," he murmured, clearly haunted by the same moments as she.

"I love you," she replied. "We'll be all right. But, Alexi. If she is sent somewhere, if the Crown by some reason engages her, I want to follow."

He took her hand, bid her rise, and then held out his arms for her. She fell into them. Percy listened to their shaking breaths taken in tandem, felt their trembling arms find rest in their entwined embrace.

"Of course," he murmured against her ear, kissing her temple. "At a moment's notice."

CHAPTER
ELEVEN

THE HEADMISTRESS WAS DETAINED NEAR THE ENTRANCE BY AN officer who explained she could not accompany Rose, and so Lord Black would have to meet a Guard member another day. "I'll wait, then," Rebecca said pointedly, taking a seat on a wooden bench in a sterile entrance hall, glaring at the gatekeeper who had made no secret of his opposition to working women in government spaces.

"I won't be long," Rose said, and hurried off.

Lord Black's door was marked only LIAISON, meaning nearly anything could fall under his purview.

She knocked and a moment later a platinum blond and silvered head appeared at the door, bright eyes glimmering with excitement. A distinguished man in his sixties, Lord Black exuded a forever youthful air.

"Rose!" he exclaimed. "Come meet someone very special!"

"Violet Rychman, I hope?" Rose replied.

"Why, however did you know?"

"Her family is looking for her."

"Ah. Of course."

He gestured her into the room, which was filled with glass-fronted bookshelves and decked with neoclassical paintings of flowers and forests. In this stately room, he met with people so numerous that Rose could not keep track: Spiritualists, artists, writers, bankers, and more. Black was a man who liked to know everyone and everything, and his position as a liaison between the Houses of Lords and Commons, with access to every cultural institution and ministry, meant he was active in more branches of the nation's workings than Rose could fathom. If Britain revolved around someone, she was delighted it was her most beloved friend.

Before his lordship's massive desk sat a young woman dressed in white with a small white straw hat, looking as though she'd been in the suffrage march. When the girl turned to face her, Rose held back a gasp. So pale she almost appeared to be sickly—save that her strength of body and spirit was palpable; a blue vein traced down each of her temples as though they were stray hairs. Pitch-black hair was pinned haphazardly beneath her hat; the girl's wide eyes were dark and flecked with a near purple glow. Eerie.

No wonder her family and friends were worried; there was something arresting and irreplaceable about her.

"Violet Rychman, my name is Rose Everhart Spire. I have seen many extraordinary things and have kept extraordinary company, so you needn't fear me; I just want to see to your safety. Thank you, milord, I'll take her from here." Rose favored Lord Black with a fond smile.

"Remember what we discussed," Lord Black said to Violet with a wink.

"Oh, I shan't forget!" Violet said, waving to him as he moved to the door. "Thank you for your kindness, sir, and I'm sorry to have been any trouble. But if you *do* think I can stop what I see . . . tell me how. We could avoid such suffering!"

"I shall," he replied earnestly. "You've opened up new worlds!" he added, beaming.

"I can find my own way home," the girl said, turning to Rose. "I made it here, after all."

"Indeed," Rose said as they left the office. "But I promised to return you and I have a feeling one disregards Headmistress Carroll at their peril."

"Oh, Auntie Rebecca seems dreadful, but that's all a façade. I know she'll be cross with me but that can't be helped. You must have to wear one, too, a façade, being a woman who works in this world. Mum says I can do whatever I like but I'd best be careful the places in which I direct my fortitude, the 'new woman' isn't welcome everywhere."

Rose couldn't help but chuckle. "Yes, that's true. Why did you seek out Lord Black, specifically?"

"Visions drove me directly to him," the girl replied. "Perhaps I shouldn't say visions as that may sound mad."

"No, visions can be very important."

"There are dark things brewing," Violet said softly, looking away. "And I'll be involved somehow. I've been trying, all my life, to prepare for something dreadful. I can't sit idly by, if I can find out what . . . how I can help. If I can, at all, stop it. I don't *want* these terrible things to come to pass." Here the girl again pierced Rose with those eerie eyes. "What good is any kind of sight if we can't do anything about what we see?"

"You sound just like my sister soul, Clara," Rose replied. "She's gifted. A blessing and a curse, it is, and questions that can never be answered."

Rose led her charge down a clerestory walk with glass paneled windows on either side with gothic arches and old stone. The click of their boots on black and white marble tiles was the only sound for a moment.

"To more directly answer your question," the young woman began, "in my visions I glimpsed papers from a government ministry. Lord Black did not recognize my description of the seal, but it is something of war."

The word "war" chilled Rose to the core, as it had the moment the headmistress uttered it. That inevitability none of them wanted.

Violet winced. Rose reached out a hand. Violet shook her head and wisps of fine black hair floated about her face, freeing themselves from her hat. When a ray of light broke through the clouds and illuminated her companion's face, Rose at last understood her name; purple glinted in her jet hair and her preternatural quality heightened. Something of the spirit world rippled from her.

"I can feel Mum's worry, sharp as a knife," the girl murmured. "It isn't as if I didn't alert her; this is absurd. What is our psychic bond good for if not to prove a reassurance?"

"As a mother myself, I can assure you, soon you'll be old enough to come and go as you please without consequence or chaperone. However, bond or not, you are not old enough for the luxury of autonomy yet. Your headmistress is waiting downstairs for you."

Violet groaned and Rose chuckled in satisfaction that adults still held sway.

That night, Rose couldn't sleep. Echoes of Violet were dancing in her head, her words glancing off her memory's ear. *War.*

If there was a war, her Vincent would be caught up . . . he was a soul too tender for war, too full of empathy. His level of it was so profound as to be in the territory of gifted, though it nearly incapacitated him. She'd teach him every cipher known. Teach him to be better than her at encoding and never leave England. Perhaps this girl's prophecies could save more lives than she knew.

CHAPTER
TWELVE

THE RETURN TO ATHENS WAS MADE IN CHILL QUIET FOR some time. Violet easily kept the headmistress's tall, strident pace. The moment they were about to wind the several alleys around toward Athens's front door, Rebecca turned to Violet and Violet's breath caught in her throat. The look on the older woman's face was so stern, so startling, so full of complex pain, it hit Violet like a punch.

"I do not doubt your gifts, child, or your conviction," Rebecca murmured. "But you are not yet a lady and cannot wish your youth away." She lifted a shaking finger to Violet's face. "Don't you *dare* be so careless with your own family that you would up and vanish should some great office call you, no matter how powerful the portent. You are called to be a daughter, too, to parents who faced down hell itself to keep you alive, through battles you couldn't even *imagine*—"

Rebecca turned toward the school and here, Violet could no longer hold her tongue, jumping in front of Rebecca, a fury in her veins.

"I *could* imagine if any of you would actually *tell* me anything about it. I've seen dead men on a battlefield every day since I can remember and you shelter me like I was some dainty flower that couldn't stomach the least discomfort, let alone tales of some mystical old glory. I'm trying to act *with* fate, not merely react. You could at least try to *help*."

She blew past Rebecca and stormed up the stairs of Athens, blinking back tears.

"You report directly to your father's office, young lady," Rebecca barked after her. Violet tore into the building.

There was no explaining the pure terror of her visions; her family didn't see what she saw. The truth was she'd run toward the first glimmer that had appeared like a solution, a way to act on something after years of reactive torment. She'd gone to Lord Black out of sheer panic after the latest onslaught, begging the heavens for someone, something, to please make the constant march of death stop before it finally reached *every* door . . . But she'd been disappointed.

Lord Black didn't know what to do with her. He was so charming, such a lovely, dear soul, and she was sure he'd keep his promise to try to stop a war if one started, but she wondered if she wasn't just some curiosity to a man like him. No one could see the urgency because at this moment, there was none. It was all in her head. "There are undoubtedly tensions, of course," Black had offered, "what Empire doesn't have them?" The sun never set and all that nonsense. When Violet again asked how she might stop what she saw, he stared at her blankly and all he could suggest was prayer.

At a loss as to what to do with all the anxiety and worry over what part she was asked to play in what she saw, Violet wished she could add a chamber to her heart and put everything the visions made her feel into it. Helplessness, anxiety, and fear. It didn't seem like anyone could come back from what she saw, but she didn't want to wish this on anyone else. She wanted to be a hero, but how could one emerge on a battlefield like she saw?

The only word that kept echoing through her mind as she

ascended the stairs toward her father's office was "sacrifice." This did nothing to ease her nerves.

WIPING TEARS FROM HER CHEEKS, VIOLET TOOK A BREATH, straightened her shoulders, and knocked on the door of her father's office.

"Yes?" her father barked. When she entered the large, book-filled room, she heard her mother's breathless "Thank God." She closed the door behind her and moved to the center of the polished floor of the grand office.

Her father had refused to have electric lights installed, so she stood stock-still in a pool of light from a tiered gaslit sconce.

"I'm sure you feel that you are an adult," Alexi began. "And there will be a time when I will have no recourse when you set aside respect for your parents in deference to curiosity, but now is not that time."

"I could have gone without notice," Violet countered. "What I was doing was important."

"Yes, you could have gone off without any communication at all, and you'd not have had the benefit of this; my present, level tone," Alexi continued. Violet had to admit, it was more level than she expected. He was a man capable of towering rage. Still, the exasperation she'd felt with Rebecca burbled up again.

"I am earnestly searching for answers to sights, sounds, and details that are entirely beyond me, beyond you, and beyond these walls," Violet exclaimed. "What was I supposed to do? Why are you angry with me for trying to understand what is, it seems, a family tradition of visions and biddings from a supernatural source beyond our reach?"

"Come to me," Alexi said, taking a step forward toward her. "Come to us. Your mother has always said to bring concerns, visions, anything, to her. To us. Are we not better suited to understand you than seeking out strangers?" Alexi stated, frustration and simple pain in his dark eyes.

"And worry you both to death?" Violet countered. "When I've brought things to you, it seems to be more a curse than any sort of blessing, and you hover all the closer around me. None of us can breathe for being too careful."

"Well, disappearing isn't how you solve this! You went so far as to say you could be *vanished* somewhere for some unknown cause, without so much as a goodbye? When you are still under our rules and care? You don't simply get to come or go as *visions* dictate," her father bellowed. "You have to be careful when searching! You're damned lucky because that man, that office, that department, could have had you arrested or committed in the instant! You cannot be naïve about the mundane world and expect it to answer questions for which it doesn't have the formula!"

"Lord Black was a helpful man in a high office who took me very seriously, I'll have you know. You could try doing the same."

"Oh, I take your insolence very seriously indeed!"

Percy closed her eyes, drew in a long breath, and turned to her husband with a gentle expression. "Alexi my love, you being who you are, when a parent or authority figure yelled at you, was extremity ever effective?"

Alexi stared at Percy. His nostrils flared. He folded his arms, wavering, glowering.

"I'm calling for our carriage," he growled. "We're going home, now, all of us."

No one dared say another word for the entire ride. Once turned into the drive, her father exited the carriage the moment he safely could. The ladies were taken all the way to the doorstep, where their patient and understanding Fred helped them out and lovingly took the horses to the stable, focusing not a whit on any of their tension.

Percy cleared her throat. She narrowed her icy eyes and Violet felt pierced right through, her mother's ever youthful and gracious face now ferocious. "You will tell me everything."

"I told you. I went looking for answers to my visions. At the end of an onslaught of terrible things, worse than ever before, I saw something, someone, I thought could help. I saw a man, a specific government seal, and I went to find him."

"That's it?"

"There are more details but I'm not sure what to share. How does it feel to only be given half an answer? Perhaps now you know how I feel when I'm only partially told about your past. Perhaps I wouldn't run away for clues if I thought I could get them out of you."

At this, Percy winced. Taking a deep breath, she pressed her hands together. "Ah." She nodded. "You have cut your mother to the quick. We need cups of tea and some time. Come. I've a long-overdue story to tell."

"I assume Father will have me banished to my room."

Percy grabbed her daughter's hand and escorted her past Alexi's study on the first floor; she stood in the doorway and made an announcement.

"I cannot in good conscience punish our daughter considering she has inherited my gifts and was acting in accordance of them. I am now preparing to tell her everything about our past. If I don't, her next act of disobedience will be exponential in scope. Our visionary deserves the whole truth with no further avoidance."

There was a long pause. A deep sigh. "As you wish. You ladies seem to control this household and I give up. I'm going to have a drink in blessed quietude," he called.

"I love you," Percy called.

There was a grumble in response, at which Percy smiled and led her daughter into a moonlit parlor where she turned into a glowing, spectral, breathtaking goddess, her name never so fitting.

Through several pots of tea, tears, and as many details as Percy could manage, she tried to explain herself, her lineage, share the confluence of forces that brought her and Alexi together, the war within Athens itself, and what the former Guard member's prophecy of "a war in the ground" may mean for them all.

There were even materials to share, letters, from the being—the goddess, presumably—that had forsaken a broken divinity to live within her mother, parts of which had flowed then into Violet. She read the hopeful missive from a dying creature hoping to live again in less troubled flesh, and wept with her mother.

She read the moving letter from Iris Parker, the chosen woman saved from an ignominious death to bear Percy, and continued weeping.

"I couldn't have shown you all this when you were just a child," her mother explained. "Don't you see that it would have been too much to take in, too much to bear? I've never known the right time to share this. All I've wanted is for you to live a normal, happy life."

"There are forces inside us," Violet replied. "Forces that have chosen us. Nothing about that is normal. We have to *choose* whether or not it is happy."

Percy drew close and kissed Violet's forehead, her cool hand clasped gently at the back of her neck. "My wise girl."

"Thank you for sharing. It is an *incredible* story. Biblical in scope, really."

"The comparisons have never been lost on us."

"And now what?" Violet asked, in awe. "The Persephone that bequeathed her name unto you foretold my visions of the war, through the Heart of her Guard. What of it now, in these in-between times as the world stews and broils its way toward a conflict?"

"A great deal of prophecy, I learned long ago, is waiting," her mother replied with a sigh, refilling their cups of tea and adding to the nearby tray two glasses of liqueur. Telling such tales required a more potent draught. Violet took to that immediately.

"You're in the place I was in my youth at the convent, at this same age, pacing the cool flagstones and keeping to the shadows as if I were one of the ghosts of the institution. This uncomfortable state is where I floated listless in the first few weeks at Athens. Things quickly changed, of course, but that may not be your path. Your visions, as you've said yourself, are of a future, not tomorrow. Right?"

Her mother looked very worried, suddenly. "The way you disappeared. Would you do that again to me? Would you just disappear if a vision told you to go to some foreign landscape?

Violet sighed. "Do you really want to know or will you fret yourself to death?"

Percy opened her mouth then shut it, like Alexi did, realizing she was caught.

"Eventually I'll have to go to Paris," Violet continued. "That being said, I'm sorry about today, about just writing a note and going off. Especially for saying I'd agree to be immediately sent away. It was a terribly overdramatic way of going about things."

Percy's pained face shifted into one of amusement. "You know, when you're self-aware, I find you utterly endearing."

She shifted and took her mother's hands in hers. "My visions have upset you as much as me. I don't want to hurt you anymore. We've tried so hard to take care with each other . . ."

"Oh, my love," Percy embraced her child. "My great blessing. You don't know how not to hurt me and I don't know how best to protect you. What a pair we are."

They just sat holding one another for a very long time.

Finally, Percy pulled back, her eerie eyes catching in the moonlight in a way that made Violet ceaselessly amazed.

"The latest vision. The one that prompted this . . . drama. Where in Paris was it set?"

"Gare du Nord. The train station. And then, out all over the world, high above it . . . a terrible scene unfolding."

"Present day?"

"No. There are . . . changes. It is a time to come, I acted hoping I could do something to stop it before it arrives."

"Will you abide the meantime with me, then?" her mother asked through tears, trying to find joy. "No one ever knows how long they have with a loved one, with a child, with anyone dear. I will cherish what I have—"

"Mum, when I am called to go, it won't be forever, it's not as though I'm *doomed*—"

"Nothing is forever and nothing is assured," her mother interrupted crisply. "Our lives are not guaranteed one day to the next so we take our time and give thanks for every moment of it. But I say, if that vision of yours is not in the immediate, is not directly tomorrow, then do what you must when you must but let's be honest in the meantime and enjoy today."

"Thank you." Violet stared her mother straight in the eye. "That's all I've ever wanted."

A curt nod and a thin smile passed over her mother's ghostly face as she shifted subjects with a determined cheer in her tone.

"Headmistress Carroll approached me recently, asking if I thought you'd be interested in taking over at Athens, when the time comes that she is ready to retire. Though that may be for some time yet, indomitable creature that she is. I said I thought you'd be a magnificent candidate. It's clear you love Athens as much as our headmistress does, which is key. I know you are steadfast and true, and I believe the safe haven that Athens has always been would flourish under your watch."

Violet beamed. "It will be an honor and joy. And I won't disappoint Auntie Rebecca or you one jot."

Percy clapped her hands. "Then that's settled!"

"Athens is magic," Violet stated.

"I know. It lives in us and we in it."

"What about Will? He loves the place as much as I do. He's helped with some of the electrical installations, one of his earliest interests. Could he take over as superintendent? Fixing things seems to give him purpose."

"It must be so." Here Percy paused. "Our light, and the power of Athens help him."

"And it is Athens that will tell me my fate."

IN THE SAFETY OF HIS HOME THAT SAME NIGHT, AS HE DRESSED for dinner, Will lashed out and punched the mirror. The voice had been particularly vile and violent, and when he'd sought Violet's help earlier in the day, she was nowhere to be found.

The idea of needing her sickened him, as he didn't feel any person should be so beholden to another. When he couldn't find Violet, he went to the seal of the Academy, where he'd first understood the building's wonders, and felt a small measure of comfort and release. Still, he felt weak for needing it at all.

Now anger surged within him, a foreign venom that created a metallic taste in his mouth and gave him the distinct feeling he was not alone in his own skin. That sounded mad, of course, so he preferred to believe that he possessed an intense temper that he had to control with a will of iron. His name was a testament to his greatest struggle: will.

The mirror shattered, generating myriad versions of his angry face and bloody knuckles. He cursed and went for a bandage. His mother would be upset when she saw him, he knew.

But at least the hissing had stopped. That unwelcome noise usually went quiet when he was particularly active. Or violent.

He liked being active. Making things. Wiring, engineering; whirring turbines, the buzz of electricity often canceled out whispers from the voice. He was eager to help the headmistress convert the whole school's wiring.

Violence he could do without. It didn't feel like it was of him, and yet sometimes, he felt it was his nature. Jekyll and Hyde.

The good doctor was preferred. He rejected the monster. He grimaced as he bandaged his knuckles. Violet would ask about his injury, of course, she was always asking questions. Just not always the right ones.

Knowing that the safe haven of Athens was only a bandage for a seeping wound, he longed to flee. The voice had set alight in him a fire for France; both his and Violet's visions urged them that direction, and he yearned to plunge his hands into the muddy dirt of foreign soil and wrestle with his demons for good. Only there and then, he was sure, would he be free of them.

No, no, my boy . . . the voice murmured with aching longing that was utterly chilling. *Only then will I be free to do with you what I must* . . .

CHAPTER

THIRTEEN

June 28, 1914

THE ARCHDUKE FRANZ FERDINAND HAD BEEN SHOT. WHEN Violet, dressed in a simple white shirtwaist and long blue skirt, read the news alone, taking an early meal at the breakfast table, she understood the cracking, splintering sound that had woken her that morning. The breaking point. International tensions would now boil over, using this assassination as a tipping point. This was the beginning.

Keeping her expression level, thankful that her parents hadn't yet come downstairs, she rose and smoothed the linen layers of her skirt, never minding that her hands trembled. Heat burgeoned inside her and she undid the pearl collar button at the hollow of her throat.

In hopes her mother wouldn't see the news, perhaps even studiously avoiding it, she placed the paper in the entrance hall and went upstairs to her room as if she were a nun taking to a chapel for prayer.

Ever since her conversation with Lord Black years prior, she'd begun training.

She had to be ready. He hadn't given her any assignment. What he did promise was that he'd carve out a place for her should it prove necessary.

In the years that had followed that meeting, she kept counsel and kinship only with Mina Wilberforce, Will, and her direct and extended family. There wasn't time for anyone else.

Studious, well-behaved, and introspective, Violet took every single class Athens offered and solemnly prepared for her destiny in numerous ways. Either within Athens's fortress walls, or in the quietude of what she had taken as her own wing in the Rychman estate, living like a person of the cloth, she cultivated her spirituality in equal parts with her physicality.

Devising a regimen, she shared her rigors with Will. He'd eagerly begun doing the same, training to make his body and mind as fit as they could be. He didn't talk about the voice but she knew it haunted him like the distant sounds of gunfire haunted her.

They swapped books on war, peace, and treaties. Digesting tomes about the human body, she made her own strong thanks to treatises on fitness, weight lifting, and strengthening exercises, using books for weights in her room at night. And she learned how to handle a gun.

Thinking of the complex international tensions across disputed borders, colonial greed, and the precarious alliances that this assassination would now strain, Violet felt more helpless than ever before, a pressure within her body that threatened to stifle the air out of her.

Reaching below her bed, she pulled out a folded blanket and unwrapped it.

Inside was a wooden box. Lifting the lid revealed a disassembled long-barreled pistol.

The equipment had been borrowed thanks to a recent visit to Lord Black. She'd gone to him out of a certain fondness, a need to maintain a relationship, and was pleased to find him as jovial and amenable as before, a ray of sunshine in dreary Whitehall. There hadn't been any updates to her visions, nor had he any news of any military front, but he allowed her this little something with which she might train, pulled from his old "war room" of supplies.

"To be clear, I'm not a man of violence," he had murmured at the time. "I want to avoid all that you have told me you foresee. But this might make you feel as though you could be ready for the unknown, so I'll not keep you from a resource."

The metal of the gun was cool in her warm hands. She assembled the machine with impressive speed, loaded one chamber, rotated the barrel, cocked, aimed, and fired an empty chamber with a click. Then she unloaded and disassembled it again; all in quick time as if she were saying rote prayers.

She repeated this task until she could breathe again.

A cool breeze over her face had her look up. Aunt Jane floated in the corner of the room, staring at her. Violet put her finger to her lips. Jane shook her head, murmuring with equal parts awe and sadness.

"My dear girl is busy becoming a soldier, when no one in England yet knows of any war."

THAT NIGHT WAS A SCHEDULED CELEBRATION AND VIOLET PUT all traces of a weapon carefully away and traded her shirtwaist and skirt for a satin gown. While the last few years had seen Violet take on many of the headmistress's administrative duties, tonight her succession would be made official.

Violet found it compelling accidental timing, as if the heavens planned to keep her mind on Athens instead of on an unfolding international stage. Thirty-some members of staff, family, and school friends gathered in Athens Academy's ballroom, where the gas lamps had only recently been converted in their sconces to electric, thanks to Will's meticulous work. When the great grandfather clock at one end of the celebratory space chimed eight o'clock, the headmistress swept to the center of the room, dressed in a lacy, high-necked cream blouse, wide black sash, and a simple plum skirt. The fuss of doubled skirts or high bustles was long gone; the early twentieth century demanded more efficient lines, graceful, with accents of lace that hadn't entirely left the last century behind.

Violet had long taken her dress cues from the severe Rebecca, simple high-necked and long-sleeved elegance in somber cottons, wools, and linens, leaving the brooding black look for her father and instead choosing blues and beiges. However, tonight she deigned to wear her one violet-colored ball gown—it featured simple, straight lines of dark purple satin with intricate folds that made her torso look like it was encased in a breastplate rather than a bodice, and a satin capelet over her shoulders.

As the clock finished chiming the headmistress caught Violet's eye and gestured her forward to stand at her side.

Rebecca withdrew a fountain pen from the cuff of her sleeve—the woman was always armed—and tapped her champagne glass. The murmurings of the room hushed for her announcement.

"Ladies and gentlemen, thank you for coming. As you may know Miss Violet Rychman here has excelled in every subject, I daresay so much that we may have bored her." A spatter of polite laughter. "But in the interest of keeping such a talent engaged and useful, considering I am no longer in the bloom of my youth, I am quite thrilled to announce that Miss Rychman is now the assistant headmistress and will very much be my peer in running Athens."

A cheer.

"To be quite clear, I am not *yet* retiring!" Rebecca said with a laugh; at this came more *hear, hear*s and *huzzah*s. "But in the event that I do, we know this school will be in very capable hands."

Applause.

Professor Rychman was suddenly at Violet's side, having

swooped there silently like some bat in a pantomime. Her father was a bit eerie like that, a product of the previous centuries' obsession with the Gothic, an aesthetic that he'd embraced fully and aged into ever more intensely. Bowing, he handed her a delicate flute of champagne.

"Why, thank you, Father." Violet smiled. He stared at her, dark eyes glistening, tear-filled; gazing at her with a staggering look of pride that nearly knocked her off balance. She'd never seen its like, and for the first time she knew he wasn't looking at her as his little girl, but as the woman who would run this venerable institution. He seemed ready to allow her, finally, to be the adult that she was.

Her mother stared at them both adoringly. If she knew that the assassination of the archduke was a withdrawal of a card from a teetering house of European posturing, she refused show it.

Violet couldn't help but beam, delighted to be at the center of this eccentric, important coterie, and feeling about this building as she did the moment she first set foot in it, when it seemed alive and welcoming her with open, physical arms.

"To our assistant headmistress!" her father cried. There was a toast, and Violet sipped, drinking deeply of joy and honor.

Several people demanded that she give a speech. Rebecca stepped aside to give her the floor.

"My friends and colleagues. I am so grateful that you are here. In this new century, when so much change is upon us, when new wonders have unfurled their banners, and new challenges lie on the horizon, what a balm we have in this old place."

A murmur of appreciation. Violet looked around her; the very feel of Athens brought tears to her eyes. "The place that for decades has been a safety for those who wish for more, for better, for peace, hope, equality . . . I've been so blessed to know nothing *but* this space. There has been nothing but Athens, for privileged me. Many of you . . . I stare out at a range of people from so many different backgrounds, places, and cultures, all here for common good and education for *all* people. Many of you came here fighting various injustices and indignities, all of you seeking the ability to teach or learn equally.

"The simple Quaker ideal has never been so grand as this place, and it will never have a fiercer defender than us. Bring me your every concern. As the world continues to change, so must we be ready for fears and growing pains, open to the students who need us most. I love this place with every fiber of my being, it lives in me, and I in it, and it would be nothing without all of you."

She turned to her parents. "In closing, I thank my mother and father as well as the headmistress, fierce advocates for students of every kind. They have in their tenures done countless things for this school that you will never know about to keep this place lit in dark times. I thank you for being the foundations we stand on today."

Her parents and Rebecca seemed deeply moved, and if Violet wasn't mistaken, she saw a flicker of blue fire race around the clerestory level of the ballroom, as if ancient forces too were applauding this affirmation. The applause ebbed and she stepped back into the shadows, feeling comfortable in the spotlight only for a brief time.

Once all the commotion and sets of congratulatory well-wishers had passed by her, she looked around, as she'd yet to see her dearest friend and most consistent confidant, her secret partner in preparations.

Marianna Page and Percy were in a corner, likely delightedly sharing memories; Edward Page and the good vicar, Michael, were laughing together nearby. Violet's father was standing in the shadows, his gaze alternating between his wife and their daughter, a pattern Violet was quite used to. But Will Page was nowhere to be seen.

She was praying Will wasn't suffering from a headache some-where when a voice sounded behind her.

"Congratulations, Violencia the Magnificenzia," Will said, giv-ing her the fanciful, over-grand childhood title that never ceased to make them smile. She turned to behold him in a smart black suit and tails, with a violet-colored tie to fit the occasion, as if he knew she'd wear this dress. His usually tousled hair was mostly tamed save for a few errant brown curls. Her heart warmed.

"Why, Willificent the Terrificent," she returned, "I wasn't sure I'd see you."

"You know I'm not one for crowds. But I've been here the whole time, trying to make sure Uncle Elijah doesn't get too drunk," he added, gesturing to the punch bowl under the eaves of the bal-cony. Elijah was holding court there; he gesticulated widely, slosh-ing a bit of punch from his glass.

Violet squeezed Will's shoulder with a white-gloved hand. "Thank you."

"Wouldn't have missed it for the world," Will replied earnestly. "Growing up, I thought the headmistress was an indomitable dragon who would rule this place forever. Startling when you realize they're human, you know?"

Violet nodded. "Utterly so. The other day, before she and I set-tled on this, the details of a service contract went right out of her head. She looked at me blankly—and you know how meticulous she is about every single maintenance these buildings need. I tell you that was one of the most terrifying things I'd ever seen. A mo-ment later she was able to recall the information, but we settled on my new role that very afternoon. She's relaxed some, knowing there's a successor in place and as she's in good health, it will be some time before I have to take over, but it's good to have a plan."

There was a long pause before Violet continued with an inevi-table question.

"You saw the papers today, yes?"

"The assassination of the archduke?" Will asked. "I did. I could feel it as though it was my torso the bullet came to rest in." He shuddered. "It's why I was late here tonight; I couldn't catch my breath."

"I couldn't either when I first read about it. This is where it begins. I know that from my visions," she said grimly. Will nodded. "The headmistress was keener than ever to announce this today, to take everyone's mind off of the inevitable . . . and to ensure I've too many responsibilities to simply vanish." There was a long, strained pause.

"But I'm going to have to go to the war," they broke the silence by speaking at the same time.

"How, exactly, do you mean to go?" Will asked carefully. "As a nurse? They won't let women close to front lines—"

"But that's where you'll be. And since when am I, or anyone around me, conventional?"

"Violet, even you, as amazing as you are, can't upturn *everything*, we don't even know what England will do—"

"We've been preparing. I'll contact Lord Black. We will live each day with a philosophy of harming no other, and yet doing what we will to stand strong against any encroaching evil."

She took his hand and watched as her simple touch did its usual trick, granting Will a rush of serenity. "Punch," she declared, and they celebrated while they could.

August 1914

When Violet came downstairs for breakfast, her journal in hand, she nearly dropped it at the sight of her mother at the table.

She was the very picture of a ghost in an unearthly realm; the sun shone softly through pale lace curtains backed with a layer of gray damask that reduced the strain on Percy's sensitive eyes. The diffuse glow lit the breathtaking specter at the table, dressed in white gauzy layers accented with lace and pearls, with ballooning sleeves gathered to a fitted lace yolk around her slender neck. Percy's hair was down in a loose braid at the back but her face was framed by voluminous, pearlescent locks.

She seemed a fragile porcelain doll. The expression on her face was one of blank terror. As Violet entered the room, her mother turned toward her, tears falling from her wide, ice-blue eyes.

The younger woman strode deliberately to her mother's side, where she saw the newspaper sitting on the breakfast table—and the bold words that had struck such terror into her mother's heart:

ENGLAND AND GERMANY AT WAR

Violet sank into a chair beside her mother. They sat in silence for a very long time, occasionally interrupted by the rattle of china as Percy tried to lift a cup of cold tea to her lips, unable to do more than shift it on the table.

Finally, Percy said, barely audibly, "This has nothing to do with you. Nothing."

Violet placed one hand over her mother's cold, trembling hand where it rested, limp, on the table. She didn't know how to refute her. It *did* have something to do with her, and she'd been waiting for it since she was a child. Now, what was to be done about it without breaking her family apart?

"Don't go . . ." her mother begged, the tiniest whisper.

Their bond made this request sheer agony for Violet. She drew a shaking breath. "I don't know, yet, what I'm meant to do exactly. To go now, right now, would be premature."

This small reassurance seemed to allow her mother to breathe. Percy nodded and wiped away the last of her tears.

"All right then, we'd best get to school!" Percy was shaking, but her voice was clear. "Rebecca has much to show you!"

Paris . . . a faraway voice seemed to whisper in Violet's ear. No, not immediately. Will was still here and her world was tied to his.

There was a sense in some households that going to war was an honor for the family. If the enemy was clearly defined, Violet could understand. But this conflict, this rush to clarify borders and establish who had the largest and best armies, did not feel morally defined for her or England.

Murky, muddy waters had whipped all of Europe into a frenzy, pointing cannons across the whole of the map; Queen Victoria's grandchildren fighting over pieces of colonial spoils as if no one were concerned that carved-up territorial prizes were in fact sovereign cultures filled with people wanting a voice of their own. The saber-rattling Kaiser Wilhelm was a jealous, insecure fool all too eager to shout above any other; to prove himself an indomitable force at any cost.

One day, one headline, one battle, one teardrop, one promise at a time.

At Athens, Violet went to her office, a plain room on the first floor between Rebecca's office and the chapel. Percy in turn made her way to the Bay Room, her own office, which felt too grand and cavernous today. She took her appointed hour with Francois, a translation student; they were translating *The Odyssey* from French to German. When they reached a scene of battle, she found that she could not hold back tears. She made fumbling apologies to the young man, but he waved his hand and looked at her sheepishly.

"No, Mrs. Rychman, please don't be sorry," the young man said, his English heavily accented by his French island origins, his brown skin slightly glistening in a nervous sheen of sweat. "I'm quite terrified I'll be sent off. It does me good to know I'm not the only one affected."

"We'll find a way to protect any of our students who wish to remain," Percy reassured him. "The headmistress, my husband, and I . . . we will keep you here at all costs. Those who must go or feel called to go . . ." Her voice broke again.

"Do you have . . . someone you particularly fear for?"

Percy swallowed. "Yes. I do."

"It's good you have a daughter, then," Francois said reassuringly. Percy tried to offer him a smile.

After the young man left, Percy paced her floors.

The spirits of the Professors Hart, a married couple who waltzed above their graves in the small Athens cemetery on their anniversary, wafted out from their bookcase and joined Percy in pacing to and fro.

"How has the whole world come to this?" Katherine Hart said softly.

"Not enough poetry!" Michael Hart said sadly, his long gray robes shifting weightlessly as he moved through the air. The ghost—like his wife, once a professor of English—looked out over the Athens courtyard. The spirit stared hard at the stately bronze angel that stood sentinel over a fountain at the courtyard center, as if willing the statue, her book in hand, to come to life and heal all with the written word. "Too many smug generals, petulant royals . . . It should never have come to war . . ."

"I'm sorry you have to weather this, my dear," Katherine said, coming close to Percy's desk, her unbound hair floating about her, her wide eyes luminous, the ghostly picture of a Pre-Raphaelite painting in grayscale. "You who have the same enormous heart as we. You who *feel* with the magnitude of thousands . . ."

"I . . . just don't know what to do."

Katherine looked at her husband, as if his focus on the angel gave her the only possible response.

"Pray," she said.

Percy nodded and set off for the Athens chapel. En route, she noticed that the susurrus of her gauzy, ribbon-trimmed skirts made more noise than the usually lively school about her. Everything, everyone, was silenced by an oppressive anxiety.

"I wonder," she murmured as she chose the less-traveled faculty paths, hoping to avoid students or fellow staff, lest her fear and worry undermine morale. No one needed to see a weeping administrator. "If the Sacred Space might still open for me . . . Come, old friend," she begged to the air of Athens that she felt was always alive and listening, "be a balm for my anxious heart, my troubled soul, let me lay my burdens at your mystical feet . . ."

Turning the corner of the long hall that ended in the white, mostly unadorned chapel, Percy began to nearly run. She was eager to enter the space, where a painted dove of peace hovered above a plain wooden altar.

This space had been a scene of trials and triumphs, of weddings, battles, and funerals. During their Guard service, she and Alexi had transformed it into their Sacred Space, there they could open the threshold between worlds made specifically for the Guard and their mystical work.

A cry welling up inside her, Percy channeled the sound into a violent, wrenching motion of her arm and hand. In response, the air seemed to snap like a whip and a dim black rectangle grew into a yawning maw. The Sacred Space answered her call.

She raced down the stone stairs at a careening pace, then tried to catch her breath at the center of the circular room below. The spectacular chamber had been created by divinity and maintained by heavenly shadows, the dark side of a glorious moon. Marching along the perimeter were vast stone columns. Beyond them, murmuring shadows never let anyone forget that here . . . they were near the Whisper-world.

Within the circle, the Guard had refreshed their powers. Prophecies had been proclaimed and made manifest. Grateful that this familiar space could witness the wrenching of her heart, Percy let her tears flow free. Kneeling where the figure of a great bird appeared in the stone as if a living creature had been gently pressed into malleable clay, Percy offered a supplication.

"I beg you, forces of beauty and truth, wisdom and balance. You may feel I have no right to ask anything at all of you, that in forsaking past divinity for present mortality I have forsaken my right to beg anything of the heavens, but I have no other choice. My heart insists I must do everything I can, my soul depends on it.

"I am sure the heavens are attending to many parents' cries for their children to be spared. Why mine and not another? I have no answer but the prayer itself. I ask for mine as others ask for theirs. Save our children from the ravages of war!"

If only there was something she could present as an offering, she thought. Dimly, as if drawing up water from a very deep well, she remembered something about blood and fire—something from her previous self that pulled at her mind. Before she knew it, she'd unpinned the cameo brooch at her throat and pricked her thumb with the pin.

Scarlet blood bubbled up, garish against her blanched skin, and dribbled onto the heart of the circle. Her blood vanished on the stones, evaporated as if she'd never shed a drop.

"Hear my prayers," she begged.

In response came a rushing, whooshing sound of wind and celestial song.

· An incredible, vaguely human form appeared. The breathtaking thing was incorporeal, a glowing, iridescent mass with a base violet tinge to its amorphous form. Soft music filled the air, as if heaven's orchestra were lifting its bows . . . Percy had seen one of these before. A Muse; one of the five beings that had taken up host in the Guard. While Alexi wielded the fire of Phoenix, Muses were his votaries, divinities of awe-inspiring wonder.

As she stared at the being, another drop of blood swelled from her thumb and plunged toward the stones. The Muse wafted a handlike form forward and the droplet turned into a glowing, ruby gemstone that hovered in the air between them.

"No more of that." An inhuman voice sounded in the air, crafted from rustling leaves and wildflower-scented breezes. "You've given the world enough of your blood through the years, milady. You bled yourself onto the stones of the Whisper-world for centuries in hopes of change. The goddess is reborn in you indeed."

The Muse grasped the ruby between vaporous thumb and forefinger before dropping the gem into Percy's colorless palm. Closing her shaking hand over the offering, Percy folded it away in an embroidered handkerchief she tucked back into her buttoned cuff.

Percy was too nervous to stand, too overcome by the being who attended her. She shifted onto her knees, understanding when the angels of scripture bid mortals in their midst to not to be afraid. To stare at something divine was staggering. Still, her plea remained.

"Don't take my child into this war," she pleaded in a tiny voice that felt drowned in the scope of this being's light. "Let my war serve as war enough."

"Your Violet's visions, milady," the being responded, its rich, reedy voice a swelling reverberation in the air, "were bequeathed by something far beyond us. It was beyond you, even. Your own divine form didn't understand the cryptic warnings of war that Ahmed, the former Guard's Heart, saw with his dear eyes and felt with his dearer heart long ago. He still wakes from nightmares in Cairo to this day."

"You know . . . nothing of what is to come?" Percy hadn't thought she could feel worse and she fought back bile.

"We have gifts and glimpses but we are not the all-powerful and the full future is unknowable. Only the Liminal edge can directly intervene and you know from your own experiences that it is unpredictable, with an agenda of its own."

At that moment, the Sacred Space swelled with brighter light and celestial chords. The rest of the Muses had followed their leader and now five filled the space, each form lit with a slightly different base hue.

"My Lady," came a green-tinted Muse, putting its hand upon its heart. "Forgive us our trouble with mortal time and its rounds. Let us go forth and see what we can do first."

"Thank you . . ." Percy murmured.

PERSEPHONE NODDED, STRAIGHTENED HER SHOULDERS, AND ascended the Sacred Space stairs that materialized to connect disparate worlds. The Muses remained.

The Heart voiced a critical question. "Is this war our fault? For resting so long? Could we have stopped mortals?"

"Humans war all the time," Intuition replied. "We've never been able to stop them, all we can do is try to inspire alternatives."

"What of the four shadows who warned us of turning tides?" Heart continued. "Do we dare seek them out?"

"I care not for the sanctity of the Whisper-world, let them tend to their own troubles and we to ours. We must go forth and *see*, what mortals need most," Intuition declared. "We are out of touch with this new century and for the sake of our charges, we mustn't be." Taking on the command that was its purview while phoenix fire still slept, Intuition instructed: "Go. Inspire in vital ways. Return with reports."

In a swirl of sound and color, the Muses dispersed into theaters of the world at war and those watching it unfold.

Intuition wasted no time. It vanished and shimmered again into being where it was drawn to the side of an English composer, Mr. Williams.

On the edge of the English coast, watching ships sail away to war, the composer thought of George Meredith's poem of a sky-borne lark as he watched his young countrymen fade into the distance and the first, transcendent notes alit softly in his ear, audible immediately to the Muse; a delicate bird on rising violin strings . . .

The music he dreamed up then was like an impressionist painting, its subject as clear as the time of day was in a Monet. The music was *just* like a lark. Ascending.

It was the most beautiful thing the Muse had *ever* heard.

This would be a gift to the world.

One victory gained . . .

But then the air around Intuition darkened and a strange light overcame it . . .

As if hurtled through space and time, and across a whole country, Intuition was thrown to the side of Art, who was thoroughly overwhelmed. Here, there was no picturesque scene. Here was immediate horror.

And there, on a French territory line held by British men, the Muses heard the most terrible thing they had *ever* heard, horrors even their vast imaginations could not have fashioned.

The shrieking of shells, a machinery scream that produced bloodcurdling human screams, then dread silence before another rattling volley of fire.

There were still more, new sounds. Sounds the Muses had

never heard, naïve to this brand of mechanized slaughter. The rumble of explosives. The varied pitches of different caliber of bullet to shell, from cannon to rifle-point.

The sounds of projectiles when hitting flesh sounded the same as it ever had; wet and tearing. And that was only one sense, sound. The Muses then saw the most terrible things a Muse could see.

Art's bluish form was shaking beside a shaking man, who was, as they would come to know, shell-shocked. Numbly, he itched at his cuff sleeve, a small louse darting out from the seam. Where there was one of the scurrying chatts, there would be thousands down the line in seams and cuffs, infesting hair and every crevice.

"Write down these terrible things . . ." Art murmured softly, even as it fumbled for words, for purchase. Art searched in the man's heart for his name, to call upon him as a voice for this madness. "Mr. Owen. Please. You must tell the world."

"What is the point?" the man asked the wind, stamping his numbed, infected feet.

"To let everyone know," Art murmured. "This terror. Everyone must *know*. Proclaim to an unready world. Make those lying safe in comfortable beds this night quake with your reality."

The man picked up a pencil remnant and noted phrases . . . *Dulce et Decorum Est*. The pointed Horace homage was clear to the Muses, the poet noting it was *not*, in fact, "sweet and fitting to die for one's country . . ." It was senseless in these muddy pits.

As one by one, soldiers died, their souls slipping up and out from their bodies, they glinted into the dark sky and winked out. To where those snuffed candle-flames went, the Muses could not tell. The full realm of mortal afterlife lay beyond their scope.

The company in the trench was bid by an exhausted commander to fall back from their positions to have rest. The Muses watched as the rain began to fall in a miserable pelt, men climbing from trenches like rats crawling out from pits. The rats came, too. For every man there was another two rats escaping the soon flooded shell holes, fat from dead human flesh and bold as thieves, crawling up from the wet pits and out from under the fallen whose innards they had been gnawing.

The unit trudged in a haphazard line for a few moments before new sounds assaulted the area and a dreadful unfolding began.

Suddenly there was screaming, and masks, and then darkness. Not everyone got their mask on in time.

Horror after melting, disfiguring horror.

A wrenching pull drew the Muses away and their background changed from wet slate gray to the dry Sacred Space. They were home, away now from the front, but forever changed.

The roaring sound of war was exchanged for the gasps, the tears, and the keening wailing of immortal beings. Devastating and devastated. They tried to collect themselves, put their raw emotions to words.

Intuition floated forward in the Sacred Space to note one new change in their environment. Its hazy form pointed to a small sliver of light hovering at the center of their circular plaza. It was a distinct force. The Liminal had connected the Sacred Space directly to its portal. The Muses were now bonded to an unpredictable actor tied irrevocably to the Whisper-world. Gazing at that crack, Intuition shuddered, knowing they were now at Liminal mercy in ways they had never been prior.

"We planted seeds seeped in blood-drenched mud," Art murmured, wafting toward its fellows, its glow flickering. "I weep for that poet's soul."

"The one we championed? He longs for a love he cannot have, I could feel it," said the Heart mournfully. "Not safely in this world that punishes his kind of desire. He will leave us poetry, but not enough, I fear . . . Not long enough in this world."

"It is . . . terrible," Healing wailed, who had been one of the quietest, the most overwhelmed of their company, wafting to and fro as if it were pacing. "These battles are like nothing that we have seen. How can I stand such senseless death? I am undone!"

"This scale is unprecedented. Human beings have been doing terrible things to one another across the globe since the first weapons were ever fashioned. The scale and the *machines* . . ."

"The gas," Healing cried. "That monstrous, unconscionable *gas* . . ."

"Our Violet must face those hells?" Heart exclaimed. "I refuse. I won't have it."

"And what of *all* those boys who have no one to champion them?" wept Art. "We cannot be everywhere at once. The theaters are insufferably vast. And will not our very own Will be dragged into this very fire?"

"Violet and Will are bound to an old foe," declared Intuition. "They have inherited the old vendetta, what's left of it, and that's for them to seek out. Their battle will pose risks we can't foresee. Until *that* gauntlet is thrown, we can't allow either of them to be sent in. A wild goose chase through hell? Not a chance. When the vision strikes Violet to her tipping point, when she takes up arms, so do we. In the meantime. Keep inspiring, whatever it takes. Sow the seeds now."

"Drenched in blood," Heart sobbed.

"What has meaning in such madness, terror, chaos, and death?" Art mourned.

"That is precisely the question their art will ask," Intuition replied, trying to keep its fellows focused and energized in their purpose when they seemed about to fall apart. "It is vital they ask it, all creative across all the fronts. Only their asking it can offer insights into how to make the world human again. We must bid them keep asking, then, until men realize they are all human . . ."

"We must rouse Phoenix fully," Memory declared.

"He'll rise on his own," Intuition countered. "He'll need every last bit of his energy until then. Our beloveds aren't youths anymore and the two children who hang in the balance are not gods. For the moment, let us fortify sacred Athens's bricks. Men will come for what Athens stands for. That's a home-front battle we cannot lose, for if the source of our power is compromised, none of us will survive."

CHAPTER FOURTEEN

As December of 1914 arrived, Violet could feel Athens despairing. There was a certain type of student that attended Athens. All were intelligent, but so were they equally sensitive. She could feel the student body struck by every report that came through, from myriad sources and languages.

She was at lunch in the mess hall, thinking it important she cast herself not as one above the students but as one proud to be with them, though she kept to her own table.

Will came to sit beside her with a heaping tray of beef and potatoes. The meals they had shared all through school comfortably gave way to their professional trades. He was dressed in shirtsleeves and a canvas apron dusted with wall plaster. As the leading superintendent, he was responsible for all maintenance across the entire premises and while there was never a shortage of tasks, Athens had never looked better.

"How are you?" Violet asked. She tried not to make it seem like she was asking after his health, but it always sounded like she was.

"This war is terribly hard on Germans living in England," Will said without preamble. "Mum doesn't know what to do or how to feel. She bursts into tears during reports from either side. She's *terrified* about my enlisting, feels betrayed. I don't know what to do."

"You don't have to enlist, Will," Violet said.

"All your life, you've known this was coming, known you would have to go over there. You're not going alone."

"Not that I don't appreciate the idea of company, but what then of your poor mum?"

Will shrugged. "What of any whose sons have gone to war?"

"What indeed?" Violet sighed.

"Mothers have such expectations," Will muttered.

"What, like when you're going to get married?" Violet asked with a laugh. Will looked stricken.

What came next tumbled from him like a release, a confession, and a question all at once.

"There seems to be a way men and women are supposed to feel about one another that I'm not sure I've ever felt, or even understand beyond the theoretical level. The way some of my classmates would talk among themselves about women . . . or even toward one another and their bodies. I'm . . . always at a loss. When I tried to describe this once, a schoolmate called me something derogatory. But I am hoping you will understand. Perhaps there is something wrong with me? Perhaps the voice and the complications therein, have made me something freakish that will worsen—"

"There is nothing wrong with you, Will," Violet insisted. "Take care with that word. My mother heard it all her life and there's nothing fair about it. You are who you are; don't take on a trauma as some sort of defining capacity. I know you as the champion unmoved by an old enemy of my family. Despite being courted by the darkest of forces, you haven't taken the creature up on its prompts. The voice and the pain it causes are separate qualities, something foisted on you by external circumstance. You are a wonder. Terrificent, my Willificent."

Violet grinned and Will chuckled, blushing.

"Don't you worry about being like anyone else," she continued passionately. "I don't. I'd like to think I'm more than just a sum of odd, inherited parts; a pawn in otherworldly games. Because of our circumstances, you and I are meant for more than world's limitations. How can we know what to say of the future and what it expects of us when the war has always been a sword of Damocles over our futures? While it doesn't have to define us, it certainly informs us and our choices."

Will seemed to be drinking in her words. Seeing that she was hitting the notes he needed, that the worry on his gentle, handsome face had eased into eagerness, she continued, with a disclaimer. "Though let's say none of this to our mothers. They feel guilty enough for our haunts and miss all the nuance. I don't want to live the life of a woman only as this age demands of her. Mum was discounted from society straight out; while more 'acceptable' now accounting for a husband and child, she remains a 'freak.' We are already exemptions. While less may be expected from society, there's all the more from fate."

"I think people have always assumed that we would marry, you and I," Will murmured with a nervous little laugh.

An unexpected, crippling anxiety seized Violet. She couldn't tell if he liked the idea or if he was scoffing at it. Her stomach twisted. She'd assumed the same thing everyone else had, of course. Hadn't ever thought for a moment otherwise. The idea of having taken his eternal presence in her life for granted was suddenly terrifying should she be proven wrong. But she continued with a certain aloofness, so as not to seem suddenly desperate. Damn her pride.

"Well, I find that assumption a comfort. Keeps us out of circles of gossip, other expectations and pressures. Our lives will be determined by our visions and voices. We will always have each other, in the unique way in which we have always been bound, inseparable. I see no reason to *change* that."

There was a long, tense pause. Violet's breath caught in her throat. "Do you?" she added. *Please say you don't want to change that . . .*

"No. No changing that," Will blurted. His cheeks were bright red. He reached out and grabbed her hand. "I can't . . . I couldn't . . . live . . ." He stared at her.

There was such a palpable, beautiful relief on Will's face. And such searing, overwhelming love. It nearly knocked Violet backward with its force. She could breathe again. The anxiety that had clamped down on her insides eased.

"But not before our missions," Violet clarified. Will nodded. "We're promised to the future instead. This is a pledge that we come back alive, to come back for each other."

Before they could address any further plans, Mina Wilberforce approached them. Her tightly wound spiral locks, flecked with a bit of gray around her hairline, were up in a black kerchief, her simple black linen dress accented by an armband; a token of mourning. There were hardly any lines on her dark skin, yet Violet felt Mina had aged a great deal since the days of Violet's childhood visits to the library. The weight of time's passage was visible in her dark eyes.

"Hello, my friends, am I interrupting?" she asked quietly, noting Will's blush.

"No, Mina, come sit," Violet exclaimed. "I miss you." She gestured to her armband. "I'm so sorry for whatever loss you have suffered."

The librarian took a seat beside Will.

"Oh, for those bygone days when our hearts were less heavy and time seemed limitless," Mina said with a similar wistfulness. "As for the mourning, it's not for anyone in particular. Hundreds, perhaps thousands, of men are dying every day in France and beyond. I've decided I'll stay in mourning as long as this dreadful war grinds on. None of us should become inured to it."

"Agreed," Violet said with a nod, relieved that the loss was not so personal.

"I've a proposition to put to you and to the headmistress."

"I'm all ears."

"I've been studying nursing. I've made connections thanks to others who wish to raise and broaden the profession for *all* people. Men of color are fighting under the flag of the Empire, in their own separate regiments and campaigns. I fear they'll get less attentive care if injured. I've tutored a few black women privately in their homes, good women of faith, hard work, and purpose. I want to share Athens with even more and help with *healing*, not the war itself. If I can use a classroom, a few dormitory rooms, books, and supplies, I won't have to keep spreading myself so thin. I foolishly hoped the war would end as soon as it began and I wouldn't have to expand my efforts."

Violet nodded in empathy.

"Any nurses of color I train would have to help tend to our own, as we'd likely not be allowed to treat white folk." Her dark eyes flashed. "Oh, prisoners of war, surely, but not our own English." The pained anger in her voice was palpable.

"That's a monstrous segregation," Violet murmured. "But I fully support your initiatives. Come, let's arrange space and supplies for you with the headmistress at once, it's absolutely critical."

Will rose to his feet. "Miss Wilberforce, I wish you the very best for a worthy cause. Violet, I'll see you around. Don't go anywhere without me, you know . . ."

Violet just smiled at him as he walked away. She and Mina turned back toward the center of Promethe Hall where the headmistress and assistant headmistress offices were features of the first floor.

"It is wonderful to have a dear friend like that," Mina said. "I have a beloved friend and I don't know what I'd do without them. I'd be groundless otherwise."

"Groundless," Violet agreed. "Why . . . that's exactly so. Our beloved roots that keep us on the ground."

"Because our heads are full of visions," Mina said, gesturing to Violet's head.

"Certainly are. How are yours?" Violet said conspiratorially.

"I've nightmares every night," Mina replied with a sigh. "It's why I have to do something. I feel the world crying out for help. I taste the world's blood in my mouth every day."

Caught by that visceral description, Violet shuddered. Quite forgetting politeness in that moment, rather than knocking on the headmistress's door, she just opened it.

"Auntie Rebecca—"

Headmistress Carroll, bent over a pot of hot tea, started at the sudden entrance, and dropped the tea strainer onto a porcelain saucer with a clatter.

"You're just as bad as your father, bursting in without any care!" she exclaimed, a hand to her heart.

"Sorry," Violet replied, chastened.

"Hello, Mina," Rebecca said, looking over Violet's shoulder. "Something important afoot?"

"Yes," Violet insisted, drawing up a second chair for Mina. Rebecca set her cup of tea on her desk and poured for her guests before taking her seat.

"Before you begin, let me show you both this paper you may be interested in signing. I put down my maiden name. I'd alter yours slightly—I don't want anyone taking an extra interest in the school, rooting any of us out should there be repercussions on the signers, but this is a very important message."

She passed over the paper and Violet read:

"An Open Christmas letter to the Women of Germany and Austria."

It was a peace initiative and had been signed by more than ninety prominent suffragists. Violet and Mina quickly added their names—with minor alterations, as the headmistress had recommended. When they passed it back to her, Rebecca said, "I'll return this to Rose Spire, who brought it to my attention. I'm sure she knows others who should sign."

"Any word from her or from Lord Black about proposing Conscientious Objection as a legal right?" Violet asked. Rebecca shook her head. Violet frowned, then said, "Mina is here to advance a cause."

Once Mina explained her initiative, Rebecca implemented it at once, designating several open rooms and the common area of the women's dormitory as now devoted to this program. Mina left in an excited, purposeful dash.

"Mum will want to sign, if you'd like to bring it to her," Violet offered. Nodding, Rebecca followed Violet into the hall.

"You can go on and speak with her, if you don't mind. I've some work to do," Violet stated, turning away quickly, feeling the seal of Athens calling her, drawing her upstairs as strongly as ever. Glad the space was so empty, she wandered to the center of the circle.

"There's so much good here . . . why must I leave it?" she asked.

Instantly she was seized by a vision. Rapid-fire glimpses of a train ride, then a quiet town, identified by a sign at the station: VERDUN.

A farm.

A black pit of hissing, bubbling dirt . . .

When she returned to Athens, she knew where she had to go.

"I have to tell Will," she murmured to the seal.

Surprisingly, a rumbling voice answered, deep murmur wafting up from below. "Wait, my child. One more attempt at intervention."

Following the voice was a trickle of blue flame that almost immediately disappeared, like a candle doused into smoke.

"Who are you?" Violet asked.

"I am *of* you," replied the fire. "Let my Muses try to stop this terror one last time. They fumble on new world's ground. Give them the holiday."

"As you wish . . ." she said softly.

At her answer, the room returned to its usual state, the seal to cool brass and smooth tiles.

Athens was alive and speaking and she would obey it. For now. Because the seal was right, it was nearly Christmas . . . Who would want to fight over Christmas?

THE MUSES PASSED THROUGH THE LIMINAL PORTAL; ITS particular, threading, sparking light reached out to them like tendrils of ivy, drawing them across into its space, then further into melee.

There was a roaring sound as if they were a part of the barrage and then there was silence.

All of them floated over a French section of No Man's Land. A desolate stretch of meters between barbed wire and the seemingly never-ending scars of the trenches, zigging, zagging lines fortified with duckboards and dripping with moisture.

In a quiet corner of the Western Front, in the bleak midwinter, along the zigzag of trenches, in the chill night air during a break in fighting, in quiet murmurs, the men seemed to realize, through the shell-shocked daze of the war, that this was in fact Christmas Eve. In one corner of a chambered trench, two soldiers murmured about trench foot and remembered to change out sodden socks for a damp pair in their pack, revealing bluish, wrinkled feet that the soldiers seemed loathe to touch for exacerbating the discomfort.

One looked up, directly at the Muses; a young man who appeared a child. Wide, glassy-eyed, the scope of him was plain as day, a readable map to the Muses' understanding; dulled from pain of brotherly loss, of love, and aches and shooting pains in his unduly battered body, ringing in his ears that sadly were no bells of the season but the damage from shelling. He scratched behind his ear, absently, lice again.

He squinted at the Heart, as if looking at a faraway star. Perhaps that's what this boy saw in it, a reminder of hope in a night sky.

"Yes, my child," the Heart encouraged in a sweet murmur. "Never forget you are beloved of the cosmos. All of you. Every last mortal."

The boy's mouth opened into a partial smile, as if he was trying to remember how the expression went after months of gritting teeth. Softly, gently, the young soldier began to sing. A jarring, amazing sound that was so human and yet so foreign amidst the sounds of fire and metal lifted into the air like Williams's lark on an English cliff . . .

Silent night, holy night.
All is calm,

A few more soldiers near him on the line joined in with him.

All is bright.

As the sound rose, so did the engagement. Englishmen joined in full-throated, keening even, an appeal, a prayer.

The Heart, glistening drops rolling across its surface, an expression of tears, turned its head at the bidding of Intuition.

The German encampments, standing, sitting, and lying listless in their trenches, were but a few meters of designated No Man's Land away from the enemy line.

Intuition could feel them stirring and it gestured to the Heart that perhaps they wanted to float a bit more between each line, refusing to take sides.

The Germans, too, could not help but hear this song they knew well. It was theirs, written by a German choirmaster who, in 1818, belonged to a congregation whose organ broke over the holiday. He was bid compose a simple tune for vocalists and guitar. It became one of the most beloved holiday songs ever since. So much of English Christmas, due to Prince Albert the century prior, had ties to Germany. This beloved song of the very same melody, was echoed across what was now a space that was every man's land. The Germans took up their part:

Stille Nacht, heilige Nacht.
Alles schläft; einsam wacht . . .

The full text was sung each in their own language; sweet and beautiful notes hung in the air as if angels had sung along.

After the tense silence, there was a slight movement on the German front.

One brave German actually climbed up the shoddy wooden stairs, stairs that had seen countless bloody offensives by this time, vertical wooden slats that had borne hundreds, thousands up and out to their immediate death by shell or bullet, hanging on the wire, close enough for bayonet . . . king, general, and kaiser alike counting on enough warm bodies to press forward to gain mere feet of land, every initiative a willingness by high command to lose portions of men along the line. Disposable. Expendable. Body after body. This German carried all that weight with him as he climbed up, stepped out, hands up, no rifle in view.

Three Englishmen raised their rifles against an approaching *Fritz* purely on instinct. Their commander gestured for them to lower their weapons.

"Is that man carrying a lit fuse?" one soldier murmured worriedly.

The boy who had begun singing shook his head. "No, it's a cigarette."

In one hand the approaching soldier held his own cigarette, took a draught, and lowered his hand again, palms open toward the British line. In his other hand, pressed between two fingers, was a tiny sliver of white in the moonlight, bright in his grubby hands. Another cigarette.

The German, an older man, a likely veteran of war before who found it now tiresome, bent, looking down open-faced, blankly, at the Englishmen who could all shoot him or skewer him at any moment. The smoke of his cigarette wafted over them in a thin cloud. He reached out and offered the unlit cigarette in his hand to the corporal at the bulwark of the trench, who reached out for it tentatively.

"*Fröhliche Weihnachten,*" the ambassador said. "Merry Christmas."

A cheer went up along the English line. This too was echoed across the German line.

And suddenly, everyone was up and out. The whole companies darted up the rickety stairs that usually meant certain death but now meant *live.*

Live and enjoy that you are all human beings . . . Together on this sacred night of all nights . . .

The Christmas Truce.

The Weihnachtsfrieden.

Trêve de Noël.

It happened all the way down the line for the next two weeks. The Muses were captivated, trying to replicate the magic of this moment and pass it man by man down the entirety of the Western Front.

"We're doing it, *they're* doing it; it will stop! This hell will end!" the Heart cried joyously. Its colors had never churned so brightly, so moved was the being that it darted around like a playful bird, like Williams's ascendant lark.

The Muses danced, then, like they used to when the world was young and the fields were the greenest.

These fields were now apocalyptic. Gone was the grass, the trees were blackened and leafless. But the cessation of the blasts and the constant tattoo of gunfire made the surreal, jagged mud pits into another Eden out of sheer quietude.

This Christmas Truce was not ubiquitous; there were spots of fighting along the Western Front; in some places little more than quiet arrangements of cease-fires were made to recover bodies on both sides.

But artists and poets, dreamers and athletes, the young recruit and the veteran soldier, every average man on the line held some part of these events in their heart. Crossing No Man's Land to exchange rations, cigarettes, stories, songs, games of sport, return prisoners, tell tall tales in broken second languages; the common experience of a shared hellscape reminded them all that they were sent there by kings and kaisers, not by one another.

The Muses tended this truce, helped strike up the song and the sport, encouraged exchanges large and small, bid artists describe and depict it all as best they could. Like poetry from the edge of madness, so did the world need to see the best of humanity on display; its commonality.

But word reached proud, comfortable seats and men were sentenced back into the mud, the roar, the terror, and the blood, and were shot if they deserted.

The Muses were crushed when the orders, like a cascading effect along the line, reloaded the dread cannons and gas crept through deadly breezes to slough off whole skins.

Slinking back to the Sacred Space, the Muses were half lit in defeat.

The Heart, specifically, was nearly spent. It had come to love these men along the line, listening to the stories of family back home, or love some quietly found with one another, the camaraderie only dire survival can craft.

"The four were right," Heart wept. "We're failures."

Despairing, broken, questioning all reason and purpose, they slept, then. They needed their strength for when Violet would come to wake them at last, when the old vendetta could no longer be silent.

WORD OF THE MANY CHRISTMAS TRUCES ACROSS THE FRONT reached Athens, via papers, sources interested in peace-keeping, by students with relatives fighting on variously held lines.

When Percy first saw a newspaper article about it, the directives had already been given to resume fighting and she immediately sought out Rebecca.

They poured a bit of bourbon into their tea and spoke through angry tears.

"Look at this . . ." Percy murmured, referencing the artist's rendition of a football game, another of men trading helmets and rations. "Here is the most heartening thing in the world. And the most *heartbreaking* thing, when aristocrats from their comfortable palaces, who will never see their own blood shed nor bloodshed on their doorsteps, consider men but cannon fodder and send them all back to shooting one another once more for the sake of three feet gained, three feet lost!

"While the death toll ticks away every second. Like the body of my old foe, Darkness," Percy mourned. "Flesh to bone. Flesh to bone. Ticking away lives . . ."

There was an uncomfortable, mordant silence between the two worried women with the weight of a hundred-some youth, and their very own, on their hearts.

"I'll contact Rose Spire," Rebecca stated. "Perhaps she and Lord Black can convince Parliament to honor those soldiers, and their wishes, more directly. And to push against conscription. If boys want to volunteer, they are most welcome to. I'll not have ours dragged away . . ."

Percy lifted her teacup. "For a *lasting* truce," she begged. The women drank.

She thought of the old nightmare where Violet and Will ticked away their lives from flesh to bone and knew that what ticked away were the last days of their safety.

CHAPTER
FIFTEEN

THERE WAS A TIME WHEN REBECCA THOMPSON-CARROLL'S pining for her own child had been desperately keen. That seemed lifetimes away, now. She was happy with her husband, Michael; the light of his heart had drawn aside the dark curtain of Rebecca's misery, driving out all her pining for the wrong man.

Athens constantly reminded her she was not without children. In the last five decades, she had sheltered more than thirteen hundred children at Athens. She contented herself with the knowledge that this was more than any individual biological mother could have done.

Her need to protect the young people in her care kept her up all night before the students returned from their holidays. The war was no longer in its infancy; hardly the quick victory Allied forces had predicted.

When conscription notices began to go out, accompanied by messages strongly encouraging those not yet called up to enlist, the quiet local Quaker congregation she had been raised in asked her to extend safe haven; as there was no codified way to protect those who did not wish to fight on religious grounds, Conscientious Objectors were without rights and subject to punishment. There were no deferments for students but it didn't mean she wouldn't try to shelter them at all costs.

On this first day of term, she brought everyone into the grand auditorium.

She asked that Mina Wilberforce stand beside her as head librarian and president of the board of directors, as well as head of the quiet nursing program for those who would be turned away at national programs. She invited other trustees and administrators of high ranking to stand with her in solidarity; Alexi was present, of course, choosing to stand more as a guard near the wings, his onyx robes blending with the stage blacks.

Mr. Kahn, head of Athens's world studies program, was less able to hide his discomfort than the headmistress. Loosening the collar around his brown throat, he gazed upon his students in the audience, and also at these sheltered newcomers, with radiant care, tears evident in his wide, dark eyes. As everyone was settling in, he turned to Rebecca and the tears fell. "We must do everything we can," he said, urgency heightening the lilt of his accent.

"I know, Sanjay. I promise my life on it."

He nodded and turned back to staring at the mix of faces before him, as if just by staring at them he could shield them from any ill.

Percy was invited to stand as head of translations, but declined, sitting instead in the front row so that her looks would not garner attention or become a distraction, Violet at her side. Rebecca felt as much drive to protect her "niece" and keep her here, safe within these halls, as any.

The chapel church bell on the other side of the hall echoed faintly into the open auditorium doors. The assembled staff, men and women of the same varied backgrounds and oppressions of which Quakers were all too aware, forces that drove them to keep open their doors, all turned to Rebecca.

Other perilous times she offered a school-wide announcement in this hall flashed through her mind; the horrific spree of Jack the Ripper, when curfews and locked doors were the orders of the day, and again to send students home early for holidays so the Guard could bring a spiritual war down upon Athens's bricks. And now . . . what to do about a *world* war that hungrily sought hundreds of thousands of young men to chew up in trenched jaws . . .

She took a breath, gathered her thoughts, and began, letting the grand acoustics of the hall help her strong voice echo down the wood-paneled aisles.

"Students. You know in what day and age you study here. Gentlemen, you are here either because you are young or because you or your family oppose the war. Welcome. But you must know that the Academy, on all official paperwork, has been renamed Athens Academy for Girls. Rest assured, gentlemen, this is only to hide your presence and ensure your safety. I would rather have you here than on the front lines for all the world." Her voice caught. Sanjay placed a hand upon her elbow.

"Hear, hear," he said quietly.

"To maintain our ruse, and keep your heads, should you hear this bell"—Rebecca picked up a small bell and rang it, a shrill and unmistakable sound—"it will be picked up by others, to ring around the premises. No matter where you are or what you are doing, report to the chapel. Once your number is complete, lock the doors and leave me to deal with the authorities. I will do everything in my power to keep you safe, and out of jail or worse.

"I have not worked so hard to cultivate intelligent young minds only to have them shot in a muddy field while barely a foot of ground is gained. Is this perfectly clear?"

Vigorous nods greeted her and she was satisfied she was understood.

As she walked back to her office, a streak of blue fire coursed around the bricks in one dizzying lap. Understood indeed, and the old forces reinforced her.

* * *

THE NEXT WEEK REBECCA RECEIVED AN UNEXPECTED CALLER. When she opened the door at the sound of a knock, who should be standing there but Rose Spire, wool coat buttoned up out of alignment, and a dazed, ruddy-faced young man.

"Hello, old friend, what brings you here?"

Rose entered, bringing with her the gentleman who resembled her. With tousled brown hair and wide green eyes, he looked younger than he likely was.

"This is my son Vincent. Please . . . can you give him a position here? I've been trying to place him in communications, coding on the home front, but as you can see . . ." She rummaged in her coat pocket and withdrew papers in shaking hands; an assignment to report to communications at the battlefront instead. "I thought, seeing as my husband and I work in government, that I could influence the situation."

Vincent looked down as if ashamed.

"How do you feel about this, Mr. Spire?" Rebecca asked.

He glanced at his mother nervously.

"You can tell her, she understands," Rose murmured to her son.

When Vincent looked into Rebecca's eyes, she was arrested by the openness of his soul. His heart wasn't just on his sleeve, it was in the air, all around them, like nothing she'd ever seen.

"I'm what they call an empath, ma'am, a preternaturally strong one, at least, so I've been told. So, I . . ."

"You'd die of a broken heart before you even shipped out!" Rebecca exclaimed. She turned to Rose. "He stays."

Tears fell from both Spires and Rose gasped her thanks.

Rebecca turned to Vincent and spoke crisply. "What's your favorite subject, Mr. Spire?"

"Alienism and the growing field of psychoanalysis, Headmistress. I have an . . ."

"Aptitude, no doubt."

"He's become quite proficient in the subject," Rose said, having composed herself. "He follows the latest advancements and has lectured at Scotland Yard and for the New York police force as well. He is interested in more humane treatments of mental afflictions."

Thinking a moment, Rebecca tapped a pen absently on her blotter. "Noble, Mr. Spire. We'll have you teach courses. I confess I find Mr. Freud off-putting, but I'm all for new explorations of the mind, especially when the world seems to be losing theirs collectively. Take a supervisor's room in the south men's hall. We are London's best-kept secret. Be sure you keep our secrets, too."

"I will take measures to protect you all from scrutiny," Rose assured. "Thank you."

"You're most welcome."

As Rose and her son left, it occurred to the headmistress that she should begin holding drills for the boys—let them practice evacuating to a maintenance cellar in case of an inspection.

HER INTUITION PROVED TRUE, AS IT WAS ONLY A MATTER OF weeks before Rebecca heard a small bell ringing loudly from the front foyer. The sound was then picked up by other small, shrill bells around the Athens quadrant.

That bell meant whatever young woman sat on watch at the entrance saw police coming up the stairs and had sounded the alarm. That had been the drill. The headmistress and Violet Rychman emerged from their offices at the same time.

"I'm going to Lord Black. If anyone is arrested he can intervene," Violet said, and dashed out toward the center of London.

Bells rang out around the school and boys hurried from various classrooms, filing down past the headmistress's office and into the chapel. The headmistress found herself climbing to the third floor instead of facing the authorities head-on. Panic choked her, pressing against her snugly buttoned blouse.

She threw herself upon the seal of Athens, appealing to whatever power might be listening.

"Please. Muses and your master, Phoenix. These children are my own—please . . . please don't let the war take them away to die senselessly. Please help me keep them safe—"

Rebecca felt a warm, tingling pressure upon her lips, like a kiss. As she lifted her head and looked up, a feather of blue fire hovered on her mouth and she was flooded with memories and sensations from her Guard years. She wondered, for one brief and guilty moment, if that's what kissing Alexi would have felt like. But she dismissed that curiosity, welcoming the phoenix fire as a long-lost friend, grateful she'd not been deserted.

"Will you help me?" she begged the fire.

"I think, clearly, it will," came a voice across the hall. She whirled around to see Alexi, standing tall and severe as ever, in the shadows.

Long strides brought him to her side in a mere moment. He reached out wide hands. The cerulean fire flew toward him as if magnetized. As if it had never left.

The moment the blue flame touched Alexi's palms, he inhaled deeply, as if smelling the sweetest of scents, and exhaled, as though sated with the most delicious of meals. He stared at her with a fresh, wide-eyed wonder, and an uncharacteristic little laugh escaped him.

Rebecca knew the strange sensation well; just being on the seal gave her a frisson of the old giddy rush that swept through her body when the Pull of the Grand Work was activated.

He stared at the fire, and for a moment Rebecca thought she glimpsed tears in his eyes; then he blinked and his expression reflected his stern ferocity. He stared down at her through wisps of rekindled flame.

"We must hide them," he stated. "Merely locking the chapel doors won't be enough. The fire knows just the place, don't you, old friend?"

Rebecca found herself racing to keep up with Alexi, whose long, furious strides carried him down the stairs and into the entrance foyer in mere moments. There, Rebecca saw that Percy had joined the young lady posted at the entrance.

"Oh!" Percy cried, turning to them, seeing the blue fire Alexi wielded in his hand. "We have help indeed!" she exclaimed. The student beside her stared at the flame in wonder.

"Never mind this," Alexi stated, addressing the gaping girl, nodding toward the borrowed phoenix fire. "Chemistry experiment."

The girl nodded rapidly, as if she preferred that answer to something of magic. Alexi, when wielding his power, had a way with making people think what he wanted them to.

"I'll distract the authorities, Headmistress," Percy assured her. "The boys are all in the chapel, I'm told."

"Thank you, Percy," Rebecca said gratefully, wasting no time in closing the distance to the chapel doors.

Percy had volunteered, when they discussed this scenario, to greet any officers at the door. Her eerie and unsettling appearance might distract an officer of the law from the task at hand, or at least gain the students some time to hide themselves.

"Boys, open up, it's the headmistress," Rebecca barked at the chapel doors. Alexi stood at her side, a fresh energy flowing from him, his eyes bright with familiar lightning. When the door swung open, the boys gasped at the sight of their fearsome professor so transformed. Rebecca closed the chapel doors behind her and bolted them.

"Stand back from the altar, boys," Alexi demanded. The students shifted around until they cleared a space between the door and the altar. Alexi cast one arm forward and the phoenix fire shot through the air like a thrown spear, creating a large, black, rectangular void. And revealing stairs leading down to an unknown depth.

"Descend," Alexi commanded.

More murmuring, fear, shifting feet.

"I told you I would protect you by any means necessary, now you go down those stairs!" Rebecca cried.

"But, Professor," she heard one boy venture. "Where does that lead? What magic is this?"

Alexi stepped inside the portal that once had led him, Rebecca, and the rest of the Guard into their Sacred Space, a vital place of life, peace, and power. He turned to his charges.

"You believe in God, my good lads? Whether you share Athens's Quaker roots or you've a different name for the divine, I offer this proof that the heavens can provide. Now get down these stairs before the headmistress throws you down, and I do not want to hear one more *word* about this."

Rebecca chuckled despite her nerves and left to join Percy at the front doors. The girl who had been standing watch stood nervously behind Percy, glaring at the officers.

The intruders tactlessly gaped at Percy and her entirely colorless hair and skin. She had proved a proper distraction. The baffled group turned to stare sheepishly at Rebecca.

"I am Headmistress Carroll, gentlemen, what can I do for you?"

"Sorry to disturb you, ma'am, but we're responding to a tip about a few deserters. A source claimed she saw multiple young men here. Eligible young men, saw them through the back gate, men who should be serving His Majest—"

"Do you not see that this is a girls' school?" Rebecca stated

calmly, pointing to the banner across the great foyer that declared:
WELCOME TO ATHENS ACADEMY FOR GIRLS.

"Yes, ma'am, but . . ."

"We have some elder male professors, yes, hardly what you're looking for. We recently had a food drive for ailing veterans, a joint event with another preparatory school. That was surely what your source noticed. You may search the premises if you like," Rebecca said, charging ahead.

"It's awfully grand for girls," muttered one officer when he surely thought the headmistress couldn't hear. But the chief mark of a good headmistress was uncanny hearing.

"Do you think you'll find me additionally cooperative by insulting my school *and* womankind all at once?"

"Don't mind McGraw, he's a dullard," offered up the sergeant.

"Clearly. You should keep a more informed order in your ranks."

Rebecca led the men about the school, one wing after another. The girl students stared at her in admiration and terror, a quality she cultivated—but now she wondered if there was a snitch among them. She would conduct personal interviews . . . and make sure every window or gate visible from the street was shuttered from now on.

The residue of phoenix fire that was part and parcel of Athens's bricks glowed slightly as the men walked by, influencing them.

Last but not least, the officers had Rebecca open the doors to the chapel. She did so obediently, but not without fear. Would the Space remain stable? She could hear an old, soft hum, the songs of the spheres, the music of the Sacred Space. Could anyone else hear that old, beloved tune?

A kind, dear voice made her pause at the top of the aisle while the officers glanced around the small, white space with golden stained-glass angels.

"Hello, my love, has the law come for prayer?" Rebecca turned around to see her husband standing in the doorway in his vestments. He always came to check in on her after making his rounds at nearby parish orphanages, and he seamlessly fell into the role of additional protection.

"No, they've come looking for young male bodies. But none to be found, eh, gentlemen?"

The officers scratched their heads.

"Sorry to trouble you and your girls, Headmistress," said the sergeant. The one named McGraw eyed her suspiciously.

"May the Lord be with you," Michael said sincerely. The officers just nodded. Rebecca escorted them back down the hall to the front foyer.

Percy had remained at the door, awaiting the officers with a smile. She opened the door for them. They took one look at her and hurried away.

After Percy closed the door—firmly—behind them, she brushed her hands together, signaling "good riddance." She donned her dark glasses, to offset the bright daylight, and placed a hand to her head.

Realizing her friend had a headache, the headmistress said, "You didn't have to do that."

"Yes, I did. We know how people react to me. It proves useful sometimes."

The two women returned to the threshold of the chapel, a glowing, warm, and wonderful place where they'd all gotten married. A place of sanctuary in so many ways. Rebecca fell into Michael's open arms.

"Thank you, you're brilliant," she murmured to her husband. "You couldn't have picked a better moment to come by."

"Down in the Sacred Space, are they?" Percy asked excitedly.

"Yes," Rebecca said with some hesitation. "I'm not sure how to tell Alexi, who is with them, that it's safe to emerge . . ."

"Well . . ." Percy shrugged. "It should still remember me, not long ago I descended with prayers of my own . . ."

She closed her ivory lids, took a deep breath, and thrust a lithe arm forward.

In response, a breeze picked up around Percy. Light began to radiate from her snowy skin, and a small black square formed before the altar. The spot grew and expanded into a two-dimensional door that revealed an inner world unseen by average mortal eyes.

"Ah. Hello, love, thank you," Alexi said from the glimmering shadows within. He turned to address the group below. "Come on up, boys, they're gone."

The students filed out, staring at the portal behind them, and at their professors, in wonder.

"If you ever speak *one word* about this—" Alexi roared. Everyone shook their heads, miming locking their mouths and throwing away keys. "Now back to class! Those of you lucky enough to be in mine, seeing as you did not finish reciting the periodic table of the elements, will be starting again from the top." A collective groan meant all was as it should be.

One crisis averted. For now. One group safe. For now. But, Rebecca thought, with a pang that made her reach out again for Michael's hand, there were so many vulnerable young people in the world, whom high command across the imperial powers continued to see only as numbers, not people. And so very, very many of them were at war.

Violet returned from her visit with Lord Black. She, her parents, and Rebecca conferred in her office, which was not as full of books and files as Rebecca's. After Percy described hiding the boys, the younger woman explained that Lord Black was sympathetic to their cause. However, a crackdown on anti-war sentiment made it difficult for him to act. He would do what he could, quietly.

"He suggests you install a telephone line so that we may call, rather than send a messenger, in times of danger, Headmistress. You *must* come into the twentieth century with us," Violet said with a gentle smile. Rebecca and Alexi scowled in tandem.

"She has a point," Percy said. Rebecca kept her scowl but made a note.

When she made a note of something, it was as good as done, and the matter was not up for further discussion. "This *bloody* twentieth century," she murmured.

CHAPTER
SIXTEEN

THE MUSES AWOKE AGAIN TO A SCREAM. THE LIMINAL HAD carried an ungodly shriek from fields of bloody mud like an alarm.

Fighting at Verdun had worsened thanks to the Gorgon's spreading rot. The Muses' old enemy had swelled from a hiss on the breeze to a full-blown storm. A poisonous rain was ready to flood the land with an ancient toxin grown more virulent with time.

The world had a desperate need for a creature of wisdom and balance.

Phoenix stirred in his own ashes, waking with an eruption of fire and music.

With an aurora of prismatic light and exultation of heaven-song, cerulean flame bolted up from Athens's bricks and flew off into the sky, high above London. Night birds bowed their gentle heads in deference as phoenix fire careened toward Hampstead Heath and settled into his asset.

VIOLET AWOKE IN THE MIDDLE OF THE NIGHT TO FIND HERSELF bathed in blue firelight.

"It *is* time," she murmured to the fire in agreement, sliding out of bed, padding silently in her nightdress to her boudoir.

She had long ago begun squirreling away small items that would be necessary in survival circumstances: tools, blades, bandages, small containers, sewing kits, wool socks, as much as could fit into a canvas bag with shoulder straps. And money, of course, but she would also appeal to Lord Black for the possibility of additional help; access to an account they would settle up upon return. She layered sensible clothes on a body that she had strengthened and toned through intervening years.

Her pistol was tucked into an under-arm holster, ammunition the bottom weight of her bag. It was her earnest hope she wouldn't have to use it, that she could get by entirely on the force of her own powers. Knowing just what floorboards creaked and which didn't, she deftly side-stepped her way down the back stair, farthest from the master bedroom, and paused.

"I'm sorry, Mum," she murmured. "I'll write. I love you both."

She slipped away, knowing that if she lingered even another moment, her resolve might vanish. Just because she knew this day would come didn't mean she wasn't utterly terrified.

Outside, at the sound of the stable door opening, the white mare turned her lovely head to see who entered while the black stallion—Father's steed—stamped a front hoof. Violet went to him and held up her hand. Blue fire licked up from her fingertips.

At the sight of the flame, Prospero II, son of her father's previous, beloved companion, bent his head. The noble creature's deference brought tears to Violet's eyes. She tacked the creature swiftly and climbed onto his back, and they took a path out onto a side road so that his hooves would not clatter on the stones of the drive and wake her family.

They'd go with her if they knew she was going, and she simply couldn't have that. In no part of her vision had she seen any friendly face or comforting presence. Had she seen them there, then she'd do this differently. She had to keep the reality of overwhelming loneliness from heightening the fear at what she'd find out there.

Out on a main road, Violet urged the grand steed swiftly onward. The fire led her and she allowed it to be the wind that pushed them through country and city as the thick of London grew before her.

The fire was within and without; the light was magnifying her, like Mary's *Magnificat*. She wasn't sure if this was the Lord her soul magnified, but she knew it was divine, ancient, and inherently good. It would be the life or death of her and there was no other way.

As soon as she reached Athens, she dismounted at the front steps, gave Prospero half an apple, kissed his muzzle, then swatted him on the behind.

"Go home and take care of Father like yours before you," she ordered. The stallion was off, directly. There was something magical about that horse and always had been; Violet felt it had somehow inherited its sire's soul and understanding. She took nothing of mysticism for granted. In times like this, she needed every scrap of it.

There was nothing strange about an assistant headmistress coming and going at any hour, she reassured herself, should she be asked to explain herself. The night watchman, dear old Mr. Rothstein, was asleep in his chair anyway, and Violet almost laughed. Tears were easily in her eyes. Sentiment threatened to get the better of her but the pull of the power in Athens was stronger.

As if dragged by an iron chain, her whole body heavy with purpose, the moment she stepped upstairs, she gasped, for the whole floor around the Athens seal was awash with glowing blue flame.

Around the fiery circle floated five incredible, glistening, prismatic, human-sized forms made of light and color. The air was full of the kind of music one imagined was made by sirens and angels, the same sounds and forces that had greeted Violet when she first realized that this seal was full of divinity.

"Hello, my child," came a rich voice from the mouthless form at the fore, a being tinted by a violet light that matched the shine in her hair. "Do you know what we are?"

"You are the five Muses. You filled the Guard during my father's time of service."

"Yes, my child. We are aware of what has plagued you and your kindred Will and we are here to help. I am Intuition. There is Art, Healing, Memory, and the Heart." It gestured around the circle at the beings floating in their distinct differentiation in hues, all beautifully luminous and awe-inspiring. The green-tinged form Intuition had introduced as the Heart flew to Violet's side. From mere inches away, it seemed made up of countless flecks of gemstones and minuscule pulsing stars. It was as entrancing to look at a part of the Muse as it was to consider the whole.

"We agree that to best protect you wherever the visions have bid you go," Heart began, gesturing with a vaporous hand, "we will divest a part of ourselves into you, imparting some of our powers each unto you."

"This is unprecedented and may be uncomfortable," Memory, a darker, deeper blue than the phoenix fire, clarified. "But we believe you of all people can handle this onslaught of gifts."

Nodding, Violet opened her arms. The three Muses on her right hand and the two on her left placed their luminous, iridescent, incorporeal palms on hers. There was an explosion of light, fire, and music, a sensory assault of beauty and power. She felt as though she leapt off the ground and returned to it, but her feet remained solidly connected—it was her soul that was uplifted. The glistening, prismatic threads of the Muses wove up her arms and planted their light within her heart. Violet felt that organ expand with each beat as her body adjusted to its new, more than mortal, capacity.

Her hands had begun to glow; her inner light had been en-riched and brightened.

The fiery form of the winged Phoenix rose before Violet's eyes, blazing, completing the puzzle of her life.

"You have a claim on me, and I one on you," came the rich, rum-bling voice, like rolling thunder. "I do not know the exact nature of the battles ahead but I will help you fight. Do you accept?"

"I do . . ."

The phoenix fire blazed over and through her, inside and out. Violet gasped as fire threaded her like a needle, making her con-sciousness expand and her skin burn with a kind of discomfort that gave way to pleasure.

Unsure how long she was a living pyre, at last the light, sound, and wind calmed and faded. When she stepped off the Athens seal, the last few remnants of Muses and phoenix fire dove back into their resting place.

Violet fell to her knees. Breathing deeply, she noticed how every sense was heightened. She would need time to adjust, but it felt right. Standing, she felt a bit woozy. Empowering, yes, but dizzy. She gave herself a moment to regain a center of gravity in her core.

There was more to do. Calmly, Violet went to her office.

Even the trip from upstairs proved her world was changed. Athens glowed. Its bricks pulsed with phoenix fire that matched her heartbeat. The dim sconces sparkled like stars and the whole Academy felt as though it had grown larger, an unknowable castle. The paintings in the foyer and in the hallway were entirely changed. What Violet had always remembered as historic scenes were transformed—angels. Every canvas was an angel or a phoenix, all painted in Aunt Josephine's expert hand, led by her Muse, each work a protective Ward of winged glory on these sacred walls.

Part of her wanted to run about exploring, but the momentum of her visions narrowed her focus. Once in her office, she changed into the nurse's uniform she'd kept in a cabinet along with a medic kit, extra shirt, boots, and a few other light supplies she tucked in her bag. From France she would send wires to everyone who would wish to hear from her.

Now she had one last personal call to make as dawn was breaking. Mr. Rothstein, who had been a night watchman since Violet was a child, had stirred himself back awake, calling out to her just as she had her hand on Athens's great front door.

"Why, Miss Rychman, can I help you with anything—"

He trailed off as Violet turned to him, ready to answer with words, but her body reacted first and she lifted her palm, blue fire held in it like a seer's crystal ball, and she spied him through the glassy flame.

"Beg your pardon, ma'am, have a lovely night." He bowed his head and turned away, sitting back down in his seat and rubbing his graying beard.

"Thank you, Mr. Rothstein," she murmured to him softly as the front door closed behind her.

"And that's how I get through to the front," she murmured then to herself, watching the fire play over her hand, rolling about it like water but clinging to her like ivy. "Is it really easy as all that?"

Of course not, she answered herself. That beautiful fire couldn't stop a bullet.

WILL AWOKE TO A GREAT LIGHT AT THE FOOT OF HIS BED AND opened his eyes to see an angel. No, it was Violet. She was on fire. Incredible, otherworldly blue fire.

"What happened . . . ?" Will murmured.

Violet put a finger to her lips. "I've not much time but I had to come tell you goodbye."

"But, Violet, you know I just enlisted. I ship out with the Reserves next week. Let me come with you now—I'll find a way to explain it to my commanding officer," Will insisted, sitting up, preparing to cast himself out of bed and throw on his uniform.

"No, no, go with your company, they won't be headed for Verdun; that's the place I've seen. British forces aren't engaged there, only French regiments. I have to go on ahead, now. Verdun and a village beyond, I'll know when I get there. It is alive in me."

"Alive . . . as it is in me? The voice?" Will was horrified. "You know that the voice is *my* enemy." Frustration darkened his ruddy-cheeked face. "You don't have to fight my battle. The war is violent and bloody. I can give over to the voice, go up and over a trench while the enemy fires, and it can perhaps, for once, be *useful.* That hope has been what's kept me going."

"You may be right. The voice might make you a magnificent soldier," Violet said. "For my part I am opposed to killing. I'll be trying to find ways to help. Great forces are awoken in me. Forces that *are* old enemies to that voice, so our battles are joined. I am augmented. You can see, surely."

Indeed, her eyes glowed with a slight cerulean light. "I see," he replied. "You've always been a preternatural being, a child of your parents, but this is a level of otherworldly even they could never attain . . ." Will admitted. He wished his claim to a preternatural edge wasn't so miserable. Violet looked glorious. The darkness within him flared and he tamped down on a pang of envy. He wanted that vicious part out of him. By force.

"If you must come to Verdun, if that too is what you see for yourself, then I will see you there," Violet stated. "I'll speak with Lord Black, so if you have to abandon the Reserve Army for our very own, personal skirmish, you won't be labeled a deserter."

"Thank you. What have you told your family?"

"Nothing. I'll write a note."

Will shook his head. "You *must* do better than that, your poor mum—"

"You can tell my family what we've shared, just . . . do it after I've gone. I don't want them to tear off after me to try to stop me, you're bad enough yourself. Remember, I don't see anyone in my visions but me and dead soldiers," she said, pained. "Reassure my parents. Tell Mum I've the strength of angels on my side. She'll likely know what happened at the seal as it remains a place of power for her and Father both, the forces divested unto me but not completely. We are *not* without resources."

Will nodded. "Violet, I . . ." He reached out as if to grab her hand but stopped short, blurting out, "I think you're the most wonderful person in the world."

"Then we're in agreement about me," Violet said gamesomely, winking. "In seriousness, thank you, and you know, I hope, that feeling is mutual." Will felt contented by this, but he still wished he could ensure that future they had said they both wanted. Perhaps marry her now to keep their compact. But he knew that seemed desperate. And that was what he refused to let the voice make him feel. He wanted to be what she needed, as she filled his every need, just her presence and conversation. Her closeness. He hoped that would remain enough.

"Remember our promise."

"That we're coming back for each other. I wouldn't forget it for a minute," Violet exclaimed, grabbing his hands in hers and squeezing tight. "It's time for me to go," she stated.

Will shook his head. "I was so sure I'd go first . . . to go ahead and give you the lay of the land . . ." Will murmured.

"I like to keep you guessing." She tousled his hair fondly, touched his cheek with her fingertips as if it were a soft kiss.

And her light brightened. So bright Will had to close his eyes.

When he opened them again, she was gone. Slipping out of the room in a blaze of silent glory to futures unknown.

BY THE TIME VIOLET REACHED WHITEHALL, THERE WERE stirrings of activity and she felt confident she'd find the man she needed already in his office. He seemed the morning sort. Wishing to test her powers and to see Lord Black's most genuine reactions, giving him no time to don a façade, Violet used her light to press past security guards and secretaries as she made her way to the office noted as INTERDEPARTMENTAL LIAISON on the door. The war formalized but still allowed Lord Black's breadth.

Knocking, she was bid enter by a genial call. When she swept in, bags in hand, he exclaimed and rose to his feet from behind his desk. While the light had been used to deflect all others, for Lord Black, she simply beamed.

"Why, Miss Rychman. *Goodness*." He stared at her. "It would appear that the more mundane façade you wore as a girl has now sloughed off and your true divine form shines radiantly in my paltry mortal office!"

"It is so very good to see you, too, milord," she said with a smile, bowing her head. "It feels as though not a day has passed since I was first impertinently asking questions of you, back when the world was a simpler place."

Black returned her smile. "Indeed. And yet . . . a world of difference," he stated, the smile quickly fading for the weight, weariness, and worry that plagued him.

"How have you been faring?" she asked gently, taking a seat across from him. He sat down heavily.

"I am so sorry, Miss Rychman," he murmured after a long pause, his voice catching.

"Whatever for?"

"That I couldn't stop the war," he said, tears in his eyes. "I tried. I promise."

She wanted to reach out, to offer a friendly embrace, wanting to comfort and reassure this gentle, dear spirit, but she only felt she could lean in and speak reassuringly. "I have every confidence you did."

"But, at least"—here Black rallied with a genial smile—"your visions have not been in vain."

Rising, the elegant man went to a wooden file cabinet, returning with an unmarked file folder. He opened it, laying it before Violet, leaning against her side of his desk, grinning like a proud schoolboy.

Inside were several layers of official-looking things. He separated out clearance papers from other items.

"This will ensure you safe passage." He offered her an identification card bearing a number, a small metal disc with the same number, and an embroidered patch bearing a regimental seal with the King's Crown. The insignia in the middle was a simple spiral with a Latin word as motto, *Iter Tenebrosum*.

Violet understood this to mean something akin to what the Bard may have translated as "Undiscovered Country." A shadowy path less traveled, but no less valid.

This was the regimental logo from her vision.

"You . . . *made* my vision come true," she said in awe. "You trusted me enough to do all this?"

"In essence." Black smiled, bright eyes glinting, fair face flushed with excitement, a lock of platinum hair bouncing free to graze his brow. "But it wasn't created *just* for you. Others will need these freedoms as well. A catch-all division that can cover supernatural ground, operating around usual governmental and society protocol and parameters? Why, that's been the stuff and business of my entire life, it was only natural I should make it so!" the nobleman

declared with joy. He gestured to the clearance papers and identification cards.

"These tactile items will, I hope," Black continued, "aid in circumstances where your gifts might fall short or you find yourself
exhausted. Thank you for doing what you can to save our nation's
soul." He looked squarely into Violet's eyes. "I do not doubt that
is at the core of your purpose.

"Thank you, milord, I am overwhelmed!" Violet exclaimed,
unable to keep from reaching out and grasping his hand in hers.

He didn't draw back at first when she touched his hand;
instead he watched as she felt her eyelids flutter.

"Are you all right, Miss Rychman?" he asked quietly.

Imagery from Lord Black's own life danced across her mind's
eye.

"My dear girl . . ." he said, somewhat awkwardly, trying to
loosen her grip on him. This drew Violet back to the present and
she released him with a fervent apology.

"I'm so sorry, milord, I don't mean to be so forward, I . . . the
gifts that took up in me are new and I'm still getting used to . . .
myself."

"What . . . did you see?" he asked. "You saw something when
you touched me, didn't you?"

Violet smiled. "I was given a gift of Memory by a Muse, allowing me to see something about you."

"Psychometry?"

"Yes. An insight into your secrets."

At the word "secrets," he rocked back, a flash of worry dark-
ening his handsome face.

"I saw your dear Francis," Violet said with a smile. "I saw how
much love there is between you and him; why you support the
fringes of society as part of the whole, all of us who may be targeted or shunned for being who we are . . ."

Black nodded cautiously.

Violet held up one softly glowing hand. "Additional gifts I have inherited for my task; a versatile light. It can Heal," she said. She placed her hand over the lord's upturned palm and focused on a small cut on his thumb. The redness of the cut lessened.

"Amazing!" Black exclaimed.

"The light can also turn away a negative force or be utilized as a protective shield. This I cannot demonstrate here, as your soul is pure. I do not know if you are gifted so much as that you *are* a gift."

Black blushed slightly and smiled, proving the point.

"I have an understanding of Art and its force as a talismanic power, for focus, protection, and shifting of energy. I also understand how to levy the Heart for ways of alchemically shifting determination, mood, and courage. I am trying to learn as quick as I can."

"I am impressed."

"These gifts used to be wielded by six mortals before my mother joined them with her own force. They may be able to take up those powers once more, I cannot say, but they're surely the group you sought, years ago. They are called the Guard and they are my beloved family."

Black shook his head in amazement. "Incredible."

He seemed to remember something and went around to the side of his desk, opened a drawer, and returned with two small quilted patches.

"Take these also." He held out the sewn squares that bore the printed seal of London on one side and a radiant dove of peace on the other. Between the two layers of fabric was a pulpy mass.

When Violet took it, she felt something much like the rush of powerful peace that Michael's power, the Heart, granted.

"Years ago, my Omega department colleagues designed protective Wards for the city, using localized magic. This poultice is such a Ward, made of various city Wards pressed together, with a bit of ivy, the most protective plant of all, carefully grown in my home. The aim of the Ward is to magnify peace and protection."

"Thank you, sir," Violet said, "these are magnificent. I can feel their aim directly." She tucked them into her pocket with reverent care.

"Go with God, dear girl," he said, raising a hand to her in benevolent benediction, "and with whatever forces you hold dear."

"And you, my friend. I've a train to catch, then a ferry to France. Should my family come looking for me, and they likely will, you needn't hide our conversation from them."

"If they ask to follow you, should I deter them?"

Violet considered this once more. She'd never seen anyone familiar in her visions, just an occasional sense of Will and his demons, but the newness of the Muses' gifts made her realize just how interconnected her chosen family all were.

"I know better than to dissuade my family from anything. If you've Wards to spare, please do all you can to protect them. The idea that I might be leading those I love into danger has lost me immeasurable sleep. I feel it is my destiny to go my own way; however, I do not presume to know the only way."

"I've Wards to spare and I'll be glad to share them. I'll have them ready when they come to call. We'll decide together what can be done."

Violet pressed her hands together in a gesture of suppliant prayer. "The Crown owes you a commendation, milord."

A deep wealth of wisdom and sadness flashed in his engaging eyes. "The Crown is beset with mortal failings. But as *our* kingdom is not completely of this world," he said softly, "I feel confident we will receive recompense. Not here, but someday in some great beyond, or in a measure for the next life . . ."

Violet beamed. She felt herself light up. Not in defense, but in care and regard. She'd seen her mother go luminous for the better, and she hoped she could do so more and more, praying that there would be lovely things in the world to go brighter for, not just shadows needing light.

At her luminosity, Black leaned back and took a whistling breath. "Spectacular . . ."

"It's a gift I can take no credit for, but one I hope will save my life—and the lives of others—when it counts the most."

Black gestured to the papers. "Once you've committed contact numbers and wiring instructions to memory, please burn the papers. The less telling information you have on you, the better."

"Will do."

"As a foreign operative, you know, I should have a code name for you." He lit up, and though not with Violet's same light, there was a similarity of glorious purpose, of kindred spirit, of old soul, as he exclaimed, "Delphi!"

"As in the oracle?"

"You are a visionary."

"Thank you yet again, milord."

"You can thank me by keeping safe." He leaned forward, tears again glittering in his bright eyes. "Thank me by doing something beautiful in an oft terrible world. Thank me by being kind."

"I wonder what this world did to deserve you," Violet stated. "You make me feel not only safe and understood, but euphoric."

Black just smiled. "The world wields infinite cruelties. People like us are born to create a balance."

Violet nodded. "And that is what I am off to determine; how best to encourage balance. We'll be in touch." She rose and went to the door, pausing. Turning back, she offered a hesitant smile. "I must leave now or I'll lose all my resolve."

"It's natural to be afraid, but we must act despite fear," Black called. She nodded, stepped outside. "Go with heaven's blessing, Miss Rychman."

"And you, milord."

Closing the door, she clutched at her racing heart, as if to keep his benediction there indefinitely.

CHAPTER
SEVENTEEN

PERCY WOKE LATE, FEELING DROWSY, ALMOST DRUGGED. SHAK-ing herself awake, she felt a sharp pain in her chest when she sat up and knew something was different about the day. Rushing to Violet's hall in the house, she listened for any sign of her, not wishing to barge in on her. She had to remember her daughter was her own woman and her fate was her own.

Violet's boudoir and bedroom door stood open. From the doorway, Percy saw a note on her daughter's bed. Already knowing Violet was gone, Percy entered the room, picked up the note, and read it.

Mummy dear, I've gone early to Athens. Don't worry.

Percy breathed a bit easier, but still had the feeling that a great shift had begun. She found another copy of the note on the breakfast table; probably left there to be sure it wouldn't be missed. When Alexi asked after Violet, Percy showed him the note.

"Ah, good then. Studious. Couldn't ask for a better quality," Alexi stated.

Percy smiled.

Violet was nowhere to be found at Athens, but then again, her work sometimes took her to other institutions. Percy refused to panic or to become a victim of fearing the worst. She asked Rebecca if she'd seen her daughter but to no avail, so she focused on her students and the rigors of language.

Between assignments that afternoon, her office door was suddenly thrown open by a very distressed Josephine. She was dressed in an indigo day dress and floral shawl, her dark hair up in a braided crown, her olive skin looking nearly green. Before Percy could ask what was wrong, a note was nearly thrown in her lap. She read, in sweeping script:

Dear Lord Withersby,
    I have been dreaming of you in a most dire manner. Please come visit me directly at this address in Grimsby post-haste.
                            Sincerely in fate,
                            Belle

"What is this?" Josephine cried. Percy stared at her blankly.

"I . . . don't know. Have you ever heard of this woman?" Percy peered back and the script. "That name sounds familiar. But goodness, how cryptic."

"If he were . . . courting another . . . I'd know," Josephine said, reassuring herself. "I'd *know*."

"I daresay we'd all know, he's not a subtle man," Percy said, trying to lighten the mood.

"But these days, these dark days, who knows?" the Frenchwoman said mournfully, her olive skin pale, her dark eyes and features looking worn, dimming her usual effervescent beauty. "I feel I don't know him anymore. Nightmares strain us both."

"Grimsby . . ." Percy murmured. "That rings a bell. The ghost." She snapped her fingers, placing the name. "Aaron Willis, the boy haunting Elijah since his death."

"The one you spoke with after I asked for your help?" Josephine added. "Wasn't that all resolved?"

"Well, I don't know how much of it Elijah mentioned. I told him to tell you all."

"Only that you'd been to see the ghost, and that he thought it would help. It seemed to, but perhaps that was just biding time." Josephine clutched at the sides of her voluminous skirt.

"The child spoke of the importance of Grimsby. He also said that Elijah would have to go when he is called. This must be that call."

The name of Belle struck Percy as like that of an old friend she would be cruel to forget. Someone from her previous incarnation, surely.

"I know," Percy exclaimed. "Let me see if Alexi will allow a holiday. We've been aching for one. Grimsby is a seaside town and we love the sea. We spent our honeymoon not far from there. That way if Elijah needs help, we will be there for him. If you find out something is indeed amiss, we will be there for you. Come have lunch with us and we'll discuss it."

Josephine nodded, holding back tears.

Percy was grateful for this distraction amidst her own odd hollowness, the echoing in her heart of a distant child, the thrum that tied her to Violet seeming to sound from a canyon, not from the city.

THAT DAY, AT AFTERNOON TEA, WILL SOUGHT OUT THE RYCHMANS. He found them with most of the eccentrics they called extended family, minus the out-of-place nobleman. All sat at Athens in the entirely wood-paneled staff room near both headmistress offices, clearly having felt some unspoken need to gather close.

Will approached them, fully dressed in his drab, umber-colored English uniform of light wool, having just come from training with his regiment. The gray-brown made him think of mud, which was appropriate, considering that's what men were fighting in. He blinked rapidly, nerves getting the better of him.

"Why, hello, Will," Percy said quietly. "You're . . . in uniform."

"Yes, madam. They're conscripting men now and I've joined the Reserve Army."

Everyone just stared at him. The vicar saluted him with tears in his eyes.

"I ship out next week," Will said, directing his attention to the headmistress at first. "I thought Violet would leave when I did; it's no secret she feels she has a place in the battle. But I fear she's gone on ahead."

"Oh, no . . ." Percy began wringing her hands; tears rimmed her icy eyes, making her look all the more crystalline. Alexi rose to his feet.

"She left me a note saying she was leaving and asking me not to tell you right away," he said, deliberately altering the facts. "After some deliberation, I felt it necessary to come to you within the day."

"Why the hell didn't you come straight away?" Alexi bellowed, striding forward.

Will winced. "Pardon me, sir, but . . . have you met yourself?"

Rebecca cleared her throat while Michael loosed a nervous chuckle. "I mean no disrespect, sir," Will clarified, "but—"

"But he can be somewhat terrifying," Michael said with a strained smile, getting up and grasping Alexi by the elbow, to see if the taller man would sit. He would not.

"What did Violet say *exactly*?" Rebecca pressed.

"She said the Power and the Light lead her onward," Will said to Percy. "Athens has bestowed great powers upon her."

Everyone looked at one another; after a heartbeat, Percy rose and fled the room. The rest were close behind her, crying of the powers of the Guard, incredulous. Will brought up the rear.

Moments later they were clustered around Athens's third-floor seal.

The headmistress closed off the landing with a velvet rope on both sides, while Percy cast herself directly onto the seal, murmuring to it. Will's heart convulsed, and it was all he could do not to run to the dear woman that he had long cherished and take her in his arms.

COLD CURVES OF EMBOSSED WINGS PRESSING AGAINST HER SKIN, Percy felt the talons through her muslin layers. She bid the powers that lay beneath to rise up to their dear old friends.

As her tears fell freely onto the stamped metal, an old sense memory wafted over her; that her tears once had been transformed into beautiful things, talismans and keys.

When she'd first arrived in Athens, she'd been desperate, needing a new start in life. Athens had been her sanctuary and more. Now she wanted to make sure Athens's safety included her headstrong daughter, wherever she was.

She kept murmuring prayers for intercession, for the Power and the Light to wake, to help them once more. Violet couldn't have taken them *all*. Pausing for breath, Percy remembered the small ruby made from her own blood—it was wrapped in a kerchief and tucked into in her sleeve. Now she drew it out and dropped it into the seal's keyhole.

The air took on a particular quality, tuned as if someone began playing a single note and the rest of the heavenly orchestra harmonically followed, creating a rich, ethereal majesty.

Next came a blinding light. An explosion of star-song and celestial chords drove Percy first to her knees, then her feet. Five columns of colored light in vaguely human forms rose from the seal, radiating divinity; glimmering and wondrous to behold.

Around the Muses coursed blue fire, in a luminous sapphire tornado. The beautiful, cerulean phoenix fire that Alexi had once wielded was a bonfire again.

Percy turned to the Guard; the tears in their eyes was proof enough that they all saw what she did. So too did Will. He was utterly awestruck and his face was full of hope and wonder.

Turning to her husband, her heart both swelled and ached at how his eyes lit up again at the sight of that fire. He reached out instinctively to grasp it. As he looked between Percy and the fire, hands outstretched in supplication, it was as if he'd been so terribly thirsty, and here was a gurgling font to ease his parched soul.

Watching him, Percy wondered if the Grand Work was its own terrible, euphoric drug. It certainly hadn't gone from their souls even if it had been gone from their bodies; a first love never forsaken in a wiser, older heart.

"Hello, old friend," came a clear voice, rumbling like thunder and purring like a cat, two distinct strata of sound. An iridescent, violet-tinged form broke from the tumultuous mass and wafted over to the headmistress. A handlike shape reached out from a vaporous limb to touch her cheek.

As if this was a signal, the other Muses moved toward those watching, each looking for the one whose body they had inhabited. Two, Memory and Healing, representing Elijah and Jane, neither of whom were present, floated above the others.

"Where is our Memory?" asked the Muse from above, looking around as if expecting that at any moment, the caustic and unpredictable Lord Withersby would pop out of hiding, flapping his ridiculous lace sleeves and cracking a poorly timed joke.

"Gone," Josephine replied, not masking the venom in her voice. "Gone to some woman."

"Ah . . . yes . . . good," Memory replied warmly. "Don't worry." The Muse floated to Josephine's side, nodding its insubstantial head at Art, which flanked her. "We'll all be together again soon."

Intuition dove away from Rebecca to float before Percy's face. The sight of it—a cloud of tiny flecks of prismatic light, gently tinkling like the tiniest of chimes—was both beautiful and soothing. If not for the heaviness of her heart, she could have stared into that lovely mist indefinitely.

"What news of my daughter?" Percy pressed.

"Your daughter was here, my Lady," Intuition said. "She has, in equal measures, some of our power. We are slightly weaker for it, but like you, my Lady, we do what we must to survive in an increasingly strange world."

"Dear Muses, I thank you for your help," Percy said, looking in turn at each spectacular creature. "Can you tell us where she has gone?"

WILL WAS GRIPPED BY ABJECT WONDER. HIS HEART, WHICH had been so careful for so long, was overwhelmed, overjoyed; inspired. He wanted to paint, move, write, sing, and compose endless odes. He nearly laughed with the sheer joy of the experience.

He felt like he shouldn't be watching this, that he had been made privy to something incredibly private and utterly sacred. But the forms did not shy away from him, despite his being an outsider. Despite the darkness that took up inside him.

Muses, Will thought. He felt burdened with terrible creativity, and deeply moved. The Rychmans and the Guard conversed directly with old gods, ancient forces, part of their so-called Grand Work. And it was so much grander than what the Rychmans had ever alluded to; mere ghost stories. They did themselves and their friends a disservice in such modesty.

As Percy begged the Muses to reveal her daughter's location, a bright, dizzying form whooshed to Will.

"Tell them," the Muse urged him in a musical whisper. "You know as well as we do . . ."

Oh, God. Will raked a hand through his hair as he drew a long breath.

"I may know where Violet is headed. A hissing darkness in the world has always called to me. More recently, it has done so from a specific place. I believe she is headed there to try and fight what wants to hurt us. Ahead of me. For me."

"A hissing darkness calls to you and wants to hurt my daughter?" Alexi took a step forward.

"Alexi—" Percy protested, grabbing him by his arm.

"I think more of your daughter than I do life itself," Will said firmly, taking a step toward the imperious professor. "I'd kill myself before I'd hurt her. She is the engine of my heart and soul. I've always known that she would be safe from the voice because she is infinitely stronger than it and a *thousand* times more important!"

There was a long, strained pause where the only sound was the Muses' celestial music.

Alexi stared Will down, hard, his eyes looking like he could incinerate the young man before him. Will stood there and didn't back down. If the voice hadn't undermined him, he wasn't about to buckle now.

"Violet and I both have had a vision of the town of Verdun," Will stated. "Though it's only French forces fighting there now, she'll try there first."

There was a tense pause.

"Then onward to France," Alexi bellowed. "What forces may join us, do so!"

The celestial light shimmered.

"Would you wish us back?" asked the Heart, diving toward Michael.

"Even when the enemy is different?" asked Art, hovering over Josephine. "When the balance doesn't mean what it meant before and we will have to find it anew?"

"Even to the point of blood and sacrifice?" Intuition asked.

"When I can only help you in scattered parts, disembodied?" Healing asked.

"Yes," came the quiet, firm, unwavering reply of the present Guard. Memory reached out and caressed Art and then suddenly dove off into the sky, perhaps heading for their missing number.

"I say, return to me!" Alexi demanded of the phoenix fire.

The professor's striking, fearsome presence in no way had dimmed from the first time he struck fear into Will's heart; despite the silver shock in his hair, despite his being a mere mortal, aging man, he remained timeless. The imperious look on the dour professor's face softened, and he added, "Please."

An aching word in a tone Will had never heard, a soft plea from a man who was desperate for these great things to help him be the protector he was born to be.

"As you demand!" the Heart declared, a rallying cry. "Miss Violet has a part of us but you shall have the rest!"

The Muses and the fire all lifted high into the air in a great swirling mass, the music in the air crested as if heaven's conductor had raised their baton, and the forms plummeted, shooting down, and with gasps were all again subsumed.

Divinities dove home once more into flawed flesh.

THE JOURNEY—BY RAIL, CARRIAGE, AND AT ONE POINT A LOUD motor car, an innovation of which he was still very leery—had seemed to Elijah to be endless.

He'd left the note for Josephine to find, of course, but he wasn't sure how she'd react. She didn't trust him these days and he couldn't blame her. He didn't know what he'd do without her; he'd never lived without her companionship and support, but this was beyond the two of them.

Dusk was falling in a bruise of a sky when the carriage slowed before the appointed address; a picturesque, seaside painting come to life.

A small, slate stone cottage with a plume of smoke curling from its brick chimney stood in an evergreen clearing at the edge of a cliff. Its front windows were set with welcoming candles lit. Beyond, a bright horizon showcased a colorful setting sun.

A round-faced woman who looked to be near his own age stepped out of the small cottage on the sea as Elijah's carriage drew near, perhaps drawn by the clatter of horse-hooves. A graying brunette with a floral shawl over broad shoulders, she was dressed in a lavender tea gown with a distinctly French pattern and design— Elijah had an eye for such details.

Elijah disembarked and claimed his bag, then paid the driver and turned to face the woman approaching him. The carriage moved away, hoofbeats fading, replaced by the murmurs of the sea past the cliffs beyond.

Her rosy cheeks were dimpled; her smile seemed welcoming and familiar, as if he were a long-lost relative come home.

"I don't know you," Elijah said, feeling foolish, "but our fates are connected."

The woman nodded and replied in a thick, French-tinged accent, "Aaron Willis came to me in a dream. I wrote to you, and it's good that you've come. Our fates entwine as a remaining mystery of the Guard!"

"The Guard . . ." Elijah swallowed, feeling himself start to shake. "How do you know—"

"Because I was you. Once," she replied, and when he gaped at her, she laughed. "Come in. There's a lot to discuss. Better over wine."

Elijah followed Belle into her cozy cottage and nearly dropped his bag in surprise. Every inch of the walls—save for the windows and bookcases—was covered in art. The themes were familiar: birds, fire, and angels.

"My late beloved, George, painted these. He was our artist, before the Muses chose you and left us behind." She shook her head ruefully. "We had such a brief time as those great votaries. But after the Muses left, some of our gifts grew even brighter; my divination, George's painting.

"I'm surprised that you don't remember me. George and I once owned *La Belle et La Bête*, your favorite café," she added in a playful pout. "You didn't ever wonder why it was so easy for you to come by that place?"

Elijah stared. "You?"

Belle laughed again. "Come."

Elijah was stunned to meet a member of a previous Guard. He had long assumed the elder Guard had passed on. Numb, he nearly tripped over the thick carpet as Belle led him into the small parlor, which had a stirring view of a twilit sea.

His hostess had wine already poured and breathing for them. A small fire blazed in the tile-framed fireplace. When they sat, Elijah gazed at her for longer than was proper.

"I'm sorry, I don't mean to stare," Elijah murmured. Belle simply offered him her charming smile.

"It is natural for the mesmerist and the artist to become lovers, you know," Belle explained. At the word "lovers," Elijah gulped and had to loosen his collar. "There's always a draw," she continued. "It's happened for centuries, two Guard members pairing up, no matter who they are, no matter their gender, identity, or status. The Grand Work never cared about that, the Muses only care about souls and the right partnerships. It seems there's a certain kind of soul a Muse goes after when hunting us. Please, tell me what it was like for you. You served far longer that I."

They talked into the night, trading stories of battles only a Guard member could understand. Belle was enraptured by a full accounting of the war between worlds within Athens's bricks, one she was proud to say her Guard had prepared them for. They shared how the café was weathering these days. They talked of worry over France, of loss, losing Jane, losing George.

Belle kindly asked after Josephine and allowed Elijah to wax rhapsodic over her in ways he wished he'd done more recently to her face. He was a better poet indirectly.

"The idea of a *world* war . . ." Belle said finally, shuddering. "It should never have come to this, such powers, on so vast a scale as to endanger so many . . ."

"And that, perhaps, is why the Grand Work retired with my company." Elijah shrugged. "The world is changing so much they cannot keep up."

"But have we exchanged the Grand Work for a worse sort of purgatory *on* earth rather than relegated to shadow?" Belle asked. "War is a unique hell. I had relatives who fought as mercenaries when I was in Cairo, for this or that battle. They were never the same. Now the world is scarred as a whole, not just a border conflict. On a scale we've not seen since Rome, since bloody *crusades* . . ."

They both shuddered and turned to another bottle of wine and more Grand Work regaling.

Having reached the wee hours, Belle bid him goodnight, offering him an embrace that lingered a bit too long. Before there was any awkwardness, she withdrew and shooed him up the stairs toward a small guest room, and he took to it eagerly.

What haunted him into the dawn in a restless tug at the

corner of his mind, however, was the bottle of blood and ash. What he did with it would be vital. What he should do with it no one had said. But he knew, as deeply as he'd ever known anything, that if he didn't do it right, people he loved wouldn't make it through this war alive.

VINCENT SPIRE, A DEEPLY KIND AND CAPABLE MAN, HAD PROVED himself useful. Since his time had begun at Athens he'd sat in on every class offered, helped any overworked professor, started a new psychology curriculum, and become the staff favorite. It was fittingly he, then, who delivered the news of additional aid.

He rushed to find the headmistress with her fellows on the third floor, careful not to go past the velvet rope that she'd used to cordon off the landing. Thankfully, most of the fireworks were out, though Rebecca's body was still in turns reeling, rejoicing, and settling from the shift of the Muse again within.

Rebecca couldn't be sure what outsiders could see of the Muses or not; a great deal of their more supernatural goings-on passed unseen by the average mortal eye. Vincent Spire seemed unaware of anything mystical, simply looked at her anxiously, waiting to be acknowledged. His gifts were all of this world and she knew his unmatched empathy could feel her worry.

"Hello, my dear," she said crisply. "Impromptu familial discussion, never mind us, please." She gestured him past the barrier and he stepped around it. "Out with it."

"I received a call from Lord Black, madam," Vincent said hurriedly. "He has . . . paperwork for you regarding a missing person?"

Rebecca glanced at Percy and Alexi, who looked both worried and relieved.

"Ah. Good," the headmistress replied. "Very good, yes. If you could return the call and tell him we'll be right over? And, by that, I mean all of us?"

Spire looked around, nodded, and made to race off like a shot.

"Also, Mr. Spire?"

"Yes, ma'am?"

"Violet is gone. We're going after her. Tell my dear Mr. Sanjay Kahn he's headmaster for the moment, as no one else has been here as long, knows or loves the place more. You're now headmaster's assistant. Don't let us down."

Vincent's eyes widened; he seemed as if he was going to explode with surprise or emotion, and he didn't know what else to do but salute.

"Good man. Now go inform Lord Black we'll be with him shortly."

"Yes, ma'am!" As he raced off, Rebecca turned to the Rychmans.

"If I know our girl, she paid her friend in high places a visit before setting off on her adventure."

Alexi clapped his hands, eagerly trading worry for leadership. "Friends, we've taken up the old mantle. Once more unto the breach and all that. Pack your bags, we leave for Grimsby tonight. We throw Elijah into our entourage and find our Violet."

The group nodded, emboldened, strengthened. Will stepped forward to address Alexi.

"With your permission, sir, and if I can manage it with my reporting officer, I'd like to report to Paris right away. I've an idea and I'd like to get acquainted with troop activity."

"Go to it. As for your unit—"

"Lord Black's special clearance," Rebecca interjected, "will extend unto you. I'll have him wire you at . . ." Rebecca trailed off.

"Gare du Nord," both Will and Percy chorused.

"I know that station was in her visions," Percy finished.

Percy rushed forward to hug Will, tears in her ice-blue eyes like glittering gems. Her forehead pressed against his cheek, she murmured, "Take care out there. Remember our light in any times of darkness. It will guide your way, I can only hope."

"Thank you," he said. "It always has and will."

THE FRESHLY REINSTITUTED GUARD WALKED OUT INTO THE London day with their spines straighter, Percy noticed, despite the worry and fear that pulled at them all.

Percy felt her age as she noticed the new century on full display as their group walked toward Whitehall. Younger than her colleagues by nearly half, she wondered if they felt a strain in walking through an increasingly alien world. The collective dress was more linear; the sumptuousness of the Gilded Age they'd known in their youth and early adulthood had now been exchanged for a certain gamesome stateliness. She hoped that style, form and function, was ready to actively take on a new world without quite discarding the predecessor.

To Percy's pleasure, the new woman was fully acclimated and on display in London, as was the evidence of her plight; bold posters and billets declared the intent for further suffrage demonstrations and the occasional daring anti-war rally. Her hope for universal rights and fair treatment had been with her as early as she could remember and she was glad movements were gaining traction.

Electric lighting had become ubiquitous in the finer parts, and there rumbled the occasional motor car—more were military-related than civilian. Percy found them to be just as raucous in their engines as a horse and carriage was clattering over stones. The early twentieth century, she decided, was an exercise in trading noises and nuisances.

The phoenix fire did Alexi good, she could tell. He looked a shade younger, they all did, less like their aging, distinguished, mid-sixties selves, and instead wearing the airs of timelessness that Percy had first come to know about them.

Rebecca led them to the proper Whitehall door and the guard inside, upon sight of the headmistress, ushered them all through a metal gate, pointing them upstairs.

"You've been expected," the man said hurriedly. Rebecca gave him a sideways glance.

"Last time I was here he gave me a lecture against women working in government," she muttered to Percy. "Lord Black must have put a certain fear of God in him this time."

Upstairs, a door marked INTERNATIONAL LIAISON was open, Lord Black awaiting them.

The platinum-haired, handsome man in a white suit with a bright yellow necktie appeared, to Percy's estimation, sunshine incarnate. To her mind, he looked to be a bit younger than the Guard's age, so early sixties perhaps, but the only lines on his face were those worn from smiling.

"Come in, I'm so glad to see you, I wanted to be sure both Spires met all of you!"

Black's office was a spacious place with a curved window that overlooked the street; a mahogany desk sat in the shafts of daylight. An adjacent receiving room was visible through paned glass doors, and both spaces were amply furnished, with marble-topped tables, brocade-covered chairs, and many bookshelves. Potted plants, ivy in particular, graced nearly every surface.

Two people stood to greet the Guard: a woman whose brunette hair was streaked with gray, wearing a long, sturdy, blue skirt, and a white, pearl-buttoned blouse; next to her, a stocky man in an auburn suit and simple black tie, his graying brown hair neatly combed to the side. The distinct scowl on his face gave him the appearance of a distinguished bulldog.

Rose and Harold Spire, Lord Black explained, had been the leaders of his Omega department thirty years prior, assigned by Queen Victoria to find the cure for death. "During that time," Lord Black confessed, "I had a habit of trying to find *you*! I had been told by a trusted clairvoyant that there was a mysterious group of ghost fighters in London and I was dying to meet you, but it seems our paths never quite crossed."

"Oh, but they did!" Michael exclaimed with a laugh. "I remember you, Elijah had a great deal of fun turning you about!" Michael kept laughing until Rebecca elbowed him. Looking abashed, he added, "Likely I shouldn't have said that."

Josephine turned to Percy and muttered in French that even though her husband was missing, someone just *had* to go say something ill-timed in his honor.

Harold Spire's scowl deepened.

"We are so grateful for your stalwart service to the Crown, milord, Mr. and Mrs. Spire," Rebecca said diplomatically. "There were things happening at that time that were not in our purview, such as the ring of devils you revealed and prosecuted. We and London remain in your debt."

"I'm just . . ." Black seemed nearly bursting. "So very glad to meet you!"

"You were an . . ." As Rose paused for the word, her husband supplied it.

"Obsession. Many a wild goose chase after you in those days," the policeman continued with a strained smile that was his attempt at a veneer of amiability.

"Yes, well, sorry about all that," Alexi replied. "You understand the need for secrecy then and now." He turned to Lord Black and bowed his head. "With all due respect for your station, I am concerned that you have aided and abetted my daughter."

"If you don't mind my saying, Professor," the nobleman began gently, "I'm an excellent judge of character. Your daughter is extraordinary and doesn't need our permission. But she was smart enough to ask for help, and to prepare me for this very moment. I am glad to be ready for you."

"And I continue to be glad for our son's place in your institution, Headmistress," Rose added. "And please"—she brushed her husband's arm fondly—"don't mind Harold. He doesn't . . . care for the supernatural."

Spire tried again to smile and failed.

"Can't say I did either, my friend," Alexi said, sharing an earnestly empathetic look, "and yet it followed us anyway." He reached out for Percy's hand and held it tight.

Lord Black had fetched a decanter and tray of cordial glasses from a glass cabinet and distributed small draughts in delicate flutes.

"The greater good matters most, not our individual beliefs," Spire replied. "To each their own, unto a fair and just society."

Lord Black raised a glass. "I'll drink to that."

The group toasted and leaned in as Lord Black opened up a map of France on his desk where theaters of present conflict were circled. From behind him, nestled between two pots of verdant ivy, he then withdrew a leather-bound folder and opened it carefully, counting the heads in the room.

He passed out papers with a Ministry office seal, bearing a King's Crown and sporting a spiral in the center, in addition to a French seal, to each of the five Guard members. Attached to the paper by a wire were metal identity discs marked simply with "Athens Brigade, London." In addition, there were small quilted squares for each of them, bearing the same Ministry seal.

Percy wondered at all of this, amazed. Black made his rounds with the items, Josephine taking two after explaining her husband was absent but would need them. "These patches are the greatest triumph of a joint English and American project. New York's Eterna division and my Omega department together devised these Wards. Wear them on your person as you would any protective talisman."

The aristocrat began speaking strategy:

"Your Miss Rychman told me that as she does not know what to expect out there, you won't know, either, so from what I've gathered, I've kept your clearances very vague, and at a level compatible across both the English and the French forces. There is supposed to be general coordination between the offensives, but don't count on it," Black muttered. Percy could read the pain that this whole affair caused him; he had a heart as sensitive as hers. "One thing I've learned about this conflict is everyone has their own agenda and everyone thinks they have the upper hand of divine right. Work with that as you will. I understand you've powers of persuasion; you'll have to use them."

He placed both hands on the map, his prominent veins looking like the topography of the land marked below them.

"Verdun," he began, pointing to the map, "carries *intense* involvement. Presently there are not British forces engaged, so you'd navigate French lines entirely. Violet mentioned visions leading here."

Black continued running his finger across campaign lines around Verdun and its villages, along, Percy noted with interest, the Meuse River. Numerous forts surrounded the town.

"Around Verdun, the lines shift, gaining and losing ground by mere feet." He sighed. "There is simultaneous involvement in the Somme with an additional combined Allied push targeted for later in the year if not enough ground is gained."

"We'll find her at Verdun," Percy murmured. "I'm sure of it."

"Along the banks of the *Meuse,* of all places, most certainly a sign . . ." Josephine offered, tears in her dark eyes, olive skin flushed with emotion. "It is beautiful there . . . At least, it was . . ." Percy nodded and the women took hands as if both reaching out for their missing loved ones.

"I'm sorry," Josephine continued, blinking back tears. "My country is being carved up like game at some terrible table, I . . . I would do anything to make it stop."

Lord Black closed his eyes and put a hand to his heart. *"Moi aussi,"* he murmured.

Seeing the map and hearing Lord Black's explanations helped Percy pinpoint the physical, psychic tie to Violet. She no longer fumbled for the distant connection. The cord was longer but she could feel her daughter at the other end again, unwinding east-ward.

"If we could press your generosity to extend to another member of our family who is involved in this destiny, milord?" Rebecca asked.

"Of course."

"Violet's other half. Will Page. He's gone after her directly while we must lag behind and collect a missing member of our company. He's enlisted with the Reserve Army but will need access to those French engagements. He will await your help at Gare du Nord. If you can explain to his commanding officer—"

"Done." Black made a note of Will's name, unit, and the station. "The Omega department gave me a wide latitude I have enjoyed in drafting up this new Ministry. I'll explain that he's been chosen for a special duty and not to expect him to report in."

"We are in your debt, sir," Percy said in earnest.

"Not at all. I would invite you all to my home for a fine dinner, but I've a feeling you'll be off. The offer stands, however."

"Indeed," Percy replied. "But I cannot thank you enough for this *incredible* help. You don't know us; you've no reason to trust us . . ."

Lord Black held up a hand. "You are legends in my book. I am grateful to Rose for having connected us and I'll do whatever we can for you on the home front."

The nobleman led them out the door and escorted them through the front gate, where he waved them well-wishes like a loved one from a train platform as they walked away.

CHAPTER
EIGHTEEN

VIOLET MADE HER WAY THROUGH THE MORE MUNDANE ASPECTS of her visions, making them into realities as firm as her encounter with Lord Black. Perhaps because she had seen these things so many times, she experienced them in flashes: the boat to France, a speedy train to Paris, men in uniform all around her. The hush of worry, the indignant sting of war on every lip, influencing every word, lurking behind every call for wine.

Between her studies of the language in school and her conversations in French with both Josephine and her mother, she was fairly fluent. On top of that, the powers within her helped in every interaction, easing her path. It would be easy to be lulled into a false sense of security—any time she felt herself doing so, she forced herself to see the aspects of her vision that indicated horrors to come.

The nurse's uniform Violet wore, coupled with Lord Black's papers and a bit of light and charm, kept her moving toward the front.

Eventually the train stopped at her destination: Verdun. On the Meuse River. The importance of the river's name had not been lost on her.

It was a charming place with a fortress gate, a high hilltop, and a sloping valley winding along a riverbank. To walk along the Meuse was indeed a comfort amidst her mounting fears. She could feel the forces within her surging at their namesake, the power of the name invoking their magic.

She took a room at a modest inn on the bank of the river, a building that appeared a bit worse for wear in these times of need. The place was clearly an institution of the town since its founding, as paintings and portraits hung in the downstairs reception and parlor area showcased several different vistas as the town grew with the inn at the fore.

Some kilometers farther on lay Fort Vaux and the trenches of the front—close enough to hear the tattoo of gunfire. That night Violet tried to sleep but could not; she lay in bed watching flashes of light, hearing the thunder that was nothing of nature, signaling only bombs and death.

This was the new way of the terrible world and its horrors.

THE QUIET OF A PLEASANT TWILIGHT WAS UPSET BY A CLATTER of horse hooves.

"Your friends have come for you," Belle said with a knowing smile, rising, and smoothing her rose-colored taffeta skirts. She had clearly dressed for company. "It will be good to get another look at them after all these years, see how they've held up!" She headed for the door with the excitement of a little girl, not an aging woman. Flinging the portal open, she ran out into the day.

Elijah hung back. "The whole Guard?" he muttered. "Why did Josie bring everyone into this?" He grimaced, thinking about dealing with Alexi.

As he expected, his wife was the first out of a carriage, managing without help, her fine French skirts of rich sapphire in a modern, streamlined style, so different from the fashions she'd worn when they first courted. The white streaks in her hair had grown wider over the years; her features, a beautiful mix of French, Caribbean, and Persian ancestry, were statelier for the lines of distinction now visible on her olive-toned skin. He loved her as much today as he had from the first.

She tore up the walk, visibly furious, and his heart jumped as though he were again fifteen, finding her at her most beautiful when angry.

When Josephine noticed round-cheeked, affable Belle standing with her arms wide, in similarly fashionable dress, she stopped. Looking at the woman's warm smile, Josie cocked her head to the side.

"I know you," Josephine said, her tone somewhat accusatory. "Where is my husband and how do I know you?"

Belle smiled. Elijah slipped farther into the shadows. Beyond his wife, he saw that the rest of the Guard had disembarked, but their bags remained lashed to the carriages and the drivers sat unmoving at their posts. Elijah wondered why all his fellows had come for him and why they seemed to have brought luggage in amounts worthy of a more epic journey than a brief trip to Grimsby. Perhaps it was just wishful thinking that made him see a cerulean glow about his friends, as if the great fire of Phoenix had rejoined them once more . . .

The simple desire for this to be true, for them to again be the *Guard,* flooded his heart so powerfully he had to steady himself on the door frame. One of his lace cuffs caught on a protruding splinter. He turned his attention to freeing the delicate, expensive fabric.

He blinked and looked again at his hand. The same glow. Hope he'd not had since the first days of falling in love nearly bowled him over. The lace caught on the frame tore loose as he wobbled on his feet.

"You know me, friends, because I was one of you once," Belle declared. "I was the Memory," Belle continued, "like your Elijah. My Guard was under the capable command of Beatrice

Tipton." Murmurs of recognition sounded from Elijah's Guard. "Do not be cross with Lord Withersby," she continued. "He is part of the continuation of prophecies bequeathed unto you by my Guard, by our very hands. Come. More of this over tea. And wine."

The Guard—Elijah's Guard—looked taken aback. The private service they had given London for decades, knowing they could share their secrets with no one, that no one else would understand, had made them protective. To hear someone not of their group talk about their business with warmth and casual openness was startling. Elijah watched them digesting Belle's words warily as they filed toward the house.

Josephine spotted him in the shadows and strode up to him on the porch as dusk was deepening. Her eyes narrowed at first; then her expression softened as he placed a hand to his heart before reaching for her.

"Hello, my love," he said. "I am glad you are here. I am glad everyone is here and can meet Belle. We must treasure those who have served as we have."

"It's a . . . trying time. Violet is gone. Gone to the war, we believe."

Elijah took in a hissing breath as the worry for the child the whole Guard considered their daughter struck him sharply.

"Where?"

"Verdun. She is going there to address some aspect of our old vendetta, it seems."

"They're all going, and you came to tell me?"

"*We're* all going and we've come to collect you. Unless you'd rather stay here with *Belle* . . ."

"Stop. Jealousy never became you, you know."

She folded her arms.

"I love you and I always have," Elijah stated. "But there's a part

of continuing prophecy that's about me. *Us,* as you and I are one."
He drew his wife close, embracing her covetously. "Let me live
into what is asked of us, please, it will do my soul eternal good."
He held her tighter.

She sighed against his ear. "Of course, my love. I believe you
and I know something will be gravely asked of us. I can feel it."

Elijah and Josephine joined the group convened in Belle's modest dining room, with its rough-hewn wood table and wrought
iron candelabras. They had just taken their places at the table when
there came a sudden burst of wind, a dazzling light, and a distinct
blast of celestial music that rattled Elijah to the bone and shook
his spirit. The candles on the tables were snuffed out, then burst
back into flame.

Before them all, its form folded upon itself as if it were a chandelier hanging from Belle's modest plaster ceiling, hovered a
bright, iridescent, shimmering form. At the sight, Elijah's heart
nearly leaped from his chest. His Muse had come for him . . .

"Hello, old friends," said Memory in a rich, otherworldly rumble. It bent a long, blue-tinged neck toward Belle and Elijah,
swiveling its head between them. "I could choose either of you
again. Leaving you, Belle, for this troublemaker here . . ."

"Oh, now—" Elijah interrupted.

"That was the hardest moment of my life," Memory barreled
on. "But it had to be done. I would take you up again, Belle, but
the bond would not be the same, not without your full Guard.

"Your companions have continued to serve valiantly on earth
and Beyond. We could not be prouder of you all . . ."

To hear a Muse speak, your muse, Elijah realized, was beyond
a religious experience. He and Belle both had tears in their eyes.
Being near it was like being near a fire while frozen. The ecstasies
of mystics were suddenly apparent to him. He fervently wanted
to apologize for having failed this Muse, for not having been a

good host to it, but his tongue was tied. Shame made his cheeks flare up in a painful heat.

He glanced to the side, feeling eyes upon him; it was Percy. He was saddened to see that she looked tired; worry dimmed her bright eyes and strained the usual smile on her colorless face. He was overwhelmed by his own emotion and the feelings of others.

"My friends," the Muse addressed them all, "what lies ahead will not be easy. You are not the youths you were when we first took you, though our presence ameliorated the more drastic effects of age and disease."

The Muse made a sweeping pass around the table, the movement sounding like the flutter of birds' wings and the pleasant musicality of wind chimes. When it regained the center, it turned slowly, considering each presence at the table.

"We are in an unprecedented time. We may need to travel to places you cannot go, use powers you cannot manifest. We ask for permission to augment you and then to leave you, as situations call for. Do you agree?"

The Guard nodded as one; even Elijah bowed his head.

"Now, don't let me keep you from dinner, go on!" Memory exclaimed, rising toward the ceiling.

"To the Grand Work." Alexi raised a glass. Everyone toasted.

Countless tales and glories were shared through the meal. The Muse did not interject, soaking up the humanity it seemed to care so deeply for, casting its prismatic, magical light through the room as if they were beneath a rotating lens of stained glass.

Belle looked suddenly weary. "We must rest." She rose and moved to the threshold. "Take whichever room and spaces you like, they've all been made up. Some of you will have to cozy yourselves or take to divans, but blankets and pillows are out and plentiful. Fetch me if you need anything, I'm just beyond the stair here."

"Thank you for your generosity, Belle," Percy called. "And for all you did that we never knew about, to get us all here safely."

Belle smiled and looked upward, perhaps thinking of her late George. "All in the line of duty, my Lady."

As Belle disappeared, the Muse floated down from its perch to address Elijah. It remained uncanny that there was no visible mouth for it to move, and yet sound still carried soft and clear.

"If you don't mind, I'll remain outside tonight. I had planned, before our Lady changed course and the field altered, to spend a lifetime with Belle. I wish to linger with her a while and tomorrow, the next phase."

It did not wait for a good night or permission before floating up the stairs after Belle, leaving a distinct glow in its wake.

Elijah looked down, feeling a stabbing pain, and masked it with one of his devil-may-care smiles, hooked his arm in Josephine's, and bid her come to bed in the guest room Belle had put him in the night prior.

When Josephine closed the door behind them, Elijah, sitting down heavily on the bed, found he couldn't meet her eyes.

"I was a failure to that Muse," Elijah murmured.

"Don't say that—" Josephine sat down next to him, the springs of the bed creaking, reaching out her warm hand to his cool one, her darker olive skin such a contrast in the dim light to his pallid fingers.

"No, it's quite clear now as it was then," Elijah countered mordantly. "I remember. How it fought within me. The night Aaron Willis died. It was trying to force me back and I fought it. I doubt it has ever forgiven me for that. I was a weaker choice than Belle, it's quite clear."

"You've atoned and then some."

"I wish I could know when it would be satisfied, but perhaps that's the point, not to do the least amount to gain clemency, but the most . . ."

"I daresay there's more to come than any of us imagined. I thought Prophecy was the end of it, what we fulfilled in Percy. But then the Athens war, now Violet's visions, what more indeed . . ." She looked away, lost in her own thoughts.

A door, Elijah thought, lying down. A door laid with blood and fire . . .

Either a beginning or an end, an uncertain journey, opened or closed.

ELIJAH AWOKE FREEZING COLD. A DEAD CHILD FLOATED BEFORE him. With a start, he sat up, and through the spirit, hissing a curse as he readjusted back to the headboard.

"Good God, child. I haven't forgotten."

The child pointed to the vial that Elijah had left out upon the small guest room table, the contents of which glowed slightly as if it had taken on some of the night's bright moonlight, or perhaps reflected a bit of the phoenix fire within.

Josephine was not with him, evidently having dressed and slipped out quietly. Glancing out the small, angled window onto the back stretch of Belle's property, he saw his wife walking with Belle, gesticulating, looking across the sea, and he heard them speaking in rapid French. There was an ache to their tones, as if they'd been dying to talk in their native tongue and share worries for their motherland. He was warmed to see this kinship.

Having been preoccupied with his own haunts, it occurred to Elijah that he hadn't yet taken into account how this whole affair was weighing on her. Her parents had come to England when she was a child, but she made regular trips back to Paris and the countryside; it was her beloved place, and it was bearing the brunt of the war thus far. England had yet to feel the pain of wounds directed onto its earth, though she had lost many men from the start. Losses and mounting conscription said this was no easy treaty; early bravado fading into mordant regret. With all sides having literally dug in, the conflicts seemed interminable. Unwinnable.

Moving to the table he tucked the little bottle into the breast pocket of his waistcoat beside a flamboyantly chartreuse pocket square. He patted it and glanced outside, where the ghost had floated to await him on the lawn.

"Breakfast first," he declared.

He descended to the dining room, where an array of breads and butter lay out for them. Percy and Alexi were holding hands at one end of the table, studying a map, and going over documents with strange seals on them, talking in hushed tones. Elijah did not disturb them. Josie and Belle were still talking in French, now on the back veranda. In the sitting room beyond, Michael was memorizing lines of scripture that pertained to peace, and Rebecca was sewing medical armbands.

Presumably that was how they would pass through doors that should be shut to them; as diplomatic and medical professionals.

No one had unpacked for this temporary respite, and any bag or item that had been brought in was ready for them by the door. His fellows started filing outside just as Elijah had a croissant in his mouth and was still buttoning his shirtsleeves.

He lingered, not wanting to leave. He was, in fact, terrified of what was next, worried the Muse wouldn't take him yet, and in some ways relieved if it didn't, if it demanded Belle go on instead— No. That was the coward's way. But in his heart, he was not a fighter. The Muse of Memory knew that. He made everything a joke because he was frankly too sensitive; everything was bluster. He hoped he could maintain a comforting mask of theatricality. Words and a bit of showmanship.

Stepping outside, looking at the ghost of Aaron who, to his immense credit, was floating serenely and patiently, he addressed his fellows that were milling about, awaiting their host.

"Before we go onward to France, as I know we must," Elijah said nervously, looking first at Percy, then at the ghost, "it's important I leave something here. A token. I'm just . . . Percy, Belle, would you . . . advise me? The bottle? What Aaron said? It's the reason why I'm here, you know."

"Yes," Percy replied slowly, very aware of the floating spirit, and Belle nodded encouragement. "The door of which he spoke. The substance is key."

Percy, Alexi, Belle, and Josephine followed Elijah farther on the lawn, toward the specter.

Elijah looked up at the sky, scratched his head, and moved to the greenest part of Belle's lawn, where Aaron's gray finger pointed to a patch bordered by two smooth rocks. Ahead, the sea. It was a grand view, really.

He uncorked the bottle of grime that had bubbled up from the Athens seal. He gazed out at the sea, then turned back to his fellows.

"Now . . . what . . . what should I *do*?" he asked plaintively. "Does this, in and of itself, make a door? Or guard a door?"

"It does both," Belle said. "Blood and fire, as Beatrice would say. That precious combination can open up a portal between worlds."

"Blood and fire," Percy repeated.

"That's what's here, really," Elijah said, lifting the bottle and shaking the contents. As he did, a shimmer of familiar blue light arced through the small glass.

"The blood of the goddess, the fire of Phoenix," Percy said softly, her words a haunting spell. "Lay it down, like the superstitious might salt a threshold; lay it out across the ground."

Elijah knelt and did so. If he wasn't mistaken, the air rippled strangely above the line he drew. A hairline crack appeared, growing into a fissure; a sliver of preternatural light hovered in the air. He rose and stepped back.

Alexi folded his arms, scowling. "We shouldn't *open* anything," he retorted, gesturing to Elijah. "The prophecy, the warning that has to do with our girl, has to do with the closing of doors. Don't *close* every door, it was said."

"One has to *have* an open door before one can leave it open," Belle said. "This is a fail-safe. I'll be here to watch it. Then there's this." She held up a brass locket and blue fire leapt up around the oval.

"That was Beatrice's locket," Percy said in surprise.

Belle smiled and continued, "It's full of phoenix fire from her time as Guard Leader. Beatrice used this from within the Whisper-world, to knit the worlds together. She paid me a recent visit and insisted it be used."

"Is she . . . aware of what's going on now?" Percy asked, hope in her voice. "We could use any and all help."

"She is aware," Belle assured her. "She only graced me with her presence for a moment, but the war grieves her. She keeps an eye as best she can, but she's trained her eye and duty to Cairo, and to the two remaining of her former Guard there. The Whisper-world is changing, too, she says, increasingly unstable. Everything is in danger."

This sat between all of them like a rock cast into a clear well. When Elijah turned back to where he had laid the contents of the bottle, he found that the spirit was gone. The small crack of light remained. He wondered if, hoped, he had set young master Willis to rest, but the child had always come and gone unceremoniously.

Memory, in its indigo form, descended from a thick cloud and touched Belle's cheek with a vaporous hand before floating over to Elijah. As the Muse approached Elijah, so did Belle, who clasped the locket around his neck.

"I believe you're meant to have this," she stated softly, tucking it beneath his waistcoat.

"Are you ready, old friend?" the Muse rumbled.

"Yes," Elijah murmured. "If you'll have me."

CHAPTER
NINETEEN

WHEN VIOLET WENT DOWNSTAIRS FOR BREAKFAST, SHE WAS startled to see a figure in a British uniform seated at the table: Will, eating bread. At the sound of her tread on the last stair, he looked up, and then jumped up. They embraced.

"I couldn't let you get too far without me," he stated. His grin warmed her heart as it had when they were children, strengthened by all the years between.

"I couldn't stop you any more than you could me." She tousled his hair. "It's very good to see you. I don't suppose Lord Black was able—"

Will reached into his pockets and produced papers similar to hers, his disc stamped with the words "Athens Brigade c/o Delphi."

"It was ready for me at the telegram station at Gare du Nord. Your contact is a wizard."

"Indeed, he is."

"What's on the docket today?" Will asked.

"I've a deep, gnawing instinct to wander Verdun. Should you find out the lay of the land, be careful at Fort Vaux, I can't say I even know who's holding it; it has changed so often . . ."

"So I shall."

"See you at dinner?"

"Here or on the line? I can assure you the food here is better."

Violet smiled mysteriously, grabbed Will's bread, and walked out the door with it. "I'll come find you."

Determined to wander now, she knew the line was inevitable. She made her way past small fortress encampments, onward past the largest bulwark, Fort Vaux, ensconced in a rolling hill that once might have been charming but now was just a muddy mess.

Onward through several villages that had already seen the effects of war, nervous townsfolk, a surely decimated population; some families sought to flee farther from the front, not everyone wishing to fight tooth and nail to their very doorstep. The French who remained were hard-eyed, suspicious, and often visibly armed.

Utilizing her gifts, she passed through mostly unnoticed. Occasionally one of the few remaining young people, their own aptitude for seeing the wonder of the world not yet entirely slain, turned to her as if seeking the warmth of sunlight. They did not truly see her but sensed her passage. Each time, Violet offered a murmured blessing, allowing a slip of light to flow from her. When the children turned back to their tasks, she imagined they did so with a little less dread in their hearts.

If only she could give each of them one of Lord Black's Wards . . . Perhaps she would write to him to have him send boxes to be distributed as if they were rations.

Fleury was the quaint village that struck her most. The irony of a village named for flowers having been turned into a barren, alien, pocked landscape was doubly tragic. She saw only a few flowers in Fleury, in the occasional window box or remnants of a home garden. The majority of the village had been turned into wide swaths of mud and rubble; land all about bore the tracks of heavy horse-drawn carts and the tire-marks of larger motor transports.

At the very edge of Fleury, Violet noticed patches of singed earth where, she was sure, firefights had taken place. Nearby stood

an abandoned stone cottage and rows of posts placed at regular
intervals, the wooden stakes connected by wire and dead grape-
vines.

The sight immediately reminded Violet of barbed wire and the
front, of a dead body she'd seen caught on wire en route. The soldier's torso and limbs had been twisted like the trunks of the
vines in this once-vineyard. One of many sights that she knew
would—and should—haunt her indefinitely.

"Would they were all vineyards instead . . ." she murmured,
moving to a dead vine and touching a shriveled leaf. It fell from
the dry stem and tumbled away in a breeze that smelled of smoke
and decay.

Walking the line of dead vines, she wondered what had killed
these once-flourishing plants. She could tell that this tiny vineyard
hadn't been directly bombed; something had done it in before the
area fell under attack.

At the end of the line, she noticed a crack in the earth, stretch-
ing out into the distance, zigging and zagging just like the trenches,
toward the monotonous, dreadful sound of shelling.

Though Violet had never heard the voice hissing around Will
as clearly as Will did, she recalled a time when it claimed to have
poisoned the earth. How much of the war and its horror should
they blame on this ugly murmur magnifying hatred and violence?
Was this very spot the epicenter of her task?

As if in response, the breeze picked up. And on it, a voice.

"Hello, old friend . . ." it called tauntingly, an inverse of the
invitation from the Muses.

This was what she had come to vanquish on behalf of Will, her
family, and the world.

"I will fight you with the collected powers given me," Violet
declared. "You've plagued everyone around me for the last time."

"It isn't about you anymore," the voice snapped. "I've a wider game. My poison has spread along a deadly line. In *both* worlds now. It can't be undone."

"This *is* your doing?" She gestured at the ground before her, and then out toward the front.

"While I'd like to take credit for the whole of the earth becoming a graveyard battle by battle, I didn't have to do much to tip humanity's scales." The voice chuckled, a terrible, ashen, gurgling sound.

"All the bright curiosity of your previous golden age, all the Empires piercing land with myriad flags, wrenching and tearing and rubbing together, friction. Every fire starts with small sparks. I wasn't the only piece of flint. You're terrible, you humans, and need to be ruled by a force beyond yourselves. You can't be trusted."

An enormous explosion just a few kilometers away rocked both air and ground. The voice laughed. "See?"

Violet held out her hand, blazing white light and blue fire. The voice hissed and retreated.

"We'll meet again . . ." came the fading murmur. "Careful," it mocked, "it's dangerous out here . . ."

Running back the way she came, she saw that the villagers of Fleury had taken cover from the approaching onslaught. Barrels of shotguns and rifles were poised out partly broken windows. She increased the cover of her light and gifts to be that much more protected. She needed to find Will, to tell him what had happened, yet felt reluctant—what if he tried to face the voice down all alone, trying to spare her as she'd done him?

Searching within herself, she found the thread of light that she'd attached to Will the day she'd left England. This point, like a pin in a map, allowed her to find, to *feel* where he was. Violet realized with both pride and concern that her dearest friend and light of her life had bravely already begun his work as a soldier, lending his hand along a beleaguered French line a few kilometers from Fort Vaux.

Descending the rickety wooden stairs where the edge of the Serpentine-patterned trench that met the supply line was shielded behind a fortified hillside, Violet kept her shields and her dissuading powers strong in order to move along the narrow, snaking path behind and between the Frenchmen in their long gray coats and glaring red breeches.

The floorboards of the trench bowed slightly with her weight, mud squelching beneath, the water occasionally pooling up red from a recent injury or death. The underground springs of France by now would only run red, she thought morbidly.

Violet followed men into a hollow chamber, where planks had been set upright, forming makeshift walls. An oil lantern hung from a jagged spike and a map was tacked up next to a French flag riddled with bullet holes. A table sat at the center of the space, surrounded by a few stools; a tallow candle burned in a holder set at the table's center. A few bunks and pallets showed that men slept as well as worked here, in this hole that served as officers' quarters.

Hidden by her light and fire, she slipped between two officers to wait for Will, who would likely report to command about troop movements. Scouting had been his skill during the little training he'd received.

She took a position in a corner, between two bunks, sitting on the floor with her back against the rough-hewn plank wall. Withdrawing her gas mask from her pack and keeping it close to hand, she listened closely to the men discussing their mission, hoping she could learn where Will was and when he might return. They spoke energetically of English aid; perhaps Will's presence and unique papers had given them cause to wonder. No, she thought sadly,

the mere two of them on their independent mission didn't consti-
tute a surge of reinforcements.

When shouting roused her, she realized she'd nodded off, for
who knew how long. It was the deep of night.

She woke to a push along the line. The warren had emptied of
officers and Violet darted out into the trench to try to find Will
amidst the madness. Magnifying her powers to full capacity once
more, she hoped to conceal herself and keep bullets and shrapnel
from tearing her to shreds. Projectiles altered course slightly to
land to the side of her, the light providing a small bubble of safety.

The barrage defied all description. The coruscation of blinding light and thunderous sound was exponentially greater than
anything she'd experienced in her visions. It was the stuff of
gods. No—monsters. Wretches. This was not how gods would
fight. Only humans, augmented by machines of terrible dimen-
sions. Machines made to kill with ruthless efficiency. With maxi-
mum force. All of it unconscionable.

She found Will, finally, in a medical tent back along the
supply line, knocked unconscious. Smoky ash dribbled out the side
of his mouth, and she could have sworn she heard the voice that
plagued him laughing amidst the chaos. Still invisible, she used
her powers to persuade the attending doctor, a white-faced young
man terrified of every tremble and sound, that Will should be kept
here until the offensive had ended, though his injuries seemed
minor, no more than a concussion.

Outside she heard an officer on watch say that the "new scout"
had alerted half the line to a shift in enemy offensives and cred-
ited Will with saving half their regiment in preparedness. Her
heart swelled.

She returned then to the trenches in hopes she could be of some
help there, with Will in a certain amount of safety. The rules of
war, as least so far as she knew, still prohibited attacking the

wounded. While this war was changing the face of warfare irrevocably, there were certain things she hoped were still considered
crimes.

Violet saw men shot, mutilated, and killed, sights, sounds, and
smells that would forever haunt her. Once all of that had fused
into a nightmare with countless fangs, adjacent to these horrors
was the loneliness.

Due to her powers, keeping just slightly out of sight and range,
she was close to the camaraderie, the life and death bonds happening all around her, forged in fire and in the quiet moments
talking of home. She would sometimes murmur along with them.

A man named Francois to her left stood beside a new friend in
hell, Evan. In the eerie moments between volleys of fire and the
shifting of orders, small conversations about pleasant things, so
surreal the juxtaposition, was the only thing to keep any semblance
of sanity. Humanity.

And just as she was getting used to them, learning of Francois's sweetheart back home and Evan coming to terms with his
own identity and how he wished he was otherwise and could live
a vastly different life, after a blinding explosion rocked the night
with fireworks and a second shout of orders, they were sent up the
ladders and into the fray.

Wave after wave of human beings. Up and over.

Up and over.

None returned.

Violet had sent anyone near her out with a slip of her light but
she soon realized it wasn't enough protection. The tears rolling
down her face were only in part due to the acrid smoke and the
faint tinge of gas left over from the last attacks.

After another wave, the offensive pushing right up until the
dawn, Violet gave a little more to the men nearest her, and five of
those eight fell back behind, injured but alive, tucked back into

the fold, jumping down into the trench's maw, nursing shrapnel wounds, insisting that the enemy's barbed wire was not, as had been expected, destroyed enough for holes to push their infantry through.

She tried to take a certain solace in the fact that her light and gifts may have saved five lives. These scenes were a part of her visions; here at the war, lending her light.

But the numbers, she realized, were against her. She was but a drop in an ocean. The war was monstrously more ravenous than she had any ability to counter. The sheer volume of it all incalculably outweighed her, and even the best-planned mechanisms to wage more effective war were fraught with failure.

Thousands of men were caught and shot to death, hung up on wires that bombs, shells, and a specific gauge of bullets were supposed to have cut.

But they didn't. And man after man was stuck. It was impossible to see from the smoke and the gas until it was all clear in the horrific light of day. As dawn broke and the bullets stopped, Violet was alone at the end of a trench bulwark. Her knees threatened to buckle under in exhaustion, and her arms burned. She climbed carefully, painfully up a broken ladder to look out into the acrid, muddy No Man's Land that was still steaming with heat from explosions and clinging smoke. As the dust, detritus, smoke continued to clear, Violet saw all the bodies folded on the wire a few meters out, many still dripping blood and other fluids. She lost count, turned her head, and vomited into the mud.

Numbly she made her way out of the trench, unsure if the cease-fire was temporary or just a pause for rest. She had to fall back. She'd been up for two days straight and she had barely eaten or drunk any water. Her body shook as if she were walking in the midst of a seizure. The cotton she'd stuffed into her ears, and the light and fire that had shielded her, did not erase the sounds she'd heard, did not keep all of the reverberations from making her ears still ring.

She stumbled across the threshold and into the quaint Verdun inn so still and devoid of so much life for such a lovely town, save for the listless innkeeper who paced a certain weary guard behind the bar in the front parlor, an old man wearing his frayed uniform and medal from the Franco-Prussian war. For some of these men, this war was just an epilogue to prior pain.

He took one look at her, in her nurse's uniform, bloodied and sooty and exhausted, and crossed himself, blessing her in French. She wanted to count for him the few lives her light and power may have saved but the numbers that had died numbed her tongue.

"*Merci,*" she offered the beleaguered man, and climbed upstairs to collapse into bed.

Violet awoke to the sound of faint crying.

There was a light near the end of her bed.

Its form curled into a ball, amorphous limbs tucked up into itself, rocking slightly, a Muse was crying.

Could there be anything so heartbreaking as a divine form weeping?

Violet didn't even have words. She opened her mouth to ask what was wrong but she was so overcome with emotion that nothing came out, all she could do was press a hand to her heart to make sure it would still beat.

Another Muse appeared. Memory floated before Violet. "What's happened to Art?"

"I don't know," Violet said, rising. Her whole body felt leaden.

"It's just too much," Art said in a small, plaintive voice. "We are not enough. Humans have moved beyond our ability to make any difference . . . The Whisper-world was right, we'll fail.

We have already failed. If we don't do better, *everything* will be destroyed."

"What do you mean everything?" Violet asked, dread creeping in to tax her aching muscles with added tension.

"Never mind that," Memory stated quickly.

"Surely you're not beyond the capacity to inspire . . ." Violet fumbled for words. Reassuring a divinity was a daunting prospect, especially when it had been proven that she wasn't enough, either, there in the trench. She wanted to sob along with the being. Thinking of one of her favorite stories, she posited a Dickensian line:

"Dear heavens, show us some tenderness connected to this world . . ."

At this Art raised its glowing head. A distinct light flickered in the room, then, and both Muses gasped.

"Liminal light . . ." Art breathed.

"Beg your pardon?" Violet asked.

"The Liminal is a distinct threshold between mortal and Whisper-world with a mind of its own, biased toward mortals. It has the capacity to transport us and show us important things. It's likely the source of your visions. Do you submit to what the Liminal would show us?"

Violet watched the peculiar light, flitting like a bird, entranced. "Of course."

There came a sound, a deep and resonant ticking, as if it were the second hand of a gargantuan clock, a fluttering shift of gears or tiles, and this came along with a distinct fluctuation of light in the room, almost as if photographers' flashbulbs were popping.

"The Liminal has access to a realm of possibility forward in time and across the present," Memory explained. "Its sense of the future constantly adjusts as mortals make their will known and their choices clear. It is showing us one probability of several . . ."

"Its clock moves us in time to see things we mustn't miss. It is an eye that never fails us . . ."

With a bright flash and a dizzying lurch, a scene was set thanks to the Liminal window, a divine projector . . .

Before them was a devastated town Violet could not visually place. Explosions had wrecked many buildings, a military installation ahead of them.

On one side of the street was a half-collapsed building. On the other side squatted a small band of American soldiers, huddled in the stone portico of a building, the country at last having joined the effort. Violet could tell their provenance from their umber-green uniforms and the insignia on their sleeves.

There was a howling sound that was not of military origin, but animal. Not human, a howl of a dog. High pitched. Keening.

Within the half-collapsed building that had been a military depot there were large cages, rent bars, and rubble. And black-and-brown-colored animal corpses. Dogs. German shepherds.

But not all dead, as the whining proved. A litter of puppies was still alive.

Their mother was lying dead, bludgeoned by a falling rock that split her skull; she'd been sheltering the pups who howled around her cooling body.

Violet put her hand to her mouth.

As she did, she noticed a flash of angled light, as if a barely perceptible fork of lightning, white and blue in hue, lit up the debris-laden ground and faded. Her light.

How could her light reach this far?

One American soldier, visibly affected, looked around, poked his head out from the building's shelter, and murmured to his lads.

Between rounds of shells, far enough off to not be an immediate danger, though sniper fire was an omnipresent risk, he ran from one cover to the next, pausing at a pile in the middle of the rubble-strewn street and again into the half-collapsed building.

Without a second thought he unbuttoned his coat pockets, tucked two pups into the wool, scooped the remainder into his arms, and darted back to his fellows.

His fellow soldiers reached out as if for bread after a fast. Puppies were doled out so each one had its own protectorate to warm up their shivering bodies and quiet their whining. The men immediately between them, retreating into the store that had been abandoned in this blitz, found a box, some paper, and made a makeshift bed for the pups, and fed them what rations they could.

The effect on the morale of the exhausted men, and the traumatized pups, was immediate. The howling was replaced by a desperate need, on both sides, to feel love. Touch. Tenderness; the purity of the distinctly unique and inimitable bond between human and canine, the keen pups, a breed known for their intelligence, seeming to realize that their rescuers had come for them, they hadn't been forgotten, frozen, or starved, their mother's sacrifice not in vain.

When the time came for their platoon to be transported out of the area, more care was taken over the puppies than nearly anything else.

"I'm going to train this one," said the American who had rushed to save them, one particular puppy, quiet and alert, with its paw resting assuredly on the soldier's hand, an immediate bond and claim, leaning forward to touch his reddened nose to the small, wet, black nose before him, an excited promise. "*Show business,* Rin. Let's get out of hell and go home . . ."

And the glass of the Liminal went dark as if closing a shutter or closing a door, the surface again roiling murky depths.

"I understand why the Liminal chose this," Art said, sounding bolstered. "Because there will always be a human instinct to protect the most vulnerable beings among you. It doesn't always win, but the *trying* . . . That's why I've never given up on you."

"And we never will," added Memory.

"But the reason for us to remain active in humanity won't change," Art insisted. "The Liminal encourages us; one brave act of love and mercy at a time. That is what we can *inspire*."

"That's how we endure the hellscape?" Violet asked.

The luminescent forms nodded. Whether the dog would indeed become a star didn't even matter. It was a tiny, helpless thing that had been saved, and if she was interpreting what she saw correctly, if enough of her powers went out into the world, it could reach across time and great distances; farther than she could know.

The Liminal light began to fade around them. Art murmured its thanks and the Muses vanished.

It would be back to the lines of hellscape the next day, the dreary, interminable drudge of it, the desensitization toward death even in the midst of paralyzing fear.

But Violet took courage from the Liminal, to wield light as far as it might go. It was her and her family against this, the greatest of villains; a senseless, sprawling war that needed every bit of the energy she and her divine cohorts could muster.

Will, of course, was her purpose at the core. But if she could cast her light wider, she would uplift as many as she could, just like the soldier and those innocent creatures.

CHAPTER
TWENTY

THE NEXT DAY SHE ROSE EARLY, FINDING THE SILENCE OF THE town and the surrounding environs almost disturbing, so bone-jarringly constant had the chaos become. Dressing in a fresh nurse's uniform, clean of blood and mud, she brought the soiled one downstairs. When asked why she wasn't in tents with her regiment, she explained she had different orders and held up her lit hand. Dazed, the innkeeper nodded and took the laundry.

She couldn't be tied to one regiment and its movements when the specific fight she'd come here for wasn't under any one general's command.

Her gifts allowed her to make her concealed way to the medic tent beyond the front lines. Not until she found Will, who was groggily waking, did she become visible.

"Hi, there," she said. Fondly, she tucked a moist lock of hair back behind his ear.

"You found me." Will smiled, reaching for her hand.

"It was only a matter of time. I've a special signal tuned to you. Like a radio wave." She fluttered her free hand, the light within flickering.

"That's wondrous," Will said earnestly. "I'm the luckiest man alive." He tried sitting up, wincing at the aches and bruises sustained in the last firefight. Violet braced him with strong arms but settled him back on the pillow, slightly elevated but not upright.

"I'm better," Will insisted. "I should go and make myself useful somewhere. It really wasn't a terrible wound. I think just my head."

"No. Your scouting saved a regiment, I heard an officer talking about it, but then I didn't want you a part of this last offensive," Violet stated. "Even if you were settled with the heavier artillery, you may not have made it. I don't really understand what happened, but . . ." Her voice caught. "Hardly anyone came back."

"I heard." Will shook his head, fighting tears. "Wrong gauge of bullets to wire. A certain caliber of bullets, when fired at the barbed wire mounted to protect ground gained, is meant to cut up the wire so men can charge through and take the enemy trench. But they didn't discharge the right caliber."

Tears blurred Violet's vision and she wiped shaking hands across her face. "Instead they just . . . ran out, thinking the wires would be cut, but they weren't. Dying, caught on the lines in a trap. Man after man . . ."

They both shuddered. The sounds of the moans of the medic tent, of the traumatized and dying, suddenly seemed unbearable.

"There's a break in fighting. If you feel up to it, come back, have lunch with me at the inn, I'll be sure you're past clearances, I have something important to tell you about the enemy," Violet said.

"Lunch with my best friend on a lovely day? What could be a better convalescence?"

Violet spoke with the doctor, again utilizing her powers of persuasion. The poor man and his dutiful, brave nurses were all worse for the wear from the massive increase in wounded and corpses. She bid Will wait a moment and she went to the doctor and then to every nurse, dazed them, and then pressed her light to each sternum, buoying them and strengthening resolve, body and soul, via the powers lent her by the Heart. The communal mood shifted in one magnificent alchemical transformation. The air seemed sweeter, as if one could taste hope.

Turning to Will, pretending this didn't tire her as gravely as it did, she smiled, and he returned the expression, full of pride.

"Light of our lives," he murmured.

Above them appeared a swelling golden sphere and Healing appeared.

"Go on, I've got the rest," the Muse murmured to Violet, its voice carrying a slight echo but in the sound of faint wind chimes. Healing wafted from one soldier to the next, leaving little golden wisps to nestle into the worst of each man's wound.

As she led Will outside, the area came under attack. The shells seemed to come from all directions; the ground around her was exploding. She spread her fiery shields as well as she could, but hers wasn't as strong for having just left so much light with the medics and soldiers in the tent.

Shrapnel grazed her legs, tearing and burning skin. Hissing in pain, she cast a ball of blue flame over herself and Will. Within it, she became a channel of luminous, silver light. Her core purpose was at her side, this man who fought a monstrous poison day by day, and that simple fact brightened her power.

The barrage continued, wearing on Violet's strength and will. Otherworldly powers weren't any match for such extended bouts of mechanized terror.

Just as she began to feel her power and energy flagging, she heard a strain of gorgeous music, the kind of tune that Athens had bled into the air, the song of the spheres and stars, the melody of heaven.

She turned around and to her extreme shock, saw her family standing near the entrance to the medic tent. Tears flowed down her cheeks as she took in the scene before her.

All were dressed as nurses or doctors in clean, pressed umber uniforms, with her parents at the fore and all her "aunts" and "uncles" ranged beside and behind them. Violet recognized one of Lord Black's ministry seals, tacked to her father's breast pocket.

Distinguished and beautiful, the Guard stood wreathed in a ring of blue phoenix fire, the protections of goddess light, and the Muses' glistening augmentations. Violet remembered her mother describing this process as the Guard's "Bind." This protective beauty would not hold indefinitely but *goodness*, it was incredible in this moment.

"There you are, daughter," her father said, setting his jaw in characteristic ferocity. "We've been looking for you. Thankfully, we were given a few tips along the way. And we've been reinforced." He held up his hand, gesturing all around him. A burst of blue fire exploded around him in a glorious, engulfing flash, and Violet gasped in delight.

"I'm sorry . . . I didn't see you in my visions, Mum," Violet murmured, throwing her arms around her mother. "I assumed I was meant to fight alone."

"Of course you didn't see us," Percy replied through tears of her own. "You've been focused on heroism in front of you. But there may be those behind you who are meant to keep you standing. The Muses have purpose for us all in this fight. Come, let's fall back."

"Thank you for bringing a bit of heaven to these pits of hell," Will murmured, and Percy moved to embrace him, too.

They retreated to a hillside that offered a decent vantage point clear of the attack. The whole Guard managed, by extending their light and fire, to protect themselves, the medic tent, and enough of the supply line that men could rally to return fire.

Once the situation stabilized, Rebecca insisted Violet get her bloodied legs tended to, and they made their way back to the Verdun inn. Violet looped her arm around Will as he still seemed foggy, though glad to see his extended family.

The Muse of Healing had hovered above during their reunion, but now lifted away from them.

"Where are you going?" Violet asked sharply.

The glowing saffron figure whirled back to her. "To another regiment. I did not take a body, for too much of me is needed. I cannot possibly heal everyone," the being mourned, "but now that you are all reunited, I must try to do what I can on my own."

"Thank you," was all Violet could manage, chastened by the being's response, as it flew off.

"I'm sorry for not telling you exactly where I was," Violet said to her parents as they resumed their careful progress back along the transport road. "You'll see soon enough why I didn't want you to follow. It really is hell . . ."

"Hell or not, we managed to find you," the headmistress replied. "I suppose I should thank you for running off and making Lord Black's acquaintance all those years ago; his clearances have been vital. We'd have been here sooner," Rebecca continued, "but your uncle Elijah had business on the coast and we had to pick him up before we could come to France."

"You're not the only one with prophetic notions these days, dear," Elijah offered from a few paces behind, Josephine keeping silent vigil next to him.

Violet could see in Josephine's face, her eyes, feel it as though it were a cloak around her, how it grieved Josephine to see her beloved France in such pain. She seemed burdened with an unspeakable heaviness. The white shocks in her hair had grown; only slivers of umber brown remained.

"You didn't all have to come," she said to the aging cadre around her. Poor Vicar Carroll, she thought, this whole scope would break his huge heart in two, she could already see the great pain in his oceanic eyes . . . They were all wonderful souls who should be enjoying cups of wine with their feet up by a fire. "I never intended—"

"The Guard has always stood for balance," Rebecca explained. "When the Muses retired, they did so without thought of a conflict of this scale and scope. This is the worst imbalance the world has ever seen. We're doing our part to try to right both worlds, this and the spirit world. Each world is rocked on its very foundations."

"From out here I fear the war, in all its fronts, has too great a momentum for balance to be restored," Violet murmured.

"We'll do what we can. We always had more sway over the mortal world but I wonder now if it isn't the Whisper-world that needs us just as much," her mother said cryptically.

A dip in the road made Will stumble and Violet righted him carefully.

"You know who joins us?" Rebecca said. "I sent word and clearances for Mina Wilberforce and her nurses. She'll get you patched up and make sure Will is indeed in the clear."

The inn was empty save for Mina sitting in the parlor, a medical kit on the floor beside her. The former librarian rose when the Guard entered, taking Violet in her arms. The two women hugged fiercely for a long moment before Mina drew Violet closer to the parlor fireplace and seated her in a nearby chair. Violet was flooded with warm memories of hours spent with this woman, learning at her side.

"There's a break in the fighting and I'm glad of the rest, grateful you're here," Violet said as Mina quietly tended to her shrapnel wounds. "You didn't have to come on my account."

"It isn't just about you, love, none of this is," Mina said with a smile that quickly faded. "How much of it have you seen, yourself, directly? Of the front?"

"Enough," Violet replied, shaking. "It's as horrific as you could imagine. Every account of the terror and ungodly noise is true. Nothing in this war is average. All of it is absurd and avoidable. There is no acceptable loss; every day when the losses were similar to other days of terrible losses, from one to a thousand, it's all unbearable. Even just this last push, the wrong gauge of ammunition to wire . . ." Tears fell from her eyes. "None of the wires cut. Men just died shot up on the wire like animals in traps."

Mina's full lips thinned. Her deep brown eyes watered.

"They won't let my three girls tend to white soldiers," Mina replied through clenched teeth. "Even ones who could desperately use them, when they are every bit as English as the whites. The French seem more eager for the help."

"Such segregations won't stand forever. We'll force them to see," Alexi said from across the room. "Widen the selective sight of privilege and power."

"We'll need to do exactly that," Mina agreed. "But right now, as people die all around us, we do what we can, save as many as we can to fight another day."

Violet wondered if Will felt the same way. She turned to look for him, searching the now-crowded parlor, but he wasn't there.

DAZED, WILL REGAINED CONSCIOUSNESS TO FIND THAT HE'D wandered far from Verdun and was near a neighboring village. He paused, mid–shuffling step. Should he return for Violet? She'd made him promise not to pursue his own darkness without her. It would seem his consciousness wouldn't allow for anyone to fight this battle but him. This was it, Will understood, standing in the eerie, deserted vineyard. Dead, gnarled vines hung on wires like tangled corpses; the ground near the vines was rent by a forking, unnatural chasm that seemed to widen as he looked at it.

Drawn there all alone, he knew this was his confrontation. His truest test.

"Get out. Get out of me and out of the earth, you beast," Will stated. "I am, and this earth is, no place for you."

The ground trembled, groaning, in response. The mud at the base of the trenchlike crack roiled, seeming to come alive with coiling serpents, their forms slithering beneath the mud's surface.

Purely on instinct, Will pulled out his pistol and fired at the shifting earth, though he nearly instantly regretted the sound, especially since the shots had no effect upon the writhing snakes. The weapon's noise could attract a sniper or worse. Seeking cover, he moved toward a copse of blackened tree trunks. From there, he looked down at fissures in the earth and realized that as the cracks trailed away toward the front, the patterns in the open earth were distinctive, the shapes unmistakable.

This trailing fissure, to his horror, displayed every type of trench. During training he'd been shown diagrams of the many ways to build one, each design an attempt to buffer both the sound and impact of explosions: Serpentine, Labyrinthine, Offset, Crab Claw, Oblique, Baffle, Bent-Axis, Bastioned and Chambered, Insets and Outsets . . . Each used a different twist and turn, creating mazes in which men ran like rats.

Now each was laid out before him as though it were a map's legend, a well from which the horrors of mankind would draw their ideas.

The ground began to hiss. Steam began to bubble up, and with it, noxious smells. Will coughed; the sting of a gas attack burned his nostrils and stung his eyes and he placed his kerchief over his nose and mouth. The steam faded after a long moment, but the hissing did not. Then, as if a new instrument in the gruesome orchestra, the hiss was joined by a voice. A familiar one. An inevitable one. Seething, all around him.

"Hello, my boy. Welcome home."

The sound of that voice *outside* his own mind, rather than lurking at the corners of his eyes, frightened him like nothing else. The absurd horror of war, its unimaginable woe, would haunt him for the rest of his days. But this, *this* was the first terror, his first memory.

The ground below Will's feet buckled, throwing him down into the mouth of the chasm, right in front of the chambered form of a trench, a grave-sized space. He struggled to climb back to the surface of the earth, but slid deeper on the moist dirt, into the chamber.

"Come home, sonnnnnn . . ." the earth hissed, reaching up as if with hands and dragging Will to his knees. "Come here, my little mortal baby . . . where you may rot with me, where poison will grow in you . . ."

"I've found you," Will declared. "And soon *they'll* be here. Between us all, we will vanquish you for good—"

"I'm part of the world now, my sweet," the whisper gurgled. "No paltry Guard can overturn what's been done to the whole world. I encouraged mortals' unquenchable thirst for war and it was so *easy* to enlarge—"

"Unquenchable is the divine thirst for peace—"

"Then why are you here, sssoldier, shooting at me? If you just let me fully in, if you just give yourself to me, you'll have peace indeed. Finally."

"I joined the war to find you and cut you out of my soul, and to rid the world of your poison."

The being that had tormented him since youth, having for so long urged him in pleading murmurs of misery and violence, was manifest before him. This lit the fire of a murderous rage. He'd refused to indulge the beast then, but he was eager to use its own need for violence against it now.

Bending down, he pulled at the moving forms, snakelike and vinelike and wriggling in his grasp, turning to ash and flaking away even as he tried to grasp them. Pulling a knife from his boot, he began slashing at the earth.

A great roar rose all around him and inside him, overwhelming him. The earth rose up, pelting him, wounding him with countless small fangs and sharp points. In an instant, Will collapsed in a pool of his own blood. As he lost consciousness he still kept fighting . . .

VIOLET, KNOWING WHERE HE'D GONE, WAS HEEDLESS OF NEEDing to rest her injured leg. Nearly sprinting from the inn, she was glad of the physical training she'd put herself through before this venture. Her family struggled to catch up.

Down the lane toward Fleury, she jogged past rubble and ruptured earth, past signs of abandonment and skirmishes, a few blackened trees amidst those still struggling to stay green and upright, hoping it was a trick of her imagination that had her hearing a low, wet chuckle, and a familiar hiss . . . Had she heard a gunshot ring out?

In the distance she saw the stone cottage, the dead vineyard, and to her horror, what had been a crack in the earth was now a chasm as wide and as structured as a trench, wet at the bottom.

With a body below.

"Will. Oh my God, Will," Violet cried, jumping into the hole, her boots sloshing in muck and blood. She rushed to his side. "Damn you," she admonished him, praying that she was not discovering a corpse, "you promised to tell me . . ."

Pressing her fingers to his throat, she discovered that his pulse was faint, but rejoiced that there was a sliver of life left in him.

Blood stemmed from cuts all over him and there was a gash on his forehead. The mud around him clung to him, weaving like vines or serpents around his limbs, snaking around his throat and trespassing into his hair. There was ash everywhere, some even trickling out of his ears. He'd been fighting it from without, but he'd been fighting it from within far longer.

Violet heaved Will free of the dirt and suddenly the earth had a face, a muddy head erupting from the muck, its gaping mouth giving forth a terrible, howling laugh. Vines shaped of mud clamped around their booted ankles and from everywhere came an awful hissing.

"Oh God . . ." came Percy's voice from above. "You again . . ."

Violet looked up to see her mother glaring down at the turmoil. Behind her ranged Alexi and the rest of the company.

Percy was a snow-white, furious, brightly lit creature. Her plain nurse's uniform and the shawl over her head were but slight shades to her inner lamp. Her pearlescent face was beaming like a star, eyes blazing past the tinted glasses askew on her nose, nostrils flared. With every beat of her heart, she burned brighter.

"It *is* you again, constantly tormenting us near and far . . ." Percy declared with hatred, her voice taking on the otherworldly quality Violet had previously only heard in the Muses. "Of course you're drawn to this terrible conflict; the depths of humanity's despair—"

"And you'll never drive me away . . ." replied the voice. "Not from here, not after all I've done, worming my way through the snake pits of the earth . . ."

"Oh, but I always do my best, don't I? You know when I'm at my best? When you're threatening my family. Now, *unhand my son*," Percy bellowed. Her body arched, bright white light exploding from her. The earth fell away; the ash vanished into the brilliance.

Behind Percy, a small, dark rectangle opened in the air—the

Whisper-world, reacting to her demands. The black, vacuous portal began sucking in the bits of its wayward daughter.

Violet lent her own light to her mother's initiative, purging the earth of the poison. Flashes of light and whips of phoenix fire, wielded from both her and her father's hand, coursed down the unnatural crack in the earth, sending dust and ash flying up into the air so it could be drawn back into the Whisper-world from which it had come.

As the evil was purged from the earth, the forces her family wielded remained within the ground. Light and fire began settling into the fissure, forking out to the greater trenches the evil had furrowed, beginning to counter the enemy's poison. Hopefully, their light could reduce the monster's toxicity, smother the flames of war, and clamp a brake on the speeding train of constant death. Violet thought of her light reaching as far as the Liminal had showed her, and she sent even more into the chasms before her.

Her father cast a rope of blue fire around Violet and Will, lifting their bodies and snapping the rest of the clinging earth away with a slap. As they rose from the ground, Violet spotted a small ceramic urn rising from the muck on an expanding bubble of gas.

"What *is* that?" Violet asked.

Percy gasped in heavy-hearted recognition at the sight of the urn. "It contained part of the body of the Gorgon we all fought before, a creature that had been reduced to ash and collected in the Whisper-world. It should have been destroyed years before. Yet here it is, far from Athens, from England, where we last saw it."

"How did it get here?" Michael asked, incredulous, his arms open, extending the heat and warmth of the Heart's energy.

"Perhaps the great holes between the worlds are bound to worsen," Josephine murmured, having withdrawn a large locket on a chain where inside an angel was painted. It was lit with such light and power it was as if the Artist held a little sun in her delicate hands.

Reaching down, Percy grabbed the urn and sucked in a breath of pain as the touch of the clay scalded her hands. With a cry, she threw it into the open portal of mist and stone where it fell on the wet slate within, breaking open. Ash flew up into the gray Whisper-world air, shifting up in an eerie, unnatural pattern until it gathered to form a cracked face bordered by ashen serpents. The face opened a blackened maw as if to scream.

"Bind," Rebecca declared and the force of the Guard rose in a powerful circle. Rebecca and Michael, Elijah and Josephine flanked each side of the Rychman family, and as a result, Percy's light shone brighter around her and the flames of the phoenix fire rose taller.

The visage began to howl like a banshee and Percy and Violet screamed right back at it, exploding silvery, blinding white fire from their extended arms like bolts of lightning; the goddess's great parting gift to their mortality.

The face splintered again, blasted by light and wind; the particles of ash flew behind the Whisper-world threshold, falling to a heap at the edge of the door. The portal flickered but still yawned open. A shrouded form stepped into view at the threshold, lifting the edge of its winding sheet toward Will's supine body as if pointing. There seemed to be no body beneath the dusty charcoal cloth and yet the fabric moved as if one were there.

"Some of her is still there, you know," the shadow said, its voice a gritty death rattle. "Kill the boy and you'll be rid of the last of her forever. You're terrible at cleaning up your own messes."

"Tend to your own world, wretch," Percy hissed, another explosion of light rippling from her body in righteous rage, snapping the portal shut.

As Violet, aided by phoenix fire and Percy's light, lifted Will's limp body, the men of the Guard surged forward, pulling him out onto the struggling grass beneath the trees. Violet joined him there a moment later.

After a pause to catch their breath, they rushed Will into the abandoned cottage, setting him on the dusty table they found within. Percy and Violet bent over him, mustering their healing abilities.

"I pray the Healing muse may return to help," Violet murmured, running a lit hand over Will's cheek, "though we're hardly the only ones who need it."

"This will take the time it takes," Percy stated. The rest of the company took to searching resources, starting a fire, and finding water.

Hours passed with no response. Violet tamped down on panic. At last, Rebecca approached mother and daughter, saying, "Mina and some of her best nurses are not far from here. We should take Will to them."

"But—" Percy and Violet chorused.

"That's an order," Rebecca and Alexi chorused in turn.

"If you expend yourselves entirely now, you risk all our lives," Rebecca said in her headmistress tone, one that made all obey. "Our dear boy is not dead, but he needs time, clearly, to heal."

There was no further argument. Alexi carried Will over his back in a fireman's hold, waving off Michael's offer of help. Back at the inn, they found a note from Mina, informing them she'd reported to a British prisoner of war encampment some distance away.

Elijah's gift of persuasion, more powerful than Violet's, presented with their papers, had the innkeeper offering them two horses for the trip.

They were stopped at the entrance of the tent at the encampment; the officer on guard took a look at the British uniform Will wore and shook his head.

"Miss," the lieutenant said to Violet, "the nurse you're asking for, and those in her unit, cannot treat one of *our* soldiers."

Violet's nostrils flared. A sheen of blue covered her vision, phoenix fire radiant in her retinas. From the breast pocket of her vest, Violet withdrew Black's carte blanche before closing the distance so she was speaking nearly nose to nose with the lieutenant.

"The nurse in question has a special commendation from *this* very special ministry, presided over by the most excellent Lord Black," Violet said in clipped tones. The officer flinched, perhaps startled by such vehemence in a woman.

"You will *immediately* revise the very foolish notion of keeping the most talented nurses away from your most grievously wounded soldiers because of an errant notion that skin color has anything to do with aptitude. These women are better trained than you could hope to appreciate. You *will* appreciate it. You will *respect* Nurse Wilberforce and her team."

The man nodded.

"*This* nurse, *this* soldier, *this* company," Violet said, gesturing to her fellows, "will not be questioned and will have your full support. So will any nurse that Mina Wilberforce, a special commandant of His Majesty the King, commands. Am I understood?"

"Yes, ma'am, entirely so." The man bowed deeply.

Violet stepped back, noting that both her mother and Elijah were standing close by, so the man was triply affected. Mina Wilberforce, attracted to the commotion at the gate, came up with a group of stretcher bearers and took charge of Will, sending him off into the quietest side of the infirmary.

"I'm sorry about that," Violet murmured to Mina, gesturing to the lieutenant.

"So am I," she said wearily. "I wish it didn't have to be done. Say a prayer over him and then be off. Can't have too many of you here."

Violet knew Mina was right—the full Guard would attract too much attention, even with Lord Black's clearance and all their powers at the fore. Violet nodded. She stood staring at the seemingly peaceful body of her dearest companion, her favorite person. She could not imagine life without him and wondered what forces he fought internally, what hooks the bitter old voice of an ancient enemy had in him. The shrouded figure at the edge of the Whisperworld, and its threat, terrified her.

She turned at the touch of her mother, and for a nearly imperceptible moment, Violet was flooded with anger that it was she who had endangered Marianna, who had passed on that peril to her son, albeit unintentionally. Her anger would have been hidden from anyone other than her mother, who saw it clearly. Percy's colorless cheeks bloomed in ragged splotches of ruby. Opening her mouth, she would either explain or apologize.

Violet wanted neither, and said, "He'll be all right. I have to believe so. If I know Will, he's now fighting an interior battle I can't possibly help him with." She fought back tears, gazing down at him. "When we were little, we confessed that our greatest fear was to be alone. Entirely alone, with no one to talk to or to hear us if we screamed. I'm so scared he feels alone in there, in his own darkness . . ."

"You've been his valiant soldier for so long—"

"And he mine. But now . . ."

"We are all tied, this family," Percy assured her. "No one is ever alone; you know that, you feel that, I know you do."

Violet turned back to Will, rushing back to squeeze his hand and proffer one of their elaborate childhood endearments. "You hear that, Willificent?" She leaned closer. "No one is ever alone, no matter where you are and on which foreign, spiritual shore you now fight. Hear me, feel me, I'm there. Our light is there, waiting for you."

Vicar Michael came over, murmuring prayers over him. He withdrew an angel medallion that was lit with the power of his peaceful gifts of the Heart and tucked it into Will's open uniform pocket.

Mina stepped into view, standing guard, her best nurse beside her. Violet knew it was past time to leave. "We will keep watch here," Mina promised.

"I trust you with any life I hold precious. Thank you," Violet murmured, before sighing heavily. "Now I have to explain to my family the true terrors of this war. They've come all the way here, but they've yet to understand. They think they can balance the scorched earth with spiritual gifts. I don't know how."

"We all must go on to the next bloody field and do so bravely," Mina replied. "We have no choice."

Violet nodded and turned away. A fresh, cool blast of air halted her as she nearly walked through Jane.

"I'll keep vigil over Will," Jane promised. "I often did when he was a child, just as you'd asked. I won't leave his side and I'll do my best to keep him out of danger." She lifted up a transparent hand and light flickered on her palm, the ghostly traces of Healing that had never fully left her. Every spare scrap of divinity would be put to use.

"Thank you, Auntie. I would like to have Will transferred away from this part of France. It carries a specific danger only to him and he's more vulnerable to it now."

"I agree Will would recover best as far from toxic ground as possible," Jane said.

"Do you think he could be wandering the Whisper-world alone?" Violet asked fearfully.

"If he is, my Aodhan will be there for him as he was for his mother. He won't be alone. He'll have a vigil on both sides."

"My heroes," Violet murmured, reaching out to the chill draft that was Jane's hand and squeezing through it, refusing to let a lack of corporeal touch keep her from gestures of affection.

Interceding again with the commanding officer—this time he was far more pliant—Violet used Lord Black's papers, along with Elijah Withersby's firm powers of persuasion, to ensure Will would not only be monitored carefully but sent back on the first steamer to England. He would be returned not to a military hospital ready to send him right back to the front if he awoke, but a private one. She knew he wouldn't like to be separated from her in this capacity, but she felt within and their souls' tether remained strong.

ONCE ARRANGEMENTS WERE MADE, THE GUARD GATHERED IN the back pews of a local church, discussing the battle with the Gorgon's ash, confident that they'd sent the remaining heart of the beast back where it belonged. Percy was kneeling at the front, near a statue of the Holy Virgin. As Violet drew near, Percy reached back without turning around, gesturing for Violet to join her. Violet settled onto her knees beside her mother, quickly crossing herself in deference to Percy's beliefs.

"Thank you, Queen of Heaven, for keeping us all safe today," Percy murmured. "I can never thank you enough for your protection."

"Thank you," Violet echoed. "Every heavenly host, thank you, and I bid you extend that protection to Will, to all of us, as we strive to do whatever you may yet ask of us."

Percy bowed her head before getting to her feet and taking a seat in the front pew. Violet joined her.

"I spent so many years worrying about these days. Now that they are upon us, I realize I had no idea what to expect," Percy said softly, taking her daughter's hand.

"Nothing could prepare us for the unspeakable amount of suffering and death," Violet replied. "Not even my visions. They pale in comparison to the front."

Shifting to a fonder subject, Violet managed a smile as she continued. "Out there. With your light, when you battled your old foe, you called Will your son."

Her mother blushed again. "I do think of him as family, but 'son-in-law' doesn't have the same potency during a proclamation. I don't mean to be presumptuous, but . . ."

"We're not meant for anyone else. Before I dare ask if you and Father approve, I should state that, being visionaries . . . I'm not sure that giving you an heir is in our stars."

Not wishing to elaborate further, Violet was relieved to see her mother did not appear concerned or surprised by her words.

"I expect nothing of you but love, health, and happiness," Percy replied. "I know nothing of heirs and lineages; I'm an orphan, born of an ancient force. What lives in you can live on in other ways. Athens is the only lineage I truly care about, and you can carry Rebecca's torch, its students your issue."

"The rest of the monster . . ." Violet trailed off, recalling the terror of that reassembling head, a constantly regenerating horror that, since it had fed on so much mortal failure and flaw, was renewed.

"Is back in the Whisper-world where it belongs," Percy stated. She didn't entirely sound convinced.

Rebecca had moved to join them. "The air is better for having leeched the Gorgon's poison from the earth," she stated, turning to Violet. "When we were the Guard, we were uniquely attuned to the balance of the air. If it was ever weighted too heavily on the side of the dead, I would get a sense that the air was off. The air is most certainly off due to this war, but it is better for what was done today."

"I'm glad to hear you perceive it so," Violet said. "And I know our light has great effect. But the beast, thrown back into its own world again . . . mightn't it grow stronger from within?"

"During the war in Athens," Percy explained, "we pummeled Darkness with so much light that eventually he was made null and void. It was a battering, a wearing down. We will have to do the same thing here with this more stubborn and evolved beast."

"That means going *in* to fight it?" Violet asked, a chill sweeping over her.

"Perhaps," she murmured.

"That creature at the threshold threatening Will . . . what *was* that?"

"I don't know. And that's as troubling as anything," she said simply, then stood, moving to rejoin the company.

Violet watched the unassuming and unlikely warrior her mother was, in her plain, umber nurse's garb, calmly glide to Alexi's side and place a blanched hand on his shoulder. There was no question that if her mother went into that abyss, she'd go in after her.

REST AT THE INN WAS CRITICAL. NO AMOUNT OF THEIR COM-
munal binding and wielding of light and fire could be spent without recovery. Violet understood why the Muses had wanted to sleep in Athens's bricks for so long.

Once she penned and sent a letter to the Pages informing them of their son's future arrival so they might be there to watch over him and, hopefully, rouse him back to full health, and offering Lord Black's name as a contact, she left the missive with the innkeeper who again looked at her so curiously as to almost be intrusive.

"Pour la France, mon ami," Elijah murmured to the worried man, who was surely wondering why this strange group of uniformed Brits, seemingly without regiment, continued patronizing his establishment. He used his gift to wipe a hand across the proprietor's haggard face. The innkeeper turned away, repeating Elijah's words on chapped lips: "For France, my friend."

Josephine was at the breakfast table in the cozy front room, hastily drawing the figure of a warrior angel in pen and ink, carrying a sword in right hand and a shield on the left. She'd done at least twenty of them, angels piled in a stack. They were beautiful and charged with power.

"I'll send one to every regiment commander across the front," she said breathlessly, feverish to create as many as she could, pushing a white lock of hair from her forehead and bending back over her work. Violet didn't know if she'd slept at all or if she'd been obsessively creating. The dark blue aura of Art pulsed from within her as if it were a visible heartbeat.

"You are living into this being," Violet murmured, staring at the angel and then at her aunt. "Where you end and Art begins, I wouldn't know." At this, Josephine smiled as if it was the first thing to bring comfort in a very long time.

As the rest of her family gathered, leaning over cups of steaming coffee, Violet spoke as her intuitions and visions had led her.

"Will isn't all we have come here for," she stated. "I think you must feel that now. I believe you must witness with me the full scope of what is happening. Let us be like a bird and find our way."

"Light the way," Josephine murmured, penning a halo around a noble head.

Violet reached out and placed a gentle hand on Josephine's shoulder. "We'll find fallback positions and from there, distribute your angels. Even as you draw them I feel their power to bring comfort."

"For my countrymen," she murmured, drawing faster. "For my land." Elijah leaned close to his wife and kissed her temple, moist from feverish work.

"Pace yourself," he whispered.

"This is our mission, the new prophecy for all of us," she said softly back to him. "You've yours, I've mine."

"Lead on, then," her father said, gesturing to his daughter, rising to his feet. "We will shield together as we move."

Yet another assault was underway when Violet and the Guard took up a position at the top of a tall hill. Stationed behind the line of the French heavy artillery and far enough from the infantry offensives, they had what was likely a safe, but temporary, vantage point. Their powers would keep them concealed for a while, so they could discern their next move.

Before them lay the full scope of the war's horror, some aspects directly visible, others needing to be viewed through field binoculars. They took in the jagged scars of the trenches, the wires and heavy artillery, the unwieldy tanks, both stationary and rolling about in barren, muddy earth. Invisible until they exploded were mines, somehow secreted beneath the enemy camp. The fortress was said to have changed hands and fallen to Germany in the night . . .

Percy, binoculars to her ice-pale eyes, scanned the lines of the trenches back and forth, over and over. A thick gray mist hung over the battlefields, eerie and ominous.

"No . . . no, no . . ." She tossed away the binoculars, clutching her head. "Is it not the gravest woe to bring *that* world upon us? Did we not fight our own war to keep the Whisper-world at bay?

Is Darkness vanquished or did he just embed himself deep in the earth?"

She turned to her company, tears streaming down her colorless face, a mottled patch of garish red angrily blooming on her cheeks, the blush of abject fury.

"They've made this whole world into Whisper-woe, carving up the very earth to match those dreadful corridors!"

Alexi placed a hand on her shoulder.

"Open!" Percy shrieked. "Tear the whole sky open!" She cast her hand forward and wrenched it to the side. "That isn't mist! It isn't fog at all!"

An explosion of white light. A thundering wave of blue fire. A gaping black hole formed in the center of the sky and expanded to a rectangle as if half the heavens were replaced by darkness. Not darkness. Whispers.

"See? What difference does it make?" she cried, gesturing to the trench far beyond, and then to the maw she had created. "The ground, the Whisper-world, the host of spirits poured over the earth, this war makes it one and the same. So it is on earth, so shall it be in purgatory . . ."

The gray mist began to rise, drawn to the portal Percy in her anguish had made.

With horror, Violet realized what her mother meant. The mist were spirits. An oncoming wave of the dead. They had covered the earth, clogged the air . . . too many to have gotten through.

And therein was their further purpose, Violet knew with a sinking weight in her empty stomach. They had to open up the Whisper-world because death needed that much more room.

CHAPTER
TWENTY-ONE

WILL REGAINED CONSCIOUSNESS STANDING IN A DARK, COM-
pletely unfamiliar place, atop a wide shelf of rock. Before him
was a glassy surface, beyond which swirled black patterns, as if he
were looking through a porthole at a churning sea of black ink.
But this was no porthole—above him loomed a huge, rectangular proscenium.

Echoing around him were the sounds of a cavern: drips of water
against rock, murmurs of an underground river somewhere to his
left, and whispers. A cacophony of whispers, carried on a low,
whistling wind that sounded chillingly like human moaning.

The glass before him shimmered and took on a reflective quality. Will gasped at the image, his familiar self, but startlingly pale
and gray, like the spirits Violet had described but he had never
seen.

"I must be dead, then . . ." he whispered. His muddy, mussed
uniform bore the bloodstains from his fight with his ultimate foe.
A fight he had lost. "Well, damn."

He could have sworn that he had heard Violet's voice, felt her
presence, his lifeline. He felt certain he had not died in that ditch,
despite the evidence currently before him.

"If I'm not dead, or even if I am, where am I?" he asked himself as the glass shifted back to clear, once again revealing the black
waters churning beyond the proscenium arch.

"Right this very moment, you're at the Liminal," someone said behind him. "While your body is on a train back home."

Will whirled around to behold a man, also gray of flesh and clothing. The newcomer wore the garb of an old Celtic warrior; a wild mane of thick gray hair tumbled around his broad shoulders and over his clan sash, which was clasped with a silver eternal knot.

"A precarious place for a mortal in these shadows," the man continued. "But, thankfully, the Liminal edge takes mortal sides."

"I am one, still, then? A mortal?" Will asked, swallowing hard.

He was unnerved, but unafraid of the answer. This new experience was nothing compared to living through a barrage in the trenches. The idea of an infernal hell was less terrifying if one had already lived it, already heard damnation in the screams of falling shells.

"For now, you are," the man replied. He smiled warmly. "The ladies down there worked some pretty powerful magic on you."

"Violet and . . . Mrs. Rychman?" Will said, assuming Percy had followed her daughter into battle with their family foe. "You know of them?"

"Yes. And Nurse Wilberforce, too." Seeing that Will's eyes widened in hope and care, he continued, "I've been watching out for all of them. You're not a Guard member, and neither is Wilberforce, but our fates are all entwined and you're all family now.

"I knew you earlier, as well. I helped your mother weather her time in these parts, before you were born."

"You're Aodhan, then, Jane's partner!" Will strode forward and stuck out his hand. Aodhan took it, his touch freezing, and they shook heartily. "I've been hoping all my life to thank you for what you did for my family."

"A thousand welcomes. I'm dreadfully sorry some of the Whisper-world was passed on to you. But you're here, and the place hasn't killed you, so perhaps in some ways we were preparing you. Divine order has a way of making accidents into blessings."

Will saluted. "I am at your service, good sir. Please, if you are my guide here, lead on and show me what you will, and how I can help from this unique position. I am still a soldier, no matter my state."

Aodhan smiled. "What a brave lad you are, to be the person you are regardless of what the Gorgon would have instilled in you. Your strength precedes you."

Will shrugged, deflecting the compliment. "I had the good fortune to be raised in the light. I knew I had to continue to live into it."

"We were all horrified about what happened," Aodhan said mournfully.

"From what I understand of this place, isn't guilt one of its great weapons? Shouldn't we try to be free of it?" Will asked. Aodhan brightened, clapping him on the back.

"Right you are, my boy, right you are. Come."

Just as Aodhan was about to lead Will into one of the entrances to what seemed to be a stone labyrinth that stretched out before them, the Liminal flickered behind them, lightning arcing across its glassy, stormy surface.

"Ah, but wait," the spirit said. "The great forces here wish you to see something."

The proscenium of the Liminal shifted to frame a view from high above the world, a distant map below. Smoke plumed up in billowing furls from countless areas, as if smokestacks were erupting directly from the land masses.

"The world at war," Aodhan murmured.

"The sheer *scope* of it . . ." Will murmured. "I knew so many theaters are engaged, I just . . ."

"Perspective. That is what the Liminal offers."

The warriors of two very different worlds stood staring at the one they had shared, a world now torn apart as never before. Borders had become sharp as the bayonets each infantry kept upon the ends of their rifles. The sobering, unifying characteristic between theaters and battalions was the common language of a sharp point of death at close range.

Will, feeling a palpable ache and fear, reached out instinctively, as if he could wipe the smoke off the map, clear the debris of battle. Before he could make contact, the scene began to change, dizzyingly fast.

The frame shifted, diving down like a raptor to a vantage point high above a specific battlefield. The focus shifted, moving past the trench lines and the barbed wire, past the blinding flashes of mortars and the tiny pinprick flares at the ends of rifles, past crumpled corpses strewn across No Man's Land, to the side of a hill. There, six bodies, faintly lit by an eerie blue and white light, moved in a slow, subtle dance.

As Violet and Percy threw their arms open, the light around the Liminal crackled again, and men began to pass through that watery glass as if stepping through a mirror. Grayscale, floating above the ground—unlike Will, whose feet were firmly set upon stone—the ghosts filed in. Many nodded to Will as they passed, acknowledging him, in his uniform, as one of their own. Most looked around, their expressions dazed, hurt, wounded, scared. Dulled and dimmed.

All across the battlefield, the smoke began to lessen, to lift. To break into component parts, Will saw, and he realized it wasn't smoke at all, but a massive cloud bank of the grayscale dead.

"That smoke is *spirits*?" Will murmured.

"Aye," Aodhan replied sadly.

And they were all coming here. So many, choking the field. It wasn't that they were able to stop the deaths, or stop the battles, that was beyond their purview. They were opening up holes in a dam, lest the world flood with the dead.

"A grim job they have," Aodhan murmured, "opening that portal, but only a Guard, our Lady Persephone, and her kin could do it . . ." Their dim, faraway figures were obscured by the incoming troops, enemy and ally.

Waves of the dead lapped at the Liminal edge and poured across, like walking through a veil of water, growing more solid as they entered the Whisper-world. From their uniforms, Will recognized men from different armies. Incoming French and British troops, even those from battlefields that were miles apart, were readier to turn to one another than they were to speak to the enemy. For their part, the Germans mostly kept to their own. Only here and there did men pause to shake hands and exchange halting apologies.

This choked Will up more than anything, reminding him of the Christmas Truce. Death made allies of men who were only enemies because their commanding officers bade them be so.

Soldiers filed through the doorways behind Will and Aodhan, heading into the stone labyrinth, crowding the corridors. Some exclaimed joyously at flashes of bright light that greeted them a few steps down the slate walks. Others wandered, starting down one hall as if looking for something, finding themselves back on the platform, then trying another path. One distant section was entirely pitch black; some spirits went there, perhaps drawn or pulled by unseen hands.

"What's going on?" Will asked Aodhan tentatively. "This place . . . it isn't heaven, and it isn't what I imagined hell to be. What is next for these men?"

"Sorting and sifting now. The peaceful at heart, those ready for rest and those who have done right by others—they can now go on to taste the Great Beyond. That's those flashes of light. I glimpsed it once, with Jane, it is everything exquisite and defies description." The rugged man smiled wistfully. "Others must try again; their souls will return to the earth in new lives. The truly listless and lost, many of those sorrowful souls remain here. Jane and I returned to this gray between because, until the rest of our family joins us, we have chosen to live on as protectors.

"But I must say, and I don't exactly know what there is to do to remedy it, this place is growing too full of spirits. This is an ancient place created when the world was newer, not built for so *much* death; so many, all at once. You can hear on the air why this place is called what it is, and the whispers carry worries of insta- bility due to unprecedented trauma."

Tumult drew Will's eye and ear. He followed the shouts, and an increasing sound of rushing water, through a twisting, turn- ing corridor of hewn slate. The sharp corners reminded him of the maze he and Violet used to pretend to run, around the hedges his father had always meant to plant . . . Perhaps his childhood had prepared him for this day, so that moving through a labyrinth would come by instinct. Grimly he realized it was also like navi- gating a trench.

Aodhan said nothing, letting him take the lead. They exited the serpentine corridor onto a broad landing. Above, the ceiling was almost imperceptible through a haze of silvery mist, but the cold wake of spirits meant there was always a chilling breeze and the mist cleared to reveal tall stone arches spanning out from around the center dais, where there was a large, empty stone throne. The throne was draped with charred fabric and ringed with a circle of crumbled, dried husks of what might once have been flowers, and beneath the stone seat lay a dog's skull. As Will blinked, the skull multiplied into three, then in another blink, back to one again, a strange trick of the eye.

A large stone tower stood behind the throne, and behind that lay a wide slate platform that led into utter darkness beyond. On either side of the platform gurgled a pitch-black river with a swift current. Will looked away when he thought he saw gaping, black-eyed faces below the surface.

Between Will and the dais was a bridge; its twin connected the dais to the opposite side of the river, with the far bank shrouded in the deepest shadows. The light in the place was diffuse and dim, only an eerie glow as if death was its own moonlight; Will looked down at his own body to see that it glowed brighter than those of the spirits around him—a sign of life, he hoped.

The dead soldiers who had not taken to the corridors were scattered about on the dais and both sides of the river, more joining them every moment. The rushing water seemed to nip at them as if it had teeth, the dank shadows in the corridors seemed to have whipping black lengths that reached out tauntingly and buffeted the gray-glowing bodies of the fallen.

The soldiers appeared shell-shocked at every new onslaught. Other shadows seemed to teem with vague forms that sported limbs and claws of terrifying beasts described in myth and fanciful text.

"Stop!" Will cried, throwing a fist in the air, thinking of how Violet directed her light, like a jab. The tormentors turned their dark heads, swiveled their ungodly forms in his direction. Shuddering at the unnatural sight, Will continued, his voice a strong contrast to the moans and murmurs that surrounded him. "These men have endured enough! They were living in hell, do not give them a new one here!

"We've had enough!"

A few cries of "that's right" and "hear, hear" went up around them, in addition to some French and German assents.

Aodhan came near, a warning look on his face.

"One thing I've learned in all my centuries here is that you don't want to do anything that draws too much attention. Darkness may no longer stalk this land as a leader, but there are old creatures who stand as pillars holding up these stones and they don't like—"

"Disruptions like I just did, you mean?" Will asked. "You might have said something."

"I didn't think . . ."

Dark shadows, swooping like great bats from every black crevice in the grand, echoing chamber descended upon Will. Everything went silent and black, his senses cut to the quick.

CHAPTER
TWENTY-TWO

ON THEIR HILLTOP VANTAGE POINT, A TERRIBLE VISION OVER-
took Violet, and she and her mother gasped in the very same instant. The Whisper-world door wavered but remained open due
to the congestion of the spirits.

In this vision, rolling away from them were countless white
crosses. Behind them was a modern-looking structure popular in
this new century, a white memorial chapel whose architecture appeared as if the lines of the Art Nouveau movement had been
given sleeker, more spare direction.

Violet found herself turning toward it and away from her fellows, drawn to its dynamic eaves, moving the distance through
the hundreds of white crosses, every step . . .

She reached the base of the memorial chapel. Peculiar windows
lined the ground level at angles that Violet found odd. She had to
look in.

Overcome, feeling a burgeoning moan of terror and pain well
within her, she put her hand to her mouth at what she saw below.
Bones.

Countless, innumerable, endless, piles of bones. A deep crypt
pit filled many feet high with nothing but bare remains.

Heaped together, nameless, many whole and more in pieces.

A section of skulls, another of arms, of legs, thousands of tiny
digits . . .

Violet knew it was a vision but that it was also true. There was no uncertainty about this future. There was this much death. There would be so much more.

An explosion brought her back to the reality that was mass death in progress.

She found her mother staring at her; her wide, pearlescent eyes, their uniqueness that Violet had found so lovely, were now unsettling.

On a thin breath, Violet asked, "Did you see?"

"The ossuary . . ." Her mother sighed, shaking violently, teeth chattering, her voice keening. "The castle of bones. The sea of bones. The *ocean* of bones . . ."

"What is it?" Alexi asked gently. "What did you see?"

"I must open up the *whole sky*," Percy wailed. "Here and now isn't breadth enough and not the only place or time."

The rest of the Guard drew close around them, and Violet rejoiced in the warmth of her compatriots as it countered the chilling cold of her shared vision.

"There are too many." Percy sobbed. "These poor souls shall choke everything and none of this wasteland will ever be green again. Instead, a castle of bones. We stand on what will be a graveyard and face what will be an unending massacre."

Michael moved close to bestow his gift, the Heart's leavening, then turned to Violet. He loosed a dove of peace into her soul by placing a gentle hand over her sternum. Both she and her mother breathed more easily, their shaking calmed.

"Not just a door. Now I understand what the Muses bid; a new kind of balance to counter what they couldn't have prepared for. A whole *field* must open up as a portal," Percy grieved, wiping her face, bolstered by Michael's offering. "I have never opened something as wide as this requires." Here came a quiver of fear, the fear Violet felt from the beginning; that she would not be *enough*.

"We'll do it together," Violet promised. "On behalf of that castle of bones . . ."

"But with a safeguard," her mother added, grasping her husband and daughter's fire-touched hands in each of hers. "Fire must stand watch. I can't let this undo the gains of *our* war. There still must be a separation of the two worlds, even in this hellscape, otherwise all is for naught." The tears began again, and Percy let them flow.

"Indeed," Alexi promised. Glancing at the ominous clouds roiling overhead, he considered their weight a moment before he sent a fork of his own fire into the sky to keep watch, a barrier and barometer.

In a burst of yellow glow, Healing returned, the Muse coursing across the field in a shimmering saffron flicker over the wounded before floating back to hover over the rest of the Guard.

With a strike of thunder and lightning, the air responsive to Alexi's own force, there was a pause in the battle. At this, Violet watched, wide-eyed as her mother pushed everyone aside and strode to the crest of the hill. With a desperate cry, Persephone threw her arms wide. An arc of white light leapt from her into the sky, speeding toward the flashes of gunpowder and the flare of cannons.

If it weren't so heartbreaking, Violet would have to have been amazed by her mother's strength. The beauty and desperation of it was so striking that for a moment, she was unable to act. Then, as her father glanced at her, Violet duplicated her mother's action, throwing light as if she were drawing a bow and releasing an arrow. Sparking silver light doubled as it traveled over the muddy fields and leafless trees, whose gnarled and twisted stumps had become alien shapes.

When the light settled, like a phosphorescent sun, over the field, Percy ripped open a wide, gaping swath of Whisper-world.

The sky rumbled as mortals shifted heavenly particulars. Percy and Violet widened the void's breadth and scope with flexed palms and straining muscles, wrenching at the growing portal in the sky.

Sweat broke out across Violet's brow, and her luminous mother was similarly damp with effort. The rest of the Guard encircled them with a binding light, lending their own force, interconnected via the bonds of phoenix fire.

The luminous gray mass of the dead hesitated at the growing maw before them, apprehension at the threshold. Alexi, in a similarly forceful gesture as Percy's, sent out a tendril of blue fire to wrap around the group of spirit soldiers that floated en masse. To Violet's eye it looked almost like an embrace, something beautiful and reassuring that lifted them toward the opening. But so many floated stock-still, terrified.

"Help them," Violet begged her family. "What did you used to do to ease the dead onward? How did you police them toward peace?"

"My dear Intuition"—Alexi turned to Rebecca—"could you enlighten the field with your gifts? I have missed the days when your gifts offered bits of sacred texts to guide the spirits."

Rebecca closed her eyes, her brow furrowing as if she were looking for something in her mind.

"Dear boys," Rebecca called out. Healing carried her words farther onto the field, its yellow hue like a small ray of sunshine floating amidst the gray, amplifying the headmistress's benediction. "Hear words from a fellow soldier. Sassoon has been divinely inspired, and in this your time of need, hear him . . ."

> *There was an hour when we were loth to part*
> *From life we longed to share no less than others.*
> *Now, having claimed this heritage of heart,*
> *What need we more, my comrades and my brothers?*

Her words carried on the air and several spirits put their hands to their hearts. Some saluted, others bowed their heads and floated forward, given their marching orders. Violet concentrated with everything she had, sending out light and fire bolster, to keep the portal wide and lit with a welcome, just as her parents remained awash in otherworldly illumination.

The first wave of dead soldiers crested over the threshold of the Whisper-world and into the arms of shadow, followed closely by another, and another.

"Where do they go from there, Mum?" Violet asked, desperate to feel that they were doing something good here at this crossroads.

"From my time in that 'undiscovered country,'" Percy replied, "each path is determined by each soul."

The innumerable, constant waves of the dead: warriors and civilians, doctors and nurses, whole villages, boggled the mind.

Percy held her hands out to keep the door open, the light within and surrounding her making her a bonfire of moonlight; silver, eerie, and raging. Her arm shook as the air resisted the rent they had created, wanting to snap closed. A door like this was the most unnatural of things, but this many dead, too, was unnatural . . . One by one, wisps wafted up toward that wide, dark unknown. Sometimes they turned. Sometimes they reached out arms to others floating that same, shimmering direction. The sadness of this dug under Violet's skin like a mine under the line; the needing to reach out toward something, someone, some soul that made any of this all right, that made anything make sense. That made anything more bearable.

The portal seeming to hold, Percy let her arms go in an exhausted collapse, turning away. "Tell me when it is over. When I need to close it. Or . . . if I even do. Or can. Does it ever stop, this terrible ugliness? How can humans have come to this?"

Suddenly, a tall, robed figure stood at the foreground of the portal.

"Take care, you who wield the old forces," a rasping old voice boomed across the field. The fighting unfortunately didn't stop or notice. The being continued, black cloth raising as if lifted by invisible arms, a shrouded reaper without a scythe. "Did your Muses not bid you seek balance?"

Alexi stepped forward to address the figure but Percy called a response instead.

"Yes, balance between living and dead is always what we seek. Here, there are too many dead. The mortal world can only handle so many ghosts before it goes mad, and what madness is already here?" Percy gestured to the field.

The robed figure mirrored her movement, indicating the Whisper-world. "Here, too."

"How, then, can we manage?" Percy asked.

"And who are you?" Alexi barked.

"Think of what built this place, mortals," the figure rasped. "What it needs to rebuild or grow. You'd best think on it, as the walls won't hold."

The figure floated away, lost to view by another wave of spirits rising into the void like mist clouding up from a lake.

"If the walls won't hold, and there are too many dead there, too, it would be as if the war we'd fought was pointless; the mortal world would still be awash in the dead, choking out the living in a spectral smog," Rebecca murmured. "Why even have a Whisper-world at all if a realm once created and defined by gods has the mortal limitations of space?"

"I don't know," Percy said slowly.

"What do we do now?" Josephine asked, her own face wet with tears, clutching her husband's hands, looking out over her beloved France, carved up and bloody.

"We will have to do this again," Percy said softly.

"And again," Violet added. "As much as will hold. They must make room."

But, Violet wondered, for how long would their fixes hold? Was there something they could put in place? They couldn't stay here, this wasn't the only area of intense engagement or heavy casualties.

Looking up again, she took a moment to send additional tendrils of blue fire, entwined with goddess light, toward the portal. As she extended the power, she felt the little poultice of Lord Black's protective magic warm upon her sternum, energizing her and magnifying the luminosity of the light. Its wisps didn't fade; instead they nestled in the corners on the portal, a warding barrier of joined powers. This gave her an idea as to how safeguards could continue on without them.

Looking down at the arrangements below, Alexi gestured to his fellows urgently, indicating an evident change in the conflict.

"Leave the portal in place. But as fighting appears to be shifting, we must leave this ridge. Guns will turn to this crest."

"Arm them with angels," Josephine insisted, patting the small leather pouch over her shoulder.

From their vantage point, the group could descend back away from the front lines and around behind.

Once Violet had consulted a map, the Guard moved in a tight cluster, the Rychmans' light shielding them as they moved behind the lines to supply chains and medic clearings. From there, they gave out gifts. Elijah's power of persuasion, continuing to prove more powerful than Violet's allotment, insisted that the men carry his wife's talismanic angels to their superiors, so that everyone might see that someone had sent them an angel.

Josephine watched, hands clasped, biting her lip as each of her words was taken into shaking, shell-shocked hands of battle-weary soldiers with graciousness and awe, the power of her Muse imbued into each paper. Michael offered the gift of the Heart to as many as he could before his shoulders slumped and Rebecca drew him away, into an embrace. "That's all we can do today."

"I drew and painted angels constantly for the Grand Work," Josephine explained to Violet as the last of the day's art was passed along and they returned to a muddy path, her eyes wide. "They were always a part of our ritual; frames I would hang in the homes of the possessed or on the walls of haunted places."

"I know. I didn't see them before, I only saw an illusion of boring historical scenes. But when I took on the powers in Athens, all those frames changed and your sentinels were revealed. They're *beautiful*," Violet said, linking her arm in her aunt's frail one.

"Never did my guardian angels carry so much meaning as now . . ." She bowed her head and began murmuring benedictions in French.

"I'm sure its weight now is unlike anything else," Violet reassured, worried for her aunt's mind, thinking of the crying Muse of Art at her bedside, when it needed to be shown hope. While the Muses said they would need to come and go from their hosts during this trying time, it was clear Art was present now in the aura Josephine wore. Still, Violet extended her own phoenix fire around Josephine and her thin shoulders, hunched with worry, seemed to ease.

Michael picked up on this act and with what little energy he had left, as they walked back well behind supply lines toward their inn, he distributed his precious gift of buoying the heart; a hand on each shoulder to smooth furrowed brows.

Violet stepped up to her parents, who were murmuring intently to one another about the events of the day.

"What was that figure at the threshold?" her father asked. "It couldn't be Darkness come again—"

"I'd *know*," Percy retorted. "We'd know. Many old things survive there, calcified spirits that were institutions of the place; one of them must have stepped up and now thinks it knows its ways better than me."

"But doesn't it, now?" Alexi countered. "It's been over twenty years since you've been in. It may be right about its limits."

"What do we do then," her mother despaired, "just let the Whisper-world sit parallel to this world, both of them choked with the dead, both of them stewing in rot for a lack of breath between? Those sad corridors *must* make room."

"It bid us remember how it was built . . ."

"By sacrifice, blood and fire, the thunderclaps of a grieving goddess's light!" Percy ground out bitter words through clenched teeth. "Is this earth not filled with sacrifice enough? The Whisper-world must take on some of that burden of these poisoned, bloody fields."

Violet thought about again mentioning the Muses' warning of sacrifice. How much would the Whisper-world ask for in order to level the cosmic scales of spiritual health? She also thought about what her mother had said at the chapel. They'd have to go in and fight back out.

ONCE RETURNED, TAKING DUE RECOVERY TIME, VIOLET TOOK to her small room upstairs and lit the glass lantern on a worn wooden desk.

Collapsing in the creaking wooden chair, she stared at the sparse whitewashed room that had seen so many of her tears and worries in such a short time. Dreading these days for years was nothing like the eternity of living them. But she needed to reach out to the man who could help sew up the wounds they would have to open. She pulled out pen and paper from her knapsack, as vital a supply as medicine, and requested aid.

My dear Lord Black,

I, your Delphi, write to you in confidence from the Verdun campaign. You likely have heard by now the ugly numbers, the grave misfortunes of this ongoing battle, sustaining the heaviest losses of any single battle thus far. The mission of my family has always been to mitigate balance between mortal and spirit world. If spirits overrun the earth, mortal minds falter in that unnatural ratio. This war is, frankly, creating too many dead. The numbers defy all other moments in history; plagues, other wars included.

So we began opening portals to what we call the Whisper-world. A silvery purgatory. Not an evil place, but one of sorrow and loss.

At Verdun, a whole sky-field needed to be opened for those poor souls. I'm sure you heard about the wrong caliber of bullet to wire.

Our Guard placed a safety on the portal to make sure the dead can pass into only, but I don't know if it will hold.

What happens when a battle resumes? If a field is taken and retaken? Verdun alone has changed hands more times than I can count, surrounding villages decimated, wiped off the map.

The Ward you gave me, one that bolstered me as I lent fire to the portal, has me wondering if you could fashion one to put in place when battles continue but we must move on. A Ward that might sense spiritual weight; a device to be a trip wire, a pressure valve, to open up the door again and close it? Perhaps your adept craft, and those of your associates, can address this? The light and fire the Guard uses can nestle into objects. I could imbue whatever you would devise.

I will continue to telegraph you our location as we go. If I can

*call I will but I'm unsure of the relay. Something of this nature
is best written and read in secret. We must prepare more fields.
    You and yours are in my heart, with thanks for all your help,*
                                                            Delphi

LORD BLACK RECEIVED THE NOTE FROM RAPID TRANSPORT A
few days after Violet had written it, applied the solution to make
the letter below the greeting visible, and was set alight with ideas.

Abandoning his office for his fine Knightsbridge estate, he and
his beloved Francis sent messages to members of his old Omega
division, asking them to come help. Together they would craft the
valves Miss Violet had requested, to be imbued with powers he
couldn't fathom, but fully supported.

Years after he had given up searching for the ghostly division
working in London, he found himself working with the Guard
after all. All the pots of verdant ivy seemed to perk up at his joy.

"We can make meaning, together, all of us, when death has
none," he murmured, crafting a fresh Ward, pressing leaves of his
homegrown ivy together with herbs, droplets of holy water from
the Anglican church where he was a patron, dabs of blessed oil
from a rabbi friend whose temple enjoyed his quiet protections, a
few sprinkles of loose-leaf tea for a bit of tradition, and grains of
soil from outside Parliament, the voice of their people. He hoped
it, once emblazoned with the Guard's special force, could be the
mediator needed between worlds.

CHAPTER
TWENTY-THREE

FIRST, WILL FELT THE COLD. NEXT, SCUTTLING SOUNDS ALL around him. There was no light in whatever cavernous space he was in, but he could hear the quiet drip of moisture on stone, and in the distance, the echoing, mournful whispers that meant he was still in the world so aptly named.

A spark from a flint lit a torch; the bright, grayscale flames looked odd in this strange netherworld. Other gray-white torches went up in a circle around him, and at the sight of what they revealed, Will held back a gasp.

Before him were shifting forms, dark silhouettes that transformed restlessly, offering glimpses of bits of scale or skin, claw or fang, edges of leathery batlike wings—the stuff of demons and medieval nightmares. Every time Will thought he grasped purchase on their form, something changed, just like the dog's head under the empty throne.

Only one of the four creatures didn't shift, a tall, unseen figure covered in a black shroud.

The closest creature, a scaly being that for an instant had the soft, beautiful face of a Pre-Raphaelite youth, save for its black, unblinking eyes, addressed him. As it spoke, its head became a giant bird's skull, beak and all. Then the seraphim once more.

"Stirring up trouble in our world, are you, mortal?" the creature asked. A long, forked tongue flicked out from its lips. "Born to be a trouble, though you had the chance to be a true leader here. If you'd listened to the voice that since your childhood was leading you to us, you could have been royalty, here. A boon, a gift, to help us into this modern age of yours . . ."

"You know me, then?" Will asked.

"Oh, we recognize the smell of you . . ." the being to the right said with a certain amount of disdain, its face hidden beneath a cowl. Will saw the stretch of a bat's wing become the flutter of a cloak in the torchlight's sharp, unnatural shafts of brightness alternating with shadow. "There's a familiar stench about mortals like you; traitors to this world, always fighting your one chance to belong."

"If you mean the voice that threatened to harm me and my loved ones, that risked my health and sanity? I want no *belonging* there," Will countered. "What do you want with me? Why have you captured me?"

"The Guard overstepped their bounds in destroying the body of our regent, Darkness, and vanquishing his throne," said the creature to the left, its lion head changing to that of a sphinx, its body shifting from two legs to four . . . "In his absence we have tried to maintain a certain order here."

"We defy any effort to make this world any more unstable just because your silly species has to go and kill one another on a heretofore unheard-of scale!" said the creature at the fore. "Yes, we traffic in the dead but we don't want *all* of yours, all at once! Have you seen what's happening? Your precious family is *flooding* us with spirits!"

"Then . . . don't keep them here, let them go on," Will proposed. "This isn't hell, nor is it heaven by the look of it. Let souls go freely where they will, where the goodness of their spirits leads them, or let them slip away to their own darknesses if that is their lot. Bid them try a second chance on earth. Bid them be at peace. Bid them into those spaces in the Far Beyond that lead to an even deeper pit than this. You'll only be overwhelmed if you greedily keep souls."

The tallest form shook its cowl and tsked, a disapproving, rattling sound. "Gazing out the windows your friends so unceremoniously rip open, we can see that our transitional space will be overrun regardless of our efforts. This place was ripped away from the mortal world at a time when populations were smaller, when the world was not capable of such massive death. If we could expand these corridors, we would. But at least we have you as leverage to do so."

Will swallowed hard. He didn't want to be leverage in this world but just as he had to fight the Gorgon in the pit, so was he born for this moment. He spoke with a strong bravado that masked his nerves. "From what I know of the Guard, while I know their duty was only to the mortal world, I can't imagine they would argue balance on either side. Let me present the issue to them."

The being at the fore hissed and gave a hollow chortle. "I highly doubt the Guard would help this place."

"Have you asked?" Will countered. "They're reasonable people." He took a breath and a risk as he dared the creatures before him. "In my short time here," he continued, "I have seen how the woe and melancholy of this place tries to cling to these dead—in some cases literally. Don't be hypocritical. If you don't want to be overrun, do something about the creatures and the shadows feeding on misery. Let souls *pass*."

"To feed on sorrow is in the nature of this place," sniped the creature, clacking its beak.

"You cannot have it both ways." Rage, like Percy and Violet's light, rose in him. "This war is an *epic* hell and my friends are risking their lives to make some kind of positive change, even if it is human nature to be aggressive. You could do the same here."

"The ways of this world are not as mercurial and easily changeable as yours," the being at the fore, clearly the leader, spat in defense. "This place is still healing from your war against it."

"Kill the boy," hissed the rear, shrouded figure. "That's our chance; his blood will open up the corridors and settle the debt they all owe for Darkness's fate . . ."

The figures engulfed Will; one wrapped a viselike claw around his neck, talon just piercing his flesh. Will tried to keep calm even as panic flooded him and he struggled against their hold. He thought of Violet's light, and as he did, there was no more pain.

Panic transformed into euphoria.

If his death could create balance, if his death could open up the limits of this space to any who needed its gray expanse, who was he to stand in the way?

Had there not been murmurs of blood sacrifice here on these stones?

Willing blood on these stones.

"Open me up, then," Will murmured. "Expand your world. If I'm meant to live through this, I will . . . I was raised by forces of resurrection."

After all, if the voice hadn't ever truly died, why should he? Perhaps he was best suited for this world after all. There was a pain, then a sense of a sweet release when he thought of Violet as the shadows closed in.

But wait, before he was made a sacrifice, he wanted to see her one last time.

Strength and desire flooded him, thinking of her light, and he heard a warrior's cry beside him. Good Aodhan. The vise grip eased and Will fled into the shadows, toward flickering Liminal light.

CHAPTER
TWENTY-FOUR

WITH A START, VIOLET WOKE IN THE MIDDLE OF THE NIGHT, hearing Will whisper her name. If he was trying to reach out to her, she opened her heart fully to him. Staring up at the heavens, she opened her arms and murmured, "Yes, my dear, I'm here, take of me, anything you need to keep you safe. We are tied forever . . ."

The feeling of connection eased, like a receding tide, which made Violet ache for him in ways she never had before. "We'll meet again," she murmured to the soul of her twin flame.

She couldn't sleep, so she studied maps and planned their next course.

Violet knew from the start of her journey, from papers and strategy notes Lord Black had included for her, that a series of enormous pushes the likes of which the war had yet to see were planned for the Somme if the area didn't come under Allied control, with British forces supplementing French troops on the northern side of the constantly shifting French and German line.

Because an escalation like this, with countless more troops, would choke the fields with dead similarly to Verdun, though they prayed not in such overwhelming numbers, Violet and her family, conferring on their next plan at breakfast, agreed they needed to open up the Whisper-world closer to this Allied initiative.

They gathered their things, left more than a fair sum for their worried innkeeper, Aunt Josephine having penned him an angel she tacked over his front desk. He was staring at it so fixedly no one had the heart to tear him away to say goodbye.

RIDING CHARTERED HORSES, THEIR TEAM PAUSED NORTH AT Charny, a small town solidly within French territory, though the entire, quaint Alsace-Lorraine region had been so hotly contested since the last century. Though no longer quite so near the front, they had moved on to the next area of heaviest fighting and were still all too aware of the war: distant shelling, transport attacks, heavy artillery fire, and the explosions of mines.

They had paused to rest in an inn on a bank of the Meuse, as had become their habit. They always gained renewal and joy from their connection to this river, named for the ancient powers that filled and supported them. Violet noticed that while her mother had calmed herself from before, she still was slightly activated in a subtle glow, her eyes flickering toward any sharp sound. There was no undoing the damage to nerves that war frayed.

A glass of wine in, Violet addressed the Somme push. While they were the only people in the downstairs dining hall, Elijah kept an ear and eye for anyone on staff or premises who might overhear or find them too interesting.

"Throwing bodies at the enemy without regard to each one being a life," Alexi said through clenched teeth. "An *inhuman* strategy."

Her father had been quieter during this whole affair than Violet had expected, but she supposed he was conserving every last scrap of energy so he could wind his fire around them as a part of their shielding. With his usual bombastic nature so restrained, his magnetic presence dimmed, he seemed but an aging man trying to keep his loved ones alive.

The determined desperation on his face made Violet put a hand to her heart to stop the ache. She didn't address this with him or offer him sentiment. He was too proud.

Mum would soothe him best, and she did, tucking herself under his arm at any moment of rest or transition. While Percy made it look as though she were turning to him for comfort and protection, Violet could see he benefited as much as she did; the strain eased at the corner of his mouth, the harrowed look on his distinguished face softened.

Her touch seemed his only balm, the silent exchange of her light with his fire. Violet resolved to burn even brighter, to afford him more ease. He was a veteran, she the fresh reserves.

She thought countless times to apologize but stopped herself. What they were gifted with, whether by prophecy or will, placed them here. It had become clear that parting the Whisper-world to thin the flooding dead was their collective mission, not something she could have done on her own. Though she had known before the others that she would be called to war, the rest had not hesitated to answer their own summons. Still, she wished she could have enough strength, enough gifts to spare them these burdens.

But then, they would not be her family if they had hung back. They were career soldiers of spectral offices and she would not disrespect them by apologizing for what they were experiencing.

In the morning they made their way north by hired carriages, seeking a British regiment added to the upper line. Ironically it was the Reserve Army that Violet sought out, the unit Will was supposed to have reported to. She said a little prayer for him and felt within her heart for the tie between them. It beat softly, far away, but strong. Somehow she knew he was fighting for her in his own way, through strange and difficult territory.

Rebecca, led by her Intuition, guided the party to the officers' quarters. Once they showed their clearances to the corporal on duty, a man named Clemens, and Elijah dazed him with a wave of his hand, they were able to study the map laid out on the officers' table.

"How are your numbers, Corporal Clemens?" Violet asked. They needed to know what to expect, how much to rip open . . .

The man laughed hollowly, responsive under Elijah's control, in a state where he was open and brutally honest.

"I have heard there were heavy losses," Violet pressed.

"Heavy." His chuckle turned into a cough. "That's one word. We lost over fifty-seven *thousand* men day one of this month, miss. All numb from there on."

Violet pretended she didn't hear her mother react in a gasp. There would be a thick fog of dead awaiting them at the front, worse than they'd imagined.

"I'm sorry," she replied, meaning it. Clemens shuddered on the stool where Elijah had bid him sit. Seeing this, Elijah drew from behind his impractical, satin neckwear the brass locket that sparked with what was clearly phoenix fire. Violet had not seen the bit of jewelry up close, but it seemed to strengthen Elijah's powers.

"Good luck, whatever you're doing," the corporal murmured, his trance renewed. "Don't get shot. I don't know what Rawlinson was thinking, that *Bon Dieu* would save all his men with some divine hand? Just kept pushing them up and out, up and over, wave after countless wave while the Maxims, line after line, mowed them down with Death's wide scythe . . ." The man began to cry.

Michael moved to him and murmured a benediction, bestowing comfort with the touch of his hand, while Violet, shaken, turned to the map. Her father was poring over the lines and positions, having tuned out from the corporal's pain, while her mother stared at Clemens in pity and horror.

Josephine had managed a new set of drawings; this time her angels were headed by a dove of peace and below, a fleur-de-lis.

She produced one now from the messenger bag slung over her shoulder and inspected the wall. Finding an empty peg next to a battered wooden crucifix—Jesus's body a bit askew—she hung the angel, lit with Art's deft hand, beside. The carved Jesus, as if in response, righted itself on the cross of its own accord. Josephine stepped back, eyes widening in wonder.

The energy in the room shifted, the oppression lightening. "Take care, Corporal," Violet murmured, directing just a pinch of light, cast from fingertip, to nestle over his rank and insignia. He sat straighter.

The Guard focused on the map. Alexi placed his finger on an unclaimed hilltop adjacent to the main press, at the edge of the line the Brits were holding. "Once more unto the breach," he murmured. Taking a second, smaller map from the officers' quarters for reference, he strode out of the tent, the others following.

They climbed the hill in silence. A wide swath of No Man's Land lay in the distance, like a muddy, jaggedly cut riverbed littered with the waste of war and saturated with blood. To one side they glimpsed a supply line of horses carrying cannons and ammunition.

Percy, Alexi, and Violet's light and fire were extended around the Guard like a large luminous tent. The Muses within her extended family were at full, each of their hands out to the side like the pictures of holy icons as they climbed to the crest.

For her family's sake, Violet was grateful that the bodies of the dead had been collected from the barbed wire. It was likely that countless bodies lay just under the soil, buried hastily and shallowly.

The stench of death was unmistakable in the air.

The second unmistakable atmospheric quality was the cloud of gray spirits. Clemens had said fifty-seven *thousand*, British alone, in just one day, and that had been weeks earlier. The numbers had only grown since then. The dead floated in clustered pools, acting partly like dense clouds, partly like leaves stirring on a breeze.

Percy and Violet shared a look and, together, they cast their arms forward in violent release. Another wide swath of sky opened to reveal the deep charcoal Whisper-world corridors that lay parallel to the mortal world. Alexi cast additional tendrils of light to nestle around the edges of the portal as a guard.

With this many dead, they couldn't wait for the souls to slip away one by one into Whisper-world corridors of their own accord in a private ceremony, a small door blinking open for one soul and winking shut in the balance of life cycles. Percy's and Violet's arms shook from holding open what Violet deemed to be unnatural and surreal, driven by this morbid necessity of volume. The thousands of spirits hesitated, unsure of what they were seeing before them. Michael said prayers over the field and turned to his wife for her unique amplification.

Rebecca called out to the clouds of the dead, Intuition bidding her give forth another poetic benediction to the Allied forces. "Heed this from your fellow fallen soldier, young Mr. Brooke . . ."

> *If I should die, think only this of me:*
> *That there's some corner of a foreign field*
> *That is forever England.*

The headmistress's voice trembled. "Go on, brave lads."

This eased many who had hesitated crossing the threshold, just another No Man's Land, and there was a growing willingness to go forward into this great unknown.

Violet suddenly noticed that on the hill across from them, a German heavy artillery squad had set up a Maxim, a multichambered machine gun that trailed ammunition out its side like a stock ticker that dispensed death instead of numbers. A cannon was rolled into place nearby, presumably to pick at the edges of the supply convoy.

Farther down the ridge, a British team were bringing up a cannon and a box of shells. They were visible to the Guard, but thanks to the angle, they would not yet be seen by the Germans.

Realizing her family would need to retreat soon, before they were caught in the inevitable crossfire, Violet spoke.

"Go on," she said to the spirits in the sky. "The field is worsening and we're running out of time."

The Guard hadn't seen Healing since their last efforts at sending the dead across, but now it returned, clearly having sensed their efforts. Its darting, luminous form, tinged with yellow yet refracting every color, herded the ghosts up toward the Whisperworld. Floating up, they looked like a grayscale inversion of descending angels.

A shot whizzed by, grazing the edges of their barrier. While the Germans likely didn't see them precisely, someone had glimpsed enough to draw their fire.

"Now would be the time to pray," Michael stated, clearly strained by his effort to keep his cohorts sane and their hearts open, so they could wield the light most rapidly. "For anything and everything you hold sacred to help us."

Violet redoubled her efforts, both arms open wide, throwing her whole body into the act, trying to effect a greater spread of the shields. She was exhausted, her muscles on fire, but panic fueled her. When her father did the same, an explosion of blue fire surrounded them all, and he wobbled on his feet from the ricochet. Rebecca moved quickly to hold him up on one side, Percy on the other.

Alexi looked at the German unit. "They're repositioning. The Maxim is turning this way. And the cannon. We *can't* stay." Sweat poured off his brow as he cast yet another wave of concentric blue fire.

"There's still too many dead," Percy stated. She strained, tugging at the air, trying to widen the portal even further. "I need time."

"Time we don't have," Rebecca countered.

"Are we trapped?" Josephine asked quietly, looking around. Only then did Violet notice she'd traced the outline of an angel in the mud with a stick and even its outlines of grit and soil appeared lighted.

Violet noticed the locket around Elijah's neck was suddenly ablaze and he stared down at it in wonder.

"No, we're not trapped!" Elijah cried. "We'll take that help most certainly," he said to the fire as it licked around him and down his arm, as if another extension of the mythic bird had come to life in a flapping of fiery wings. "Perhaps our dear Belle has lent us her prayers on this day, far across the Channel. Oh!" he said again, grabbing Violet's arm and turning her to face what had opened up behind her. "Look!"

A narrow door to the Whisper-world, just wide enough for their group to enter single file, had opened behind them. Across the corridor, a bright green field. England.

"So that's what the whole Grimsby business was about," Elijah stated. "Look everyone! Keep up your strengths but look! Don't close every door . . ."

Everyone turned to him.

"But . . ." Michael began hesitantly. "We're not supposed to go *through*. Only Percy has been inside the Whisper-world safely, Rebecca only for a moment . . ."

"We do see the other side," Rebecca countered. "The Whisper-world can't affect you unless you let it."

A figure across the way stepped into view, holding up a hand. "Belle!" Elijah called.

A second shot tore the fabric of Violet's nurse's uniform and clipped her bicep. She bit back a curse, dug in her pocket for gauze, and tucked it against the wound, sealing it as much as she could with the small amount of her healing gift. Done, she adjusted the armband over the small wound, turning it so the bloody part was on the underside of her arm, hiding it from her mother's sight.

Next, she reached under the folds of her nurse's apron and drew her pistol. Her right arm screamed in pain from the injury as she lifted the weapon, bracing her right wrist with her left hand. It seemed likely the opposite hill was too far away, but she'd shot for distance many times, even with a handgun.

"Violet, what are you—" Percy gasped beside her.

"This is a war and we're being shot at!" She aimed for the far side of the Maxim and fired twice. The men ducked, then brought the machine gun to bear. "Well, damn."

Rebecca placed her hands gently on Percy and Alexi, who were still radiating power toward the field. "We must go, we cannot hold this line."

"But my country . . ." Josie murmured. "Our light was helping heal both the air and the soil, didn't you see? Will we abandon it?"

Violet thought back to that pit in Verdun, when the light of the Guard issued forth from the cracks in the earth, helping reverse some of the poison the Gorgon had laid there. Perhaps she could give one last push to send light into the carved-up earth before they retreated, in hopes of helping the living and the dead.

Returning her weapon to its hiding place, she reached within herself, every muscle in her body aching, every sense strained, every fiber of her being stretched and stinging. She thought of the day at Athens when powers first came alive in her, and this sense memory doubled the light within her. The prismatic effect of the Muses entwined within her widened, and she sent this refreshed blaze directly out like its own cannonball, directed to the trench itself, where it landed like a mine blast, but in light and a chord of heavenly music. The light spread down the trench like a dam bursting, sending water down a sharply twisting river.

There it would go, healing into the future, all the way across every line and border.

"The light," Violet exclaimed, grabbing Josephine's cold hand, "will heal what was poisoned, it will just take time." Violet wiped a damp sleeve over her sweat-soaked brow, a dizzy spell threatening to send her to the ground. "Now we *must go.*"

The group moved toward the hovering portal.

"Steel yourselves, all," Percy warned. "Don't wander. Focus only on England ahead, don't look around. The Whisper-world's power is in making you feel powerless. Do not give that place pause. Do not attract undue attention. The world will likely awaken to our presence—we won't be strangers long, and there's now a cross-breeze created in this portal. Am I perfectly clear?"

The company, all pale and nervous, nodded. But a tattoo of gunfire spraying dirt across their hill had them jumping through.

The light and fire still encompassed them but lessened when they all stepped into the Whisper-world. Elijah lingered at the threshold, waiting for Josephine, who was still staring out at the field of wretched woe.

"Look, Elijah," she said through her tears. "The light. The light of the Guard, love and fire. It *is* spreading across the ground, slowly, isn't it? Wounds do heal." She offered kisses, her hands tinged with Art's deep light, blowing them out toward the distance.

"Yes, love, now come away . . ." Elijah said with mounting concern.

"But I've a prophecy, too," she murmured. "Dreams I never told anyone."

"Auntie, come!" Violet gestured them ahead, into the wet, slate-gray corridor of stone where silvery mist hung in the air as if it were spider-silk hanging before them in intricate wisps and then dissembling as their mortal bodies stepped through.

The Whisper-world, this close, gave honor to its name, the air, the wind, the breeze, everything around them whispered, beckoned, and mourned, in a growing, cresting sound. The shadows were deep and all of them moved.

Violet was in awe of the realm.

Rebecca and Michael were paces ahead, hurrying through the corridor fastest, the first to make it to the threshold where Belle helped them down.

Percy and Alexi ahead, Violet in the middle, she gestured emphatically for Elijah and Josie to come away from the French side and join her, when the little illumination the corridors shed went out and an enormous shadow blocked their path and all the light.

"You send all the dead through and you dare to think *you* can pass, too?" came a brittle voice from the shadows.

"Who's there?" Alexi called, his hands bursting bright with blue fire. Shadows in the murk shrank back, and the fire illuminated the same tall, shrouded figure that had cautioned them from the portal before. The whispers of the world were growing louder, cacophonous, sounds of woe and confusion echoing through the stone corridors in a maddening din.

"Who are you?" Violet demanded, stepping forward in lockstep with her mother, both of their lights firing up from within them. They had already broken their cardinal rule of not attracting attention in the Whisper-world. The gray realm reacted in rattling hisses and scuttling shadows that slithered about, nipping at the hems of their pants and skirts.

"If you rule in Darkness's stead," Percy continued, "all we ask is a peaceable solution to what I'm sure neither of the worlds had ever bargained for."

"I am one of four Keepers here and it isn't in our power to expand the depths. Responsibility is shared. Look," the spirit demanded. "The walls are straining." The shroud moved to point to a fissure in the stone. Grit was falling from its crack as if the whole world vibrated from an ongoing tremor.

Violet looked behind at where there still was light, the portal still to France. Josephine still stood at the threshold, staring between the shadows and the mud as if trying to judge a distance, Elijah whispering to her to come away, although the spirit blocking their path had Elijah hovering on the edge of retreat.

"We *told you* sacrifice is required," the shroud growled. "Else we'll have to send all your poor dead right back out again, cover France and beyond with all the excess we can't house."

"But sacrifice is everywhere," Violet declared, exasperated, her arm throbbing in a fresh roiling wave of pain. She tried to muster a flicker of healing light, pressing it down, taking an edge off the burn.

In a frightening moment, the being had closed the distance between Violet and Percy, and a sharp, unseen point was being driven into both their breasts, just below the hollows of their throats.

"Our limits are governed by the blood of the divine!" the entity gurgled. "The blood of divine hosts will do! If you're so committed to expanding the worlds to spare the minds of an already mad world, then you won't mind sacrificing yourselves to save the surface of your precious earth. We tried to take your beloved little Will, but he weaseled out of our grasp. But taking *our Lady* is even better . . ."

The driving point, a burning claw, was an overwhelming pain

and Violet couldn't reach for her gun, she couldn't move for the agony. She gritted her teeth as her mother cried out.

"Take me," Alexi barked, stepping forward and grabbing at his wife and daughter, trying to pull them away, but invisible claws held them fast. "Phoenix was your first casualty! Don't you want to best him again? I'm right here!"

Violet couldn't turn her head to look but she was suddenly awash in a blaze of blue fire that hit the being squarely in the center of its winding-sheets.

Cerulean fire made concussive contact with incorporeal shadow. The claws retracted and mother and daughter were thrown violently against the wet stone wall. Another surge of agony from this collision against her wound; the murk of the Whisper-world was seeping in, gnawing at her skin like a pestilent insect. But Violet knew her body was strong, having prepared for strain and toil. Her mother threw an arm forward in a punch of light raining down in a reinforcement for the line of phoenix fire.

Just after the blow of goddess light landed and the shrouded form seemed to retreat, a movement caught Violet's eye and she turned to see that Josephine was even nearer to the French threshold again, her arms open. "Auntie!" Violet admonished, rushing back for her, Elijah at her heels.

"I've seen this moment. I understand. I *am* the angel. *Pour la France*," she murmured, stepping one foot on mortal soil and one still in the Whisper-world. Elijah did the same, but enfolded Josephine with his own body.

The screaming sound of a shell. Violet anticipated a dreadful secondary blast of sound and concussive force and so she used what felt like the last of her energy to rip loose a burst of her own light and fire, throwing the three back into the Whisper-world fully. There was a cloud of ash and smoke that accosted Violet's lungs and she coughed, but her power had a magnified and rippling effect. It was as if just that one casting of her unique mixture of goddess and phoenix light had brightened the whole interior of the realm.

Violet reached out for her aunt and uncle but struggled for purchase; the portal to France was now obscured entirely by smoke. Josephine and Elijah were finally visible through the smoke and they turned back to the corridor, moving ahead to England.

The floor was suddenly so much slicker and Violet nearly slipped.

The walls continued to undulate as though they were made of fabric. The vibrating tremor now steadied, and it sounded to Violet as though a thousand doors were being opened on rusty hinges. A horrid fascination gripped Violet, to see this; the world was *changing*.

But pain sharpened her focus and she reached out for Josephine and Elijah, pushing them forward. As she stepped over the threshold to Grimsby, her hands met only air, and she tumbled down onto the green field beyond . . .

CHAPTER
TWENTY-FIVE

FOR A DREADFUL MOMENT, HOVERING AT THE THRESHOLD TO Grimsby, Percy had lost track of Violet in the explosions of light and ash, in the mist, the murk, and the quaking stone, but she was flooded with relief as she saw her daughter tumble through, blown by the buffeting wind of phoenix fire, Alexi forcing them all through with his power. Though Violet had her hands on Josephine and Elijah, as if pushing them through, she suddenly fell, and Percy tried to steady herself on Alexi so they didn't all fall in a messy tumble onto the verdant grass of Grimsby beyond, such a welcome color of life compared to the muddy gray and blackened earth they'd left behind.

Her light fully radiant, Percy righted herself, Rebecca and Michael immediately at her side to steady her. But there was no longer any Keeper in the corridor, only the trembling Whisper-world. Did it still threaten to collapse? Was she wrong in thinking it looked wider, brighter?

Elijah and Josephine were the last to exit, even though Violet had tumbled out with them; they still stood at the threshold of the Whisper-world.

No, they didn't stand. They floated.

Grayscale. On either side of them floated their Muses, Memory and Art, disembodied.

"Darlings . . ." Percy murmured, her heart faltering, her stomach plummeting in a sickening lurch as she stared at two forms that had taken on the distinct pallor and properties of spirits.

"Look at what I managed," Josephine murmured. "I did it. I *became* the angel." She bit her lip, grabbed Elijah's hand, and gestured around her.

The Whisper-world's constant gray had indeed lightened. The corridors themselves seemed almost luminous, as if lamps had been lit behind slate curtains, and down the endless, winding corridors it almost looked as though a dusky dawn were breaking. A pulse of white and blue light, phoenix and goddess fire, seemed to bounce down lengthened corridors. The cacophony of the dead settled back into the whispers the world was known for.

There was a single, solitary color visible amidst this lightening of the realm, bright streaks along the stone floor. Amidst all the grayscale flowed a flash of red forming a shape.

The angle of the corridor was such that Percy could see the shape being made; crimson rivulets stretched into a striking outline.

An angel in blood.

The form of Josephine's wartime angel was spread out onto the Whisper-world stones.

"The Whisper-world expands after all," murmured Memory. "Well done, beloveds. Stay safe, now." Art gestured to its colleague and the forms disappeared into Whisper-world shadow before the Guard could ask anything further of them.

The corridor between Grimsby and France had reduced to a mere two feet instead of a long hall, the smoke of the bomb blast having cleared. Along the hilltop they'd come from stretched the same bloody outline of the angel across the jagged soil, but from its sword snaked light.

"I had to," Josie explained, floating at the portal's edge. In the bright sun of Grimsby, her lovely form was now luminous grayscale, transformed, dressed in one of her favorite old ball gowns; death's garb was always a sentimental choice. "Sacrifice. Blood and fire. It meant more from me, for my country."

"No . . ." Rebecca murmured. "No, no, no, no . . . this cannot be . . ." She rushed forward and tried to grab Josephine by the arms, but her hands went through her old friend's body. Michael went to her and enfolded her as she collapsed against him.

Alexi put his face in his hands and doubled over in the grass.

Belle stood to the side of the portal, her hands over her mouth.

"We felt no pain, friends, our bodies were immediately dust from heaven's fire, our ash swept into the Whisper-world, food for its growth." Elijah addressed his fellows from the threshold. He stood there so he could be heard. The moment he stepped across, only Percy would be able to hear him. "I was ready. I've been ready ever since I made this door, since our turn at prophecy was revealed. How blessed is our company to *know* that death is not the end?"

"I'm so sorry," Alexi cried, still kneeling in the grass. "That I was not strong enough—I thought you were right with us—"

"As did I," Violet cried. "I *shielded* you, I thought—"

"No," Josie exclaimed. "It was my choice! *Pour la France!* For each world we are beholden to. Elijah didn't have to do the same but I knew I could never stop him from loving me to the end," she said, and turned and pressed her ashen lips to his before turning back to her fellows. "Alexi . . . look at me."

He did.

"You've always been our leader," she continued gently, "but you've always taken on too much that wasn't your responsibility. I chose to be the sacrifice demanded of us. Now the Whisper-world expands with willing living blood and the sanity of my nation, and all affected by this terrible onslaught, might be helped. The dead will have someplace to go. The living may live less haunted."

"I should have foreseen—" Violet mourned.

"You did, Violet, that's how I knew what to do. I have lived into this angel, you wise visionary."

Percy recalled hearing Violet's murmur while watching Josie drawing. She watched her daughter's face, harrowed, guilty, awestruck. And then, suddenly, Violet was staring through and past them, tears in her eyes. Was she seeing something Percy didn't?

Percy turned back to the portal, looking again into the Whisper-world, following her daughter's line of sight. A flash of a familiar face, quickly covered by a dusty black veil.

"Will!" Violet cried. "*There* you are!" She threw herself into the Whisper-world after him.

"Violet!" Percy responded with the same urgency, following her daughter through the portal.

Glancing back, she gave her husband an apologetic look and saw him as he tried to follow them, an anguished sound strangling from his throat, but Rebecca and Michael seized him and forced him back.

Even phoenix fire that clung to his body held up a luminous hand, blocking him. Percy was suited to travel deep into this world, her husband was not. She knew Rebecca and Michael would take good care of him, and all their Guard who now were spirits, too.

Percy turned back toward the gray depths, her heart aching for all that had just transpired and worried for what her children would need ahead.

"WILL!" VIOLET CALLED. BEHIND HER WAS THE THRESHOLD TO Grimsby, bright and clear. All around her was moist darkness. She had leapt in, driven only by instinct and panic. This war and these forces could not take Will, too.

"Shh, my dear," her mother said, startling her—Violet had not realized Percy was there. "Remember what I said. This isn't the place to announce yourself. Whatever blocked us before won't like us being back."

"Mum," Violet admonished, "you didn't need to come in after me." She placed her hand on her mother's, noticing how markedly colder skin was here.

"I was built to weather this place," Percy insisted. "You don't know what to expect and I'm not leaving you here alone. It's because of me that this place has a hold on you and Will to begin with."

They stood in a long, dim, charcoal-slate corridor; the walls ran with narrow rivulets of moisture that might as well have been tears, weeping walls that made Violet shudder.

"I saw Will," Violet insisted. "I think he was trying to reach me but something dragged him away . . . Oh, God, please tell me he isn't dead."

"His mother wasn't when she was in here. I trust his body is healthy and sleeping. Now proceed quietly and with caution. The magic that got the Guard through to Grimsby cut out many of this world's traps but I don't know how many of the old ones still remain."

Almost as if on cue, a rush of water came around the corner of the corridor. Crests of frothy foam appeared, sharp as teeth, chattering and cackling. Violet stepped up onto a jutting rock, carrying her mother with her. The eddy passed beneath them, stray bones floating by. The river of woe swept the detritus of decay along on mysterious currents to estuaries unknown.

Where Violet's injured arm was pressed to the wet rock, the gash on her bicep stung again unbearably, as if the moisture seeping through the sleeve of her dress also had teeth. Her wound was now Whisper-world infected. She clamped back on a cry of pain, not wanting her mother to know she was still hurt.

When the water ebbed, the women resumed their search.

"This place is *entirely* surreal," Violet stated, trying to take her mind off the pain.

"It is partly dream, separate from our reality, but very much of its own mind . . ."

A thunderous sound came from ahead of them at the intersection of two corridors. A battalion of grayscale soldiers marched past, likely fresh from the Somme, the damp floors no different from those of the wet trenches, beings of habit even in death, marching into some unknown battle of the soul.

The stone walls around them shifted and parted, revealing the core of the Whisper-world. The overwhelming, echoing space was a limitless cathedral nave of stone, distant arches like a gray rib cage lifting into shadowed heights. A center walkway divided a rushing river; a dais set before a stone tower stood at the end of the walkway, a pearlescent sheen over its gray stone.

"Ah, yes," Percy said, her tone steel. "Here I am again at the heart of the Whisper-world. But I see now that its surfaces are brighter, broader, more open, for what Josie and Elijah did—" Her voice broke.

Violet took her mother's hand. "There will be time enough for grief, Mum."

Her mother nodded and continued explaining her surroundings. "That was once Darkness's throne," she said, gesturing at a fabric-draped mass on the dais. "What sits there now, I shudder to think . . ."

"You don't think much," said the same rasping voice that had been taunting and making demands of them. The voice was everywhere around them, echoing off every stone. "Your kind just *feels*. Reacts. If mortals were capable of true thought beyond themselves—"

"Two of my kind just bled all over these stones, giving their lives for the sake of both worlds," Percy said, her voice breaking as she barreled on. "Don't you *dare* say another word about self-ishness. If you're going to admonish, reveal yourself!" Percy commanded, her inner light brightening.

The mass before them shifted. What was fabric became large, leathery wings, then mist, then feathery plumes, then thick black cloaks. At the fore stood the unshifting shroud. The three figures behind were changeable; chimerical forms transforming between many recognizable parts of creatures of lore, a dizzying vision of rotating parts, and at the center of the mass stood Will, hands behind his back, a wide claw over his mouth. Violet visibly suppressed a reaction and Percy squeezed her hand.

"If you'd like your friend to live," replied the voice, "for his roaming spirit to return again to his body, you will agree to the truce."

"Truce?" Percy asked. "Are *we* at war with *you*? I didn't think so, not anymore. Believe me, we want no more war. Who *are* you?"

Violet stared at Will. He stared back. Stay strong, she thought, willing him to hear her. Her own light brightened.

Violet realized she had a hand on her gun. Useless in this world. Perhaps her small knife in its forearm harness. She could draw blood again, expand these stones . . .

Another figure rushed up to the side of the dais as if he'd been running the whole Whisper-world over. Violet recognized him as Jane's Aodhan, the tall Celt, an ancient Guard healer who had been vital to their cause.

"Leave this young man alone," Aodhan called to the figures. "You steal him from my watch only to torture him?"

"Our concern," the figure clarified at the fore, shielded in a cowl and robes, hands flickering between scaled digits and curved talons, "remains balance. You have overrun us here and while yes, now there is more room, now there is more *misery*. The unprecedented horrors of this war oppress and terrify beyond belief.

We will not be punished for the mortal mess of your wars indefinitely."

"Then let the spirits *go*," Percy replied. "This world's instinct, its compulsion, is to hold onto melancholy, regret, envy, and bitterness. *That* was my enemy's food, and he was greedy, sending countless spirits into the mortal world to feed on unrest. Relinquish that diet. Especially now that there's so much more of it."

The forms stared, squirmed, shifted. The being holding Will lowered its claw. There was a dreadful silence.

"I said the same thing," Will stated. "I freed myself but they snatched me back again. I'm not sure they know *how* to let go, Mrs. Rychman," Will said softly. "Can we help them do so?"

"It used to be . . . long ago . . ." explained the tall form, in a tone that carried with it eons of exhaustion, "that the queen of these parts would . . . manage the balance on her own. When she was here."

There was a strained pause. A form to Will's side, looking for all the world like the grim reaper in a hulking cowl, stretched a skeletal animal's claw out from its billowing black robes in a searching gesture, as if grasping for words.

"We've not her gifts," the Keeper continued, "and we do not have the force to send spirits out into your world like Darkness did."

"We are just . . . lost monsters with no other place to belong," came the quietest of the voices, a birdlike creature before it was batlike. "We don't want to rule as Darkness did; we would like better for this world, and the next. But we don't know how."

"Ah. Well, I have it on good report that your queen is . . . not as she was," Percy said quietly. "What remains of her can help. But hand over my son or you'll get nothing."

The entity clutching Will hesitated a moment before throwing him across the distance with a preternatural strength and he tumbled forward, Violet rushing to grab him. He held onto her tightly as he steadied himself. He looked tired and bruised, but otherwise all right.

Once Percy got a good look at Will, she stepped forward.

Violet watched as her mother closed her eyes, a flash of pain working over her alabaster face, and then a smile, a soft breath of relief. "When the old memories come back, suddenly everything is clear. What you need of your once regent, take of her."

Percy went utterly, blindingly luminous, letting loose the force that had taken her body and forsaken something ancient and divine in order to close a cycle of pain.

It seemed these creatures wanted to close that circle, too. Violet couldn't look directly into that blinding, goddess light, so she turned to Will, who was so beautiful when lit by it.

Will nodded at Violet. "Show them who you are," he murmured. "They used to understand your light and know how to make use of it. Remind them. It's your lineage, too."

Violet moved to stand beside her mother and did the same; joining in full incandescence.

Through the light, she could begin to see . . .

The soldiers, civilians, nurses, all spirits within view were affected. Some reached out, others murmured prayers, hands to hearts. Others responded to the myriad corridors leading off from the main cavern as the halls began to change from a shadowy pitch to something brighter and more colorful. Others responded to the beckoning call of flickering lights and were drawn off into new boundaries, perhaps to start again. Other souls simply faded, slipping away into a blank, peaceful nothingness.

The sounds of change, release, murmurs of joy or of acceptance could be heard in a new cresting wave of whispers, giving the world a sweeter tone than the unsettled chorus of stifled sobs and suffering moans.

"Peace, release. As you will . . ." she murmured to the spirits. Her light could be seen brightening the depths of cavernous shadows into the far reaches, past limitless stone corridors that had recently expanded their capacity.

"You are our Lady and she lives on indeed," said the smallest voice in wonder, its shifting form settling into that of a tall, black, wading bird, a great dark heron. It coursed the dais perimeter, tilting its head toward the shadows. "There is care, here. I can feel their hearts. I recall, once . . . what human beauty was like . . . before we closed our doors and rejected tenderness . . ."

These words struck Violet to the core. Purely on instinct she strode forward, crossing the distance of the landing to stand before the leader of the creatures. Beneath the hood was mist and nightmare, but she stared into its cloudy mass and the harder she looked, the more still a figure it became; an ashen, human-shaped shadow made of onyx flecks, granite dust that floated in a vague form of a body bound by spiderwebs.

"Our family was given a prophecy not to close every door. Through all this pain, through all this suffering, I shall not close my heart. For Mother and for me, the heart has been the most important door of all."

She held open her arms, inviting any of these dramatic, sorrowful things to embrace her.

The leader shifted its cowl as if tilting its head, looking between Violet, her outstretched arms, and Percy. A rasping, choking sound came from its depths. A drop of water, then another, fell onto Violet's skirt. After a moment Violet realized the being had manifest tears and the sound was it weeping.

"Forgive us, my Lady, her legacy." The four knelt in deference. "It has been impossible for us to regain what was lost so long ago. Bitterness clings to us. We do not know how to cast off its potent veil."

The shifting figures settled not into any distinct creature but into the same iridescent, shining, basic bodily forms as the Muses, though these were in varying levels of grayscale.

"Ah," Percy said in understanding. "You're the four who ran away, in ancient times and the dawn of this world. There were *nine* Muses once. You. It's you. Now I understand. There are forces who would like to see you again, I'm sure."

A distinct, resonant voice sounded from the shadows and the whole space around them took on a new, peculiar light, refracted as if tiny gemstones hung in the air, all celestial fire and gentle, harmonic chords ebbing softly against the grating whispers of this grayscale land.

"They know us," Intuition said. "It was we who were blind to our old friends."

Violet turned to see that the Muses had extricated themselves, having left what remained of the Guard and wafted in. Here, the colors of the five Muses were not eliminated. Dulled, but not extinguished; the Whisper-world could not tame their inherent vibrancy.

"At first we were cowards and hid in shame." The leader at the fore could not lift its gray head. Its voice trembled. "We wandered the earth for ages until we slunk here and were allowed to stay, taking on façades, trying to make meaning . . ."

"Cowardice it may have been," Intuition began, "but you rose to the challenge of a kind of balance even we didn't understand. But through blood, fire, and light, forces greater than even we have seen fit that the worlds will continue, beautiful and terrible, with beautiful and terrible mortals and spirits on both sides. As it has always gone. But we'll never let the world be just one thing. May mortals keep surprising us, hopefully for the better."

"Let this be a setting of broken bones. A healing of scars,"

Memory added. "While the wars rage between cultures on Earth, let us not dig any trenches here."

"My lady." The least vocal of the four forgotten Muses approached her, a form of charcoal and pumice, shifting flecks of gleaming obsidian. "We never stopped loving you. If you can believe us. We helped you, sometimes, escape back home to heal. When shadows lifted you up or eased you down into the mortal world when you bled all over the stones . . . that was us."

Memory reached out an incorporeal limb and cupped an amorphous hand around this prodigal Muse.

"Then I thank you and I must trust you, as ancient forces," Percy began carefully, "to work together, now, for the mutual benefit of both worlds."

"Yes," the nine Muses murmured, forming a circle of color and ash at the dais.

Violet reached out and took her mother's hand, then Will's, and they stood a moment, still shining their light.

Aodhan, having stood his watch in the shadows, lifted a hand to Percy when her eyes caught his spectral gaze and he crossed toward them, nodding at the lost Muses, they finally having earned his respect.

"While the keepers may have handled him roughly and ran him about, I never lost track of him, and Jane's vigilant with his body back home."

"Our guardian angels," Percy stated.

A distinct light flickered down a corridor nearest them, beckoning. Violet recognized it as their ally, the light of the Liminal edge.

Percy turned back to the reunited Muses. "Now I take my family safely home, as we've grief to bear and healing to be done. There is still a war on. That is not a matter of debate. Blessings to you all." She bowed her head and they bowed in turn. She turned and walked away, curving around to where the Liminal light was leading, Will, Violet at her side, Aodhan joining them.

"Aodhan, bless you for all you've done," Violet stated.

"He's been my hero against that capricious lot," Will explained. "I'd have been taken down and bled dry or driven mad by those four several times by now if he'd not fought for me."

Aodhan shook his head. "No, it's you who fought for yourself. You stood strong against them and understood them. No one in centuries has been able to be such a diplomat. Only you got them to this place to accept our Lady's succor."

"I can feel them," Will stated. "I understand. I was born to."

He turned away and coughed onto his sleeve. A bit of ash remained there.

As Violet's eyes widened at the sight, Will reassured her. "Seeing as I woke up here for a reason, I've been using being here as a way to force the last of the poison out of me. To fully heal. Your light is the last of it. I'm finally safe for you."

"You always were," Percy and Violet chorused. Percy continued, "No amount of toxin could have eclipsed your noble heart. The fact you fought it always was safety enough. Bringing that understanding here, I've no doubt, helped reunite the Muses. Our diplomat indeed."

Violet had never seen Will look so proud.

The corridor was about to open into the Liminal clearing when a sudden, blasting gale of wind powered over them with a hissing, rattling roar. Violet knew the sound, and as the hissing drew close, Will tensed, his eyes going wide. His expressive face showcased equal rage and fear.

"No," he murmured, and in that, Violet heard the little boy who had grown up fighting this monster and was desperate to be rid of it.

Violet reached out a glowing hand, lit with all the powers the Muses had granted her, and cupped Will's cheek. He leaned into her touch, bolstered by her raw power.

"We're done here," Violet called out to the rattling shadows. "You won't win in either world."

"When will you learn I'll *never* be done with you!" cried the diminished, splintered voice of their family's eldest enemy, little more than some grit and an echo, a bare idea in this ancient realm she had once nearly ruled. Only the Gorgon's old vendetta seemed to keep this dread thing ticking, clutching the last gasps of pathetic envy.

Percy shuddered as if something were coursing through her. Her vision shifted as her eyes went luminous.

Violet knew this ancient wretch had never beaten her mother yet and could not now. Together their inner forces always bested eternal hate. Will stood beside her, his jaw set, his eyes full of fury, his own fists raised to fight.

"I've told you in every one of those jagged trenches where we've cast our light that *we* are done with *you!*" Percy cried, brightening to full capacity in a wicked flash, as if she were the core of a fork of lightning. "We've reversed your poison across the land," Percy growled, the air around them crackling with ferocity. "You will. Relinquish. Your. Hold. Forever." With a swift backhand, she sent her light out in an arcing whip. Violet, who had been watching closely, mirrored her motions to double the impact.

Accompanied by a thunderclap, a blinding explosion of light that was so like the bombs that had been falling on the mortal plane rocked the whole of the Whisper-world. The ringing echo of it reverberated for a full minute. Even the whispers, the inherent respiration of this land, were blasted silent.

"I will *silence* that old bitch if it's the last thing I do!" Percy shouted.

Violet sputtered out a convulsive laugh. Aodhan and Will echoed her. Percy's cheeks flushed. "I know that's unchristian of me, but I'm *very* weary," she conceded. Everyone laughed harder.

"I've been aching for you to say that for years," Aodhan exclaimed.

The Liminal's grand proscenium arch opened before them. At the top of the arch, where a theater might sport some great finial or angelic flourish, hung a vast clock capable of manipulating mortal time. Behind the Liminal's glassy pane, the murky darkness roiled, like the tumult of ink in water or swirling, thick smoke.

The moment the space caught wind of Percy's light, there was a glowing flicker from within the pitchy fog. Suddenly the surface cleared, showing two images side by side. On one side, Will's body rested peacefully in a white hospital bed, Jane floating at his side. On the other, the remaining Guard comforted each other on Belle's lawn. Josephine and Elijah floated at Michael's side as the Vicar placed a halting hand on Alexi's shoulder and Rebecca stood sentry before the portal to the Whisper-world.

"If I leave with you . . ." Will said, "what happens to my spirit and my body? Will I be whole again?" He tried to sound valiant but fear was evident in his voice.

Aodhan gestured toward the massive arch. "That is a question for the Liminal."

The light of the portal sparked; the images blurred and spun, forming a whirlpool of streaming color. Violet felt a pull upon her body.

"It is ready with an answer," Aodhan stated. "Go on, friends. Go on and *live*."

A violent wind surged around them, and Percy, Violet, and Will were pulled into the abyss.

CHAPTER
TWENTY-SIX

WHEN VIOLET QUITE LITERALLY TUMBLED INTO THE WHITE room, falling to her knees beside Will's bed, a startled gasp sounded behind her. Her sudden appearance quite surprised Marianna, who had been sitting vigil over her son.

Even Jane, floating watch over Will as she had promised, exclaimed in shock.

Violet's efforts to transfer Will home to England must have worked; Marianna couldn't be here otherwise.

"Violet!" she exclaimed. "How in the *world* . . ."

Rising, turning rapidly about, Violet searched for an open portal, for her mother. But there was just a white wall and her mother was nowhere to be seen. The Liminal must have divided them and returned Percy to Grimsby. She prayed that was the case and that the rest of her family were safe and holding up as well as could be imagined.

"Marianna! I . . . can't tell you exactly how I got here. We're in England now, yes?"

"Yes," Marianna said. "Somehow, wondrously, he got shipped home. But you . . . you look like . . ."

"Hell, I'm sure," Violet muttered. "I was . . . in a firefight."

"I've seen too many strange things in my life to be surprised, I only rejoice to see family," Marianna exclaimed. "Will is alive but in a coma and the doctors don't understand why."

"When I tumbled through, did you see any glimpse of him?" Violet asked. "His spirit returning to his body? It may take time for him to wake."

"I saw a bright light and felt a blast of cold air. But look." Marianna gestured Violet to Will's bedside and they flanked him. "His color is better now. He was so pale . . ." She pressed a hand to his cheek. "He's warmer, too," she said excitedly. "And his eyes . . . move behind his lids. He's been still as death . . ." A tear splashed onto her son's cheek and a slight tic of his muscles responded as if in reflex.

"These are all very heartening signs," Violet said.

Much like grief had hit her mother in a visible blow, so did the loss of Elijah and Josephine hit Violet in turn, but she said nothing for the moment, she focused instead on her heart lying out before her. She'd taken for granted that Will would be all right, having been so conversant with his soul.

But there was no guarantee. Panic flooded her. Going between the worlds, being absent spirit and body was an extreme state. There could have been damage done.

"Do not fear," Violet assured, as much for herself as Marianna. "Will is so strong and *very* brave. I was . . . with his spirit in the Whisper-world. He helped us navigate it. He'll be all right."

Marianna nodded, looking away.

Knowing any mention of the Whisper-world was an emotional subject for Marianna, Violet continued in hopes of easing her burden. "Had you and Mum not gone through what you did, Marianna, none of us would have made it back to the living alive or with our wits intact. You saved us, really. It isn't a place for mortals, and yet you both inoculated it for us."

Marianna considered this for a long moment. Finally, she nodded. "Then some terrible things have . . . their redemption. I am glad . . ." She rose, shaking, clearly overcome. "I will . . . tell the doctors he's regained his color, at least. And . . . someone should take a look at your arm. That's . . . unnatural." She walked away as Violet took a seat before Will's bed.

In all the dramatic tumult Violet's wound had taken secondary focus, a supreme mental feat, but the pain returned in a sickening swoop. She looked down and felt bile rise in her stomach. The wound was seeping with blood and Whisper-world grit.

Once she sat, the weight of exhaustion was like an anchor, and fiery pains coursed down her arm. It looked like she'd brushed against thick soot, her arm now a swath of black. Looking closely, it was more like tar. A dizzy spell threatened to crumple her.

Blinking, she tried to steady herself as the room went gray. The temperature around her plummeted and she was lost to either vision or a visitation.

The room remained, Will lying still remained, but everything was in grayscale, as if they'd never left the Whisper-world. No other figure or presence could be seen, but a whisper at her ear chillingly illustrated the point that the world she'd just escaped was a mere heartbeat away.

"Your wound, your blood is bound up here, with us," said a familiar, small, birdlike voice. "You could stay here, be our queen. We'd like that." The long-lost Muse took on an ominous tone. "We'd want that."

Violet's pulse pounded in her ear. Her arm freshly burned as if she'd been hit by a bullet all over again. She thought of Will and her mother, of their diplomacy, of the careful dance one had to manage with ancient, lonely creatures. They weren't human and Violet couldn't try to convince one as if it were.

"I'm sorry," Violet said, "I'm fully mortal and only borrowing powers. I am not incarnate and I could not be what you wanted. The ancient age is long gone. I opened my arms to you not so that

296 LEAHNA RENEE HIEBER

you would take me as one of yours, but in a gesture of good faith as you turn another leaf."

"You'd best treat that wound, then," the creature said sadly. "Because the Whisper-world will call you, haunt you ceaselessly until you're healed. Just ask your heart."

The mention of Will was enough to rally Violet's strength into sharper focus.

"He isn't yours anymore," Violet said gently but firmly. "We've made that clear. Our family belongs to this world alone, while we yet live."

"So be it. Your world, then. But if you change your mind," the Muse offered, "should your violent, *absurd* world finally break your mind, your heart, your spirit with its constant need for conflict and pain, we're here. This whole gray world is here, often making more sense than the senseless mortal realm."

"Your hospitality is noted," Violet declared and turned her head to the wound, wincing, the burning sensation having traveled all up her neck.

Hovering her hand over the wound, she mustered healing forces and her own mixture of powers in an effort to fully cleanse the clinging murk, the cloying residue that was the unfortunate side-effect of dealing in the Whisper-world.

There was a flutter of color across her vision and the gray was replaced by sterile white, the room returned to mortal hands, but there was still a Muse at her ear. This time, Healing had come, murmuring apologies for being spread so thin. Another flicker of Healing's yellow glow and she was again in the room alone with Will, the pain easing for the additional help, the Muse gone again.

"Miss, I'm sorry." A flustered nurse in white came in ahead of a blustering Marianna who was trying to make excuses for her. "I don't know how you got in here—"

MISS VIOLET AND THE GREAT WAR

"She's supposed to be here," Marianna said as if that were perfectly obvious. "Not to mention she's—"

"In a military nurse's uniform in an English civilian hospital—"

"I can explain," Violet said, trying to stand without wavering.

She fumbled in her breast pocket for her identification, the card and stamped metal tag that bore Lord Black's Ministry, and handed it over. There was a tense pause.

"I . . . I'm sorry to have troubled you. How did you get *in*?" the nurse said, incredulously.

"The same card," she replied. Never mind it was a doorway between worlds. "Could I have a bandage?"

"Yes. Of course." The nurse hurried off to procure one.

"A doctor should take a look at it—" Marianna called, going after the nurse. Violet nearly stopped her but she was out into the hall when Will's eyes fluttered.

Violet rushed to his side. He opened his eyes and smiled.

"You're back," they chorused, then laughed.

"I thought for a moment you'd gone back into the Whisper-world," Will clarified. "So I waited for you in case we had to fight our way back out."

"Thank you," Violet murmured. "I could never have weathered this without you, my driving purpose."

Tenderly she reached down for his hand and he pressed her palm between both of his.

The moment they touched, she felt a clear and palpable relief that she saw mirrored on his face.

"Violet," Will murmured. "Promise me all the time we're given. I won't ask you to be anything you don't want to be, to do anything you don't wish to do.

"I just don't want to lose you to whatever the world demands of you. I want to be able to hold your hand, to have you rest your head on my shoulder. I want your embrace to shield me from the cold. That . . . that will see me through.

"It's what has seen me through, all these years. Your light. Your simple touch. Will you grant me that forever?" He dared lift her hand so that he could softly kiss it.

"Treasure of my heart," Violet replied, tears in her eyes. "Our hearts have always been part and parcel. I love you."

"And I love you," Will murmured. He smiled.

Violet almost gasped. She'd never seen quite that look on his face. He was well and truly healed, rid of his demon entirely. Indeed, she saw her own light reflected in him, as if the Whisper-world had blended some of their gifts.

"For the first time in my life," Will stated, "I feel at peace." He looked suddenly pained. "It seems unfair that there is still a war."

"The light will turn it back, but like the Gorgon's poison, it needs time to work," Violet assured him. Will nodded. "As the Liminal returned me to England, I hope to help Lord Black with Wards that can help maintain the light we sent across the fields and continue the process of healing and balance the doorways."

"Would you go back to the front to do so?" Will asked, his brow furrowing in concern.

Violet shrugged. "I've no vision to guide me now, I'm running purely on instinct and the slivers of powers within me. The Guard is"—she fought back tears—"splintered, well and truly finished. They can never go back. As for me . . . I just don't know."

He reached out and seized her hand, his eyes wide.

"Then marry me. After that, you may ask your powers that be," he stated.

Violet leaned in and kissed him softly on each cheek, his forehead, and finally a soft press upon his lips. "I shall," she whispered. "*You* are my vision of the future."

Marianna hurried back, a baffled, flustered doctor in tow, exclaiming when she saw Will awake.

"You've done it, Violet," she cried, rushing over to his bedside and clutching him. "I knew he'd rouse to you."

"Hello, Mum," Will said with a smile. "I'd never leave my favorite ladies behind."

The beleaguered nurse returned with a bandage and a doctor.

"Ah, thank you," Violet stated. "I'll take this and be off, though if you could be so kind as to show me to your nearest washroom."

"Where do you think you're going—" Marianna and the doctor chorused.

Violet waved her Ministry badge again. "Don't worry, 'tis now but a scratch. I must report to my superior," she replied. "And see where my family ended up."

When she was still protested, she held up her hand and the light of Memory flickered across the field of vision, and the three went silent; only Will was left chuckling softly. "I'll see you very soon," Violet promised. "If you're well enough to be discharged, come to Athens. I'm not taking a moment with you for granted ever again." She turned to go, but Will calling her name had her turning back.

He placed his hand upon his heart, then gestured to her, as if his heart went with her. She did the same.

WHEN VIOLET APPROACHED THE GUARD AT WHITEHALL, EVEN with the use of her powers, the man was wary.

"Who are you here to see?" the man in uniform asked gruffly.

"Lord Black," Violet replied, showing her identification card.

The guard bobbed his head and gestured that she ascend the stair to his floor.

Walking down the lush red carpet, she noticed that the door

to Lord Black's office was slightly ajar. Knocking lightly, she said quietly, "Milord? Delphi reporting to Control."

"Delphi!" A moment later the door was thrown open and she was swept in; Lord Black shut the door behind her. Lord Black's power was ebullience; not a soul could speak with the man or keep his company and withhold a smile, it was positively preternatural.

"Your door was slightly ajar, pardon me, I wasn't sure . . ."

"You never know the things you hear when people think doors are closed!" he stated. "Considering there's so much about my life I'm forced to hide . . . here"—he gestured around him—"I shall be open. For all its faults, I love the world and don't want undue barriers between me and it."

She smiled. "You, milord, are a light and we need lights like you like never before. If there's anything this century needs . . ." She sighed and took a seat across from his desk.

"Tell me everything," he bid gently.

"I've looked hell right in the eyes, in the teeth, sir; the devil is an artillery barrage." She looked away, shuddering, feeling and hearing all the assaults all over again. "Many will be coming home broken, if they come home at all. Qualities like yours can help them find their way again. Lest they lose all hope for humanity."

"Who could blame them? High command has undoubtedly made men feel like they're mere numbers," he said angrily, coming around the desk to sit across from her. "When did you return to London? The Wards for the battlefields are nearly ready."

"Good. They'll be of help, I'm sure. I arrived today via . . . a shortcut," she said with a partial smile that soon faded. "We"—sudden tears welled up—"lost two of our rank. At the Somme. We were overwhelmed."

"I'm so sorry . . ." Black murmured. "Is there anything I can do? Transporting of bodies?"

Violet shook her head, thinking of the blood angel and all the

ash that had clouded around her; the Whisper-world was their cre-
matorium. "It was a . . . unique situation. When you live a life
with ghosts, life and death are bittersweet. But they died helping
the cause of the living and the dead. Thanks for seeing Will safely
home to a hospital here."

"My utmost pleasure. Has he recovered?"

"Presently. There was a shift the Guard effected at the Somme.
Everything has a pendulum of sorts and I think we wrenched it
back the other direction in both worlds. I hope."

"Sometimes hope is all we have for certain."

"Truer words were never spoken. While the Guard has sustained too many losses to continue opening portals to the dead
ourselves through the rest of the war—may the horrors end soon—
the forces that have guided the Guard since ancient times have
promised they will maintain the spirit world as open and stable,
despite the unprecedented numbers.

"It would help, of course," Violet continued with a mutter, "if
high command would stop sending men up from the trenches as
if they were water and not actual humans."

Black nodded sadly. There was a pained silence.

"I don't know that I thought I could stop the war, out there,"
Violet murmured. "But I feel like I've failed nonetheless."

"The *war* is a failure. Yet hubris insists, impossible to kill,"
Black replied. "We can't stop all of humanity's worst urges wielded
in the unfeeling hands of brutal empires; all we can do is try to
put brakes on its runaway trains. I think you've done that, out
there, in ways no mere mortals could."

Violet nodded. This helped.

"I must try to find my family now, but I had to thank you. We'd
not be alive or have made any progress if not for your papers and
clearances. I confess, I also came for absolution. Thank you for
helping me not feel I disappointed you, heaven, and the world."

"It is an honor to have served the Guard!" he exclaimed. "A dream of mine, really."

"Send word to Athens when the Wards are ready. If we've imagined this right, you and I, I can imbue each box with the mixture of light and fire that the portals are so responsive to. I'll need to charge them at Athens, where the power is strongest. It's been stretched too thin during this process."

"Indeed. Once powered, I'll order them laid near strategic points where loss has been heaviest; your light will continue to lend the balance that has been your mission. You'll hear from me shortly, once the Wards are assembled."

"Thank you, milord."

THE FRONT DOOR OF ATHENS ACADEMY WAS LOCKED, PER orders. Turning the key felt like she was opening the door to heaven.

"Miss Rychman, welcome home," Vincent Spire said the moment she stepped into view, standing up from behind a wide desk that blocked entry; posts and ropes extended the barrier on either side. He saluted.

"Why, Mr. Spire, when you were asked to help watch over the place on our behalf, we didn't mean you had to be right at the door . . ." she said with a little laugh.

"Thousands of my peers are dying on the front, madam. I am privileged enough to be spared. Least I can do is be vigilant on *this* front."

"Well, I'm heartened and grateful," she said, as he came around the desk and shifted one of the ropes to allow her to enter. "And so very glad to be home."

"We're glad of it, too," he said.

As Violet moved under the center chandelier, drinking in the grand main foyer, she felt the building react to her, as it always did, its lights brightening, its heights seeming to soar.

She raced upstairs, relishing the feeling of her palm on the familiar, precious wooden banister. She was eager to reach the seal; a place from which she thought all things possible. Despite that desire, she paused to latch the velvet rope behind her, blocking off the foyer. Then she nearly threw herself across the cool floor toward the motto of knowledge and light.

At the center of the seal lay a small stack of papers. Each inked with an angel. Josephine's work; manifest from the beyond. What a wondrous magic. Tears flowed down her cheeks as she scooped them up in her arms.

"I've missed you," she exclaimed, collapsing upon the eagle, feeling its beak press to her cheek like a kiss.

"Welcome home, child . . ." Athens seemed to say, their two connected hearts speaking to one another.

She was a child of her parents and a vessel of the gods.

"What now?" she asked the fire. Having taken this ancient power out into hell itself, she didn't know what else to do.

"Rest, child," came the rumbling of Phoenix. "You did what was needed, at the highest marks of casualties. The Guard is now but fragments and I'm withdrawing your power. We all have our limits. Rest and work for peace."

Blue fire poured from her pores like sweat, running in rivulets back into the seal.

"Let me keep just a little," she murmured to the fire. "For strength and sanity, to charge Wards and to help keep hope alive."

The fire seemed to agree and when she turned her hand, a little flame rose from the center of her palm as if it were the sacred heart, her hand the wick of a great lamp.

"Thank you," she murmured.

As the power flowed out of her, she allowed the horrors to slough from her form, the grit and ash of trench and smoke, debris, and human fear, caked into her skin and fresh in her mind in gruesome images; she wanted to purge every nightmarish sight and sleep for a decade. She'd never be rid of the scars, but then she never should be, lest it demean the sacrifices made.

She thought to move from the seal but couldn't bring herself to, thinking about what many soldiers notably said upon return from this war in particular. The unnerving quiet.

There was a terrible emptiness within her now that she was no longer augmented by ancient forces and the visions that drove her between worlds. The *roaring* quiet.

Every sense that had been made fuller by the forces that took up within her was dull by comparison. Her body was far more relaxed but it felt so much smaller.

She understood now why the Guard spoke with such aching conflict about their time in service. You were full of power, and yet it called you to harrowing dangers. She was now a more peaceful body, and yet a lonelier one. When connected to fire and the Muses, your heart beat with the thousands that had come before, called to a sacred, curious task. One's own heartbeat was such an insignificant thump.

Violet had no idea how long she'd been there until a soft voice and quiet footfalls echoed across the hall.

"There you are," came a relieved voice. Shifting, forcing herself to sit up, Violet turned her head to see her mother rushing over to her, Father at her heels. Helping her up, her mother then held her tight, her father folded in around them both. Rebecca and Michael followed and stood near, the vicar murmuring thanks and praise the moment he caught sight of her.

"There *you* are," Violet countered, wiping tears from her face. "I assumed the Liminal routed us where needed most. Will is recovering, how are you?" Violet asked the four Guards who remained. The whole experience seemed to have aged them all immeasurably.

Before anyone else could answer, three spirits wafted across the floor toward the group. "They miss *me,* of course," Elijah stated, wafting over to them, Josie smiling at his side, Jane on the other. Their grayscale forms were not attired as they were at the moment of passing but instead how they would wish to be seen. Josie floated in a lovely gown of the previous century's style, Jane in a simple dress, and the lace cuffs of Elijah's ostentatious frock coat fluttered as he gesticulated. "But now I can tease Alexi indefinitely, without corporeal constraint, and he can't even hear me to retort."

Alexi eyed him. "He's taunting me, isn't he? I assume whenever that inexhaustible mouth is flapping he's at it again." He held up a hand lit with blue fire as his fellows chuckled. "This may work on you yet," he stated with a smirk.

"Oh, Auntie, Uncle—" Staring at their spirits, Violet's eyes teared up again. It was clear from the swollen eyes of the rest of the Guard that they had done their fair share of weeping. Seeing her family again in such an altered state was fresher for Violet, and she blurted through her tears, "Again, I'm sorry I didn't—"

"Guilt is no currency here, not when fate deals the hands it will, like it or not." Jane stopped her. "Believe me. Our souls are all here together, here at this place of power, and for that we can rejoice."

Violet nodded. There was something she could offer that would cheer them all and she turned to Michael.

"Vicar Carroll, will you marry Will and me? As soon as he's arrived?"

The assembled company lit up.

"Of course, my dear girl," Michael exclaimed, his oceanic eyes now filled with happy tears. "My joy and honor."

"Nothing fancy," Violet clarified. "Just the simplest of pledges, here in the chapel, with all of you present. A promise made on these beloved bricks is all the more fuel for our protective fire. Soon after I'll charge Lord Black's Wards to be placed along the perimeter to keep what we've wrought in place until the war's end, but not to keep the Whisper-world open indefinitely."

Her hands trembled and her voice broke as she lifted Josie's angels that had been so spectacularly left for her, turning to the beautiful floating spirit who beamed as Violet clutched them. "These, too. We'll send these along, too."

"I remain inspired," Josie stated softly, blowing Violet a kiss on the cool draft in her wake.

"Your father still has the phoenix fire." Percy smiled and ran her hand fondly along Alexi's arm. "He seems loathe to let it go."

Alexi shrugged. "It hasn't let *me* go."

Violet studied him a moment. "You could let go of some of the pain. Even if you lose the fire, you shouldn't carry the pain."

He shook his head. The loss of lifelong comrades of another war meant he would never let go of certain pains.

Violet had grown up with Jane a ghost. This created an innocence about death so close to her. Grief was relative but the bond of a Guard was closer than blood. She, like her mother, could generally hear the spirits. Her father would never hear the Withersby clan again, constant verbal jousting and all. He should indeed keep the fire and hold it close; a friend he couldn't lose and could always feel.

Alternately, any innocence Violet may have had about death at large, death unchecked, death as sentence passed by blind generals bent on inane practices—that all had been blasted with shells and stung by gas, hung out like a bullet-riddled corpse caught on a wire and left to turn to dust.

While the constant sounds of war she'd known all her life were only now receding from Violet's inner ear, noise was replaced by memories, every other sense. She wished she could have left what she'd seen behind as the powers that augmented her drained away, but there was no scrubbing away the trauma. Thank goodness for the blessed bricks of Athens and the soft hum of its constant power to offset the nightmares.

As if sensing her, Rebecca reached into a fold of her skirt and pulled out a set of keys on a brass ring, grabbed Violet's hand, and pressed the set into her palm. Her hands seemed so much frailer.

"I'm retiring, dear girl. It's past time and it's your turn now."

"Thank you, Headmistress."

"My old apartments are on this floor, you know, just waiting for my replacement." She gestured beyond the foyer where archways led into another darkened wing.

A movement at the top of the stair had Violet turning to the handsome man in a freshly pressed uniform. Will saluted her from the landing.

"Returning for duty, ma'am, and ready to take your hand."

"Come." Violet gestured to her family. "Let this man and I bind our hearts"—she pressed Josie's art to her chest—"with all these angels to witness."

CHAPTER
TWENTY-SEVEN

IT WASN'T FOR ANOTHER FOUR YEARS THAT VIOLET COULD FI-nally let go of the unnerving quiet.

On June 14, 1920, the British Symphony Orchestra premiered *The Lark Ascending.* Having heard a report that the composer, Ralph Vaughan Williams, had written it in 1914, inspired by Mer-edith's poem and watching ships sail off to war, Violet knew she had to attend, as she had done with any work relating to the con-flict. Scars could only lessen by massage, treated with salve to bid the flesh be less bitter.

She went by herself. Father was feeling poorly so Mum was tending him, and Will was caught up fixing failing electrical wir-ing at Athens as superintendent. He demanded she treat herself to something beautiful.

Buying a ticket for a shadowed corner slightly set apart, she knew she would cry and wanted the peace and anonymity to do so. When the lights dimmed, Violet felt that something sacred was about to occur.

From the moment the single violin floated its notes out into the void of the theater, the impressionistic quality of the music brought a lark exquisitely to life and floated it out over the audi-ence. Time stopped, allowing nothing but spellbound beauty.

Beneath the floating violin-turned-bird swelled an orchestra of wind, a surging tide of emotion and staggering depth. Violet hadn't heard anything like it. She'd heard a critic familiar with the piece say "it showed serene disregard of the fashions of today or yesterday. It dreams its way along" . . . and it did. As it dreamed along, taking the listeners under its wings, Violet noticed luminous colors shifting over the sleeve of her blouse.

Looking up, she was surrounded by the Muses. The audience was thankfully oblivious to the lit forces, rapt in the fluttering creature being audibly evoked with exquisite care.

Intuition had its amorphous hands to its mouth. They had clearly had some part in inspiring this piece and here they were to see it grant peace.

What a transcendent experience.

It was true that Art prevailed exiting the war, as a general principle as well as the ancient force propagating it. Art was the only way anyone made sense of the senseless. The Muse itself had become more robust; Violet could even see that its blue was richer in color, its form larger even, as if it had grown to fit the staggering need.

So many things suffered in the war. An enormous number of people were dead and the world still grieved. But art was a reminder of civilized survival and became the way the world learned what really happened, there in the depths of the soul's bleak nights.

A mere news report couldn't capture horror. Not even the dread motion picture footage. The only context was wrought and written words. The aching songs. The absurdist art asking: what did anything matter if human life mattered so little? The blood-drenched poems.

Every beautiful moment she would witness, see, taste, hear, encourage, was a gift of a Muse. Often one would appear purely to bow its head at her, bidding her enjoy life as a mortal under their protection. As all mortals were their charges, if they took the time to look at beauty and live in radical hope.

Radical only because there was so much hopelessness in the state of a battered world. Radical for something tender to exist in a murderous universe. Radical to think hope could actually be down there in that box of evils, left behind when all else fled. Ready to ascend.

EPILOGUE

IT WAS TIME.

The doctors were baffled. He didn't look particularly ill.

But when Alexi had turned to Percy and said, "I believe I am dying, love, let me retire and come hold me?" she sent for Violet and hadn't left his side since.

That had been three days ago, and doctors had come and gone. Violet brought water and soup, whatever they requested. He had spent most of those days in a listless half sleep, stirring ever so slightly, noticing that Percy was holding his hand or had her arm around him, and he seemed contented back into a mysterious delirium.

Percy had not let go of his hand, propped beside him on the wide bed, arms wound around his neck, since the declaration, having maintained contact every second possible, save for a few moments of necessity. She was terrified that if she let go for even a moment, he'd somehow slip away and she wouldn't be there with him for it.

"So many years with you, beloved," he murmured on the third day of his fading, suddenly grasping at a moment of clarity. "What did the spirits say to you, at the end of that terrible night so long ago when you saved my life? When you agreed to marry me, what did the spirits say?"

"They said that eternity awaits, love. Eternity awaits."

"And so it does . . ."

With that he closed his eyes, a breath slipped from him, and he did not breathe again.

Violet stood against the wall, ashen, her hand over her mouth, then both hands, creeping over her face slowly, as if she couldn't bear to look.

Will had been keeping a respectful vigil across the room in a chair, and he rose, moving silently to her side, tucking an arm around her waist.

There was a tiny sound in the back of Percy's throat. It rose and grew. An unbearable sound, the unraveling wail fashioned only by loss of the most passionate of love. This was no mortal love, it had crossed centuries to live in these two bodies and now one of them was gone . . .

Michael and Rebecca were downstairs cooking dinner for the family, and upon hearing Percy's cry they rushed up to the open door of the bedroom. Seeing Percy crumpled over Alexi, Rebecca turned into Michael's embrace at the threshold, her face immediately in her hands, stifling her own sobs into his shoulder.

A low rumble sounded from the bedroom. Blue fire erupted from Alexi's body, wrapping Percy in a winged embrace, lifting her up from Alexi's body. She struggled against it, choking on her tears, fighting to throw herself back on her husband's body.

The phoenix fire held fast and propped her up, her pearlescent hair blown back in the gentle breeze of the fire while wisps of the cerulean flame dried her tears, never minding they kept flowing fresh.

"My love . . ." the fire rumbled. "My light. Be not afraid and be not sad . . ."

As the fire spoke to Percy, the grayscale, luminous form of Alexi lifted from his body and his spirit floated up, up away from the bed, looking around at the room and then at last turning back to his wife. At the sight of his spirit, Percy stopped struggling with the fire and tried to reach up to grasp him.

His spirit, upon catching her eyes, smiled. "My love and light . . . you know better than anyone that death is just a beginning. My body was tired. My spirit is not."

Percy froze, unsure whether to try to grasp his incorporeal hand and feel its chill, to speak with him, or to still hold onto his mortal coil.

Alexi stared in wonder at what stretched out before him, visible through the open door and out into the hall. It was as if Percy's keening wail had summoned them; the Rychman estate was flooded with ghosts.

Suddenly, all the spirits that had been keeping a certain respectful distance from the family lest they seem like vultures or reapers in and of themselves, swooped in around Rebecca and Michael. Jane, Elijah, Josephine, Aodhan, Beatrice and her husband Ibrahim, and other Guards began filing in behind them.

A whole receiving line from all the Guards that ever were, century after century, culture after culture, a world of Guards, all of whom had fought together, all of whom had come back together to honor the last Leader of their ranks that had taken an ancient practice into a modern world and was leaving it there to pass into obscurity.

Violet and Will came to Percy's side, helping her stand beside the floating ghost of her husband over his own body.

"Look, Mum, look how dearly he is respected," Violet said through her tears, watching the endless receiving line bow and kneel in deference, the faintest of hints of blue fire still wafting about the whole premises, a phantom flame clinging to the spectral host.

"And you," Will added as the Guards after paying respects wafted to Percy and bowed or curtseyed again, many adding "my

Lady" or another term of deference and adulation in any of their various languages.

This went on for an interminable period, the family just holding onto one another, staring a bit bewildered at all of it. At the very rear of this impressive queue were the Muses. They said nothing, only swirled around Alexi's spirit and his family in light and music.

"We love you and always will," the Heart said. "Thank you for your service . . ."

The forms swirled around and faded, their inherent music lifting into the air as their shimmering light thinned like a draining fog.

Rebecca and Michael came close, embraced Percy and Violet, and murmured that they'd have dinner ready for them and cleaning done, were downstairs whenever they needed them. Numbly, Percy murmured thanks.

Finally, they were alone again. Alone with the dead body of the most important, imperious man they'd ever known, his spirit still hovering, eternal.

A small dark spot in the air grew at the foot of the bed until it became a rectangle the size of a narrow door. Beyond, gray wet stone and a cacophony of whispers. But, thanks to the reunion of the Muses and their coalition, the feel of the place, what was emanating from the portal was brighter, the whispers were song, the air was warmer.

But it was still the Whisper-world and it had opened for Alexi.

"No, no . . . not yet . . ." Percy whispered, shaking her head, waving a shooing hand at the portal. "Not yet, please . . ."

"Don't worry for me, my love," Alexi's spirit said, reaching down a grayscale hand to run over her colorless face.

"How strange," Percy gasped, staring up at his form. "For we who have dealt with death our whole lives, that it should *still* be so foreign and terrifying to us when it is our beloveds . . . I don't know what to think, what to do . . ."

"You are not without me, love," he countered. "You know I will be by your side every moment, until the heavens see fit to have you in this similar state. But don't rush that. Take care of my girl . . ."

Percy reached over and grasped Violet's hand again, both hands cold and trembling, splashed with countless tears.

"I . . . don't know how to contain this . . ." She turned to her daughter, panic in her eyes. "When the goddess's light awoke in me, it nearly killed me then. This . . . I am breaking apart anew . . ."

"Mum." Violet reached out, brushed the disheveled pearly hair that had fallen from a loose bun back from her cheek. "It's all right." She gestured to the narrow portal. "Go. Why don't you go with him, and see where the corridors lead him? You can travel there, you were built for it. Even our Jane glimpsed the Great Beyond and came back for us. So, just . . . come back to me."

Will said nothing, just placed his hand upon Violet's shoulder. She threaded her fingers through his. "I'm not alone."

"See him through to the undiscovered country," Will added with a smile. "See what wonders may await. And let us know when you'll be back for dinner."

Percy stared at them. Then at the portal where Alexi floated. Back down at his dead body.

"If there ever was a time when mankind needed to be able to shift between life and death, it is this century and this time," Violet said quietly. "Live your gifts and lend your light between every world."

"You would . . . not mind?" Percy said in a tiny whisper.

"Mum," Violet choked. "*Go*. This will ease your pain. Transition it. All I have ever wanted, my whole life, is to never see you in pain."

"I love you and am so lucky for you," Percy murmured, kissing Violet on the forehead. "I'll see you soon."

There was a blaze of blinding light so powerful, Violet and Will had to turn away. When they opened their eyes again, they were alone with Alexi's resting body.

A number of apropos biblical and Shakespearean thoughts came to Violet's mind to help wrap her head around grief and the mordant material of a resting body once its light had gone out.

The end of an age. The Victorians were fading into the modern age and the last Leader of the Guard was gone forever.

And yet, what light there had been.

What fires were there yet to be lit from new and innovative forges . . .

The world was mere kindling awaiting sparks to catch holy fire.

The strange and beautiful lessons taught by her family were exactly the kinds of salve she wished for the world as it healed its myriad scars and gingerly lifted bruised Hope out, the last to remain in the box of evils. To live as blazes of glory, fearless in the face of an ending was, indeed, only the beginning of another journey. Transcendent.

Author's Note:
On History and Meaning

About the Muses' Grand Works in the book, the references are a few real-life moments where humans have been most particularly inspired:

Ralph Vaughan Williams's *Lark Ascending.* The composer was watching English warships as described, and was thinking of Meredith's long poem, "The Lark Ascending," and wrote a piece for violin and orchestra that would go on to be one of the world's most beloved pieces of music. On the anniversary of the September 11th attacks on the United States, *The Lark Ascending* has been one of the most requested songs to be played on NYC's NPR station. On a personal note, when my parents brought me home from the hospital as a baby, they made sure *The Lark Ascending* was the first piece of music I ever heard. It is definitely something that evokes a transcendent spiritual connection and has from the first.

"Silent Night, Stille Nacht" being sung between the trenches is a true story, as is the whole Christmas Truce across most of the Western Front. It forged an unexpected armistice driven by this camaraderie of soldiers that in some cases lasted almost two weeks. This was broken by higher chain of command and the war resumed.

Wilfred Owen, featured in the scene where the Muses urge the soldier to write, remains one of the most prolific and celebrated poets of the war, despite the short time he lived. The stanzas utilized in the text are taken first from Siegfried Sassoon then Rupert Brooke.

The litter of German shepherd puppies from a bombed-out shelter is a true story. One of those puppies would indeed go on to become the greatest movie star of his day, Rin Tin Tin.

The Verdun ossuary vision was inspired by my trip there. It is just as overwhelming as I tried to capture. Of Verdun's seven lost villages that exist now as only jagged earth and lines of eerily symmetrical trees replanted by the forest service after the war, with posts marking where the buildings once stood, I was most enchanted, moved, and entirely struck by Fleury. The jagged earth overgrown with grass is so alien, the verdant green such a contrast, the peaceful quiet the most opposite of the hell that wiped the place off the map never to be rebuilt.

The basis for Josephine's wartime angel drawings, an angel with sword and shield, is taken from what would become the 1919 World War I Inter-Allied Victory Medal, designed by James Earle Fraser, set on a rainbow ribbon, and given to any who fought.

Forgive, by the graciousness of artistic license, my being open and loose with general battle dates for the sake of the needs of the Guard. Countless books and resources exist for all the war's specifics. Out of myriad research materials, one of the most visceral and moving resources I utilized was John Ellis's *Eye-Deep in Hell: Trench Warfare in World War I*.

The horrors were real. So is the art.

Peace be with you.

We'll meet again.